Leaning Towards Infinity

SUE WOOLFE

LEANING
towards
INFINITY

*How my mother's apron unfolds
into my life*

Faber and Faber
BOSTON • LONDON

Library of Congress Cataloging-in-Publication Data

Woolfe, Sue.
    Leaning towards infinity : a novel / Sue Woolfe.
        p.   cm.
    ISBN 0-571-19939-9 (paperback)
    1. Mothers and daughters—Australia—Fiction.   2. Women
mathematicians—Australia—Fiction.   I. Title.
[PR9619.3.W65L43   1997]
823—dc20

96-44133
CIP

Cover design by Milton Charles and Lisa Falkenstern

Printed in the United States of America

*To Gordon who leans towards infinity
every now and then*

ACKNOWLEDGEMENTS

THIS BOOK WAS A LONG TIME IN THE LIVING AND THE MAKING, AND MANY PEOPLE TOOK PART KNOWINGLY AND OTHERWISE. FRANCES BECAME A MATHEMATICIAN BECAUSE OF MY FRIEND GEORGE KOSOVICH WHO TALKED TO ME ABOUT MATHEMATICS AS I HELD MY BABY. AT THAT STAGE, LIKE HYPATIA, I HAD NO KNOWLEDGE OF MATHEMATICS, BUT I'D ALWAYS BEEN HAUNTED BY THE SUSPICION THAT MATHEMATICS IS A MIRROR METAPHOR OF WHO WE ARE.

KAY FREER, GORDON GRAHAM, KATE GRENVILLE, PHIL KUTZKO (IOWA UNIVERSITY, AMERICA), PATTI MILLER AND MARION PIERCE (ALSO OF IOWA UNIVERSITY) READ EARLY DRAFTS OF THE NOVEL AND ENCOURAGED ME. PAUL DAVIES KINDLY CORRESPONDED WITH ME WHEN I DIDN'T EVEN KNOW WHAT QUESTIONS I WANTED TO ASK. FRANCES' EVENTUAL MATHEMATICS WAS GUIDED AND COMMENTED ON BY PAULA (BEASLEY) COHEN, ADRIAN NELSON OF SYDNEY UNIVERSITY AND BY MIKE WOOLFE, AND SHE COULDN'T HAVE FOUND HER NEW SORT OF NUMBER WITHOUT THEIR GUIDANCE. PETER BOYLE ASSISTED WITH HER PHILOSOPHICAL IDEAS, AND JILL FLOYD WITH HER THOUGHTS ON MOTHERING.

I ESPECIALLY WANT TO THANK PETER BISHOP, JULIA STILES AND LYN TRANTER FOR THEIR PATIENCE AND GENEROSITY IN READING AND EDITING SEVERAL VERSIONS OF THIS BOOK. MOST OF ALL, I WANT TO THANK THE LITERATURE BOARD OF THE AUSTRALIA COUNCIL WHO BELIEVED IN THIS WORK BEFORE ANYONE ELSE, AND THROUGH FELLOWSHIPS AND GRANTS GAVE ME THE TIME AND SPACE IN MY LIFE TO WRITE IT.

Some of the Story

Great Grandmother Johnson   Great Grandfather Johnson
(a wet-nurse)   (profession not remembered)

No one remembers their Christian names now because for fifty years they called each other Mum and Dad. They were Irish-born Roman Catholics.

Violet Johnson b. 1910   Daniel Fernandez b. ?
(Seven other siblings, but   (No birth cert.
lost to this history because   Factory owner. Emigrated
they called her Jewish fiance   from somewhere in Spain.
an infidel and worse, a loose   Knifed and left to die in
fish)   Grafton, NSW, in 1935.)

Juanita Fernandez b.1929   Frank Montrose b. 1925
(housewife and secret   (handyman, Blue Mountains
mathematician)   Mayor)

Matti Montrose b. 1947 (missing)
Frances Montrose b. 1950   Harry Craig b. 1950
(English teacher and   (Professional mathematician)
amateur mathematician)

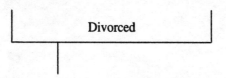
Divorced

Hypatia Montrose b. 1973   Jim Williams b. 1972
(mother,   (Fell from cliff 2006.
biographer of Frances   Rumours of foul play persist)
Montrose)

Zoe Montrose b. 1994
Frances Williams-Montrose
b. 1996
Jim Montrose-Williams
b. 2003.

More of the story

It's a little known fact that professors of mathematics daily receive large clumsy envelopes from people claiming they've made astounding mathematical discoveries. It's easy for a professor to tell at a glance that the senders of large clumsy envelopes are not respectable mathematicians, because they'd have a departmental secretary, who wouldn't dream of scrawling a professor's name across an envelope in biro (sometimes misspelling it which could be overlooked but to misspell professor is very revealing). Moreover, on these envelopes there isn't a return address printed in neat letters on the top left hand corner. It is also a little known fact that the voluminous contents of these large clumsy envelopes are seldom opened or the voluminous contents glanced at. Professors would tell you that people who post fat unsolicited clumsy envelopes crammed with mathematics are cranks.

At the turn of the century there was such a crank, Svrinivasa Ramanujan, an Indian who like many other senders of large clumsy envelopes had no formal qualifications. He'd behaved oddly since childhood, when his parents had to employ a policeman to take him to school or he wouldn't get there. He'd failed every examination he ever sat. Instead, through his adolescence and youth, he spent hours each day on his porch scribbling mathematical formulae on a tiny blackboard, often rubbing them out when he'd lost interest in them. Eventually, in 1913, a friend encouraged him to send his formulae to three eminent professors of mathematics in England—E.W. Hobson, H.F. Baker and G.H. Hardy. His painstakingly legible letter began

Dear Sir,

I beg to introduce myself to you as a clerk in the Accounts Department of the Port Trust Office at Madras on a salary of only 20 pounds per annum. I am now about 23 years of age. I have had no university education but I have undergone the ordinary school course. After leaving school I have been employing the spare time at my disposal to work at mathematics. I have not trodden through *the conventional regular course, but I am striking out a new path for myself.*

Professors are busy people and Ramanujan's letter had arrived in one of those suspicious envelopes. Anyway, what could a clerk in a backroom office say of interest to a professor of mathematics? Any glance at the history of ideas will show how unlikely it is that great ideas—those that survive—come from cranks.

Professors Hobson and Baker never replied to his letter. However, the third mathematics professor on Ramanujan's list was G.H. Hardy, an obliging Cambridge professor who rather liked things unorthodox and unexpected, and rather disliked smugness. History has recorded exactly what G.H. Hardy did on the day the envelope arrived because it turned out to be one of the most important days of his life. He opened the envelope, glanced at the mathematics inside and decided it was strange. He picked up the newspapers instead, but they were more dreadful than usual. It was a slow news day. King Edward's dog had died: the professor didn't like dogs. A Mrs Buxton had been adulterous with Lord Crowley: the professor didn't like Lord Crowley or ladies. So he did a few hours of his own mathematics, he ate a predictable lunch and went out with the usual crowd to play a dull game of tennis. There he had a spectacular win. Who can know how great an effect that little tennis win had on our civilisation? After all, the vibrations from the flutter of a butterfly's wings in Africa may change the rainfall of the world. We do know that all through the ordinary day the mathematics of Ramanujan's letter nagged at Hardy. It was strange mathematics, and bewildering, but was it more than that? Maybe it was a hoax, to make him look a fool. Ramanujan's formulae hinted at surprising new mathematical methods, but he hadn't sent proofs. Then came Hardy's little afternoon triumph at tennis (indoor tennis, to suit the English climate). Hardy strode back to his study in high spirits to look again at Ramanujan's peculiar formulae. Many of them were unlike anything that would've occurred to a conventional mathematician. Many of them Hardy couldn't prove, even though he was England's most eminent mathematician. By high tea, he began to think he was rummaging through the mind of a genius. By supper, he knew that some of the formulae weren't merely brilliant, they were almost supernatural. Before midnight he wrote that though he hadn't plumbed their depths, they must be true, because no one would have had the imagination to invent them.

A century later, Ramanujan's papers are still being plumbed for their secrets, and cosmology and computer science depend on his ideas.

What about Professors Hobson and Baker? History has not bothered to tell us how they spent the day that the envelopes arrived. For the rest of their lives, at three in the morning when only the remorseful are awake, did they writhe? Did they know they'd missed their chance of immortality? Did they ever open the envelopes?

But this book isn't the story of Svrinivasa Ramanujan in 1913. It's the story of Frances Montrose, an Australian woman who'd never had any formal mathematics training but who in 1995 carried across the world, inside a borrowed suitcase and amongst ball dresses, a bulging three hundred and fifteen pages of revolutionary theorems, and something else no one knew about—the beginnings of the discovery of a new kind of number. The contents of her suitcase had the power to turn the mathematical establishment upside down. But in her heart, she carried such burdensome memories, she was almost mute.

I don't intend to describe anything of the mathematics of Frances Montrose since only six mathematicians in the world understand it and they disagree with each other. (One of them currently has a libel case against another for name-calling over a particularly contentious result of the Eighty-first Montrose Theorem.)

There's another difficulty. I have no knowledge of mathematics.

But perhaps mathematics is a mirror of the mind, and I can tell you about her mind, and her memories. I pieced together her story over many years, and while we were drying the dishes together and cutting up vegetables for soup she told me all sorts of things she was too shy to tell other biographers. I've included many of her meanderings and her stops and starts, assisting the reader when I felt assistance was necessary, but my radical departure from other biographers is to reveal my special knowledge of Frances Montrose.

After a lifetime of heart-searching I have decided to include not only the diary of her mother, the unknown genius whose secret work laid the foundation for the Montrose Numbers, but also my letters to Frances Montrose. The reader will discover that my letters were the turning point in the famous missing four days before Frances Montrose turned the mathematical world upside down, and after my revelations, conjecture about what happened in those four days will be finally laid to rest.

I have told the story of Frances Montrose as if I was her. Some have said this is a liberty but they don't appreciate how well I knew her. Knew her through and through. After all, I was her daughter.

Hypatia

CONTENTS

THE REMAINDER OF A LIFETIME

THE BEGINNING OF
A LIFETIME

HOW IT SEEMED TO BEGIN

I think it all began because of the shape of my mother's breasts. And it definitely began with something my mother wrote on the margin of a page stuck on the wall: Frege said that the line connecting any two points is already there before we draw it. Underneath it, she'd made two dots, pressing the nib of her fountain pen so hard the swelling scarlet ink stained the white paper. She always wrote in scarlet ink until she went mad.

And of course, there was the advertisement. Many things became linked because of it, in the way that you might be sitting in a cafe and suddenly a stranger stands at the door in an ordinary brown coat, but because of the fall of light on the brown coat you cry out, fragments from the past are linking and unwinding in you.

Or a man might walk across a room wrapped in a white towel, with windows behind him, nothing more momentous than windows, and mountains are behind the windows, only mountains, but their light is turning him emerald, turquoise, purple—so he moves inside a jewel, and tears start in your eyes.

The advertisement went like this:

WANTED: Radically new ideas about mathematics, to be read at an international mathematics conference. Perhaps, as an outsider to university mathematics, you have been figuring out revolutionary mathematical ideas that seemed too outrageous to make public. This is your moment. We want to hear from you.

The conference was to be held across the world from me, in Athens, and hosted by an Australian university who regretted

3

'that mathematics had become the exclusive province of academics, an old men's private debating club.'

The conference was to be held soon. Applications had to be sent to a private box number, judged by the university, and then

'the person with the most intriguing theories will be invited to the conference, fares and accommodation paid, to explain them.'

I've often thought since of all the people who answered that advertisement. You'd have had to be living a particular life. On the edges, waiting, maybe not knowing you were waiting.

I saw the advertisement in the magazine on a colleague's desk, one of those cold blustery May days when trees outside the window were tearing the sky apart.

I bundled up my scribbles, three hundred and fifteen pages of them, and sent them off. I'd found the way to rescue my mother at last.

The next two issues of the bemused magazine were besieged with letters from suspicious readers. Why had the invitation been made? Was it (some readers darkly suggested) an attempt by the university to prove it was not an elitist institution? Or to prove that it should be elitist, to demonstrate that all mathematical amateurs are lunatics? Was mathematics going round in tired circles? Was new blood needed? One reader suggested that the chosen one might be like Archimedes drawing his last diagram in the dust, engrossed, silent, absorbed, while his assassins crept up behind him. (The reader was of course only alluding to poaching, and certainly not suggesting that a murder might take place in the orange Athenian night.) The choice of Athens was mocked—was a university down underneath the world making some grab for credibility by recalling mathematics' ancient and romantic past? Some readers (ecstatically) remembered Svrinivasa Ramanujan, described (commonly) as a poverty-stricken young Indian who found a textbook on the streets he swept and changed the history of mathematics. Another reader urged that the organisers invite the world's press. The lucky amateur could wake up in his (the letter was particular in its choice of pronoun) hotel room to find his name and his theory made famous.

The magazine was still publishing letters about the competition when I received my invitation. My mother's work had been chosen.

OPENING THE INVITATION

It lay on my doorstep, inside my shut front door. It just looked like a bill. Coming in from school, I pushed it aside with the brown leather toe of my shoe. It skidded under an armchair and may have stayed there for months so that I would have missed the conference and this story would never have happened. But a few evenings later as I scribbled as usual, my work on my lap, I angled the armchair more towards the light. On the gleam of the floorboards lay the envelope.

I'd thought that from now on, all there'd ever be to my life would be the dailyness of it, the roar of the garbage men down the tunnels of narrow city streets, the empty clang of the front door behind me as I left for work, the mumble of gossip in the staffroom that stopped when I walk in, the slumped teabags puddling the sink, the vegetables limp and damp at the bottom of the fridge.

The hope that my scribbles gave me every night, the despair as I crossed them out over breakfast in the morning.

I'd watched the other teachers wiping the crumbs of sandwiches from their desks and chattering about their busy weekends. I'd been eager to offer them lifts home if their cars broke down because I liked flicking open the books in their living rooms and peeping in their bathroom cupboards. Once I saw a poster on a colleague's toilet wall: This is the first day of the rest of your life. I remembered the sentence from when I was young. It seemed to make sense then. The poster was spotted with age now, as my hands would soon be, and hung limply from one blackened pin. In the mirror as I washed my hands the poster was back-to-front. I would've followed its advice but as I watched the rush of water, I wondered if I knew how to change anything.

In those days, I sat too deep in other people's armchairs, words jerking out of me, staying long after my welcome wore out, searching between the pauses of my colleague's words, in hope of what I'm not sure. I was seldom invited back when dinner parties were considered.

A mousy person, I heard a hostess say. Not much to her, do you think?

I combed the newspapers every day; you can imagine me at my kitchen table, a cup of coffee near my hand just a punctuation point in the long drone of the day, something to cradle in my hands. For years I'd searched the faces of people on the bus, the corners of their mouths. I sometimes travelled way beyond my stop just to keep up a conversation with a stranger that always withered into silence. I watched laughing people go into their houses and shut the doors behind them and afterwards I stood alone beyond their noise of light, wanting to knock on the door and say: Let me in, let me be part of it.

But I just walked back home, my steps ringing out against the empty letterboxes.

At school, it was known from a departmental form I'd filled in that I had a divorced husband and a daughter with a funny name, grown up and gone.

So she's managed to have her fun, I heard the men say one

day in the staffroom when they didn't know I was there behind the lockers, and the word jostled their trousers so the material needed easing across their thighs.

But she saddled her daughter with the most pretentious name, said the economics master.

What? asked the young student teacher, whose name was Winston.

Hypatia, said the economics master.

Hypatia was mangled to death with oyster shells, said Winston. Is that what she wanted for her daughter?

I left quietly. So much of my life had been spent trying to find the new numbers my mother's work hinted at. I was running out of time. I only had a few months left before I became a brilliant forty-five-year-old woman who'd saved her mother, a mouse no more.

When I opened the invitation, I saw what I'd always known from mathematics, that a new universe comes into being when a space is severed.

About Hypatia the ancient mathematician

It's true that Hypatia, the ancient Greek mathematician, was murdered by oyster shells in 325 A.D. She was the first eminent woman mathematician that anyone seems to know about. But she'd become dangerous to Cyril, the Patriarch of Alexandria. She'd studied under Plutarch in Athens and then she'd become head of the Neoplatonic school in Alexandria, where she taught philosophy, geometry, astronomy and the new science of algebra. She had a huge following, and distinguished students came from Europe, Asia and Africa to hear her. Cyril was fearful of her popularity and her religion, and incited a mob of fanatics, who dragged her to a church, murdered her with shells, and then burned her. This happened at the height of her fame, when she was 45. All her writings have been lost.

Grandma Juanita named me Hypatia. But I turned out barely able to add up-
Hypatia

IRISES WAITING TO BE COLOURED IN

At school, I had to ask the headmaster for time off immediately. He was sitting with his legs on the desk. He'd been a mathematics teacher with a fast promotion. We'd seldom spoken. I was only an English teacher.

The magazine that carried the advertisement was on his desk, and the pages with the readers' letters were spread open. I couldn't resist glancing in that direction, and every time I did, a line of print spangled the air.

'A poverty-stricken young Indian who found a textbook on the streets he swept,' I read.

He managed to find his staff file without moving his legs. I could tell this had taken a lot of practice.

You English teachers, you've got no stickability in this job, he said, so I get you all mixed up. When did you first come here?

Fifteen years ago, I told him.

See, people think I'm an organisation man, he said. But what I really am is an ideas person. And the big ideas are in mathematics.

I know, I wanted to tell him.

'Modern-day assassins crept up behind him,' I read.

Clare Fletcher, a mathematics teacher, wandered past the open doorway just at that moment. She was large, statuesque, fun-loving. Her skirt floated behind her and lingered for a moment inside the room, twinkling at us.

8

The headmaster swung his legs down from the desk.

Miss Fletcher? he said. She paused. Her skirt caught up to her and wound around her legs.

You called? she answered.

Miss Fletcher, he said, I was just saying to er—he checked his file for my name—I was saying that the humanities people should be brought up to date with ideas, the big ideas of the twenty-first century and you, your sudden presence reminded me, we mathematics people, you and me in particular, you no doubt saw this ad about big radical ideas, I'd thought of sending them in a little something, you and I could host a couple of evenings, full pay of course, you'd be free to talk about whatever comes into your, may I say your pretty little head—

Pig's arse, she said.

She floated away. We both gazed after her.

A woman of the times, he murmured.

We sighed together. He remembered me.

And what ideas have you been teaching today, Miss, ah? The placement of the comma?

Irony, I said.

He bent over to riffle through his filing cabinet for a leave form and for the first time I saw how languidly his eyes moved. Disappointment had drained them of colour, so his irises were outlines, like a child's picture book, waiting to be coloured in.

Like mine.

My mother's digressions

My mother's mind was probably never one of those minds that travel in straight lines. Who knows? That may have been the secret of her greatness. I know she had a very strong spatial sense which

9

she inherited from her father, that's my theory, and this allowed
her to do—but I'm jumping ahead. Anyway, in her old age, she'd
sit up in her queen-size bed (she'd become plump with love and
success), and bang her pillows into shape with her wrinkled hands,
and digress.
    If you want to know what happened at Athens, go to page 64.
(Some might say that digression is to be expected of a
mathematician, that mathematics is a digression.)
Hypatia

THREE FAREWELLS

In any journey there are many farewells. One was to my lover
Guy. When I walked into his room to say goodbye I knew at
last what a room would be like where love could happen.
There'd be white-framed windows opening onto a haze of
light. The space inside the room would be honey-warm. The
man inside the warm space would want to know my
mathematics.

We sat on Guy's unmade bed. On the sheets my fingers
touched grit.

I didn't know you were interested in sums, he said.

One day, one day, I promised myself, I'll find a proper
lover. I'll spend my life lying close beside him, skin moving
against skin as we sigh, the ripples, concavities, undulations
of warmth like dry ice. That shock as the hand moves into the
everyday air but isn't disappointed, the thrill will still be there,
it'll linger, I will still stretch my fingers out to it. Some parts
of his body will be always mysterious, I'll have to learn them
again and again, like a familiar house that in a dream has
acquired unexplored nooks and crannies, so that the dreamer
says: Why haven't I gone into that room, sat on that balcony

and on that shadowy window seat? He won't say: Can I come into you? He'll say: Would you like to enclose me? He'll melt into me, and my muscles, flesh, heart, mind will enclose him. We'll talk as we move gently, we'll talk mathematics. And afterwards, we'll watch the ceiling roses, how still they are, their fixed petals.

That's what I thought then.

I told him that I wanted to tell him about my mother's work and what I'd done with it. He dismissed that with a shrug.

What's there to tell about a mathematical theory? he asked.

When you first brought me here, I wanted to tell you the story of my life, I said. So you'd know who you'd be making love to. Like new lovers are supposed to do.

And I stopped you? he asked.

His hands moved so easily on his sheets, they made me furious.

You said: Will it take long? I answered.

This wasn't the room. This wasn't the lover.

And yet there are such stories to tell. I might have told him about my mother's breasts. They had such abundance, impossible to mute, even under stern dresses they pushed the cloth regally. Such grand stillness, they seemed not blind, but knowledgeable. And when she pressed me close, there was no impact of bone. Only softness, that could go on whispering forever, like a confession.

I might have told him about my mother Juanita, when she was young and as beautiful as light. Or so I thought then.

I'm always thinking of a tunnel of mirrors, the way an image swims all through the tunnel, as absolute as water. But eventually there's interference, the glass distorts, the light trembles, the image drowns as if it had never been.

11

SEANCES AND MATHEMATICS

My mother explained to me that Zeno, a young man who lived two and a half thousand years ago in the Greek city of Elea in Italy, believed that the world of sensation is an illusion, and to discredit everyone's belief in the sensory world he tried to show that motion is self-contradictory, or at least a succession of stills, not the smooth transition we think we see. He put to his contemporaries four paradoxes that have been discussed ever since, and used in some form in all theories of space, time and infinity. Socrates who lived at the same time was irritated by him and dismissed him and his friends, the Sophists, but he was unable to answer Zeno's arguments.

One of Zeno's paradoxes was The Dichotomy. 'There is no motion because that which is moved must arrive at the middle (of its course) before it arrives at the end.' The second was The Achilles: 'The slower when running will never be overtaken by the quicker; for that which is pursuing must first reach the point from which that which is fleeing started, so that the slower must necessarily always be some distance ahead.' The third was The Arrow: 'If everything is either at rest or in motion in a space equal to itself, and if what moves is always in an instant, the moving arrow is unmoved.' The fourth was The Stadium: 'Two rows, composed of an equal number of bodies of equal size, pass one another on a race-course as they proceed with equal velocity in opposite directions, one row starting from the end of the course and the other from the middle. Thus a given time equals its double.'

I don't understand these entirely, but that's what mum told me. I'm sure they're very interesting.
Hypatia

Even though I'm your mother, I don't know how to tell you my story, it's blurting out of me, and I promise you it's worth your while, if only I knew how to begin. I'm a name to some people, but that's the problem. It's as if my life folded neatly behind my name. As if you could shake my name, and out would fall a proper life. But it wasn't like that.

Especially when Juanita's lover . . .

But I've never known where a beginning is.

There are those four vital days when I went missing in Greece just before my talk that turned the world upside down. It's known that I sped away in the back of a taxi cab and people have made wild guesses about where I went and what I did that inspired me so much. They traced the taxi driver, but all he could remember was putting me out on a dusty road somewhere near the mainland coast. There's been speculation that I found on that lonely road a stranger, some say a man, some say a woman, older, younger, handsome, pretty or beguilingly ugly, and that I had a love affair that tore my fears away. Other stories have me drunk and sleeping in parks, or hiding in an expensive penthouse. So perhaps I should begin with what really happened in those four lost days—that in a house echoing with the ocean, I peeled potatoes with an old woman more mute than me.

Or perhaps I shouldn't begin there. Perhaps I should show you Juanita when she was young. There's a certain room I could take you to. Our loungeroom. It looked a lot fresher then. I'd open the door, nudge you to go in. She'd be sitting near the window, leaning into the light. You'd know where you wanted to sit, you'd sit near her, your armchair would almost touch hers. She was like that when she was young, someone people wanted to sit near. I always wanted to sit near her.

But there's a photograph I'd show you, look, here she is at seventeen, too haughty to turn her beauty to the photographer. She's a young girl waiting for happiness, the daughter of a widow with a fortune, the daughter of a refugee who'd been knifed.

So perhaps that's where to start my story, after all.

When Juanita's schooling at the convent was over, her mother, my grandma Fernandez, came to take her away. Juanita hadn't seen or heard from her mother for ten years. No letters, no holidays back home, no visits. In school holidays she'd sat on her hard bed in her tiny cell, hiding scribbles on paper amongst her prayers. Now she turned her head away when her mother spoke, in case this stranger with pearls bumping around the circles of her neck expected something of her that she wouldn't know how to give. All she'd remembered of her mother was her comfortable farmyard smell, and now she smelled of expensive perfumes. She would've known how to talk to her father, if he'd come. He'd have still smelled of farmyard. They would've laughed about the goat he'd given her, his face crushed around the eyes like brown velvet with laughing. She would be the spit and image of him one day, she was a chip off the old block, they used to say.

Her goat used to always skitter inside, sliding on the polished floors. Seventeen-year-old Juanita was shocked that her mother now had nothing to do with her memory of her father, but of course they weren't part of each other, whatever the church said about man and wife. And of course he couldn't have come to take her home. He'd died before she'd come here. That's why she'd been sent here. It was a fact as slippery as a lie.

You wouldn't credit how busy it is, being a widow, Grandma Fernandez said to the nuns in her best accent which she put in her mouth of a morning along with her false teeth. She hadn't greeted her daughter yet because it was that hard to think of something to say after ten years, you wouldn't credit. Juanita was paler and purer than she'd remembered, like a marble statue in a cold church.

14

Indeed, the nuns said, and blinked the remark away, and talked about Juanita instead.

Juanita's surprised us all, said the younger of the two nuns, her lips fluttering prettily in the breeze of her voice.

Once she'd settled in, said the other nun, perhaps the mother superior, Grandma Fernandez couldn't remember which was which because it had been so hot being driven here in the Humber, she'd have preferred the first-class carriage in the train with the possibility of male glances, but she'd wanted these nuns to know who she was.

She's had of course a while to settle in, added the nun. Ten years.

Grandma Fernandez realised she was expected to nod. She nodded.

She seemed like the others, the young nun said. Despite her—despite everything.

Here the pretty nun faltered, and blushed, so that she was white and pink and mauve. Grandma eased the pearls across her throat, and was glad of the decision to bring the Humber.

The older nun folded her own pale hands across the stern folds of her garments.

She began saying strange things, said the older nun.

Grandma in the new pause considered this.

Like what?

About numbers, said the younger nun.

Oh numbers, smiled Grandma, who was glad to smile and show she knew a thing or two.

One day we found her laughing at her sums, said the younger nun.

I'm not surprised. Grandma Fernandez sniffed ostentatiously at the memory of her schooldays. I often laughed at sums myself.

In the brown corner, Juanita spoke.

Excuse me—Juanita looked from one nun to the other. She didn't know who to address as mother, now her own mother had appeared at last.

With them. Not at them or about them, with them. I laughed with numbers.

The three women stared at the oval amber of Juanita's face floating in the brown corner.

When she was only nine, said the young nun, Juanita had such an intuitive idea of how infinity lies between each number that she could see Zeno's argument that Achilles in a race against a tortoise could never catch up to the tortoise because he had to get halfway in the course before he got to the end, and he had to get to a half of the half and a half of that ad infinitum. Juanita looked at me brightly and said, So a door never shuts.

Doors go like that after rain, said my grandmother.

The nuns told Grandma Fernandez that Juanita's strange ability with mathematics had frightened them. They'd prayed hard.

So we'd know where your daughter had got her gift from, explained the mother superior.

Grandma Fernandez stiffened, remembering that she too was again a mother.

Got what gift? she asked. Who gave what to her?

Why, that's the point, said the mother superior. We decided that if she did wonders for our accounts, we'd know it came from God. Otherwise—

Otherwise? demanded my grandmother.

She did wonders for our convent, said the mother superior smoothly. Absolute wonders. We're a poor order, but because of your daughter's mathematics we've refurbished the building and doubled our enrolments.

Grandma Fernandez was horrified to find her gloved fingers automatically clutching her pearls at the mention of poverty. She willed her hands to drop casually to her smooth, wool crepe sides.

So we called in a professor of mathematics, said the mother superior. Once a week. He's told us that sometimes he asks questions of Juanita that he can't answer.

Well if it's just questions we're talking about, any fool can ask questions, said Grandma Fernandez, who didn't have all day to hear about a convent's accounts after she'd paid a king's ransom to these nuns in the last ten years.

Outside, in the real world, you have to have answers, outside a convent it's answers you need up your sleeve, she said, letting her voice fall to show that she'd heard enough.

She insisted on struggling with the heavy entrance door alone just to prove she could deal with the reality that lay beyond their cool brown rooms. Grandma Fernandez swung out of the convent in a chic whisper of wool crepe. It was good to leave that pretty young nun behind. She probably had her lipstick hidden somewhere under her wimple, thought my grandmother darkly.

But out in the sunshine, there were comforts. Even though she was large-boned, even burly, at least she'd had the love of a passionate man. That was something those nuns would just pine for. And now at night she had her ex-husband's money under her mattress, to fondle as if it were him. And once a year, on the anniversary of his death, she gave herself a pearl, sometimes mounted in a dainty droplet, sometimes in a ring. Just one a year, for comfort. Pearls were becoming to the larger figure, any shop girl would tell you that. As palely elegant as the moon, as smooth as mother's milk.

You deserve it, after the way I left you, she heard his kind voice say at the seances she often went to.

And the way the dogs were lately, she needed all the comfort going.

There's a shininess about Juanita that makes her look morally scrubbed, thought my grandmother, sweeping ahead of Juanita into the waiting Humber, knowing the prickle of the rounded eyes of nuns at the upstairs windows.

So scrubbed, perhaps you could say God has smiled on me for marrying a Spanish Jew.

She turned to the stranger her daughter.

You'll put your sums to use to help me with the dogs, she said.

The sheep dogs are still alive? asked Juanita joyfully, remembering her goat.

I'm talking about greyhounds. On the track. You can tell me about the odds, said Grandma Fernandez.

She was so pleased with this thought, she touched Juanita's arm. The last time she'd touched the girl was when she was seven and leaving for the convent, and the time before that was when she was a baby. They weren't a touching family. The girl didn't flinch or murmur, so Grandma Fernandez became bolder, and lifted the hair from my mother's forehead.

You are so young, she said in surprise. There are no lines on your forehead.

My mother was able to recite, as the Humber swept through the suburbs: 'Next to the sanctification of the soul comes the cultivation of manners. A young lady should avoid wrinkling the forehead. A wrinkled forehead is often the mark of a melancholy temper, or of a haughty mind.'

She recited it with irony, but my grandmother nodded with gravity, and made a mental note to avoid wrinkling her own forehead. She hoped too much damage hadn't already been done.

Aren't we going home? my mother asked when she saw no green countryside rolling away out the window.

We live in the city now. The men with knives can't find us here, my grandmother told her.

My mother Juanita remembered all her life the moment the Humber swept into my grandmother's driveway. My grandmother's city house was dauntingly grand, without paddocks and jacaranda trees.

I don't suppose you brought my goat, my mother said.

Now that my mother suddenly belonged to the world, she wanted to find knowledge at university, but Grandma Fernandez didn't want to waste the fees. A beauty like her daughter would soon be married, and what good was education then?

Besides, no matter what Grandma Fernandez dressed her in, my mother continued to look like the daughter of a Spanish Jew.

There's no knowing what the university ratbags would do to you, with your face, said my grandmother. Not that there's anything wrong with looking like your father. It's just that the men with knives . . .

Her voice softened.

She could still have lustful thoughts amongst the rounded pink cushions, though she wasn't sure if it was sinful to have lustful thoughts of the dead. Not a question you could ask anyone, if there was anyone to ask. Certainly you couldn't ask it of a nun.

She allowed herself a titter.

He was such a passionate man, he couldn't stop himself, she often told Juanita, who blushed like a nun. He had to marry out of the Jewry, because he had to have me.

She was roused from these musings by the next amber

cup of tea that the maid brought in, with sunlight slanting through it.

The trouble is, those university ratbags might bundle you onto a boat and send you back to Hitler and you wouldn't have a chance to explain that your mother is a good Irish Catholic, she said. Don't think anyone would help you. The government wouldn't help. They'd all be in it together.

She was pleased with the quivering darkness in her daughter's eyes. The girl seemed to have inherited his terror, those dark nights when all that could calm him had been her own plump, comfortable body. He hadn't minded her big bones.

Every day the two women would sit in the pink parlour, and my mother would obediently turn the pages of my grandmother's form guides and use her mathematics to calculate the odds of Gumleaf taking out the Empire Cup. My grandmother thought of the convent Juanita had made rich, and kept her plump fingers crossed.

But with the dogs, my mother never even got a near miss.

After the war, when my mother asked my grandmother if it was now safe to go to university, my grandmother took her to seances instead.

You meet the smartest young men at seances, said my grandmother, her own longing so fat you glimpsed the lonely white sheets of her troubled bed.

Grandma Fernandez had taken to calling for her own mother Great Grandmother F Johnson at the seances, and when that reedy voice filtered through from the dead, she'd request a racing tip.

It was a remarkable thing that Great Grandmother Johnson, who'd spent most of her life as a wet-nurse, could speak from the dead about dog racing so reliably. Grandma Fernandez claimed the old skeleton had come up twice with winning tips and three times with a near miss.

It goes to prove, Grandma Fernandez nodded as my mother's mathematics got it wrong again,

If you want to know what dog is going to win, you don't go to Einstein.

I'll admit it now: I was the envious daughter of a mother so beautiful she shimmered into light. Was it envy that pulled me into mathematics, to be better than her? Or was it adoration? Or were the envy and adoration part of each other?

My mother and Grandma Fernandez went to the photographer. He'd watched many young women through his lens, their hands leaning on his painted pedestal, their long fingers tapering like water. He watched my beautiful mother, her terror, her power.

Your beauty's a danger to you, he said.

Later, tinting the photograph, he spread pink on my mother's quivering cheeks and on her forehead (that later wrinkled deeply in thought) as if he was licking her with his own pink tongue.

Years later, when Grandma Fernandez died, my mother inherited the photograph. It was the only thing she inherited, apart from a china dinner set. Great Grandmother Johnson must have lost her touch in betting. Perhaps she had other journeys to make. All Grandma Fernandez's money was lost to the dogs.

The photograph was put away in the sideboard drawer. I got it out often, hoping something had changed in the balance of things. Nothing did. She stayed beautiful, and I stayed plain. We both smiled urgently.

In the seances Juanita reluctantly attended, candlelight flickered across the faces of intense young men.

Their eyes look like frogs' eggs, objected my mother.

Candlelight is seldom flattering, despite what love songs say, said Grandma Fernandez. Particularly around the chin. Not to mention the shape of the nose. Sometimes it's made me almost give up on seances. But apart from the dogs, what else is there to do?

Buttressed between the sad smell of her mother's perfumes, and the hopeful smell of a young man's semen, Juanita considered the shine of oil on a grand painting of woodlands. Someone's dead aunt was chattering. The young man beside Fernandez followed her gaze.

The leaves, murmured the young man to Juanita, the leaves were magnificently executed. Weren't they?

They look like a hairpiece to me, said Juanita. Stuck on. That could slip off, any moment.

My mother's beauty taunted. The young man leaned towards her.

Tell me what else you see, he murmured.

So Juanita was forced into something like truth.

I was looking at the oaks, she said. Their roots.

Roots, chortled the young man, wondering if this was a joke a lady should tell.

I was wondering if there's a connection between the roots and the trees' heights, she said. And if the connection is numerical, and how do you begin to think about it?

Despite her mother, Juanita saw in the candlelit painting a path out. Or perhaps because of her mother. She hadn't thought of a path out before, although she was clever. But now she knew that to follow the path would require her mind, a few books, and a mentor like the admiring professor at the convent. Then she could become a proper mathematician.

She stumbled onto another path, through another gate. In ten weeks she'd married my father instead, whom she met at a Saturday night square dance. Once my mother decided on something, that was that.

He's a working class man, Grandma Fernandez roared in her upper class accent,

with no prospects. And he's got nothing in common with you.

This seemed at the time a reasonable judgement. Juanita was a mathematics prodigy, and my father couldn't count past ten.

DRESSING AND THE SOUL 1

A further digression, but at least you find out that my mother inherited not only her mathematics, but the wrong face.
Hypatia

In the week before I left for Athens and the mathematics conference, the suitcase on my floor gaped like a panic-stricken mouth. Clothes fluttering off hangers in my wardrobe were suddenly preposterous, though I'd worn them for years.

It doesn't matter what I look like, I said to myself. The thought only made me panic more.

I rang Clare, the mathematics teacher from school. I hardly knew her, but she was a good dresser. She said she'd come over right away. I'd almost hung up when her voice fluted: Why did you win?

I was still finding an answer when the phone went dead.

I sat at my kitchen table with my new mathematics calculations. They were littered with toast crumbs and stained with coffee cups. But I couldn't concentrate, I kept jumping up to clean spots off the fridge, and wipe water off the sink, and even when I forced myself to read, a breeze through the window made me look up to watch the skitterings of white clouds as suddenly buoyant as me. A space was opening up inside me as expansive and full of light as the sky.

Clare screeched to a stop and left her car in the middle of the street. I'd watched her do this at school, with the traffic filing around her abandoned car and becoming a procession for several blocks until the arrival of a policeman and a tow truck. And even then, Clare still laughed. I'd always tucked my car away as if it had never been guilty of use.

I'm going to be like her, I say. After Athens.

Clare dragged dresses from the front and back seats of her car, piled them on top of a bulging suitcase, and kicked the car doors shut with a high-heeled foot. On my stairs, only her hair could be seen sticking out above the froth of brilliant dresses. She stopped in my hallway, box and all, looking at a photograph of my mother. It was the one of Juanita that the photographer had coloured ice-cream pink. I'd hung it so no one would miss it when they came in the front door. I was hoping someone would say we looked alike. No one ever did.

I've been putting off telling you about my face. You would have met many like me, and not even noticed. Your eyes would run past me in a group staring out of a photograph. You would bump into me at the supermarket queue, even if we shared a bus seat you'd think you sat in it alone. I should've had amber skin, black hair, wide black eyes, like Juanita. I have a long earnest nose and a red face. I've gone through my life looking embarrassed.

Goodness, who's this? she asked of the photograph.
My mother, I said.
She shrieked with laughter.
You must have taken after your dad, she said.

She didn't take long to get to the point. She dumped the suitcase down on the kitchen table and said,
You know nothing about mathematics! You've never studied it.
I read the old books my mother collected, I said.
What? A few old books? she asked.
A laundry full, I said. She'd put them in the laundry because Dad never went there.
But old books, she said. Out-of-date mathematics!
Out of fashion, I said. But beautiful.
My voice was thick with its beauty.
And I read her mathematics notes, I added quickly.
Your mum's notes? she laughed.
She'd stuck them up as wallpaper—
all out of order, I said.
A pink bodysuit slid out of her suitcase and onto my table.
But that's not how to learn mathematics, said Clare, her hands on her elegant hips.
Learning mathematics is like climbing up a tree, she said. First you've got to know arithmetic. Algebra builds on arithmetic. Geometry builds on arithmetic and algebra. Calculus on arithmetic, algebra and geometry. Topology is an off-shoot of geometry, set theory and algebra.
You can't just pick it up.
It seems to have worked, I said.
I went to the tap to fill the kettle for tea.
Everyone knows amateur mathematicians are maniacs, she said. When I was doing teacher training in mathematics,

amateurs were always writing letters to the mathematics lecturers. She faltered as I turned to face her.

I was on their side, she said. The amateurs of course. Once we asked a lecturer: What if one of these amateurs really has found a way to construct an antigravity shield and you ignore him? And he said: Well, that's one of the risks the mathematical community is prepared to take.

You think I should be ignored? I asked.

Why didn't you ever talk to me at the school about your mathematics? I'd have liked a bit of real conversation, she said.

In case you said what you just said, I answered.

I held up the pink bodysuit against myself then.

You couldn't wear that, she said. You've aged first around your neck. Pity.

She opened her handbag and tucked the pink bodysuit inside it.

But she couldn't let the thought go.

Why did your mother collect old books? asked Clare. Why did she use her notes as wallpaper?

I couldn't tell her then, I couldn't say it. I can't tell you yet. Some memories are too sadly lived to talk about, as if the pastness of things is just an illusion. But I told her about my mother's lonely childhood in the convent, and how numbers were her companions. That softened her, as I knew it would. People always indulged my mother, even when they didn't know her. Clare was suddenly laughing again and pulling a cream lace dress out of the suitcase.

What do you think? she asked.

Against her shapely body, the dress rustled and swooned.

You think I should get up and explain her ideas in a balldress? I asked.

There's always balls at these conferences. I think, she said.

I pulled the dress on. In my dented silver teapot, I saw my reflection, the wrong face sticking out of an overly-frilly dress. It should've been my mother's face.

Clare tweaked at the bodice.

The trouble with you, she said, is that you've got no breasts. Same as me. I wanted that huge-breasted look, with nipples— out here.

She stretched her arms in front of her and twiddled her fingers as if she was turning dials.

I could've had an implant, I suppose. But I wanted that huge-breasted look that says you're huge accidentally. In spite of your modest intentions.

A gold bangle slid slowly down Clare's arm. Many men must've watched that slow slide. She watched me struggle out of the dress, fumbling the buttons, catching the zip in my woolly hair.

It's genetic, of course, she says, untangling me. You just live a different life if you've got good breasts. They determine it.

She pushed out her own stylish bosom, swathed in smooth crossover pleats.

That's probably why you became a serious mathematician. Amateur of course.

She pulled a dress of stiff gold brocade out of the suitcase. The grandeur of it, the gold threads woven with white, and my reflection in the teapot, jolted words out of me.

When I was very young, I said, I fell in love with the story that it was Einstein's wife who discovered $E=MC^2$.

Clare laughed.

All the great discoveries aren't made by amateurs, she said. Einstein used esoteric mathematics about the curvature of space that a wife wouldn't know.

She was a top-notch mathematician, I said.

Clare's smooth arms went around the brocade, cradling it.
They both loved mathematics? she said.

She rocked the brocade dress as if it was a dancing partner.

She knew she was the wrong mathematician, I said. She knew that anything is not just what you can prove, for who's to believe a mere proof? And to a salon of eminent men in those days, from her mouth it would've seemed like the gibbering of a chimpanzee.

Clare's face was soft with the hope of romance.

She kept silent for love of him? she asked.

For love of the equation, I said. Its immortality.

Clare put the brocade down.

You need to vibrate for brocade, she said. You're not the vibrating type.

She picked up a red satin skirt. She was still thinking about my mother, I could tell.

Why didn't your mother finish her mathematics by herself? she asked.

She had a lover, I began. A mathematics lecturer. But she also had us. My brother Matti, he was supposed to take over where she left off.

He didn't? she asked.

So long ago. My brother Matti was so long ago, Matti and the lake. I still can't talk about that either. Not yet, anyway.

I took over, I said.

She was watching me, waiting.

One night, I said, it was dawn, the traffic was just beginning, birds were twittering in the tree outside my window, someone down the road was revving a car—and there it was. I'd used some geometric devices I'd invented. They gave me a spatial sense of what I was doing. They helped me to change a theorem in one place and keep track of the changes happening at the same time to the theorems in other places. My mother didn't

28

have those devices. She didn't seem to have that spacial sense. I found the conjecture she'd been searching for.

I took a breath to cover all the unsaid words.

I'll always remember the jarring of that revving car. And then suddenly, the peace. It seemed to go on forever. I couldn't go teaching for a few days. I stayed in the peace. I got there, I kept saying to myself. She's there at last.

Then what did you do? Clare asked.

Nothing, I said. Till this competition.

I touched the dress, its softness.

We were both sipping cold tea. I knew I should get up and heat the jug again, but Clare murmured:

It must've been pretty difficult, what happened between you and your mother. Fancy your mother having a lover!

He didn't stop there, I said.

There was a long silence in the kitchen. We listened to the warbling of my old fridge.

Did you hate him? Clare asked.

I thought about hate, what love and hate had done to my family.

I was only thirteen, I said.

The fridge cut out.

My mother's armpits

It was the day after I began bleeding that my mother's lover first came to our house. I've heard it doesn't usually happen so early in life, the daughter's discovery of her mother. But the way he leaned there, it was impossible not to know, a child instantly knows about possession. The moment before I arrived, his eyes had been dancing with my mother's eyes, that dancing when bodies cling all the way down, yearning. They were standing at opposite ends of the kitchen but their eyes had looped across the black and white lino of the kitchen floor, across the squares scratched by too many chairs, too many withered conversations. I walked into the stillness at the centre of the dance.

I had come through the house because there were none of the usual noises, the iron's sigh, the rush of tap water, the scratch of the scrubbing brush, the tired squelch of my mother's old slippers on the newly mopped floor. It was a silence that clamoured, an indrawn breath you remember as deafening all your life.

As I arrived, my mother was huffing as she looked at him. Perhaps she had told him not to come to the house. And there he was, leaning against the doorframe. While she leaned against the old green stove, her ally and enemy and constant companion, now scrubbed free of her wrestles with it. She wore her old dress that only the family was supposed to see, and her quilted apron with the squares she'd never added, and her hair flossed out of its pins and fell over her cheeks.

There's a first time in her life when a girl sees her mother. My mother had been just a consciousness to me till then, a will that wasn't mine, she'd floated at that point down the tunnel beyond a mirror's reflection. She had lived for me in a succession of moments, like numbers. The prickle of a hairbrush in my hair. The nudge of her hand as she buttoned my shirt. The strict stiffness of the sheets she still tucked in at night. The admonition to eat one more mouthful of carrot amongst the smell of meat fat at dinner. The reminders to put my socks in the wash, to tidy my room, these moments had been my mother, till then.

Now the man who was my mother's lover leaned against the doorway of my father's house. My father had built the doorframe, he'd built the house, just as he'd promised my

30

mother he would when he'd been a bachelor at the Saturday night square dance at the School of Arts hall, with a carpenter's pencil stuck in his pocket, and a piece of blank paper. He took paper and pencil everywhere all his life: he needed his subterfuges. And my mother was there because in an act of great daring, she'd run away for the evening from Grandma Fernandez's house and her seances and her dog races. She'd braved the men with knives. She was looking for the path for her life.

I don't know what my father was wearing. But my mother kept her dress of that night all her life, its pearly pinkness like a shell that could be full of air, or echoes, because a shell can sing. As someone later said to me, in some dresses there are promises but you never know which dresses will keep those promises. My mother, a fragile shell herself, was ready to break herself, to shatter, anything to leave her mother. And here was my father, out on the School of Arts porch in the silver sheen of stars that died millions of years ago, see him slowly pulling from his pocket his flat carpenter's pencil and the blank page crumpled by his body's sweat.

The stars, he said to fill in the silence while he drew, are . . .

—words failed him, like they often do me—

. . . grand, he found at last.

Near him, sipping the orangeade he'd stutteringly bought her, my mother stood amused, wondering, waiting.

Some of them died ten million years ago, she said after a while.

But the light's still coming to us. From nothing. We're bits of stars ourselves, she added.

I can see, said my father.

He was drawing on the paper a promise so precious to him

he could no longer look at my mother's beauty. He drew all he knew about love. He drew the house he'd build for her, if only she'd give him her life.

It'd be on my land, he said. A nice bit of land near a lake. I'd put a porch on, so you could sit and look at the lake.

What are the dots you've drawn at the windows? she asked. Our children, he said.

Children! But there are thirteen of them! she said. Didn't know I'd drawn that many, said my father. Is thirteen big?

She nodded absent-mindedly.

It's quite big, isn't it, the number thirteen, he said. I never had a head for big numbers.

My mother should've listened more carefully to him. But all she said was: I could hide there.

He should've listened more carefully to her.

She didn't keep the drawing, why should she, she'd come home at last, the daughter of a refugee.

That's how she told us it happened, me and Matti. She'd tell it over and over again, as if she was trying to explain it to herself.

The way I do.

Now the man her lover leaned against my father's doorframe like a rock that was needed to shore up a wall. His sleeve was rolled up to his elbow, with a cuff loose and flapping. He hadn't seen a need to visit in buttoned-down cuffs and a tie. I was tall enough to reach up to his armpit, his arm was a bridge I had to duck under to see my mother. The excitement of his sweat under his arm hit me like a slap. In that slap, I looked at my mother with his eyes.

You see, my mother and my mother's lover began life for me. That's when it began, after all. So that's where my story should begin.

My mother at the old green stove put her hands up to her hair, to fasten it back. She was always lifting her arms like that, even when someone was waiting for her to answer a question, lifting her round arms behind her blue-black hair and leaning back her head to pillow her thoughts. Her loose sleeves fell back. I saw her armpits, before this they'd been just a blur of flesh while I waited to hear if I could go swimming in the river, if I could go out with Matti, if I could stay home from school.

Her hands were fluttering about her hair, searching like eyes for hairpins, her sleeves were falling back when he said: Would there be a cup of tea in the pot?

His voice was careful, like the rehearsed voices of the men on ABC radio. My mother lifted her hands right behind her head because she'd remembered she had her apron on and it was tied at the back of her neck. He gasped. I looked up at his face, to glimpse the quiver in his lips. I looked back at her. I saw that even her armpits were beautiful, I gasped with him as we gazed together at the black shining coils of hair nestling secretly till this moment against her candle wax skin. I saw with her lover that she lowered her eyes while she thought, so that you wanted to bend to peep up at them, the way they moved mysteriously behind thick lashes like the lake at midnight but darker still with her musing. I saw with him that she thought with her whole body, that long after the noise of the question had faded she found her answer with a timing that was voluptuous, like the majestic pace of an equation as it moves deliberately into its silent conclusion.

She pulled at the ties that held her apron at her neck and then she untied its bow at her waist. She shook it off, folded it so he couldn't see the missing two squares (kept on the mantelshelf and dust smeared) and put it on the table.

We're out of milk, she said. You have milk in your tea—
she glanced at me and then back at him—don't you? she asked
him as if she wasn't sure.

I was sent down to Bev Roberts' corner shop for milk for
the cup of tea that my mother's lover needed. She'd probably
already decided that he would be her lover. Touching roadside
angophora gums that glowed gold in the afternoon light, I
found they were as warm as bodies. I kicked stones over the
cliff in wonder that there were things I'd never noticed before,
things all around me.

Loss opened up a chasm inside me. I was as lonely as I will
be in the moment of my death. Suddenly I knew that my
mother would never belong to me.

Don't misunderstand me. I don't blame her lover for what
happened to us. Love and fury flow like blood in families,
darkly, silently creeping underneath, almost forgotten, then
gushing out as white and irrefutable as death.

My grandmother's armpits

Grandma Fernandez's armpits were shuddering white flesh
punctured with blunt black hairs as she lifted her arms to pin
large hats to her thinning scalp.

My mother introduced my father to my grandmother on the
South Coast platform of Central Station in front of the curtained door of carriage 3, the first-class carriage of the train
to the Dapto Dog Races. My grandmother had demanded the
introduction, but didn't know how she'd spare the time. There
were more important things to attend to than the ambitions of
an unsuitable man. Then she'd remembered the lull at Central
Station while the driver's assistant messed around stoking fires
and the driver strode down to lift his hat to the passengers in
first-class carriage 3.

Juanita arrived punctually at the door of carriage 3 with my father as she promised her mother she'd do.

She was so nervous that as she touched the jiggling flesh of my grandmother's arm, she forgot my father's name.

This is my mother, Juanita said to my father, introducing the elder to the younger first, despite the good training of the nuns. She wished the nuns had been there, so she could have explained that she was gasping for time to remember her intended's name. But no name came. All she could say to my grandmother was: This is him.

The fires were roaring, the guard was about to whistle. My grandmother only needed to glance at the man with no fortune, no proper profession and no name before she took action as her husband would surely have done if he hadn't been so untimely taken. She lifted her dimpled fist with its milky pearl rings and punched him.

Who do you think you are? she said. She always spoke evenly in public because she was a lady. But with a voice so trenchant against the vague circle of faces and the blurred megaphone voice shouting all aboard, that no one, no one would think that in the dark mornings at three o'clock, she'd asked the question of herself.

That'll learn you, she told him as she towered over him.

She comforted herself early the next morning that it had only been a little wobble in grammar.

And as my father lay with a bleeding nose on the gritty platform amongst the belching smoke that smelled of hot train, as his best hat rolled on its brim, as my grandmother's crepe dress greyer than smoke whirled around her large-boned but ladylike legs, as her sleeves whispered back into their proper place, as she stood over him irrefutable as any steam engine, my father glimpsed her armpits. He must have wondered at all those thorns.

Undressing and the Soul

A week after my mother's lover first lounged in our kitchen, Matti and I stood at the crack in the bathroom door. We were home from school with some childhood ailment. Perhaps my mother thought we were down the long hall in our beds reading books.

We had a huge old-fashioned white bathtub with feet shaped like a mythical bird's, once golden brass, now streaked with powdery green. My father had found it in a house he'd renovated. Nobody else wanted its quaint splendour and he'd dragged it home, humping it along the dusty roads because to drive it would do in the springs of the ute.

It's for you, he'd said to my mother. You soak yourself in that, you'll have no more worries.

He touched her cheek with his blunt and grimy fingertips.

Until he began to suspect she had a lover, he was as indulgent as bathwater with us all.

My mother leaned back in the water, and her pubic hair was as spiky as a hairbrush, it could comb thought. She tipped her head back, the hair on her head floated in wet black streamers behind her. She had the sort of beauty that stills thought. I've taken her walking on city streets and discovered faces straining out of buses to watch her, the circles of faces like fixtures on the buses' sides. I've seen her come into a room and everyone turned to watch the patterning of light and shadow on her face.

Matti came into my bedroom smiling feverishly, his hoarse voice was heat in my eardrum.

He's looking at her in the nude, he said.

He pronounced nude as nud-ee, he didn't make it rhyme with rude. It made it ruder, almost a blasphemy.

Who? I asked.

Her lover, he said.
What's a lover? I asked.

She sat in the bathtub facing us but unaware or uncaring.

She moved a languorous wash cloth against her amber roundness while her breasts rode high and ballooned in the water white with soap. She lifted an amber leg and the water flowed down her smooth roundness, making it rounder, smoother, she lifted her arms and her breasts followed, high on their bulbous weight, and the purple nipples rose on their creamy richness, and the water flowed, caressing, shining.

I took turns with my brother, moist with terror that we'd be discovered, hot with a secret rush of urine between my legs, breathless to be buried in her, to be her, to be instead of her.

Matti nudged me to look at her lover. I saw his legs at the end of the bath, his buttocks on its rounded edge on a folded white towel so he wouldn't get his trousers wet. He was reading aloud to her. Her lower eyelids sagged to take in the words. There was no other sound, just his voice and the occasional drip of the brass tap in all that unheeding water.

He didn't read from a book but from a set of loose-leaved pages in a brown folder. The words filled the air. I've remembered them all my life. His voice rose and fell on a staircase of music, he was at home amongst those words as an organ at church is amongst the patterns of Bach, he was in love with the words, as much as he was in love with my mother's beauty, I was sure by the way his foot against the bathtub's side moved with their rhythm, even when he was just looking at spaces between words, at blue ink on white paper. He was reading Cantor's theory of infinity to her.

'My theory stands as firm as a rock; every arrow directed against it will return quickly to its archer. How do I know this? Because I have studied it from all sides for many years; because I have examined all objections which have ever been made against the infinite numbers; and above all because I have followed its roots, so to speak, to the first infallible cause of all created things.'

That's a lover, I breathed.

I knew when I was thirteen years old at a bathroom door, I would watch this picture again and again for the rest of my life. The woman my mother with her floating breasts, the man's legs resting so easily on the white bath's edge, his voice reading the quiet, astonishing words. I would take the picture apart a million times, each segment of it—the dripping tap, the pale fall of light, the shiny white tiles behind. I'd touch and revel over each piece all the years of my life. I'd put it together in another shape, so I was there instead of her. Sometimes in my dreams that bathroom would become a cathedral, where her beauty and Cantor's words rose together like birds into flight, like the shape of prayer.

From then on, I had no choice.

A good thing for a girl

In which my mother agrees to take the wrong pathway. (I'm afraid that this is a digression upon a digression. But what choice has an earnest and loving daughter?)
Hypatia

So much of a life ebbs from memory like a body of water. I remember being seventeen, facing into the bright wind that twinkled across the university's green lawns. Juanita, my mother, was grey and puckered already, long before her time.

It was one of her good days. My father said that on her bad days she had nerves. She hadn't had nerves for weeks. My father and I had become very careful of her nerves.

Watch out, she might start imagining the men with knives, he'd warned as I waited for my mother to put on her hat. It was a story he'd told me many times—how Grandma Fernandez had scared her daughter silly and that was why my mother had developed nerves.

I can manage her, I'd said loftily to my father.

After all, I'd won a scholarship to university. My father had been uncertain that I should take it. No one in the family had been to university. It wasn't what girls in his day did. Then he saw that it was called a Commonwealth Scholarship.

I suppose if the Commonwealth wants you to go to university, he said with sudden respect, it means that the Queen wants you to go.

We didn't dare tell my mother about the scholarship. She wouldn't have wanted the government to know about her daughter, let alone the Queen.

My Commonwealth Scholarship said I could study anything I wished. I knew what I wished. I'd read that most of the great mathematicians of the past had made their discoveries while they were young. Because my mother was now framed with sunshine, I was sure she wouldn't object to my plans. After all, her thwarted youth was long ago.

That must be the Great Hall, I enthused, checking my map. I was ready to admire the very stones.

My mother had her hand on her hat, a silly boater, I noticed for the first time, flapping sailor-blue ribbons. I regretted her hat, but she was oblivious, as she usually was of all clothing. Her hand on it was firm, not trembling. It was the moment for my big announcement. But she turned her back on the nineteenth century Great Hall, and sniffed and said that the building was not great, merely pompous.

You'll be able to teach Literature when you leave here, she

said. There was a curious quality about her voice. Later I realised that she'd been rehearsing these exact words for years and now was her moment to say them.

Literature is what a nice girl studies, she said. And teaching is good for a girl who mightn't keep a husband. (She didn't realise then that she was daily losing her own.)

But I don't ... I began.

I was facing the wrong way. It was useless shouting into the wind.

A group of girls passed as we stood in the shadows of the old building, they flung long hair blonde as sunshine over their shoulders, they could catch and hold sunshine in their hair, or toss it away. They had careful upper-class accents, proper mothers, proper family lives. They were pretty. They'd keep husbands.

My mother struggled with her hat in the wind.

And you're likely to pass Literature, she added. It won't be too rigorous.

Now her eyes gripped mine like a promise. She knew how flattered I was when she smiled at me. How fearful. She slipped into my father's slang. He wasn't there, but she knew how to call him into being.

You know what Dad says: If you stick your neck out, you'll get it chopped off.

She saw how I trembled, but she chose to decide it was only the dark shadows of the wind.

I want ... I began again.

I touched her hand, but it was too cold to acknowledge my pleading.

That's fixed then, she said.

I need ... I said.

You need to be able to earn your own living, she said. In case you're left on your own. Besides, she added, what does need matter? When has need ever mattered for me?

There was a pause. The wind changed direction, streaking me with cold. Or perhaps it was what she whispered then. I knew these words too.

Don't hurt me, she whispered.

Suddenly her hat was whirling out of the shadows and away, out into the sunshine and I was chasing it yelling, I chased it all over the green and gold lawns amongst the neat groups of students lounging, and when I caught it I would have willingly thrown it up into the wind again to run away from my mother. But I could scarcely breathe without my mother and I didn't know how to live in any other place than the place she'd made for me.

What we both need, she said, is a cup of tea.

While she sat at the table and I went to the counter to ask for a biscuit for her, my mouth was full of words like little black currants: Let me get to mathematics in time, let me get there in time, let me get there in time.

In those days, I could sit down calmly with a biscuit on a plate and smile at my mother, because I thought I could throw away my life up into the air, and there'd always be more life left to study mathematics, like endless ribbons trailing up into an infinite sky.

I studied every night to become a teacher of Literature, but I only scraped through exams. I liked nothing I studied, I spoke to no one. Amongst the hearty greetings called across the university lawns, my face was redder than ever because I had no friends. I hid in the toilet between lectures when it was too far to walk to the library to hide. One day, I made myself go to a beach picnic advertised on a university noticeboard. In the banter about sandwiches and beach towels, surely I would get into conversation. I stood under straggly trees, too shy to join the group though I recognised faces. But wading alone in the yellow shallows of the rolling sea was a small spindly man with dark stains on the bottoms of his rolled-up trousers. I waded nearby so that if the group looked up from their laughter and tumbling, they'd think I was with somebody.

To my surprise, he spoke to me.

I forgot my swimmers, he said without looking at me, so I could hope he hadn't noticed my red face. I kept turned the other way. I didn't know what to say back, but a seagull squawked loudly to cover my silence. His hands weighed down his pockets.

I am, he said as if he knew it was a credential,

a mathematician. Harry.

It seemed possible to talk to a Harry who'd forgotten to take his swimming costume to the beach. He took his hands out of his pockets as if he had something he could give me, something I couldn't give to myself. I looked at the bubbles winking around my legs, and found my voice telling him my name, and what I was studying. He nodded briefly. It wasn't important. What was important was that the water swirled around us both. After a few minutes, we held hands, and the relief of being people who held hands felt like love.

We married immediately in a nondescript room with a cleaner as our witness. I hoped we would soon talk about mathematics. But we never talked about mathematics because mathematics is doing, not saying, or that's what he said. He was always a stranger, but at least every night I thought the stranger belonged to me. On the night Hypatia was born, he sat on my bed. He was still a small spindly man, but it was one of those mattresses that dent easily. My body fell towards the hollow that he made, and his car keys fell from his pocket. He said he'd been patient through my pregnancy, but now he would go to the other friend he had, a man. I had my mother, he said, so I'd be fine.

It took me a while to find my voice.

Why? I asked. It wasn't the firm, confident thing I should've said, but my daughter beside me was squalling.

He shrugged. He gazed at the redness of my face.

He has my heart, Harry said.

What does that mean? I asked.

I don't know, he said.

When he'd gone, I found his car keys in the sheets. In my exhaustion I allowed myself one angry act. I threw them into the bin. He didn't come back for them.

When I rang my mother she said: Good.

By then Dad had left her for Bev Roberts.

We're the sort of women men leave, she said.

She spoke with regret, but proud tears pricked my eyes. It was the first time in my life that my mother had linked herself with me.

DRESSING AND THE SOUL 2

In the sixteenth century in Bologna, there lived a man who was a mathematician, a doctor of medicine, a gambler, a horoscope caster (including one for Jesus Christ), an author of a masterpiece in algebra and, my mother said, a thief. His name was Cardano. His life, his mathematics and the study of mathematics itself was changed by a local mathematics contest. Antonio Mario Fio of Bologna in 1545 organised the contest to solve cubics and quartics. (I don't know what they are either. I could never concentrate long enough to follow my mother's explanation. But I'm sure they're not as interesting as their story.) Each contestant had to give some money to a notary, and whoever solved in thirty days the most problems out of a collection of thirty could collect all the money. A Venetian mathematics teacher, nicknamed Tartaglia (which means stammerer—he'd developed his speech impediment during a French attack on his native Brescia but that's another digression) had worked out a formula for solving any cubic, and since the questions all turned out to be cubics, he won the prize. He didn't allow his stammer to stand in the way of his honour. With the money from his win, he hired a poet and a musician to sing all over Bologna how great he was, but what he told them to leave out of the song was his theory of the cubic. This was all too much for Cardano.

My mother said that Cardano got his sweetheart to wheedle the formula out of Tartaglia. Tartaglia wrote it down for her, she wrote it down for Cardano, and Cardano wrote it down for the world. Cardano credited Tartaglia, but the world hasn't noticed that.

My mother had sympathy for Tartaglia not just because his mathematics became famous through a competition, not just because it wasn't really his mathematics, but because she blundered into her great discovery the same way that he'd blundered into an extension of complex numbers. By his time, complex numbers had been known for some centuries, but according to her, he must've been thinking about them and getting nowhere and he thought: All right, I'll let myself use the square root of a negative number here even though there's no such thing—and suddenly there was a new labyrinth of mathematics.

At least, that's what she told me.
Hypatia

Clare's voice drifted into my mind.

You were explaining how you'd rebelled against your mother.

I looked around the kitchen, which was, after all, my own, not the kitchen of my childhood. Not my mother's kitchen in my father's house.

Eventually, I said, I decided I had the right to work on her mathematics.

My voice was adamant in my hushed kitchen.

She'd gone so crazy she couldn't.

Clare's mouth drooped as she fingered the dress. Against the sequins of the blue dress, her slender fingers were careful not to catch a thread.

When you read out her work, it'll probably change your life, she said softly.

Excitement was a rush of spit in my mouth.

No, I said. But I'll be able to end something.

She looped tendrils of curls behind her ears.

The trouble with mathematics is that I wanted it to be about something, she said. And it wasn't. At college we were taught to think only about what follows from what. Then one day at school I was calculating something, like how fast a pea has to go before it punches through a ham sandwich. And I thought, well this is very interesting, but who cares? The pea?

There are moments in every conversation that are like hinges.

I had to say it then.

My voice trembled out of me.

I've made a discovery of my own, I said.

I suppose I expected something to happen. Something extraordinary as if the world is tugged at by our thoughts. Nothing happened. The ordinary sun still poured in through the window, past the burnt-out stubs of African violets. Clare stayed preoccupied only with sequins around a neckline.

They're all held on with one thread, she said.

Another discovery my mother didn't see, I said.

If you caught one sequin on something, half the dress would go bald, she said.

It's an extension of her conjecture, and she never got there, that's why she didn't see it, I said.

I don't want my dress going bald just because you get caught up in some theorem, she said.

At first I ignored it, I said. You see, I needed something to be true. So I worked hard to prove it, and I did. Then I kept going. It was taking me in another direction. And I let it. I'd invented these geometric tools that became very useful—

Another direction to what? she asked. Her voice was angry again as she examined the sequins so they flashed.

To her work. I felt that's what I should do, finish what she wanted . . .

We both sighed.

But I just sent the judges her work. Her conjecture. The one I found for her. Now, it seems like nothing at all. Even though it's won the competition. Compared to what I've found since. Now, it's as if I'm standing at a window. The curtains are drawn. But I'm pulling them apart and looking out.

What at? she asked.

I'm in an undiscovered country, I said, and I'm like a blind person. There's something up ahead of me, and I don't know what it is. I'm feeling with my hands a bit sticking out here, and a bit going in there. Maybe over here is an arch. Maybe over there is a tunnel. It's like something that might be a labyrinthine cathedral.

Her face drifted down to the dress.

There are bones in the bodice, she said. You're probably not experienced with bones. You've got to make sure they're in just the right place or you'll look like a lampshade someone's sat on, she said.

I'm like Cardano. I think I've found a new kind of number that will explain many mysteries, I said. Or at least, things that have seemed mysteries.

The fridge began again, humming the ordinariness of the day.

I thought we had enough numbers already, she joked.

A dish on top of the fridge started rattling. Neither of us moved to stop it.

You mean, asked Clare, you've noticed new connections between numbers? You don't mean an entirely new sort of number?

Yes, I said.

The dish was rattling imperatively.

I've found the first number, I said. I'm now looking for the second one. If I can find it then I'll be sure. One number proves nothing. But if there's a second one, there's a pattern. A pattern that's been needed.

I watched her swallowing my answer.

That sends shivers up my spine, she said.

She reached for the rattling dish.

You'd better take the best dresses we can find, she said.

Her lips drooped, as if she was about to be kissed. Slowly words formed.

When I was a kid, she said, I kept hoping one day I'd wake up and hear loudspeakers on the roofs of Holden utes and people on the radio shouting. They'd all be shouting the same thing, and horns would be blowing. It's all right, they'd be shouting. Come out of your houses. Living's not pointless after all. We've discovered that mathematics is real.

But it isn't, I said. We're just making it up.

Then I thought, she said, if mathematics isn't real, there's numbers. At least they'd shout—we've discovered that numbers are real.

But they aren't, I said.

No, she said. They're not.

There's nothing to hold onto, I said.

No, she said.

Nothing, I said.

47

No, she repeated.

Except my cathedral, I said. Maybe my cathedral is real.

She smiled lopsidedly, opened the flap of her handbag, and pulled the pink silk bodysuit out.

Take it, she said. Your neck's not so bad, really. Take everything. But try to get to your second number before you give your talk.

She got up.

At least you'll have your moment at last.

She came around the table and kissed me. Her hair fell warmly over my face. In the tremble of her lips, I thought too late about her anger that I won the competition. It was the first time I realised that none of her evening dresses showed any sign of wear.

If you take them, she said. Maybe they'll actually matter.

Her voice was so sad, I asked for her suitcase as well. It bulged with the promises that gold brocade and scarlet taffeta and midnight purple satin make, with the moment she hadn't had. There wasn't much room for my own clothes.

Watch out, she said as she left my kitchen. You'll be overtaking your beautiful mother.

COFFEE AND ABANDONMENT

I arranged to meet you in an inner-city cafe, do you remember? I thought I'd arranged it to tell you that I'd won the competition. I took a lot of care in dressing because I always felt in the wrong with you. I decided on one of Clare's unassailable dresses. If numbers are unnatural, so is motherhood. Do you remember, when you arrived you looked around to see who'd noticed me.

Mum, you hissed, where'd you get that appalling dress?

You banged a pile of letters down on the shine of the table, bound with string, the ends dangling.

What are they? I asked.

Letters from me to you. Telling you what I think of you. I wasn't going to have you read them, then—they're not in your way, are they?

Your eyes were suddenly tear soft and I wanted to lean over and snuggle you into me because I knew at last what I needed, I needed your strength to tell Juanita what I'd done. But I didn't know how to do it. Even when you were little you were always wriggling away.

A delivery truck outside roared its motor.

No, they're not in the way, I shouted over it. I immediately knocked them off the table. By the time I'd retrieved them, you were pulling off your scarf and your neck was white and stiff. You were holding a squinting baby on your lap.

Meet your grandma, you said to her.

I have to admit that I'd even forgotten you'd given birth.

Let me hold . . . little . . . the baby, I said.

Zoe, you had to remind me.

Zoe, I repeated.

You thrust the baby at me. I was astonished at her warm, compact weight. But even then, I have to admit I was trying to wind the conversation around to the conjecture to impress you, my daughter who wriggles away.

What conjecture? you asked.

There were bowls of chocolates on the counter nearby, and against the glinting wrappers on the chocolates, emerald, crimson, purple, I saw that a conjecture which had consumed Juanita's young life and mine might mean nothing at all.

It's about—

You were reaching over the table, impatient, straightening your baby's bib.

About mathematics, I sighed.

Do you remember what you said?

This conference of yours is probably a scam.

I remember nuzzling my face in Zoe's downy hair, it could wind around me, this warm sweet milky baby smell of my granddaughter, and cushion me. I must've said that I'd read about the milky smell of babies. Words were jerking out of me, like they always did in those days.

We weren't good mothers in our family. Bad mothers make bad daughters. It seems to go on from generation to generation, I said.

A waitress interrupted us.

Tea? I suggested to you. You always drank tea at home. And what about bread and butter, remember how we used to eat all that bread and butter.

You and the waitress exchanged smiles.

We don't serve bread and butter, said the waitress to me.

Of course they don't, you said.

You ordered cakes that I feared might be too rich.

Be daring for once in your life, you said to me.

Of course you were only joking.

Eat up, I said because I was a mother, your mother.

It's a pity, you said, that you haven't bothered to see your grandchild before. You've missed some important moments.

There was a crumb on your perfect lips that you weren't going to wipe off.

Would it help that I've just made a breakthrough on a new kind of number? I said.

No, you said.

And of course you were right.

The coffees came then, chocolate-sprinkled white froth on them riding high. We both eased into a smile and I glanced at my watch. Most of the cakes had been eaten and the coffee should take no longer than twenty minutes and then I'd walk down the street into my new life. Little Zoe made a grab for the prong of my cake fork. When I whisked it away, she began to cry. I jogged her.

Look, I said to you. A baby's crying mouth is the shape of infinity.

Rattling her won't help, you said. But then you added: I remember what you said once.

My muscles knotted in fear for what you'd say, they always did, and I saw why, it swooped on me, this understanding, like a bird suddenly swooping through the open doors and sitting on my shoulder resplendent in Clare's dress. I never believed you loved me. I never believed my mother loved me. The two seem intertwined.

What did I say? I asked you.

That mathematics holds you closer than a lover, so you forget everyone else, you said.

Ah, I said, pleased.

So I stirred the froth into my coffee, all the froth that was there and Zoe curved her tiny arms around me, a curve like the nestling of leaves into the soil, and I began again to hope that I could draw strength from you to face my mother. But you said,

Wasn't I your child?

You reminded me that I'd said I hadn't experienced that warm, milky smell.

Your voice was so smooth it didn't even jolt the air.

So I explained that I had accepted help in your first year. I was on my own struggling with a job. Then, because I had to speak into the pale light of your eyes, I reminded you that at least you weren't abandoned at the convent like your grandmother, or farmed out like Grandma Fernandez because her mother was so busy.

Another mathematician? you asked and too late I saw a bitter twist on the edge of your smile that I hadn't noticed before.

A wet-nurse for other people, I said. You've always resented my mathematics, I added.

Who did you abandon me to? you asked.

I explained that I'd thought a baby would comfort Juanita.

Grandma! you shouted. That mean old witch!

Your grandmother gave you her house, I said. And your name, I added because it was a caress Juanita had never given to me. At least she must've been prepared for you to be a mathematician.

My name! So Hypatia's her fault! you shouted. What happened between you and Grandma?

My heart thumped.

Why are you always placating her? you shouted. Why?

I wish you could've known her better. No one ever called her mean before, I said. Some people would've called her—

I finished my coffee before I could speak, I needed all its strength.

Sometimes the past seems not to exist at all, I said. At least, not the way we lived it.

I was standing, still holding your baby, but I was pushing my bag over my shoulder.

I found a diary in Grandma's house, you said suddenly.

My bag flopped back onto the table.

A diary of what? I asked.

You don't get a mention, you said.

That's likely, I said.

Juanita had pasted in some old school work of your brother's. Some sums. I never knew you had a brother.

You looped my bag back on my shoulder and your hand lingered there till tears stung my eyes.

You never asked anything, I said.

Why haven't we ever talked? you said so softly, so sadly that your voice began seeping into my skin.

I was hoping—we could've talked, you were saying.

I want to, now, you said.

Why now? I asked.

The baby, you said.

Perhaps everything could've changed but I made the wrong move. I held Zoe out to you because I was too close to tears to give comfort, I've never known how to give comfort. I held you out the wrong way, I suppose. It made you angry.

She's not a sack of potatoes, you said. Anyone would think you'd never had a child.

We heaved with rage and tears in those days.

I meant—the baby has taught me ... stuff, you said over the baby and a burst of noise from the espresso machine.

Give me the diary, I said.

It's back at home, you said.

Can you get it to me before I leave? I asked.

It's about her and Matti. You weren't even thought of, you said.

That's likely, I said.

I left to face Juanita with you calling after me: At least don't leave my letters behind.

They didn't look as if they'd be any help, lying on a cafe table and scattered with cake crumbs that were, after all, nondescript.

I didn't see the diary until long afterwards.

SOME PEOPLE WOULD'VE CALLED HER BRAZEN 1

It was 1963, the age of breasts, when my mother's lover first leaned against the doorframe of my father's house in our mountain town, and my mother tidied her hair, and took off her quilted apron.

Down the dusty road, on the giant cinemascope screen of the town's only movie theatre, the cleavages of Sophia Loren and Elizabeth Taylor were plunging ravines where green water might rush from creeks overhead, where children with hot brown bodies might slide dizzy and shouting amongst cool ferns. In front of our upturned faces, breasts ranged with the splendour of Old Testament mountains where fierce holy men lifted their eyes to find their god. The giant hands of screen lovers lingered near those ravines, hoping to submerge their gauche uncertainties and clamber out stronger, braver. I panted in the projector's whirring light, pressing the cobwebbed pattern of my thin bony ribs in hope.

Then my mother bought a bra. She'd had other bras before, thick troughs of slimy brown sateen that on the dripping Monday washing line could have been used to feed oats to the horses of my grandmother's childhood.

I was with her when she bought it in the town's lingerie shop of grey shadows and white discreet boxes, and a shop assistant with a laugh of polite surprise behind the calico curtains. I sat in the shop and watched the calico curtains ripple with elbows and knees and then with my mother's bent head.

A perfect figure, my dear, said the shop assistant to my curtained mother. If you don't mind my saying, the sort that an artist would love to paint.

The shop assistant rationed herself one of her cultured

laughs at nothing, a general purpose laugh perhaps at the surprises a wintry morning can bring. She emerged putting on her glasses with one hand now that she was no longer pressed close to my mother's creamy flesh. In her other hand she held a white lacy bra by its hooks, as if it was a fish she'd pulled out of the river.

She called it a brassiere and managed to pronounce the word with an Oxford accent, so that it seemed a scholarly piece of clothing.

You have a very beautiful mother, she said to me, or at least to the grey shadow where I was sitting. Her tone was at once congratulatory and consoling.

My mother's mind was not on her daughter in the shadows.

And, my mother said. And, I want one of those pullovers that the girls in the city are all wearing now.

There was something so carefully nonchalant about her tone, my own skin tingled. My mother hadn't been to the city for years. She never began sentences with *and* or finished them with *but*. The nuns had been very insistent about it.

Something cosy? suggested the shop assistant.

Something silky, said my mother. To show off the line of the bra.

The shop assistant blurted another surprised laugh, but this one had purpose. After all, my mother was a married woman. But she caught it, this laugh that exceeded politeness, and buried it in the rustling of tissue paper.

My mother, shopping later in her lacy bra and the silky blue pullover, was awesome. Outside the pub, men's eyes watered with longing as they held their amber beers, I heard the noise of their eyes like lost lambs bleating, and as we walked away I turned to see them still nuzzling, although there was only her diminishing blue back. My headmaster outside the post office lifted his hat and fondled her name in his mouth as he'd never done on Parents' Nights when she'd worn thick clothes to ward off the cold.

Good morning, Mrs Montrose, he said. How are you this morning, girlie?

Girlie, she said to me afterwards, completely missing the point.

He must be feeling his age.

Boys on motorbikes looked up from their boasts of petrol tanks to watch her pointed hills far more exhilarating than any hill track they'd dare to climb. And the startled butcher wiped the brown blood off his hands and threw the stained cloth out of sight under his counter before he weighed up our pound of veal.

I popped in a couple of kidneys, he confided to my mother's breasts as he pressed himself against the counter. A special for you today. No charge.

My mother's head arched so proudly, she was the only one who had no thought of her breasts, they were now further from her thoughts than the distant horizon into which the grey-green hills rolled. I knew what she was thinking about, the way a child has knowledge of her mother. It was two days after the visitor had leaned against the doorway. She was so young, she didn't even have lines on her neck, she was only thirty-four. Now I can see how young that was.

I went outside the butcher's shop and looked at my mother through the window, at her figure, the word the shop assistant with the laugh had used. She'd made my mother's body sound like a number. Infinity, I decided, looking at my mother framed by the lamb chops, that was the number. My mother, the shape of infinity.

But no one had noticed that since her girlhood, until him.

AND SO THERE WAS MY MOTHER
TO FAREWELL

*My grandmother, Grandma Juanita, in old age. You won't find this
story in the other biographies-*
Hypatia

In any journey there are many farewells. And so there was my
mother. I had to tell Juanita that since I'd put her away in the
old people's home, I'd worked on her conjecture.

I had a plan, I make many plans, many lists, those bright
pages taped to my fridge and my walls, they fall in any breeze.

I'd go on my way to the airport. Then, in the urgency of
separation, surely we'd sit close to each other at last and I'd
pleat up my life to tell her, as if I was an innocent girl in
skirts whispering who I'd like to dance with. For years, our
throats had been thick with conversations that wouldn't begin.
So instead we'd say There's enough meat left on the bone for
a stew. That tidy-up has done the house a world of good.

Wrong words that clung like greasy dishwater on the hands.

We sat on the verandah. She was the youngest of the
people at the home. Her skin was petal soft, smoother than
mine.

I'll be away for a couple of weeks, I began.

There'll be no one to take me to the lake, was all she said.

The lake, always the lake, that sullen stillness.

These days she meant the ditch down by the laundry block.

She didn't ask where I was going. She'd brought her
handbag out with her and she fussed inside it for her handkerchief. She wouldn't accept mine.

We haven't got long before the plane, I said.

But she couldn't talk without her handkerchief, so I went
to her room, which curved so tightly around her it had taken

on her smell as if she'd always been there, as if those years at home didn't happen at all, and I panicked to see piles of old ladies' clothes because I needed to be taught again and again that she was old, singlets and panties washed too often and sagging, the pink nylon ribbon trims unravelling. I was running out of time to possess the body of my mother. All I could take from her room was her handkerchief.

This is our moment to talk, I said.

Hah! she shouted. Her thin old lips curved like a snake. You've been announcing moments, she said, since you were a child. As if they're moths you could hold in your hand, despite their dusty fluttering.

There are moments when everything changes, I said.

I've never known moments like that, she said.

So I should've known to go away then, but I sat watching, as if it could all be different, watching her hand moving over her bodice, touching buttons, touching her breasts, her hand moving without curiosity, unknowing. She always lived apart from her clothes. I think she didn't even notice their touch on her skin. But her hand's movement on her dress was essential to me, to who I am, as dense to me as numbers.

Mum, I pleaded. I was going on with my plan, I lifted her face to mine, but her eyes wouldn't grip mine. They slid across the paspalum-flecked lawn to the washing lines, and beyond, to the ditch. She was pretending it was his lake. And suddenly she was shouting, The birds!

Only later did I realise that her voice had always clung to me like pleading.

The tree at the laundry block was shouting back, full of birds' cries, it seemed to have inside it as many birds as leaves. She was struggling out of my hands to walk down and stand underneath it. All I could do was follow.

It had rained recently and the ditch sang with mosquitoes.

Inside the laundry block, washing machines whirred. The tree arched darkly above us. But there was a single cry from deep inside the tree and a flurry of birds flew out so fast she couldn't see which branches they came from.

My mother was running around the tree saying: Look, look, it's from there, that's where they are.

And I was shouting above the shouting tree and the humming machines and the mosquitoes: There are things we've got to say to each other.

There was a rake leaning against the tree.

Watch out for the rake, I said. She didn't hear me. She said: We've been together for a lifetime. You don't get birds like this every day.

There was another flurry of birds and she was calling: I can see the leader, although she couldn't. There was no leader.

She ran around the tree again.

Watch out for the rake, I repeated. She ignored me.

There was another cry, another flurry of flying birds, another cry, another flurry, until the sky was as dark with night as the tree.

There's still more birds hiding, she cried.

My mother swayed and peered in her old brown dressing gown, and I stood with her, silent in the dark, until we were both as dark as the tree.

They'll have dished up my dinner, she said suddenly. Off you go.

So I said it, the way it shouldn't have been said.

I worked on your work, I blurted. It's taken years. But I found what you'd been looking for. I formulated your conjecture. In fact, I've formulated many. Lots of related conjectures. The fact that there were many, that's probably what confused you. Oh, I wasn't saying you were ever confused. But look, I'm a geometer and you're not, I don't know where I got it from but I had a spatial sense you didn't, you had so many formulae to keep in your head, you couldn't keep track of them but I could, I invented some geometric objects that simplified things—I'm not saying this well, but I also found—

Her eyes swung into mine, widened with memory, quivered.

You didn't take the reasoning far enough, I said.

My voice was as smooth as her skin, once I'd said it.

You didn't—can I explain what I did? I said.

The muscles around her cheeks clenched.

You didn't realise—you couldn't have realised . . . I said.

She was swallowing, what was it, words, anger, the past. The flesh on her old throat waggling.

I went back through your old books, the books in the laundry, I went back through them all, and your notes, and your arguments against . . . his . . .

Her face, her mouth, the pores of her skin closed, her face was like a stone that could be hurled at me. Her arm came up, my mother's arm that once cradled me, the loose old skin shaking. She'd grabbed the rake, the rake she hadn't noticed.

You had to stop because of Matti, I shouted. My voice was ringing as loudly as the birds. She'd lifted the rake over her head. My mother's trembling old arms, and the rake so absurdly high it scraped leaves. Towering over me, trembling. I knew what she was about to do, I'd been waiting always for this moment, and I waited then.

You had to stop because of me, I shouted.

I was waiting for my mother to kill me. For what I did to her back then when I was thirteen years old. I wasn't watching the rake's arc, I wasn't ducking, I was watching my mother's face that was once so beautiful.

There was an appalling crack, and pain that belonged to me, didn't belong to me, belonged to me again. I was on the ground, breathing dirt. Little billows of dirt lifted off the earth with my breath. Near my mouth were my mother's toes in velvet slippers worn down with innocence. Far above me, a lone bird sang in the tree with determined jauntiness.

You're lying on the bulbs, my mother's voice came to me at last.

Matron put lots of bulbs in last week, and if you keep moving your toes you'll break their tiny hope of life. And each bulb is unique, there's not one quite like it in the world. Matron said.

As I drove away, someone had switched on the verandah lights and she stood in a pool of yellow. She didn't wave. She turned to check the soft soil of the bulbs, that I hadn't ruined them. Before I'd reached the corner, she was on her old knees smoothing the soil to comfort them.

On the way to the airport, I saw her in my mind, she filled the taxi, my mother. She'd drunk from a cracked glass and it had shattered in her mouth. She'd turned her electric blanket up and set fire to her bed, she'd gone down to the ditch by herself in the dark.

The last call before boarding was sounding but I was finding a phone box, finding coins.

I formulated it for you, I said.

She didn't know what I was talking about.

Of course she was all right, just exhausted, I always exhausted her, the only peace she'd get from me was when she'd gone from the earth.

My mother, my love, my emptiness.

I scarcely remember the person I was when I was young. These letters talk to me about a very different self. But I feel the biographer must sacrifice herself and include all material, no

matter how discomforting. It's never been told before that Frances Montrose took my letters with her to Athens and they were in her suitcase when she ran away. They were absolutely pivotal in her life. In fact, they were the turning point in those four lost days that everyone speculates on, but knows very little about.
Hypatia

MY FIRST LETTER

Grandma Juanita's house

Dear Mum,
I just gave birth. I thought you might be interested. Though you're probably not, since you didn't come. Don't feel too bad. The father didn't either. I'd have stayed away if I could, but somebody had to be there.

I'm not ready, there's something else I have to do, I kept shouting to the nurses. They just laughed and tidied their hair under their cute little caps when the doctors came by. They said it'd soon be over. So will my life be, I screamed. You can scream and scream when you have a baby. That's the one good thing about it. That explains why some women have lots of babies. A few good chances to scream. I'm a bit hoarse still.

When they brought her to me afterwards, I looked around at all the other mothers sitting up on their beds. Every breast in the room but mine was roundly ample. Just the pressure of a tiny finger, still wrinkled, making a glossy dent on those glossy globes, and milk would gush. Whereas my breasts were heavy with reluctance. I didn't know how to feed my baby. I mean, how would I? How do you know anything?

Offer her the breast, they said, as if my breast was a plate of cheese at a party. But I did. It felt a very generous act, this offering of my body to a stranger. It was a surprise when the baby's cheeks ballooned with sucking. Even then, I couldn't believe it. When everyone went to dinner and left their white rumpled beds behind, I licked the milk off her pursed lips. She scarcely noticed the dry brush of my tongue. Her blue eyes held as little judgement as the sky. She just assumed she'd arrived in a world where mothers licked their own milk. It was sweet. Watery. It didn't taste like milk. It didn't really taste like love either.

Well, how would I know? After a childhood with you. And that's the problem. You can pretend you love a man for a while. Pretend to yourself. But how do you pretend to a baby?

I'm too tired to be angry with Jim. When I told him I was pregnant, did he cheer? Did he smile? No. He sulked. I was the one to be blown apart with pain, and he sulked. I had to comfort him!

He doesn't come to Grandma Juanita's house much now. He's in the city doing research about camels for his new play about Australian desert explorers. Apparently lots of people went off on camel expeditions and got lost. I know where he's doing research. It won't be very useful. You don't find out much about camel expeditions in Cheryl Cooper's bed.

When my baby sucks, my vagina contracts. It's like sneaking an orgasm. If you breastfed in public, say on a bus, you could sneak an orgasm on the bus! You could be chatting to a sweet old lady about her garden while your vagina was going whump whump whump.

Why didn't you ever tell me this would happen? What else haven't you told me? Sex, lust, vagina—these aren't words we can say to each other. That's probably why you didn't come to the birth. In all our talk, birth is an immaculate conception.

She's just finished sucking, her tiny hands feeling my emptying breast, as if they want to learn me. As if she's wondering who I am. Her toes curled in pleasure. And then she fell away, satisfied, like any lover. I thought I'd better give her a name before the nurses came back from their goulash. So I called her Zoe. That means life, if you don't know. It's about all I can give her.

It mightn't look like it at the moment with my breasts dripping milk and my hair stuck with cotton wool, but my destiny is to be *great. Perhaps I'll be a great artist like Georgia O'Keefe or a great writer like Austen. I may even be a great composer, and I'm going to learn to play an instrument very soon. The baby will just have to wait its turn. I won't leave my destiny till old age, like you have, doing something you should've done when you were young, at the proper time. You didn't get accidentally pregnant like I did. You wilfully ruined your life. Anything rather than stand up to your mother. So you did sums in our time. My time. Sneaked them. I watched you scribble secret equations on the backs of envelopes while you burned the porridge black. What are you writing? I'd ask. We need butter, you'd say. But it wasn't a proper shopping list.*

Sums—how I hate them. Even when I was little, I gnashed my teeth at your scribbles. You wondered why those bits of paper so often went missing. I lost them. Buried them in the garden. Burnt them on the back porch. Flushed them down the toilet. Threw them into the wind. I wanted you to be a mother, a mother writing real shopping lists.

This is fun, writing you a letter you'll never see.

Hypatia

TRIUMPH

Another mathematician of extraordinary intuitive power (besides my mother) was Bernard Riemann in the nineteenth century. He decided not to tell the world everything that he knew about mathematics, and in an anguished note left amongst his papers he said that much of his work derived from something which he hadn't managed to simplify enough to tell. However, he was responsible for one of the most famous mathematical upheavals. He dramatically challenged an essential axiom of Euclid's that had been accepted for two thousand years. Geometry has never been the same since. It inspired the challenging of other established axioms, including Einstein's challenging of classic axioms of physics, which led him to invent his special theory of relativity.

My mother had a great natural sympathy for Riemann. To protect the anonymity of the boors that attended the Athens conference so pivotal in her life, she invented the term Non-Riemannian Hypersquares. I've noticed it since in a book called The Mathematical Experience, *but I'm sure my mother didn't.* Hypatia

All I remember about the next week is a succession of moments. I suppose someone greeted me at the hotel in Athens when I stumbled in from the other side of the world at five in the morning. The details of my life's beginning. I was told that the mathematics conference was about Non-Riemannian Hypersquares. I'd never heard of Non-Riemannian Hyper-squares. But there were many areas of mathematics I'd never heard of. There was a tall, thick glass of orange juice with frosting on the outside. My room number was 377, a Fibonacci number, a good omen surely because as a child I pretended that I'd been born before Fibonacci and discovered them, I'd run full-skirted shouting through the fields when I'd seen their patterns in daisies, the Frances numbers that show that nature is mathematical, after all. And my hotel room, a room so white it was like the photos of peace in travel brochures, so warm you couldn't believe nights have ever been cold, so smooth my feet ruffled the carpet like an explorer's. The curtains were heavy, newly washed, not the intimate smell of old dust in folds. The sheets billowed when I moved my legs.

I've always slept with my eyes open.

I didn't wake you, Harry would insist when he wanted sex. Your eyes were open, watching me.

But that pristine room said: Begin again.

The secret hope that I'd formulate my mother's conjecture

one day was a small tight thing I could hold when I was jostled by crowds at the traffic lights and by eyes of men too close on the peak hour trains. When Harry walked out. When love curdled one more time around. And at night, when the fluorescent street lamps spiked my bed with light so coldly blue I could almost hear the shudder of the city in it, there, in my mind, the hope of finding her conjecture was my only comfort. I'd have been thinner than air without the hope, less than that. The air knows how to continue.

I kept believing that it would be thrilling, the moment of telling at the conference. So thrilling, the air would seem triumphant, and ordinary trees outside the window would shift with my joy. The sun would be shouting in triumphant stripes as I walk to the microphone, there'd be stripes of shouting triumph on the wall, on the lectern, stripes of light on the glass jug of water, stripes of triumph in my eyes. There'd be rustles at first, a cough, a sudden scrape of a chair, people turning the pages of the programme while considering their lunch, fish or meat, wine or water, or perhaps neither, an assignation instead in the next bedroom with no promises that love lasts. I'd be a little breathless, a little high-pitched ... But what's she doing? Eyes, minds focus as she draws. She's drawing on the whiteboard a pattern of such fierce, austere beauty, you might think God is real.

She drops the pen and it falls into a room so silent you can hear the triumphant shouting of the sun.

But after an hour or two of sleep, I saw that the morning had the ordinary grey indifference of cities, as if what I'd done for my mother didn't matter. Beyond my white curtains I saw the grey concrete footpaths below, the fierce city buildings that chop away the sky. I saw the glum road, the heavy air. My hand slipping on window glass, I saw a waiter in a tired dinner suit hose the chairs and tables of a street cafe, careful with his shoes. Two motorbikes roared by. The waiter put the hose down on a wet table to straighten his bow tie. There was a squeal of brakes at the traffic lights, and a crunch that might've only been my heartbeat. The waiter didn't bother to turn to see, he was holding the hose so it jutted out from his crotch, he was leaning backwards to pretend the water was leaping out from him. It leapt across the empty barrows of a vegetable market, it was suspended in a silver rainbow over the rounded red roof of a tiny church. It pattered to the ground near the feet of two worshippers shuffling at the dark arch of a church door, feeling in pockets for money to light a candle. The old man handed a coin to his wife, and as I grasped the shine of glass, their skin touched and I remembered the way flesh clings to flesh in its moistness. The waiter turned off the hose, laughing to himself.

Something was toppling at street level, I heard the sound between one truck's rumble down the street and the next. Beside the hotel was a yard where white dust floated. There was a pile of rubbish, a shed, and rows of strange shapes flaring white in the grey morning. A man came out of the shed humping a block of marble, he was naked down to his rumpled shorts, his hair and eyebrows were scurfed with white dust, white dust caked the sinewy twists of his neck, as if his head was screwed on, like the top on a bottle. He leaned the marble block against a wall. In the silence that traffic lights make, I heard the chink of tools. His hammer hit the chisel. His hands moved with knowledge on the marble, and little eddies of white dust rose and fell at his feet.

He was rounding an O. He chiselled another letter. I peered into the grey morning. OINOZ, I read.

My Greek dictionary almost translated it for me, there's a word something like it, but not quite.

Family.

And that's when things started to go wrong.

The stonemason turned, perhaps he saw me against the window glass, he tipped his hat to wipe his head. I almost expected him to wink.

So I went back to bed and slipped under the sheets, and they billowed around me comfortingly. I was burrowing into that softness, trying to find that fringed edge of the morning between sleep and waking.

The image of the past swims into the floating present, like the image through window glass of a lit candle in a church archway. The past, they say, has nothing to do with the present. It all happened a long time ago. It's over. But the present wavers and drowns because of a stonemason carving family on a tombstone, and winking, just at a moment of triumph.

The pitiless dark

There were the nights of creaking floorboards. You know that my mother's father, your great-grandfather, was Spanish as well as Jewish. He'd been persecuted in Spain but he escaped to Australia at the turn of the century with only his scars and his terror and a stone in his pocket from the mountains of his childhood. To build a fortune, making chairs in Sydney in a rusty shed that became a large and ringing factory. In his wealthy middle age, he courted my Roman Catholic grandmother, Grandma Fernandez, and he lay in her white comfortable arms in her childhood home amongst purple jacaranda trees on the long, yellow plains out West. He changed his name saying it was too hard for the locals to pronounce. In many ways he hid himself. Some said that my grandmother was his best disguise.

But my grandmother said: I brought out the passion in him.

If he'd lived on, I would've kept him faithful and that's something you young generation can't do. He wanted me and he
didn't give a fig about marrying out.

But he'd been pursued for something he'd done in Spain, or
hadn't done, or maybe just because of who he was, not that we
ever knew that either. The men with knives found him. One
night he died on the street in the township, stabbed. No one was
suspected, no one convicted. So Grandma Fernandez gave their
only child, Juanita my mother, to the Catholic convent.

It's God's will, she said, folding her gloved hands comfortingly in the back seat of the Humber as she drove away.
She hadn't much liked being a mother but she didn't tell
anyone that, especially God. She needed help from Him in
return for her gift. She hoped the help would start immediately. She didn't head home. She did what anyone would do
in the circumstances. She spent the rest of her life gambling.
She drove straight to the Dapto Dog Races.

At seventeen, when my mother left the nuns, she was a Jew
without other Jews, because she was a Jew from her father's
line, not her mother's. So she wasn't a Jew, not really, only
her amber skin and her blue-black hair and her aquiline
nose and her memories of her father and his midnight face
of fear, a Jew without Jews amongst all the ghostly grey
gum trees of an Australian mountain town, gum trees that
in the night seemed full of watching eyes when Hitler was
killing Jews of mixed descent in the cities on the other side
of the world. His troops could come here, she knew how
small the world is, she knew it had contracted for her father
in his youth, and she'd seen it contract at seven years old
when she kissed the pearly sheen of his dead face. She
wasn't a proper Catholic either, though the nuns had taken
her in. She belonged to no people, and she feared everyone.

The fear ended up taking over her life, as if it was her who'd been stabbed.

But you know this already. You see, I kept telling her story over and over, as if the telling could've freed me, so I could begin my own. That wasn't how to do it, but I didn't know that.

There was a time early in her marriage when my mother walked carelessly through the township, examining the fish brought from the city on blocks of ice, looking at their sad, dreaming eyes, turning the slippery bodies over and saying to the fishmonger:

Two, please,

like any other housewife.

She'd examine the vegetables grown by the Chinese brothers in their tiny garden you could glimpse between the slats of the fence.

They're such precise gardeners, she whispered to me once as she fingered the green frills of parsley. They turn the earth with such tiny knives.

Beautiful vegetables today, she'd exclaim aloud, and they'd laugh together, the Chinese brothers and her, as if sunshine and brown earth and vegetables were the cleverest things on earth.

Marriage and motherhood seemed to have healed the scars left by her father's terror.

But that time ended on the day when my mother and I walked down our dusty road to Bev Roberts' shadowy shop for some cornflour she'd forgotten to buy in the township. This was before her lover turned up, perhaps before she'd even met him, perhaps why she took a lover. I don't remember much about that day, at first just another day in the layers of childhood days. I only remember that my mother was going to send me to the shop alone, but as I reached our gate she caught up with me, because of the sunshine she said, it mustn't be wasted. She hummed as we walked along, and I hummed with her, I'd have liked to walk hand in hand but my mother didn't like to touch, after a childhood with the nuns she wasn't used to sweatiness, she said. Our voices held each other's, and I made myself happy with that.

My mother was standing amongst Bev Roberts' grey-skinned pumpkins cut to show off the orange flesh. I was sidling up to my hopes of red lollies from the glass jar on Bev Roberts' old wooden counter. My mother with her worn purse with the edges flaking leather, waiting for Bev Roberts to swallow her last sip of tea and turn and realise we were there. My mother clearing her throat. Bev Roberts turning. A crumb of carraway-seed cake on her lip. Her mouth open like a gash. It's made me forever frightened of open mouths, of speech, words, books, literature.

What are you doing sneaking into my shop? Bev Roberts' open mouth shouted. You reffos, can't trust any of you.

I heard the shock in my mother's breath first. The words from Bev Roberts' mouth seemed to take longer to reach me although she was shouting.

Then my mother was wheeling on her heel in the shop, not seeing me, abandoning me, my mother's face streaked silver with tears, my mother who never cried in public, my mother running down our road, her skirts flapping around her like the wings of crippled birds. I was running after her, calling, stumbling, frightened, stones flying under my feet.

Wait for me, don't leave me behind.

But she didn't turn to me until she'd got home, to the brown shadows of the broom cupboard.

Afterwards in our kitchen Dad knew Bev Roberts couldn't

possibly have said that, and as I looked at the tight muscles in his face, I was no longer sure either.

Mrs Roberts is kindness itself, he said. Her blood's worth bottling. You misunderstood. She just said—his arms stretched wide in the enormity of kindness that was Mrs Roberts' stout body—what would you like in all my shop?

She knows you're not a reffo, he added.

My mother cried louder, for Dad had abandoned not only her, but her father.

By evening Dad wanted my mother to go back to Bev Roberts' shop and apologise.

The poor woman must be so hurt, he said.

That began the nights of the creaking floorboards, and then silence spreading through the house with the stickiness of fear. The moon fingered clothes, books, a towel flung over a chair, a raincoat hanging on a door into grotesque shapes.

She's gone, I'd know. She's not coming back.

I'd swing my legs unwillingly out of bed. Surely she's coming back, wasn't that the door clicking.

This was before the lake. Before her lover.

There'd only be black silence. Only a low murmuring that might be a lost animal, or the lost wind. I'd wait, hoping for a scrabble of stones on the path. Only silence. And then the floorboards would creak in the dining room.

So she was sleep-walking again, I'd know.

I'd pad through dark rooms, not daring to switch on lights lest I wake her, my arms out in front of me to ward off furniture, walls, her. One night I got as far as the cold laundry and found her there, her eyes wide open and staring, she was plunging white sheets into the copper, and memories had settled on her as dense as a shroud. She'd stoked the copper and lit it, fast asleep. Outside, steam ambled up to the sky, which was just a black bedsheet.

Room after room I'd walk in the meandering house that my father built for their life together. In the blackest room, in the pitiless depths of the house, there was a white patch on the floor that was my moaning mother. She was grasping the wooden legs of a chair.

Daddy, she said.

My confused hand brushed hers in the darkness, her skin so chilly I shuddered. She clutched at me, my warmth, she slid her hand up my arm, she found the thickness of my crouching body, she clung. Her eyes were as open as a mouth, as if she was ready to swallow anything that would set her free.

When will it be morning, Daddy? she asked.

I found a voice that was far older than my years, because comfort is always a pretence, the soft-fleshed human hope against the jagged edge of chaos.

We'll be all right, I said, in the voice that wasn't mine.

I knew you'd come back, Daddy, she said.

In the cold black silence of her need, fear drained out of me. I planned the journey back to her bed while she leaned on me. It was merely a matter of willing obedience and strength into my body, I partly lifted, partly dragged, partly carried her, it was my mind's will against my body's shriek-ing. We moved ponderously through the dark and watching rooms. To get beyond a doorway was the next triumph. In the hall she lifted her head, her glittering eyes searched mine, in all that blackness her eyes still glittered, she found a source of light and drew it to her. For a spine-tingling moment I feared she'd know I wasn't my dead grandfather. I don't look Spanish. I'm as Australian-looking as Grandma Fernandez, as my father. But her eyes saw nothing.

I knew you wouldn't leave me, Daddy, she said.

I pushed her head with its soft hair against my neck, to

mute her. Stumbling on floorboards, we got at last to her bedroom, to her bed as her eyes stark in the moonlight. My father, on the far side of the bed, thundered and gurgled in his snores. It didn't occur to me to wake him or my brother for help. This was my mother's family secret. I disentangled her arms, she fell on the bed, I fell on top of her, I stretched out my hand and saved her at the last moment from my tumbling weight. She snuggled into the sheets, the blankets, and turned her face away from the moon's cruel searching. I tucked the gentle sheets around her as her father would have done in her childhood, and in that moment, there's history.

I never told her that I did this. Perhaps she never knew.

A gladbag of secrets

For a while after Bev Roberts' outburst, my mother became a gladbag of secrets, a thousand tatters of secrets lay tossing in the air of our living room, dining room, kitchen, laundry, my parents' bedroom, my bedroom, Matti's bedroom. These secrets didn't go out past our gate, into the street, into the township. I suppose she'd learned about secrets in her lonely convent cell, but she'd imagined that after marriage to my father, there'd be no secrets at all.

For a while after Mrs Roberts and before her lover, we lived in a twilight house, the blinds always drawn, the electric light always on. We became the only family to lock up in town, three locks each door, a chain, a deadlock and a bolt.

When there was a knock on the front door, someone with a job for Dad, the visitor wasn't asked in. Visitors were never asked in.

I'm out, she'd say, every time there was a knock, and if I was alone in the house with her, she'd hide.

She'd hide like a child, running, panting, she'd knock over

jars in the pantry, hangers would clang as she stumbled into the wardrobe, brooms would crash in the broom cupboard.

It takes a while to undo three locks on a front door. Even then I had to wait for my mother's prompting.

Now, she'd say. She'd whisper so as not to be heard, but her whisper was fear sharp enough to tingle right down the road into town.

When I opened the door, the sudden dazzle of sunlight would almost knock me over.

I don't know where Mum is, I'd say, to the adult on the step, or the child with a note.

Don't want your mum. We want your dad, they'd say.

There'd be a crash behind me.

What's going on in there? they'd ask, ducking their heads to see around me.

But often they'd already have thrust a piece of paper in my hand. So I could read loudly

Our drane's busted, please come ASAP.

If they ask any more questions, I'd think, I'll tell them how to spell.

But usually I'd stretch my lips into a polite smile and say, Dad'll be there tomorrow, for sure, and I'd slam the door before there was another jingle from another coat hanger.

She'd come out of hiding when the front gate squeaked shut. I wouldn't notice she'd been amongst the brooms. I knew she didn't want me to. So I'd clamp my eyes on anything, on the canisters, on the Billy Tea packet that said 'Hello mate', on the Rosella biscuit tin, on the helmeted Silent Knight on the fridge door, on the kookaburra picture on the stove. On the squares of the lino floor.

She'd come out combing nightmares like spiderwebs from her hair with absent-minded fingers. It was as if her night-time nightmare world had unreasonably invaded the ordinary sunshine. We didn't speak about it, we'd pretend it hadn't happened, this jagged tear in the fabric of a day. I was frightened to ask questions, she never offered answers. Her hiding was another of the unspoken things in our family. Then she'd sigh, she'd turn to the stove, the saucepans, the kettle, the ordinary dinner threatening to burn, she'd pick up the patchwork apron of her household as if she'd never put it down. After a while she'd say:

Goodness Frances, we've run out of sugar again. Why are we always running out of sugar? Go down to Mrs Roberts' for a pound of sugar, quicksticks.

She'd raise her glossy eyebrows for a second after she spoke, daring me to take the ordinary moment further. I never did.

She never hid from customers when Matti was in the house, or Dad. It was some strange comfort that she was only herself with me. I had two mothers, the day mother and the night mother, and nobody knew her two selves but me.

It's a good thing Matti wasn't home, she'd say. He's the spit and image of his grandfather. If the friends of Hitler came, they'd take him away too.

There was, however, school.

Every day after school, my mother waited at our kitchen table, her lushly rounded arms folded on the laminex. I leaned on it. She held my chin in her fingers so she could talk right into my face. Her fingers on my skin were adamant.

What did you say today? she asked.

My ambition was to keep my mother's eyes calm, but every day after school I watched the golden cobwebs inside them quiver.

I took a breath. It was so hard pretending to be normal in

a playground with this mother at home. And then at home, pretending I hadn't tried to seem normal at school.

At lunchtime they were only talking about birthday cakes, I said.

Birthday cakes, she repeated. She lifted her arms behind her head to cradle her glossy mane of hair while she considered birthday cakes, the cobwebs were quivering now to consider the possibility of betrayal.

Already I was quailing.

You'd better tell me everything, she said.

The slow ticking of the kitchen clock measured more than time.

You talked? she prompted.

I had to take my turn, I said.

On her apron, a fraying thread from the raw edges of her unfinished apron trembled.

I only told them what cooking pan you use, the one Dad found in that house he fixed, the heart-shaped one, I said at last.

The heart-shaped one, she repeated, considering the glittering spaces of her kitchen, where no dirt or smear betrayed her like her daughter might have done.

Everyone uses heart-shaped pans, I said, but my voice was like time running out.

What else? she asked.

Guilt was waiting for me, I saw now, along the dark path of this inquisition. The moment in the playground when, wanting to be one of the girls, I had betrayed my mother.

Everyone said what their mothers put in cakes, I said slowly.

You said we use sugar? she asked.

Everyone uses sugar, I said.

I don't want them to know how we live, she said.

Her apron over her breasts was billowing with her breathing.

Did you say lemons? she asked.

Everyone uses lemons, I said.

There was a pause. I spoke quickly, to seal it off, this inevitability I now saw we were racing towards, the betrayal under the peppercorn trees.

It was just an ordinary conversation, I said.

Nuts? she demanded.

We were speaking fast now, my mother had reached the moment I betrayed her.

Everyone uses nuts, I argued, still hoping.

You said we use the nuts for flour, she said, she breathed, she knew.

I said we use the nuts for flour, I whispered.

You know they don't do that here, she said. We do it the way his mother did it. Your grandfather. Your great-grandmother. Your real family.

But this is a different country, I argued. We weren't born there, we didn't know his mother, we were born here. You've never even been there.

I have, she said.

I laughed, as if it was funny.

Only in your head, I laughed.

In his head, she shouted. Don't you, a mere child, tell me what matters, she said.

I was hot from answering her back, we were wrestling, mother and daughter on the gleam of the laminex table, I wanted so much to make our family like the other families in the town.

My life is his, she said.

But he won't know, I argued.

Her head jerked.

He isn't here, I said.

He's dead, I shouted.

The word she'd known for twenty-eight years hit her like a slap. She fell to the tabletop, her face, her beautiful face hidden in hair, my mother was groaning with my word.

Why? she groaned. Why do you find so many ways to hurt me?

Her hair was unpinned, it collapsed gently, it slid along the tabletop. I didn't dare touch it to comfort her. There was a gap between my hand and the sheen of her hair worse than a sudden silence on the asphalt at school under the peppercorn trees. I thought of the girls at school, the way they tossed their brown and gold and ginger hair so easily, as if they had a right.

You don't know what it's like, she said suddenly. You don't know what it's like to be the child of an immigrant.

You're a child? I said.

Of an immigrant, she said angrily. Immigrants make you know they left home for the hope they had in you. They weren't just running away, they were escaping for you.

She gathered herself up, even in that moment she loved explaining, she put all her body into it.

You're responsible for all their past, all your life.

She buried her glossy head again.

The next generation goes scot-free, she said.

And then she said the worst words possible.

You know what's wrong with you? You're your father's child.

After a while she got up, she wiped her face and hands on a teatowel, she slammed down saucepans. She didn't look at me. Then my brother came in, rollicking from school, and she was laughing with him and pouring milk and tumbling biscuits from the biscuit barrel. She gave them to him with relish, my mother trusted my brother. My brother wouldn't betray her, not ever, because my brother was her child, even though he was a liar. Perhaps because he was a liar. And of course, he was beautiful, like her.

She never asked my brother what he said at school. She never asked my father what he said at work, as far as I knew. I was the lonely keeper of my mother's terror.

And now, all day in the silent house while we were at school and Dad was at work, my mother's lover learned the shadowy configuration of our living. His bare feet found the very knots on our floorboards, the worn threads on our carpets. His hands felt the bumps in our mattresses, the folds of our blankets. He knew the secrets of our cupboards, he knew even the dresses frothing in my mother's wardrobe, the secrets in the cake tins. He heard the mind of my mother and her memories and her history. Daily he learned by heart her secret, magnificent body.

He didn't know about my mother's terrors, I was sure. In fact, after he came along, my mother's terrors seemed to ease. For a while.

At some moment in a tunnel of mirrors, there's interference, the image wavers and drowns as if it was never there at all.

But perhaps that's not where to begin at all, for who knows where a beginning happens? And dare I suggest that Grandma Fernandez's life was a reason for it all? Or Grandfather Fernandez's death? Sometimes the best reasons are no reasons at all.

THE IMPORTANCE OF POTATOES

My mother was peeling potatoes when I first went to tell her I was bleeding. I stood on one leg at the kitchen door. She was unaware of me. She worked in total absorption, the knife moving so fast over surfaces, the peel coiling down into a sink full of water. Then she dropped the peeled potato into the water too, so the white floury shapes floated like breasts in a bathtub. I stood slapping flies, finding phrases, abandoning them. It was wrong in our family to talk about bodies, to see bodies, to have seen her breasts. They had to be covered with patches of words.

My bottom's broken, I said.

My mother lifted the peelings, streaming water, in her hands, before she pulled the plug, and turned.

Broken? she said.

She was just beginning to lift the peelings, the water was rushing silver, cascading in rivulets between her amber fingers. The peelings were high above the sink now, she could have been holding an offering or giving thanks to a god. It could have been a celebration.

But it wasn't. She became methodical. Now she insisted on order, the rituals that postpone. She had to find newspaper, she had to wrap up the peelings in several sheets of newspaper, she had to sort out the newspaper because there was an article she wanted to keep if she could remember what it was. She had to wash the sink out with fresh water, she had to dry her hands, she had to find a clean tea-towel to dry her hands.

When I came to her, everything always took time. With me, she had some private agreement with emotion, a slow negotiation with loss.

At last her hands were dry enough to talk to me.

It's taken you forever to turn into a woman, she said.

She fingered my hair, the way people touch when they're thinking: I ought to do this now. And I grabbed her clumsily because I sensed that at this moment, some concession would be given. She flinched, she prised off my hands.

Will the bleeding make me prettier? I asked.

You'll break my bones, she said.

Will it make me smarter? I asked.

Hear that? My neck's cricking.

She struggled away from my grasp.

My mouth tried another question, but there were no words. Her breath drew in, she was waiting, the muscles of her face pulled as she waited for me. Dread moves across some people's faces as wind moves across trees. I found the question.

Will it teach me what you know? I asked.

She dropped her arms. She went back to the pale potatoes.

Next time when you're peeling potatoes, can I do them with you? I asked, despite this.

Of course, she said.

Just like that? I demanded.

Just like that, she agreed.

She never called me and after our agreement, I didn't want to wander in. I'll wait for her, I thought sulkily. She didn't call. She didn't want me to know what she knew even about potatoes. I never peeled potatoes with my mother.

MY SECOND LETTER

Grandma Juanita's house

Dear Mum,
Zoe looked up at me from her sucking today and her eyes met mine. You know what happened? Her eyes went wide with surprise. The last person she was expecting to see above the milk was me!

I tried to explain it to her. I drew a line with my finger from my nipple to my face. But I suppose it's hard for a baby to be

interested in abstractions like cause and effect. She just went on
sucking.

Sometimes she turns towards sounds. Yesterday I blew my nose.
She turned to look. That was all, just a simple turn of her tiny
head, and my heart went spinning.

She's just looked up again. We held a gaze. We shared it. I
almost forgot to breathe. The baby, the baby melts my bones.
When I look up from her at things, they seem to have the haze of
possibility she has, the newspaper folded on a chair, a fork with
bent prongs on the table, a leafless branch out the window, they
seem to merge with me and lose their hostile edges.

I think I might be in love for the first time in my life.

I'm wasting so much time when I should be writing or painting
or something, if I'm to be great. But yesterday, I couldn't leave her
crib. I sat five metres away from her and I didn't move till she
woke. All I wanted was to be with her.

Soon I'll get on with my destiny. I've just got to get the hang of
things, how limply or sumptuously it hangs, my new life.

I wasn't expecting any of this. You always seemed so miserable
about having me.

Hypatia

LOST 1

At the manager's office, I knocked at a little window of corrugated glass, the sort that's meant to stop people peering in.
I wanted to ask about the day's lectures, I didn't want to miss
anything of the start of my mother's new life. I peered into
the circles of light and made out a long sofa and empty
shelves. Just then the door burst open and a man put his head
out and shouted at me, the angry sound of languages you don't
understand.

I tried to ask questions but we had no language in common

and he was one of those people who turn their eyes up and ask heaven for patience while you stand wondering if you should ask for some too. Then I saw a sign in English about a lecture with arrows pointing the way. They seemed to point into my past. I leaned on the wall.

A young man passed me, stopped and said: Have you had a funny turn?

He had a smooth face and a gold chain slipping on his unlined neck. I was anxious for him to know I hadn't turned forty-five yet.

It's just the heat, don't you feel it? I laughed. And I haven't had any breakfast.

There'll be coffee and buns before the talk, he said. He kept walking, so I lolled against the wall. He looked back over his shoulder and caught me.

You've got to look after yourself, you're not as young as you used to be, he called.

He was to stab me many times with words.

Another mirror

In the year that my mother's lover arrived, Matti became more beautiful. I noticed it then, I noticed it every morning. He looked off into distances a lot, his skin taut, his dark hooded eyes intent on some secret ambition.

His beauty never showed on photos but it's there, hard-edged in my mind. His face was an amber jewel, chiselled in planes so you waited for the angle that would show the light inside. He became identical to her. Sometimes, coming up a road, walking from the bus stop, you'd start to call out Mum, until the unimportant differences became distinct. Whereas I was the daughter of my father. Strangers to the town didn't believe I belonged to my mother.

My mother said that when she looked at him, she was looking into a mirror.

You were born so delicate, she would say, her arm on his shoulder as they watched clouds shift light over the lake. After you came out of me, the doctor said I wouldn't rear you. Then suddenly, one day it was over, one day you shuddered into life.

They kept watching the clouds. He never turned to look at her. He'd heard it all his life, this affirmation that he existed before his memory began, the same words, the same intonation, the same pauses, we could say it with her, a recitation.

That day, behind the curtain of their linked bodies, I said: And me?

She didn't twitch, she didn't look around. I had to repeat the question. At first I didn't hear her reply. Her back was towards me. Her voice was stiller than the lake without a breeze, darker.

You know I love you. But you're almost standing on my heels, she said.

Matti was son and daughter to her, he used up all the need she had of children. His hair was so black it was purple in the shadows, like hers, as he sat on the kitchen stool wobbling on the bricks of the backyard, she could never bear to cut it short, after her scissors it still moved languorously in its length, secretly, sumptuously, like hers. His eyes behind the brown transparent irises were like a spider's cobweb on a gold morning, like hers. And his arms, hands, they were amber shining and rounded against a sky singing with blue, against a lawn green with winter rain, against a white wall, a white bathtub.

His hands moved like a dancer's promising more, he'd

copied the delicate movements my mother had learned from
nuns. The boys at school called

Dago Girlie, dago girlie

after him, and I saw how he quivered, but he smiled to tell
Mum, his lips red as if he'd bitten them, his eyes so black and
hooded as he told, till I saw the cobweb behind them,
patterning.

That day she smiled back at him, you could see from the
smile that memories were starting.

When my father died, I began to feel that I was chosen, she
said.

We knew these words too, another recitation.

When she sent me off to the convent, she said, something
was snickering inside me.

Matti scratched his ear.

A deep voice, like my father's. It said I would do something
that people would remember forever and ever, she said. That
would change history.

She was still smiling, sadness stretching across her face with
her smile.

You'll have to do it for me, she said to him.

For your grandfather, she added.

After all, he was the one who was her mirror.

In the silence, blowflies droned heat, then winged out the
door. The garden rustled only in a drench of sunshine. It was
a relief when a customer came knocking at the door to ask for
Dad.

I tried not to be jealous of my brother, how could I be,
when he looked so much like my mother. My father didn't
rate as an ally. I'd look down at the round rims of my
shoes pressed firmly into the ground. Leather shoes, even
scuffed, look important. But the certainty of my importance
softened all the way up my body and by the time it reached

my eyes, it was a poor drooping thing. Whereas there were two of them.

Together, they were my link with emotion.

And then, the lake.

LOST 2

I roused myself to follow the arrows for the 10 am lecture by Gerard M. Gaunt on Non-Riemannian Hypersquares. I'd read about Gerard M. Gaunt in one of my mother's newer books, and beside his formulae she'd quipped in her red ink: Is this why it's tragic? Is God Gaunt?

What do you think about when you're trying to hurry beyond your past and into the start of a new life for your mother's work? That tomorrow or the next day people will be following arrows with my name mother's name stuck up on the very same spot that held the name of Gerard M. Gaunt.

To Juanita Montrose's work, as formulated by her daughter, they'll say to each other.

A cold wind blew through me, as if there was a draught. But I would like Gerard M. Gaunt to be in my audience tomorrow or the next day, whenever I'm scheduled, listening to the explanation of her work. I allowed my daydream to drift, I pictured the face of Gerard M. Gaunt hovering in the floating sunshine and saying, what would he say?

Your mother's work is so stimulating, young lady, that I'll reconsider my theory.

There were tables in the anteroom piled with empty coffee cups. An urn was bubbling, but the lecture room was rustling with people chatting in different languages, rustling, finding blank pages in notebooks. Gerard M. Gaunt was already at the lectern, smiling, pink cheeked, white eyebrowed, not at all as

I'd imagined him, a Santa Claus of a man. I left the temptation of the urn.

Come in, my dear, Gerard M. Gaunt said to me. Surely some gentleman . . .

It's the Australian genius, I heard someone whisper.

I hurried to a chair up the back row, stumbling past knees, bags, jutting notepads, biros. My chair legs scraped the floor.

You may wonder at my interest in hypersquares, Gerard M. Gaunt was saying. But one never knows when a tiny backwater may become a grand and raging river, sweeping all of mathematics with it.

Exactly, I wanted to shout. That's what will happen with my mother's work.

The audience listened to him respectfully, leaning forwards, rubbing the stubble on their chins and examining their fingernails.

That's how they're going to listen to me, I said to myself. I was too excited to concentrate. I'd become a good daughter at last.

Dancing for her lover

Everything in my childhood seemed to happen in the summer, winter, summer after my mother's lover first lounged at our kitchen door. Perhaps it wasn't so, perhaps time took a particular shape because of his shape, the particular angles of his body as he leaned one elbow against the doorframe, one hand on his head, one hand on his hip. That's how it seems now. Sometimes, after I'd come home from school, the silent dust in our house still whirled with his footfall, his smell, what was it, books, pages, sweat, the smell still lingered between the sheets of my parents' bed, sheets so scrubbed they were thin and soft, but now crumpled deep down where my mother hadn't pulled them straight, and it surely was his teaspoon, not my mother's, upside down and dripping a puddle of milky tea onto the silver sink.

Have you started having milk in your tea? I asked one afternoon, holding up the spoon.

You could make me a cup of tea now, said my mother, in answer. She was peeling carrots.

I've been trying it with milk and without milk, she added. And today I'll have milk and two sugars, nothing like a change.

Peelings of carrots thrown into a bin under the table glisten when sunlight's behind them.

I became a fossicker, a rummager, a spy, one of those people looking up through their eyebrows, their face twisted until they think to rearrange their mouths.

At night, in my room at the back of the house my father built for my mother, at night I danced for my lover. I wrapped a towel around me, a towel that had been boiled in my mother's copper, a towel as shamelessly white as any in a hotel. I stood in front of the glass doors that opened out on to the dark garden, the doors as black as the garden, as black as the lake beyond, a black mirror. It wasn't my body in the black glass of the doors, it wasn't my eyes I saw with. I'd taken my mother's body, and I saw with the eyes of my lover. I slipped the towel down the ordinary white tree trunk of my body that I'd known since I was a baby, but now I discovered that my chest was small breasts of promises, shell-tipped promises that, like my mother's dress, could sing. I slipped the towel past the spider-webbed pattern of rib bones, and now there was my curving waist, I measured it for him, see, it's only two hand spans, for my lover, only the span of his large man's hand. My navel that once held me so close to my mother that I fed from her food, now I saw as a cave where his penis could linger, enticing, swelling. Look at my hips, my lover, my pelvic bones show the swelling of a woman's hips, my rounded calves, my slender legs are pathways to his place of entry. I touched my skin under the new curling pubic hair, touched it gingerly, a tongue between my legs protruded, a kitten's tongue, that's what my lover saw. I thought till now I was an empty slit. For him it glistened luxuriously, like cut fruit on a pale bowl. Like a tongue tasting the last lick of ice-cream. I stroked it, pulled at it, and tasted my fingers, to know the tingle on the tongue of my lover beyond the black mirrors of my dance. At the thought of his ardour, I couldn't put off the moment of ecstasy, I was convulsing, in the black mirrors I watched myself convulse. I tried to give my ecstasy voice, and I was appalled that no words came, but my eyes were rolling into my skull in the lonely pleasure and bliss was falling around me like white light.

When my hand was drooping wetly, and my thighs were streaked with silvery threads, I lay on the bed and pulled the covers over. I was not my mother, and beyond the black mirrors, there was no lover's face, just the blank bodies of white trees in the faceless moonlight, and beyond, the black threat of the lake.

That summer moved imperceptibly into the belief: the only real adventure for my life will be to become my mother.

Lost 3

My mother, the words were drying on my lips as I rocked on my chair in the Athens conference room. My head had lolled forwards until it had to jerk backwards.

What's happening? I blurted to the man sitting next to me, a red-faced Scot. My voice was thick with sleep.

All around people were jostling to get out the door.

He got up, stood with his hands in his pockets studying me.

I wiped saliva off my chin.

It's been a bit difficult to tell, with the racket of your snoring, he said in a broad Scottish accent. But I'd have a guess that it's lunch.

Outside the dining room door was a sign in Greek. I wondered if it was about the conference schedule, or even about mathematics.

PLUCKING SOMETHING OFF

No one who is not a mathematician, said my mother, can come under my roof. Plato wrote that on the gate to his Academy. She joked that she ought to put up a sign like that over the kitchen door.

She always helped Matti with mathematics but often she'd drift off and begin dictating something else, her face lit by the drift of white curtains at the window.

Mathematics is just about picturing things, she said.

Instead of fiddling with formulae and co-efficients, you just have to look at the pictures in your mind, how they correspond, she said. A formula comes out of that.

Matti's pen would slip on the page.

I thought Euclid was bad enough at school, he grumbled.

Her face came back to his, still in its dream of white curtains.

Euclid's just the foothills, but when you struggle to the top, you'll see.

Her face was pointed with hope for him.

You'll see.

She softened.

You think my mathematics is as beautiful as Euclid's? she asked.

He looked in horror at what she'd been dictating.

Is this just stuff you made up? he asked.

Euclid would've had a scribe as well, she said.

We're getting somewhere, she said. Together.

On those nights, our dinners were wreathed in her smiles.

They have such actuality, triangles and squares and points, she said. No wonder the ancient Greeks built them into their minds instead, it must've been such a relief.

There's something that passes between the parent and a particular child. I never knew what it was. I was always running between their faces too late, I couldn't pluck it off to share it, it had seeped into them, become part of them.

But I comfort myself: if I'd been that particular child, if I'd been allowed to be her scribe, I wouldn't be here. Love whispers so strangely, we often can't make out what to do.

Matti let his hair fall over his face as he packed up his books. Then he flung it back. He'd thought up an argument. How would Dad feel, coming home to a sign like that when the right angles of his built-ins have gone all wrong?

He wasn't usually on my father's side. He was on no one's side, he owed loyalty to no one except himself.

FAME

There was a woman near me in a white tracksuit and an explosion of vigorous blonded hair, watching me struggle with the sign in Greek.

Do you want me to read it for you?

She was standing closer than most strangers would, with a wistful face but the deep brown authority of a voice stained by thousands of cigarettes. She translated, her warm eyes eager to please me.

Conference breakfast 8 hours to 9 hours. That wasn't what you were expecting it to say, was it?

I wanted her to please me because she was the same age as my mother.

You're right, it wasn't, I said.

She laughed hoarsely, charmingly.

It must be wonderful to be you, she said admiringly. You wouldn't have ordinary concerns. Your life must be like living in a rainbow.

There was a swell of noise from the dining room as someone opened the door to go in. The woman kicked the door shut with her running shoe. It was grubby but authoritative. She looked more like a tourist than a mathematician. She carried a video camera. I was trying not to stare at her, because I'd assumed till that moment that all women mathematicians would look like my mother. But the brightness of her face warmed me, that another mathematician admired me.

Oh, I have very ordinary concerns. I laughed. I don't even know what Non-Reimannian Hypersquares are. Do you?

It wasn't a concept that came up in Lost Property, she said.

Before I could ask her what she meant, she leaned towards me and corrugated her wrinkled lips into a whisper: I wanted to welcome you to this conference. The others won't.

They won't? I found myself whispering back.

Because of the competition, she whispered. Most of the mathematicians thought it was mathematical maoism. The peasants invading the institutions.

Invading, I repeated. I jerked into a laugh, I had to struggle out of panic.

But they're clever people here, they'll look at the idea, I said. The idea is what matters. It's not like in Ramanujan's day.

I was struggling against the memory of what Clare said, the tattered brown envelopes from amateurs thrown on a professor's floor.

Ideas don't queue up like people and file their way to the front, she said. There's a lot of pushing and shoving in ideas. Some even get trampled to death.

She'd kept from girlhood a pretty way of throwing back her head when she laughed. Light bounced on her chin and a smudge of face powder. On her a smudge was not a mistake, she made all unsmudged faces look dull.

At that moment the dining room door banged open and shut behind another eddy of noise and a man dressed in a Hawaiian shirt. He walked past, then looked back at me.

Oh no, you're not the winner? he shouted in an Australian accent.

My face was redder than ever with pride.

She is, smiled the woman in the tracksuit.

Blimey! he shouted. Just my luck!

He strode off, shirt flapping.

The woman held open the door so the clang of plates and roar of conversation rushed out at us.

When I read about you in the *Sunday Times,* I knew you'd be victorious, she said. Even though they treated the competition as a joke—

A joke? I repeated. My stomach was quaking.

It isn't the usual way great mathematics comes to light, she said. Is it?

You're not a mathematician, are you? I said to her.

I worked in Lost Property all my life, she answered brightly so that it sounded like the sort of answer anyone could expect at a mathematics conference.

Creating a mathematical model of Property Loss? I asked.

No dear, she said. I just stood behind a counter and gave people back their things. No one ever came for this camera, so the boss gave it to me as a golden handshake. He didn't like unclaimed things hanging around. Made him look as useless as he was. So I decided to make films that explain.

Explain what? I asked.

She roared deeply again.

If I knew what needs explaining, it wouldn't, she said. But what I'm pointing out, dear, is that many mathematicians struggle for years to get published in one of those tiny magazines that only get read by five people. They're the five contributors. You haven't given your talk yet and you've already reached millions. So the mathematicians are a bit put out.

I struggled with disbelief.

Do they know you're here? I asked.

Oh they'll take all comers, she said. In fact, they're rather messianic about Non-Reimannian Hypersquares. It's a wonder they're haven't got spruikers down in the street in front of the hotel.

I should remind the organisers that I'm here, I said, to end the conversation.

You'll interrupt a discussion about golf, she warned. The word's out that since last year's conference, one of them has scored a hole in one.

I laughed.

Mathematicians at a conference would be immersed in mathematics, I said.

No one looked up at me as we walked in. Young men and

two or three women were stirring coffee, chewing lumps of meat, eating pasta, buttering bread, spooning soup, drinking Coca Cola, yawning, stretching, talking. We dodged a man tipping his chair back so it teetered.

The woman in the tracksuit pointed to a group of men sitting at a small table in the middle of the room.

Apparently they're everyone who's anyone in Non-Riemannian Hypersquares.

But there's only six of them, I said.

The hotel had trouble finding a table small enough, she said and roared with hoarse laughter again.

The men were leaning over a sheet of paper. As I came closer I saw it was a diagram.

Excuse me, I said to one of them, a man with a red-striped bow tie. I'm Frances Montrose.

The man looked up from the diagram and nodded a greeting.

Good, good, he said. He looked back at the diagram.

I won the competition, I said.

Was there a competition? he asked. I'm glad I didn't go in it. I never win anything.

I did, I said doggedly.

What did you win? the man in the bow tie asked me. I could see he was humouring me, waiting for me to go.

Here, I floundered. I won being here.

He looked at me uncertainly, but his neighbour turned and whispered in his ear.

Excuse me, said the man in the bow tie politely to me. I watched his lips twitch as his neighbour continued to whisper.

The one in the Hawaiian shirt! said the man in the bow tie to his neighbour.

His neighbour nodded.

There was a pause. The man in the bow tie turned to me.

In that case, you'll need your lunch, he said and he turned his back.

I battled through the crowd to the buffet.

The woman in the white tracksuit looked up from propping her camera on the counter. There was a puff of desolation in the muscles around her mouth.

They weren't discussing mathematics, she said.

I think they were discussing how to best hit a ball out of a sandpit, I said.

They'll get around to mathematics when they work out who's clever and who's not, she said. Console yourself with food. There's stiffado, fasoulakia me kreas, kota yemisti, melintzanosalata, spanakorizo—

How is it you learned Greek? I asked. It seemed as if she was going to be my only friend.

Someone left a Greek linguaphone on a train, she said. My Sanscrit and Hindi are pretty good too.

What are you going to eat? I asked her.

Chips, she said. I hate foreign rubbish.

I piled steaming mounds of pasta, meat and beans on my plate. I put my plate down to wipe steam from my glasses. Amongst the din, I seemed to make no sound, it was as if I was walking in a country where the meanings of my past had loosened, they'd become as silent as floating leaves.

Then beside me a man was shouting:

nyet, nyet

roaring victory, while his neighbor fumbled matchsticks in an arrangement on a table, his face flushed and awkward with concentration. The victorious man swung his legs, and his shout was like the iridescent feathers of a farmyard cockerel catching and holding light, turquoise, gold, scarlet, all the light there is.

My father's favourite saying tumbled into my mind, the way

it does when I least want it to: Don't stick your neck out beyond your class. Or you'll get it chopped off.

Suddenly a cup toppled off my crowded tray and smashed on the floor. The din in the room paused as I bent to pick up the pieces. A woman in a yellow uniform came over, she was fussing around me, taking the broken china out of my hand. But there were still broken pieces on the floor, and she was unused to a miniskirt, her legs were goosepimpled and stuck with veins like the branches of trees, she was pulling at the wrinkles of her short skirt, trying to hide her embarrassed legs, uncertain how to bend.

The woman in the white tracksuit hailed me from a table. She was framed in window light like a prophet. I walked towards her illusions, unloaded my tray and sat down. She said her name was Adele.

We might as well stick together, she said. Can I tell you about the Winged Victory of Argos? The Winged Victory is still joined to the boulder she came from.

She lifted her hands to her face and bent, she was looking through an imaginary camera at a statue.

When you see the Winged Victory, you see the stone, she said. You see the whirling white dust back in the old days, you know that the stonemason watched her edge into life through the day, and then when he went home he dreamed of her. You know that he dreaded the whiteness of his life when he'd finished giving her a life of her own. So what did he do? He left her incomplete, bound to him always in the stone.

Out the window, the sun moved, fizzled.

What are you doing at this conference? I asked.

That's what I'm telling you, I came because of you, she said as if it was obvious.

I was filming the Winged Goddess all over Greece. Then I read about you in Argos. I put down the newspaper, I went back to my hotel, I had a whisky, I ran my bath. I was buzzing, I guessed what was going to happen here. A genius able to turn the known world upside down and everyone ignoring her. That would explain a lot. Not everything. But a lot. I whispered to the universe: Should I go back to London? Or should I stay in Greece? And would you believe, it answered. Most of the water fell from my legs and do you know what was left?

I waited for her to tell me.

The shape of a map, the exact outline of Greece, she said. On both legs.

There was a thud down at street level, then a crash. She stood up to investigate, still chewing.

It's a stonemason, I said without looking. Carving the names of the dead.

It's a significant place for mathematics, she said.

Her eyes dreaming out the window were dissolving buildings, churches, even the stonemason's carving into the shapes and shadows of her hopes. She sat down and mopped up tomato sauce with her chips.

Archimedes might have run through these very streets, she said.

But this is Athens, I said. Archimedes was in Alexandria!

She sat down. But she was in her dream, and it was wafting towards me like the smell of meat.

When I was young I used to think of him running naked through the morning light from his bath, his big penis swinging—boom-a-boom—and he didn't care, she said. He was so excited by his idea. That's genius, she added. When someone says something extraordinary, we all get a feeling for a moment that we're gods.

She looked wistful and uncertain again, shifting her knife and fork uneasily.

We float, I said, in spite of the forces that could submerge us.

Pardon? she asked.

Archimedes. The bath. What he realised in the extraordinary moment. The physics that showed we float, despite the forces that could submerge us.

In the street below, there was another chink of marble falling. We both listened to the chink, it held us, this tiny sound.

You could give me an answer to something, she said.

She put down her knife and fork, rummaged in her pocket and pulled out a piece of paper for me to read. But she was too excited to wait for me, so she read it herself:

The desire on one hand to go on and on, to lean towards infinity. On the other hand, to be caught, completed, with no more yearning.

I took it from her. I read the words again. I couldn't keep eating, I couldn't look at her, I who taught literature for years couldn't move because of a few words scribbled down on a piece of paper. In the hush of the room, the words were forming around me, shaping me.

What do you think? she was insisting.

It's probably from something important, I murmured. I was smoothing down the folds of the paper possessively, the words rubbing against my skin.

Oh yes, she agreed. A pigskin handbag. Found on the New Cross line. It's amazing what's been found in handbags. It links things, doesn't it?

I sighed.

It links what? I asked.

It shows, she said, that everything's in patterns.

She glanced up at my dull face, and hers faded a little.

There was another chink of sound as marble fell again.

I guessed that they'd ignore you, she said. A genius able to turn the world upside down. I knew it'd explain things. Not everything, but a lot. I'm going to get it all on film.

What would it explain? I asked.

What people know seems real, she said. The rest seems improbable.

You did a lot of thinking in Lost Property, I said.

There's only so many ways you can arrange fifty umbrellas, she said.

But did you ever look at them? I asked. These umbrellas?

I was always staring them in the face, she said.

But were they on a shelf against each other? I asked.

Usually. To save space, she said.

In a straight line? I asked. Were they all different?

More or less, she said.

She was gloomily puddling a chip in more tomato sauce.

If you'd decided to arrange your fifty umbrellas in a new line, you would've had fifty ways to choose the first umbrella and forty-nine ways to choose the second one. That'd be two thousand four hundred and fifty choices for the first two umbrellas.

I was using my knife and fork to show her.

I see, she said.

Then you would've had to decide which would be umbrella number three from the forty-eight umbrellas in the old line.

I used the sugar spoon to show her.

After you'd decided, you could've picked up that umbrella from the old line and put it as the third umbrella in the new line, I said. And you'd still have had forty-seven umbrellas left to choose from and arrange in the new line.

I suppose so, she said still puddling her chip.

Then you could've chosen umbrella four. Then five. Then six. If you'd picked up all the umbrellas one by one like that, you'd have a big number of choices. If you want to know how many new lines you could've made, you have to multiply all the choices together. You get a number with about sixty-five characters.

That might've used up some time, she agreed.

She bit the chip in two.

Of course you could've stood them on their points and blu-tacked them together, I said warming to the subject.

I never thought of blu-tac, she said.

Say if each umbrella had ten ribs, I said. You'd have had five hundred ways of choosing the first rib to use and four hundred and ninety-nine ways of choosing the second rib. Of course it would've been complicated because you wouldn't have been able to blu-tac just any rib. Some of them would've got in the way.

They never gave us blu-tac, she said.

But you could've blu-tacked the first rib of umbrella one against the first rib of umbrella two. Or you could've blu-tacked the second rib of umbrella one against the second rib of umbrella three. By the time you'd got up to fifty umbrellas, that would've been quite a lot of arranging.

I suppose I could've requisitioned blu-tac, she said.

Of course you could've smashed the umbrellas, I said. If you'd decided no one was going to claim them, you could've smashed them into fragments.

We didn't usually smash them, she said.

But if you'd smashed each umbrella into fifty bits, you could've started arranging all over again. Just choosing would've taken a while. You'd have had two thousand five hundred bits to choose the first bit from. When you'd decided on that, there would've been two thousand four hundred and ninety-nine bits left. By the time you'd decided on the first two bits, you'd have made six million choices. And then you would've got to arrange them. You could've put, say, bit one of umbrella one against bit two of umbrella one. Then bit two of umbrella one against bit three of umbrella two. Then when you'd worked your way through the bits of umbrella one, you could've started on umbrella two. Then umbrella three. Then umbrella four. For fifty umbrellas. Or on other days you could've put bit one of umbrella one against bit one of umbrella two. Or against bit one of umbrella three. Or four.

We'd have had to employ someone else just to arrange the umbrellas, she said.

In the end, you'd have had a really huge number, I said. I paused. No wonder living is so difficult, I said.

But I was just talking about umbrellas, she said.

She finished eating her chips, got up and left the table. Her piece of paper still lay there as if it wasn't important. I put it in my pocket.

I don't know what magnetises events to each other, or why events that might have passed unnoticed in another person's life became momentous in our family. Over and over again I traced them, these events. I've said: Other sons are selfish. Other husbands don't know their wives. Other mothers have lovers.

It happened when I was too young, too unaware. After my mother's lover lounged at our kitchen door, perhaps my father and Matti were trembling with his presence and I saw nothing. Just as my mother saw nothing of the townspeople's reaction as she walked so resplendently through the town, only aware of the movement of her mind.

My father left every morning, as he always had, to do the household repairs that were the gossip of our lives, the stories of other people's disrepair.

Every evening, my mother questioned him closely at dinner, it was their bond once she had committed herself to him in a blinding white defiance of her mother.

You don't believe it was a burglary? my mother asked of the Williams' battered front door that they'd come home to after a night at the Bingo in the Catholic church hall. And Dad would feel with his fingers the shine of his fork or the weave of the tablecloth, it was impossible for him to talk without his fingers stretching and moving as if he was always measuring, and he'd say:

No, he didn't think so, and nor did the insurance company, they wouldn't pay, they believed old Williams had stolen his own cache of money hidden behind the hot water heater.

My father flung peas across his plate, catching them with his other hand as they fell onto the tablecloth as competently as a wicket keeper.

How can they imagine no one would find out? my mother would ask, in those days she chatted to him as amiably as any traveller wandering in a foreign country and passing time with a local before setting out for home.

And so she considered closely the hole in his plaster wall that Bill Collins punched the night his pregnant unwed daughter ran away, the suspiciously overworked bathroom at Mrs Dwyer's although she lived all alone (how can one widow have a dozen showers a day?), the new shed at Collins' farm that was going to be a pickle factory but after three bad seasons with rain at all the wrong times it burned down, another insurance job. Dad, who'd been working on

the Collins' drains, was sent to assess damage and he'd
arrived before the police. You could see the footprint of Mrs
Collins' cousin in the mud just where the fire had started.
My father said the cousin must've stood right there at the
door with the kerosene can, my father could even make out
the brand name of his shoes. And he drew the letters in his
gravy to show us

olaffuB

Oh, Buffalo, Mum said.

This cousin, continued Dad, had been walking around in the
mud for days, and I'd been looking at this name on his footprints and wondering what fool would manufacture shoes by
the name of olaffuB.

He looked up, distracted by Mum's voice: Which way round
does an f go?

At the end of the table I was pulling a loose thread on my
sleeve, I was jealous, chafing.

I thought of the way my father always painted ceilings blue,
he'd insist upon blue as if it mattered.

But the walls are green, a housewife might argue.

Sometimes she might soften her argument with a waggle of
her finger.

Blue and green should never be seen.

She'd smile at me for endorsement.

But my father would nod no.

When you wake, you'll think you've died and gone to
heaven, he'd say. A blue ceiling is what's needed for the spirit
to rise.

Now, at the dinner table, while my father swallows, I want
to shout at my mother: Why did you waste yourself on him?

Every morning, my father would get up early, and stoke the
stove and make a cup of tea and a piece of toast, and take a

cup in to mother before he left. I'd come in later, and the tea would still be there, unwanted, a brown stain around the white cup as I emptied it down the sink. My father would pull up in his ute at people's houses, his customers, he called them, knocking on doors while families were still dressed for sleep. Vulnerable in crumpled pyjamas and housecoats stained with egg yolk, they'd wait while he investigated their damp walls, broken gates, battered doors, leaking gutters. Then he'd ask for a talk in the living room with the whole family. My father believed in the rituals that rooms promise, his message for the family was too important for him to stand loose-legged on a leaf-strewn, cracked doorstep. There'd be a pause, my father was good at pauses. He had a sweet smile, that flew slowly out of his face, and through the pause the smile would come to rest on you, especially you. He knew that now was not the time for talk about prices, not in the slanting morning sun still hazed with dreams. He leaned both hands on the dining room table, with the family gathered round, and he'd begin to draw.

You've got to see your house, he'd say, as it was meant to be.

My father, as you know, was good at drawing dreams. He could draw a gutter wrapping around a house as protectively as arms, he could draw a back porch so peaceful you could touch the summer breezes. The family would breathe and smile and say yes, they wanted to believe that all the pleasure that their lives had refused them would be made possible by the strokes of my father's flat carpenter's pencil. Soon, they'd be chatting to each other in that quiet nook, this family who hadn't spoken to each other for years, soon the chaos of the children would be kept at bay because of that new staircase, soon a wife would cry out in pleasure at last as her husband held her because of that new bedroom. My father knew the power of his pencil, it was impossible not to in the glowing circles of faces, and he was businessman enough to do the sketches most exquisite with hope for the most expensive jobs. Afterwards, the family would often hang my father's sketches under glass on their walls, the blueprint of how their lives almost became.

People in the town said that he got straight to the heart of things, my father, and perhaps he sometimes did, even if the renovations ended up a little out of kilter.

In some quarters, he was even forgiven for marrying my mother.

If she hadn't been such a looker in that swarthy, reffo way, she wouldn't have got a man like that, I heard Bev Roberts say one day while I fingered the hessian on her potato bags, out of sight below her counter.

Sometimes he'd take me with him, his assistant he explained to his customers when he guessed that the drawing of dreams wasn't quite enough, and I'd do the measuring up while the family watched him realign in his sketches their more important lives.

I'd do it impatiently. Out of school time I wanted to be with my mother. She was the one who'd teach me to be a mathematician I was sure. Because, despite all the red and white and green counters my mother moved around on the kitchen table, despite all the lessons my mother tried to teach him, my father would stop when he counted to ten, suddenly with no more fingers. Everything to him was a length from an outstretched little finger to this freckle, this mole, this scar. His body was irrefutably there, so much more irrefutable than numbers.

He'd peer at the numbers.

All you have to do is count up to ten, she'd say again and again. Ten is our base number. Thirteen is just ten and three extra ones. Thirty three is three lots of ten and three extra ones.

She was always ruling the backs of envelopes into columns for him to look at, columns of units, tens, hundreds, thousands, tens of thousands, hundreds of thousands, millions. Her writing was an angry writhing, but her voice was even.

Once you can count to ten, you can go on forever.

But my father got stuck on thirteen. Later, I wondered about that. Thirteen was a number that kept coming up in our family, so you thought, ah, there's a pattern. Then you were tricked, for there was no pattern at all.

You know what numbers look like to me? I heard him say one day to her. Sticks. These numbers aren't anything. They're just little sticks thrown on the ground.

On the day I was born, he had to go to the corner shop for milk for himself and Matti. My mother had left out the exact change in piles before she'd gone to hospital, a pile to spend each trip to the shop for milk. But there were always dangers lurking.

How big's the new baby? asked Mrs Roberts from behind the till. It was early morning, she was still brushing her hair, struggling with the tangles from her new perm.

My father paused, one of his sweet smiles winging out.

How many inches? Mrs Roberts persisted.

My father's mind twisted to remember what he'd heard the Sister at the hospital say, but numbers were the crackling of a foreign language.

I'll show you, he said, he was always showing.

He reached for the white paper Mrs Roberts used to wrap lollies into funnels for children.

She's as big as your hairbrush, he said, and he drew a baby and Mrs Roberts' long-handled brush, the baby more soft and round and milk-perfumed because of the bristling hairbrush. Mrs Roberts hung his drawing near the till.

She'd cluck her tongue when people asked.

How many dads would do that? she'd say. They broke the mould when they made him.

She'd look at me meaningfully.

Your father doesn't know some things, she'd say. But by golly, he knows what matters.

My mother never went in Mrs Roberts' shop after Mrs Roberts shouted at her, so she never saw my father's drawing, and no one ever mentioned it hung there. It yellowed slowly through the years, it mocked my teenage bravado, another image of the secrets in our lives. I had been thirteen inches long.

My father's ignorance of numbers was another of the things never discussed at home. Once after I'd been fuming at Dad's drawing near Mrs Roberts' till, I'd said to Mum: If Dad wore sandals, he could use his toes and count past ten.

But all Mum said was: Feet aren't needed. The Venerable Bede in 735 AD counted to 9000 on his hands, just by bending his fingers.

She began clanging saucepans on the shelves as if they were Dad's head.

Then Matti came in, and she forgot about dinner, and showed him how to do it. She took a long time to adjust Matti's fingers, and she went over and over it, laughing him out of his impatience, testing him again and again, as if she was afraid that, despite everything, he was in danger of not turning out like her.

I thought of 59049 instantly, but it took me all the time she adjusted his fingers to say it. I knew I shouldn't say it, it was not mine to say, it was Matti's to say. I still expected him to be our mother's wish, for her sake. Finally, when my mother was giving up, the subject was almost drained of its interest, I blurted:

Only nine thousand? He could've put his fingers three ways-up, down and bent. Then he wouldn't have had to stop at nine thousand! He'd have got as far as 59049.

Their faces hovered above me, remote, as two remote identical moons. I knew then I'd never have her heart.

How did you do that sum? my brother asked me.

For the first and only time, he was curious about numbers.

I swallowed. I couldn't look at my mother, the brightness of her face.

It's just three raised to the tenth power, I said.

My voice was getting thicker. Soon it would grind to a halt, and I'd have to look at her.

Did you multiply or something? my brother persisted.

Her cheek muscles flickered. Her eyes widened and narrowed. The corners of her lips darted. But no words came out of them.

So I said it then, what I'd known all along.

You tell him what we do, I said to her.

There was a dizzying silence, no rustles, no twitches, no flutterings. Even the kitchen clock seemed to suspend time. My mother lifted her arm, her beautiful, rounded arm. She looped it around him.

Mathematics is about ideas, not numbers, she said to him. Once you get past the first hurdles, you don't even have to add up.

Even the cleverest amongst us are moved by the simplest passions.

But now, when my mother and I stood in the kitchen alone, I waited for a covert smile. A small pressure on my hand as she passed the teatowel. A look flung over her shoulder as she got the baked dinner out of the oven. A hand nuzzling my waist as I watched with her for the postman. I piled plates quietly so I'd hear her indrawn breath before she began to speak. I stood in the laundry while she pounded white sheets in the copper's steam.

Don't you have anything to do? she asked.

One day I waited while she sliced green beans.

She looked up, the whites of her eyes blank. I was at the door in the same spot where her lover had first stood.

If you're just hanging around, you might get busy with the broom, she said.

I picked at a bit of paint, I shuffled words in my head, like numbers they had relevance only to each other, they'd insist their relevance to the world was random, purely miraculous.

Get on with it, she said.

I took the broom out of the cupboard, the one where she hid. I began sweeping. Behind her silent, intent body, I took large swipes at the spotless floor. The broom end was arching wildly, like a torch it lit on all the objects in the kitchen, the way her lover's glance must every day, the furnishings of my mother's shuttered and secret life, these ordinary things, the cannisters, the kettle, the chairs, the Royal Doulton teaset that my grandmother had sent as a wedding present two years after the wedding she hadn't attended.

That's not how to do it, shouted my mother.

I was sweeping, sweeping, and knocking over a chair. There's too much stuff in here, I was saying. There's no room to move.

The broom end poked at gardenias rammed into a jar on the kitchen table. They tipped, the glass broke, a dribble of water on the floor became a puddle.

Now look what you've done, my mother said.

My fingers were clenched on the broom, like teeth.

What were flowers doing on the table? I demanded.

Nothing wrong with a bunch of flowers on the table, she said.

You never put flowers on the table, I said. Not before.

Before when? she asked.

The air was full of words and her wide caverns of eyes, so defiant, so vulnerable, anyone could steal her away, my mother, my child.

I wish I could replay many moments, to change my part in them. But each moment became an intrinsic part of our pattern, and a small shift would have made a pattern so different, it wouldn't have belonged to who we became.

Before now, was all I said.

We've never had gardenias before now, she said triumphantly. The bush has never flowered.

I memorised the shape, shine, weight, smell of gardenias in a jar on a kitchen table. That evening, I went out into the garden in the freckled moonlight. While crickets sang, and Matti and mother washed and dried the dishes, I examined every bush, I fingered every cool leaf, one by one. There was no gardenia bush in our garden.

Liars, gossips and secretive people make you think you're special, you alone are at the still centre of their talk, you are the one who won't be lied to, gossiped about, you won't be excluded.

In the shadows of the night garden, I saw that my mother's secrets were also from me.

BEING HEARD

The next morning I woke knowing something fundamental had changed, so fundamental the sky was lower, the traffic more monotonous, the air damper. My watch showed I was too late for breakfast again, but this time I rang for room service. Breakfast arrived so fast I suspected it was meant to go to somebody else. But I sat up in bed, the covers rolled up to avoid toast crumbs, the tray so busy it was like a child's picture book with tabs to lift, but there was only sugar and milk and hot water and fig jam underneath. I made six fingers of toast last a long time, struggling to find yesterday morning's elation. I shuddered with the bitterness of the American coffee. I left a little in the cup to prove I'm a lady if anyone should look. Then I pushed the tray to the other side of the bed and sank back. But the coffee had steeled me against further sleep, I was as odd and upright in the bed as a gargoyle.

And that's when I started saying it over and over, as if I already doubted it: This is the second day of the beginning of my mother's new life.

The words got me into the shower and dressed again in my crumpled clothes the colour of walls and out into the corridor only a little late for the first lecture. The signs on the walls announced the morning's speakers, 9 am J. Thung, 10.30 am S. Fu, but someone had scribbled that those were cancelled due to a plane strike in Abu Dhabi. Someone called C. Denver was pencilled in to speak first, followed by J. Symonds, who also only rated a pencilled inclusion. In front of J. Symonds' name, a red pen had written (MISS) and underneath a black pen had written in a different handwriting (GET IT?).

There was a draught in the corridor, one of those early autumn breezes that puckers and goosepimples the skin. But I merely hugged my arms around my thin chest, because when

I've become a good daughter, no winds or storms will touch me.

I glided open the lecture room door, late again, but there was no need for silence. The room was in uproar. I found an empty chair next to a man on his feet shouting:

You might whinge about non-determinism but at least it can give you an idea on curvature.

No one reacted to this because at exactly the same time someone else two rows behind was shouting, It's got to represent the continuum, can't you see?

Immediately, a group of six men from all over the room were on their feet shouting against each other, and someone behind me was saying, This isn't new, it's been recognised in lots of different contexts, you haven't done your homework.

I looked at the lecturer, C. Denver, the man who hasn't done his homework, and remembered that he stopped in the corridor yesterday to speak to me. He had a child's face, rounded and fresh and pink. He glanced from one interjector to the other, all the time holding one hand behind his back like a waiter, and saying quietly whenever there was a space of silence

OK, OK, perhaps that wasn't the best example...

and

I guess what I'm trying to say...

and

Will everyone agree at least that a truncation has taken place?

and

There's a theorem I don't yet have but if I did, it would validate this.

Each time he got no further because a new explosion of argument broke out.

Softly and regularly so they soared over our heads like

thoughts, someone had begun throwing paper planes.

Then a man in the audience walked up to the whiteboard as if it was his lecture. He picked up a texta colour and began to invoke theorems, scribbling calculations on C. Denver's whiteboard.

I can't think without a pen in my hand, he explained with his back to C. Denver who hopped from one foot to another like we used to in the playground when the ground was hot and we had no shoes on. There was a clock on the wall which he watched, wondering if they'd leave him time to read his theory. The interjector talked on and on. At last, at 10.00 am, when the staff were rattling the morning coffee cups, C. Denver heaved a sigh and bundled together his papers. He tried to make a noise doing this, but the interjector kept lecturing and only stopped when someone called out Coffee Break!

The interjector summed up his argument and bowed his head to the audience's applause. C. Denver saw me gazing, and smiled a twisted smile that suddenly I wanted to help straighten out. There was a tremble in the close textured skin under one eye.

Thank you, he said as if he was speaking to me, and disappeared out the door.

The man next to me, grey-headed, bow tied and still pleased with himself, turned to me and said companionably,

He should've responded to my hint on curvature. He didn't put up much of a fight, did he? They oughtn't to send postgrads to these things. They just can't manage debate.

He got to his feet. I stayed sitting on my chair in protest. But we didn't find out what his theory was, I said. Now we might never know.

The man thrust his hands in his belt, stuck his stomach out and exploded with laughter.

Theories! he roared. Everyone's got theories. You're obviously not used to this. Debate's in the interests of good mathematics. Mathematics is a debate, an impersonal game.

I was stern in my chair, remembering the young man's gentle face.

But a game must be played fairly, I argued.

The man laughed again, and backed away down the rows of chairs, kicking them.

Where did you come from? he chortled. Mathematics isn't a Sunday School.

He pretended to hold a champagne toast as he turned into the coffee room.

It's a glorious game and let the best man win, he shouted.

I stayed in my chair and waited out the coffee break alone.

BEAUTY'S WAITING TO SNEAK UP ON YOU

I was a child riding back from Mrs Webb's house, prickling with shame on the torn seat of the ute.

Why couldn't you fix her hallstand? I was nagging.

My father's pale eyes watched the dusty road. Sometimes I wondered whether it was all the guarding of his secret innumeracy that drained the colour from his eyes.

We're not in her class, he said.

Mum is, I said.

Mum, he said, belongs with me.

He changed gears loudly. It sounded like a slow grinding.

But you knew what needed doing, I was saying.

I could've nutted it out, he said.

Then why didn't you? I said. I was shrill with impotence.

Mrs Webb was the doctor's wife in a huge house lapped by a green rolling ocean of lawn. I'd stood with my father on carpet so lush it could have gulped me into its soft heart, while my father, hat in hand, had scratched his elbow in front of the eighteenth century carved oak and grunted: Not a job for the likes of me.

I'd seen Mrs Webb's fat eyes quiver at this dusty man my father in overalls washed too many times. Her fat eyes flicked off him and back, and off again, as if he wasn't a proper object in her house. Diamonds quivered against the fat flesh of her neck.

I wanted to scoff: Diamonds! Before the sun's properly up! like my school mates would have done.

But instead I smirked at her ancient fat. I would never grow old.

My father drove for a while against the dust.

That old wood, he said at last. It was worked with a tool that's no longer around. My granddad did carving like that, but before I was old enough to ask him how, he went.

Where'd he go? I demanded.

He passed on, said my father.

Died, I corrected.

My father ignored me.

They hurled his tools into the coffin, special tools, my father said. He wanted it that way.

Sometimes the shapes of my father's mouth stirred me with sadness.

So no one could build things like he did, said Dad.

He stopped talking for a moment and we watched the road together.

That's the way of our family, said my father. He gave nothing to my father and my father gave nothing to me.

His mouth was still shaped like sadness, like a dark window with a child left outside. He steered around a pothole that had been there ever since I could remember.

117

I didn't want to tell her that her hallstand was once much more beautiful, he said. It probably had a row of flute players along the top. Down on the shelf on one side there was probably an old man sitting and remembering. And on the other side there was probably a shepherdess dancing, her skirt flying.

How did you know that? I said, softer now.

Sometimes, he said, when you put your hand on a bit of old wood, a bit of old oak, especially, from an earlier time, oak that's been cut and carved the way it ought to be, time in the wood is different, it's stopped, you can feel the hands of that other man, the man who carved it. You can almost feel his breath, still in there, still misting the wood. You can feel his mind moving, thinking, just a little further, just a little more, easy does it.

I watched his hands, the way the steering wheel kept jumping out of them, but he controlled it despite stones.

When you make something beautiful, you pretend it's your doing, he said. But the thing is, beauty's out there, waiting to sneak up on you. It comes up of its own accord. I wish my grandfather had admitted it to himself. He thought he could own it.

Now in my father's ute I saw how his shoulders slouched, I saw for the first time how his eyes ended in wrinkles, I saw the hair greying above his ears. It turned into me like a chisel, those lines, that hair, that slouch. That shape of the mouth. That grandfather, that father.

And as the chisel turned, I was shouting: Why don't you talk like this to Mum?

The chisel was still turning in my stomach, and in its agony I was saying the unspeakable in our family.

Then she wouldn't care that you can't count, I was shouting. None of us would.

I'm not sure what happened next, but there was a jerk, perhaps a rock under the wheels, and at the same time my father whipped around to me, his eyes straining, and the car raced across the road and up an embankment. We were going so fast, so slowly, I watched death come. I found words to pray as we raced to the cliff top.

Let me live so something beautiful in mathematics sneaks up on me.

Father screeched to a stop. Three metres away, the cliff fell away into valleys a long scream away, all that was in front of us was the empty air. We sat on the edge of the world, panting.

Shut up when I'm driving, he said.

There was a jaggedness between us that was almost hate.

A DRESS JUST LIKE CLARE'S 1

After C. Denver's lecture, it was Miss J. Symonds' turn. I saw her out in the anteroom sipping coffee alone. She was wearing a blue shining dress that showed her knees and a lot of her rounded breasts, and I'd thought of how Clare would approve. She was the sort of woman that men call pretty, but another woman notices the defiant edge of her jutting nose and the fierce way her hair is pulled back. I said hello to her because we were the only two women in the room, and she said hello back in the sort of American accent that makes me think of warm honey. I could see she was gearing herself up, especially when she turned her back to everyone, took a silver hip flask from her handbag and poured a nip of whisky into her coffee. She caught me watching her, and we shared a smile, and mine faded into the thought: Will it be like this for me?

When she arrived at the lectern, she had to find out how to

lower it, and she fumbled working the microphone and switching on the overhead projector. I was surprised no one came forward to help her, but it was a warning for what was to come.

Which way is on? she mouthed to herself, until she remembered the switch on the wall. And all the time her blue satin dress strained to barely conceal her short, lush, large breasted, wide hipped body. I was beginning to think she chose her dress precisely because it clung to her, supporting her in her defiance. The audience, all men except me, sensed this strength beyond her prettiness, there were rustles and whispers, and when she said Good morning, the polite murmur didn't quite drown a languorous response from a German voice in the front row. It was meant to make us all think of warm bedrooms. I heard it the way you sense words in a language you don't speak, when even your skin seems to reach out and touch meaning. She pretended not to notice, but the corner of her mouth tightened.

She straightened her back and squared her shoulders and decided to take her time writing theorems on the board first. For a few moments there was only the squeaking of her textacolour pen. She straightened up, and opened her mouth to speak. But someone called out

Well, well! A girl of many talents!

There was a rush of embarrassed male laughter and her lips twitched.

Give the lady a go, someone shouted.

She cleared her throat. Somewhere in the ceiling, a water pipe gurgled and rattled, and in a room behind us, a phone rang insistently. Her arms pressed against her sides, making them support her body like her dress did, and then she began her lecture. She was barely through the second theorem before a man jumped to his feet saying:

I must say, has anyone noticed that this theorem is an alle-gory for the theorem on meeting times?

I'm not going to talk about meeting times, said J. Symonds but the man's voice boomed without a microphone.

If everyone, he said, puts down on a piece of paper the time that they can make it to a meeting, you can prove by this theorem that the meeting times written on all the bits of paper will stabilise. But what you can't prove is that anyone will know it has stabilised. And the whole point of planning a meeting time is that everybody knows when the meeting time is.

The man looked around him for agreement. J. Symonds managed to say into her microphone (which she was grip-ping with white knuckles, she was not going to give it up like C. Denver had to): So there's no point to your inter-ruption.

But is there any point to this lecture? the man boomed.

But another man was shouting: You can't link the first theorem you've written up with the second, not now!

He jumped to his feet to explain. Half a dozen people called out to agree or disagree, and J. Symonds flicked a switch and suddenly she wasn't a small figure in shining blue, she was a black shadow huge on the whiteboard behind her, and she was saying into an abrupt silence:

Gentlemen . . . ladies. This isn't my invention, this is clas-sical mathematics. There's been a misunderstanding. There is a part in my reasoning that's historically young because I just worked it out late last night, and I found some nice things on the way. Please sit down and listen and you'll see what I mean.

She smiled absently, the smile of someone deeply pre-occupied with mathematical thought despite a shining blue dress, but she was fragile too, and her lips began again to tremble. Some of the men heard the preoccupation in her voice, and sat down. She looked at the others still on their feet and then she spoke soothingly to them, as if they were children.

You'll see, very soon, she said. Trust me. Just wait. After all, the whole subject's about contemplation.

Not only breasts

My mother was holding the curtain away from the window to see if the postman had been. There were letters spilling out of the box but she was staring beyond the fence at the shadows in the sunlit bush, those questions.

We used to sing them, the times tables, she was telling my brother Matti. He was drawing on the margins of a comic.

Singing the times tables was like singing the national anthem, she was saying. It was wonderful, a hundred kids' voices, the little girls going high, the bigger girls blaring to be loudest, and some of them losing rhythm and racing, and the nun dragging the swell back with her arms as if it was a ship on ropes so we sang together, it felt like a hymn. It gave me the feeling that God cared about seven times seven.

My brother kept drawing.

Some things burn in your mind. Every time you try to answer a question, you discover more things you'd like to know, she said.

My mother laughed at the questions she'd like answered.

And you can't keep track, she added. Of what you know, and you don't know.

We listened to the sound of Matti's pencils.

It's the silence when I think, that's what I love, she said.

She paused.

I'm in love with thinking. I don't mean thinking things

through or thinking things over or thinking things out, she said.

Only the crackle of the fire made a sound. I tried not to fidget so she'd go on.

Thinking itself, she said.

But it didn't matter what sounds Matti and I made, her voice had that echoing quality of someone talking to themselves, or perhaps she was too close to the windowpane. There were little puffs of mist where her voice had been.

Thought, she said.

Something boiled over on the stove. She turned to the sound as if it was coming from a long way off.

It's as abstract as death, she said. All the mess of life removed. And what's left, it can go anywhere.

When she talked like this, I was filled with unbearable sadness.

The milk's burned, my brother said.

My mother's head jerked. She looked across at him from a long distance.

It stinks, he said.

I mightn't be genius enough, she said.

Her mist on the windowpane was already fading.

A DRESS JUST LIKE CLARE'S 2

The men standing up in the conference room looked at each other, daring each other, who would sit down, who would defer to her and let her speak. No one wanted to be the only one to sit. Then the youngest wavered, and clanked down in his chair and the rest followed, and J. Symonds had just linked her first equation with her second when a young black man in the back row jumped to his feet and called, Miss! Miss!

He sounded so like a schoolboy that everyone looked around, smiling.

Could you explain whether Miss on the sign outside was an indication of your marital state, or was it a hint that we shouldn't have bothered to attend your lecture? he called.

In the chaos that followed, she stood aside, turning her notes over and flicking through them. Eventually there was a pause in the interjections and she said:

Now, if you'll all bear with me, I'll recap what I said, so you'll be able to follow the next part. Because the next part—

she smiled proudly

—is quite a leap.

I think it was her pride the man couldn't bear, her pride inside her tightly-held shining body. She was bending down to the whiteboard, but his voice ripped through the air, yelling out in a sing-song way,

I can see a nipple, I can see a nipple.

There was a terrible silence. J. Symonds straightened up, her face seared with fury. There were bubbles of spittle at the corners of her mouth.

Is that what's troubling you? Don't you know about nipples? she roared at her audience, and I could hear the indrawn breath of men shocked that a shining blue dress could contain such a loud voice. But there was a greater shock. Her fingers moved to the buttonholes of her bodice. I suddenly knew what she was going to do as she stood defiant, fuming, her fingers jabbing the buttonholes. I wanted to yell out

Don't

but who was I to yell out? I hadn't found out how to live, not then. Suddenly she was standing with her breasts bared and bobbing up from their confinement like children jumping out from hiding into the middle of silence.

She gazed around at her audience, tense, fierce, beautiful. The only sound was the rustle of her dress as she rotated, glaring at us all.

Now you do know, she said. So let's get on with it. She calmly tucked her breasts back into her bodice, did up the buttons, and went on with her lecture.

MY THIRD LETTER

Grandma Juanita's house

Dear Mum,
Zoe's sleeping well, much better than other people's babies, and I'm sitting in Grandma's sunny bush garden and the writing's coming easily as if someone smarter than me is inside my head. The nappies leap on the washing line strung between gum trees and it's so quiet I can hear a bird's wing fluttering, the crinkle of twigs as leaves drop. Even the washing basket near the open door looks like peace. I think about that other child inside me, my heroine. Maybe, maybe, it's possible to be both a mother and a great person.
Bits of a new character drift in. People talk to her and I write down what they say. I'm not sure where they're talking, so I manufacture bedrooms, bed sheets, tables, apple cores, lips, verandahs, candles, even the people's feet, in the most cavalier way. I go from elation to horror at the presumption of it, but I must write on, it's leading me, I follow, I'm trying to map this bewildering landscape inside my mind. She's unwinding in me, my heroine, I love her, in the haze of my mind she twitches and glows.
Sometimes my heroine seems like a mother to me. With a baby, I feel so unmothered.
Whenever you were silent, bossy, irritable, morose, punishing,

I'd say: She was probably like that with Dad too. Harry. That's why I haven't got a father any more. I waited every birthday for him to write to me, so I could arrange a secret meeting with him against the harbour walls in the Botanical Gardens. It would be near an overgrown bed of red gladioli flaring. I'd tell him how you were still in the thrall of your mother. It must've driven him crazy, I'd say. It's driving me crazy too.

He'd say: She should've married her bloody mother!

I practised saying in front of the mirror:

Can I go home with you?

He never wrote.

There were moments in my childhood when you'd shake yourself free, remember that you were my mother as well as her daughter.

Then you'd ask what we should do today.

So the sun would shake gold into the room and swirl while I stroked your hand and tried not to cling to it. If I didn't cling too closely, you mightn't go away.

You always went away.

She was your first, your only love.

In the black night my fists are clenched so tight, the blood in them flows yellow hot, and I promise myself I will never, never be like you.

And then in the morning I wonder if you said that when you were young.

Hypatia

ANOTHER STRANGE COUNTRY

Seminar: Infinity and Non-Riemannian Hypersquares 12 pm room 128 said a sign on the wall. Some wag had scribbled underneath

By popular demand.

I moved through the corridor of the first floor with trepidation, because I was going to the country of Non-Reimannian Hypersquares, ringing with unknown formulae which I'd try to follow like a traveller leaning on a bar in a foreign country listening to a spot-lit singer and trying to mouth the words, to be part of the song, to touch some part of that country, to be able to say afterwards, I belonged. I walked softly, I didn't even want to disturb the dust, I wanted to belong amongst those real mathematicians so much. The shining corridor meandered on and on, but there were reassuring skid marks on its lino and boot scrapings along its walls. I opened the door of room 128 at last to find a man and a woman lying on a bare mattress. In that moment when they turned their heads to gaze at the intruder, my eye snagged on detail, like a skirt catching on a fence, it seemed very important that the mattress had black and white stripes like pathways, and that some of the stripes were thicker and bolder than others.

They both yelled at me so I didn't ask where I was.

I slammed the door shut and ran up the stairs to the second floor, and opened doors more cautiously now, but all I found were fat, friendly piles of towels in cupboards.

At last there was an unnumbered door opening onto a room with white plastic chairs ranged neatly around a whiteboard on an easel, a jumble of coloured texta pens and a duster on a tray. A lace curtain moved at a window, barely touching the sill, guarding the room against the traffic noise below. I sat down and watched the lace curtains of my life, their passivity. Adele came into the room, her camera at her side. With the onrush of air, the curtains billowed and fell. I smiled to see her, and patted the seat beside me. We could sit together through the seminar.

There's something so still about you, she said. You're right for this place. You know the word I hear most often in Athens? Perimeno. I am waiting.

She smiled lopsidedly.

You look like someone who's always been waiting, she said.

Will I be giving my talk in here? I asked her. She seemed to know everything, she was like a cat, checking all the secret places, sniffing and measuring with whiskers.

Probably, she said. They could only afford to hire the big room for the big boys.

We giggled conspiratorially, as if girlishness could protect us.

It doesn't matter, I said about the room. It's the way mathematics was done in the beginning. Scratchings in white dust.

She switched on her camera.

I'll close in to a tight shot, if you'll try to look deep in thought, she said.

I heard the camera roll, I blinked obediently at the white curtains. I thought about how my mother would've turned towards the room with her back to them, she's always hazed in a light more luminous than the light that falls around other people. My image of her can't possibly be real but she strode through my nights and days, gathering meaning, all the meaning there was until I could do nothing but live her life over again. I've learned her by heart so well, every ripple of her, the way she stood at window curtains gathering the meaning of the room into her body before she spoke.

My mind drifted with the white curtains, but Adele's voice kept insisting into my thoughts. She was using a BBC accent.

There's a diagram drawn on the ground, she was saying. The person who drew it is squatting to get closer to the diagram, he's almost part of it. Behind him there's a semicircle of armour and swords, but it doesn't matter. You know any second death will lunge, but it doesn't matter. You know any second that the body will be covered in dust, and maybe even the diagram will be trampled, but it doesn't matter, because it's been discovered, that's the point, the picture is about the moment when something from the timeless world broke into ours.

Archimedes, I interrupted. He was killed by soldiers. And maybe it did matter.

Adele broke off.

If the understanding of the diagram was something only he could have, I said. If he invented its meaning.

She paused.

What are you waiting in here for? she asked.

I'm wondering if we're in the wrong room, I said.

The camera clicked off.

Wrong? The others have gone up the Parthenon, sightseeing, she said in her ordinary voice. They're not telling you anything, are they? They'd be sweating down the hill by now. Go up to the roof garden. Paul's up there. He pretends it's his office. He's cranky he hasn't got a proper one. He's been looking for you. Anyway, from up there the Parthenon is an abstraction, and isn't that what a mathematician would prefer?

Who's Paul? I asked.

He might know what's going on, she said. He talks loudly and looks in a folder a lot.

Grandma Juanita's house

Dear Mum,
I'm only writing to you because there's no one else to talk to. Jim's still with the camel expeditions in Cheryl Cooper's bed, I suppose. So I'm on my own. I suppose we're always on our own, really. Funny how a baby makes you think of that when all you can do is just sleep and wake and feed and the nights are tacked on to the mornings, and sometimes, for a change, rain splatters the window glass.

You see how alone we all are, but you don't want the baby to feel that, so you exhaust yourself trying to prove that she's not alone, and the more you do that, the more you know how truly alone you are.

She woke me at dawn with her little bird cries. Zoe, my tiny bird.

But I have to tell you that though I adore her, walking around this house with her is so lonely, there are times when I don't want her at all. She goes to sleep after a feed and she wakes with her bird cries at the merest whisper of my pencil. Then she stays awake for the rest of the day. A day with only a baby for company is a day of dread. All that gets me through each day is the hope of a bit of time to myself. I hold that hope more closely than any mother does a baby.

But today, she whimpered for ten hours. It was freezing outside, so I walked her around the house. It's only a little house, the house Grandpa built Grandma. Maybe his heart wasn't in it. The walk takes no more than sixty seconds if we go slowly, the nook where I write and paint and where I'm going to learn the violin, the kitchen, the loungeroom-dining room, the bathroom, my bedroom, the nook where she sleeps. Back again. Her nook, my bedroom, the bathroom, the loungeroom-dining room, the kitchen, my nook. This was no way to get through an afternoon. I picked up a book as we passed the bookshelves to read as we walked. Zoe wailed. I put the book down. Nook, loungeroom-dining room, kitchen, bathroom, bedroom, other nook. Other nook, bedroom, loungeroom-dining room, kitchen, nook.

Look at the furniture, I told her. See, that's a table. That's a chair. That's a ratty old TV set.

She wouldn't look at the changing perspectives as we walked, she only looked at me. I stopped at the goldfish bowl, at the big windows looking out onto the bush, and the kitchen clock on the mantelpiece, and the golden fire, and at the oven to pretend there might be something in it. Just in case Jim meant to surprise me with dinner once when he stayed overnight. And then forgot. I switched the oven light on and off. On and off. That was really diverting. The dread came over me in wafts like mist.

All the time it's me that she watches. Her trust in me is spikes of ice. Is that how you felt about me?

I don't think I can take this loneliness. It's rotting me. Why didn't you say it was so miserable?

Hypatia

A SHELL CAN SING 1

I went up to the roof garden just as Adele suggested and sat down, cowering like a child banished from an adults' party in the night, with music and laughter and streamers. I was miserable because the mathematicians hadn't invited me to go to the Parthenon.

It doesn't matter, it doesn't matter, I whispered to myself. I was ashamed to be cowering, but shame made me cower more. Amongst the blue tunnels of shimmering air that swooped around the roof garden I said:

You've stood with your mother where no one else in the

world has stood, you've seen with your mother what no one else has seen.

That didn't help. The air shimmered on, as it always does.

All I could do was go in silence and wait for the whirling fragments to settle, just as I did a long time ago, the afternoon when I ran home to catch my mother and her lover making love.

The only thing to do

About sex, there comes a time when imagination isn't enough. I was determined to find a lover like my mother's lover. None of the boys in town would do, he'd have to come from out of town. On the footpath outside the corner shop where the teenage girls giggled and the boys on motorbikes squatted puny against their machines, I watched the highway traffic with such determination that Bev Roberts came out from behind her counter, drying her hands on a limp tea-towel. She stood on her step to look at the sky.

It might rain, she said. Your sweet father doing work outside?

She'd lately taken to speaking of my father as if he was a little boy.

I don't know, I said, though I knew very well he was laying brick foundations for a new corner shop down the other end of town. That was likely to be outside.

He's contributing a lot to the progress of this place, she said. His blood's worth bottling.

I didn't want to take my eyes off the traffic. She sighed, looked meaningfully at the sky again and went inside.

On the other hand, maybe it won't rain, she said over her shoulders, and I noticed how fatly they sloped.

Then, miraculously, a Customline braked outside the shop and a man leaned out.

Want a lift? he asked.

I stared. He wiped his nose with his hand, this man my longing had conjured up.

Want a lift? he had to repeat.

Maybe, I said.

My feet wouldn't move, despite the wonder of his sudden arrival, because his face was thin and peaked and his hair receded from the top of his head as if it had slipped in disappointment, that's how I saw it then, and his eyes were turned down at the corners like a kicked dog's. I'd been hoping for elegance. This man was like the wish in a fairytale gone wrong.

Bev Roberts came out to her doorway again.

You alright, love? she asked me, looking at the man, a stranger to town.

I looked away from them both, up the road to the horizon, where my rapture would begin.

I've been waiting for him, I said truthfully.

The frowning face of Bev Roberts hung like a moon in the car window as we drove away. But I sat on car tools he hadn't thought to move. He was a flurry and bony wrists, grabbing at screwdrivers, saying: You wouldn't want to hurt your lovely body.

Lovely, it had a shocking sound. Lovely, his tongue slithering on sharp brown teeth as if he wanted to hurt to make it more shocking, his hands stretched tight and mean on the steering wheel, and the way he smiled into his own face, it was raw, brutal, red, tawdry, it exhausted me, wherever he'd take me. I knew it wasn't where I wanted to go.

You want to do it now? he asked suddenly. You fussy where? I know a place, it's OK.

I was throbbing with shame that he should speak to me like this, when surely he was speaking about love. My blood was pounding, shouting:

Get out, get out.

But I said nothing, did nothing, my legs were glued to the vinyl of the seat, even to wriggle them was hard unless I pulled and then they'd come away with a loud, rude thwack. This seemed important, not to make a rude noise. I tried wriggling my legs. I glanced at him, to check if he'd heard.

Your first time, that's my guess, he said. Is it?

I wanted to ask:

At what?

hoping he was meaning something other than the little I knew he meant, but the words wouldn't come out of my mouth. It was unbearable to catch his eye, I stared instead at his glove box, it had no lid, it was crammed with papers, bills, empty envelopes. On top of it all was an empty Chiko Roll wrapper stained with grease and still crinkling. He must've just put it there.

A virgin, he laughed. I bet you're a virgin. Must be my lucky day.

He laughed to himself, I wasn't meant to join in.

But you'd know a few tricks, he added. Your girlfriends would've told you things. Swapping stories in the playground.

He laughed.

Yech-yech-yech.

I stared at the Chiko Roll wrapper, its greasy sadness. You know some tricks? he asked.

I shrugged. It seemed quite sophisticated to shrug.

One day you could introduce me to your girlfriends as well, he said.

Yech-yech-yech.

The Chiko Roll wrapper crinkled again.

My blood shouted: But you don't know whether he should take off his clothes first, or whether you should. How quickly, how slowly. If he should undo your buttons, if you should undo his. You don't know anything. And he'll know you don't know.

I stared at the stones in the road, how they rushed underneath us. I longed for them to rush up and cover me. Why hadn't I ever asked anyone, why didn't I know who should undo whose buttons? It seemed an enormous omission, as if God himself might look down and thunder at me on the vinyl seat: You should have found out who should undo the buttons.

My blood shouted again: And even when you get past the buttons, even when the clothes come off, what happens then? Do you lie on the ground by yourself? Or do you lie down together? You'll have to ask him. Imagine asking him.

Not far, said the man.

There was yellow wax in his ear.

I stared ahead instead.

The Chiko Roll wrapper slithered in the glove box. On the corner of the wrapper, there was a smear of dried yellow. A bit of Chiko Roll. No. It was too yellow. My stomach turned. It was ear wax. He'd been cleaning his ears just before I got in the car. Making himself into a dandy. I heard my father's voice in my head, my dear, humble father in his overalls stained with grease and paint:

He's been prettying himself up.

Stuck on the vinyl seat of my destiny, my stomach grinding, I suddenly wanted my father. To have had my father there just then, laughing at this man, I could've cried for that.

Then traffic lights turned red outside the butcher's shop and I was yanking the doorhandle and falling onto the stones of the road and staying there on all fours while he accelerated

135

away and I was choking in the smoke of his car.

The butcher was staring out of his window between the white cardboard squares of Specials For Today. He saw me, his eyes widened, he waved and hurried to the door. But I was running beyond him, past his shop, past houses, running to my father, my racing feet scattering like water the shimmering blue mirages on the road.

I got to his building site. My father was mud spattered, as smelly and comfortable as an old armchair.

Nearly lunchtime, he said, leaning on his spade and wiping his forehead and nodding to me like an old friend.

You can stay and share my sandwiches if you like. I think Mum's given me corned beef. That make you happy?

The only thing to do was to run away from school to spy on what my mother and her lover did. One day after lunch, I didn't go back to class, I couldn't run fast enough, I knew she was with him, the sudden knowledge a mother and daughter have of each other, a knowledge that filters through the cells of the body.

Grey trees and shadowy clumps of ferns fell away as I ran, these were until recently the playthings of my childhood, the scarlet tips of new leaves and the orange lanterns of bottle-brush flowers. It's not so much that I was running as that under my determined feet, my childhood was falling away. Every secret in our shrouded house had to be pushed apart, like the white sheets on my parents' bed where she would now be lying with her lover. I had to learn, this was the moment, I had to see, smell, taste sex, I had to examine their pulsations and stains, I had to see the human animals they were, I had to see his veins standing up on his neck and his penis, I had to see his muscles, her muscles, which were taut and which loose. I had to know the exact angles of arms and legs, where

136

his hands were this moment on my mother's body, where his legs were, his balls were, his penis was. Where the kisses of her mouth caressed, what her fingers slid in and fondled. I had to see how he held her silent tongue.

I'll creep in through my window at the back of the house, I'll slither across the floor of my parents' bedroom as my mother writhes and moans with her lover, I'll hide under the bed as they pound, I'll hide in my mother's wardrobe where she hides.

I stopped behind the hydrangea bush at the steps of the verandah. They weren't in bed.

My mother stood on the verandah beyond me, side on to me, her elbows out from her sides, her head tipped to one side. She was standing at the cane table to pour tea, the way she always did it, extravagantly, like a conjuror, the pot held high and then sliding smoothly down the slant of the tea's long and golden stream. She'd poured tea every day like this since I could remember, it was part of the pleasure of being at home, my mother pouring a cup of tea.

My father poured it like that, she told me once, to amuse me so I'd drink it. He'd boil grasses for hours and make them into tea, to make me strong.

Now she was pouring tea in front of her lover, the special secret way that belonged to our home. Shock oozed out of me with sweat.

If I moved my head, there were more shocks, until I was jagged with them. He was sitting with his legs crossed at the knees like a woman's, not a man in our township would have sat with crossed legs like that. His trousers flowed down the long slant of his legs as precisely as the tea from my mother's pot, in elegant folds as if he'd asked the tailor to cut the cloth for this exact moment. His back was to me but I saw with a jump of my heart the side of his cheek. It was a young cheek.

He was younger than my mother. A boy, she'd call him. And he wasn't newly shaved. No man I'd ever known would've come to afternoon tea unshaved. The stubble furred his smooth skin as endearingly, as flagrantly as pubic hair. And on his head his hair was a riot of curls that ended in a rim moving against his neck like lace. Every man in our township had short back and sides, wet with grease, so ugly they could never be accused of prettying themselves up, oh no. But this man was pretty, and all my father's judgements were wrong. His shirt bloused away from his body, so that if I stood above him and peered down, the way men in American movies peered down women's dresses, I knew I'd see the muscles of his back, so round and smooth they could have melted my fingers.

My mother's young lover was as beautiful as God.

He cleared his throat urgently.

I know, my mother was saying in answer to something, words so ordinary that I could have brushed past the blue heads of hydrangea flowers and told my mother I was there.

Tell her now, amongst the usual rattle of teaspoons.

Tell her now, while she was putting the teapot down on the tablecloth and handing him his cup.

They were using the unused cups from my grandmother's tea-set, my mother's only heritage besides her photo. And the saucers. And the plates. And there was the matching teapot, with a band as gold as the squares of velvet meant for my mother's unfinished apron.

I can imagine it all, she said. There was a gap of quietness, and creaks of chairs. There was a soft rustle of silk that wasn't just her voice.

My mother was wearing her pink shell dress. She had taken it deliberately, for this moment, out of its mothballs. She'd chosen it for him. I could tabulate the exact progress of my mother's morning. She'd washed it, drying it carefully on a hanger, then she'd ironed it so no crushes would interrupt the flow of her body. She'd bathed, she'd brushed her midnight hair till it floated, she'd pushed the tortoiseshell combs into it. She was so close I could see the little creases along the seam of her dress where she'd moved the iron too fast in her excitement. My mother's dress that she last wore when my father asked her to marry him. My vain, tormented mother who knew that a shell could sing.

The dread of beauty

A digression on a digression. But what can you do with a mother like mine? Sometimes I felt like throwing up the pieces of her story into the air and letting them fall randomly. But no one would read them randomly, that's the problem. You'd make meaning of the order
Hypatia

Before her lover, my mother and Matti would pick at the scab of her beauty, like children on a back step picking at sores.

She was ironing a shirt she'd just brought in, sweetsmelling of soap and sunshine.

I'd dread it, she said to Matti, and the iron sighed with her sighing, and moved up and down the ironing board with her thoughts.

I'd dread it so much, at afternoon teas after the seances. If they asked me a question, I'd have to remember what they'd been saying before, I'd have to chase after the receding sounds. Because what I'd been concentrating on, while they were talking, was their eyes darting, measuring me, the exact concavities of my face, the exact convexities. The men jockeying to be the one seen talking to me. And the women calculating: if they parted their hair like mine, if they tied a knot in their scarf like mine.

Matti smoothed out his hair in the mirror. He'd begun to look in mirrors lately, he'd begun to be critical of the way our mother cut his hair.

You made a cockscomb stick up, he fretted. It wasn't sticking up before.

He saw our mother in the mirror, her words still on her face though the sound of them had gone.

They were admiring you, he said.

He kept ducking his head this way and that in the mirror.

They weren't admiring me, she said. They were admiring my beauty, that's all.

She put his shirt on him, pleased how it clung to him in its ironed warmth, pleased at the male roundness of his chest. But she kept picking at the scab of her beauty as she shook another shirt out of the ironing basket.

If people think you're beautiful, she said, they feel you're part of them. The part they almost were. You're as familiar to them as their underwear.

Am I making this up? Was she really ironing when she said this? In my memories of evenings, my mother is always ironing. She must have done other chores but down the years it's the memory of the iron's sigh with the heat whirling and settling as she rested it on its end. She moved her feet under the light globes that never seemed strong enough as the years went on, the way she had to peer, she clipped back her glossy blue-black hair that slid out of its combs in its richness, she warmed her hands on the blanket where the iron has been, she gazed out the window into the lonely night, and she sighed again.

My mother ironed everything, towels, washers, sheets, her fingers moved lightly over cloth, adjusting a tuck here, a fold there, it was an abstract order she was adjusting in her mind, I knew. She'd iron the unfinished apron she always wore. On her body it looked as if things are meant to be incomplete.

You've ironed wrinkles into the collar, Matti said. He took off the shirt. So she ironed it again.

You'd do better, he said, if you put your mind to what you do.

She didn't hear him, they were often like this, two singers in an opera, balancing a see-saw of sound.

When people say you're beautiful, she said, they make it sting like guilt. As if you should have done something with your beauty. As if they've given you a pearl that was theirs, that you should've worn with gratitude.

There was a pause. She looked over at me, picking paint off the doorway.

Beauty is no passport, she said. Don't worry.

She turned back to him.

So don't worry about your cockscomb.

All those years I kept looking in mirrors in the hope I'd find my face had shifted. It seemed reasonable to expect I might inherit, if not her beauty, at least her long eyelashes that made her eyes into stars. At least the slenderness of her neck, like a flower stem. At least her nestling ears.

My face didn't shift, and still I couldn't learn the lesson of my mother's life.

I longed for her life instead.

After her lover arrived, my mother began to linger in the town's chemist shop. She'd never bought things for herself. When she bought us new toothbrushes, she kept her old one, its bristles over the years as curled and soft as the eyelashes of a child. But now she took the spare tiles out of the bathroom cupboard where they'd waited for years for Dad to finish the bathroom edging. She put them out on the lawn where Dad would see them when he mowed, but he mowed around them and the piles made yellow squares on the grass. She brushed cobwebs off the bathroom shelves. Over weeks, jars began to accumulate. Moisturisers, cleansers, cottonwool in pink and white balls. Powders, perfumed soap coloured like jewels. Perhaps her lover bought them for her, I don't know.

The wound of my mother's beauty was healing. Her lover was healing her.

The only thing to do 2

Now at the afternoon tea her lover breathed, that little huff people make before they speak, when their mind is on their thoughts.

It was as if, he began. He paused, and there was another rustle of silk. That was the sound of my mother restraining her dress, and the silk rushing out between her fingers to disobey but she wouldn't allow it, my mother wouldn't permit a flutter of silk to mute the voice of her lover.

I used to like solving equations too, he said.

There was something about his voice, what was it? A feeling I already knew but couldn't name. Was he trying to impress her?

It seemed to me, my mother started, faltered, went on: It seemed when I got to the resolution of an equation and everything was balanced, there was a sound like snow falling. A silence deeper than silence. That makes you realise that before, there was no silence at all.

Her lover re-crossed his legs, this time from left to right, I heard the material of his trousers slide along his smooth thighs. My grandmother's teacup rested casually on his knee, but his fingers gripped it tight, as if it was a thought.

You know how snow falls, my mother said. So fastidiously. Not letting a leaf evade it. So gentle, so insistent. That sort of silence.

My mother's speech was full of shy pauses, not the way she spoke when she was telling me to clear away dishes.

There was a creak of cane, her lover was leaning across the table, nodding. I knew he couldn't nod too much.

That's how I used to feel it.

My mother's words jerked out of her. Then her voice came stronger, as if she was learning to sing.

And I'd feel in the midst of it, at rest, she said.

My mother's hand bumped one teaspoon against another. In the jangle, she remembered that they were having afternoon tea.

Drink up, she said. Or it will get cold.

Of course, he said.

They sounded relieved to speak about drinking tea.

She held up the teapot and poured her own cup of tea slowly to measure her thoughts. Perhaps it had always reminded her of her father, every pot of tea, and I never thought of it before, her memories always there even in a stream of tea.

My father, she said suddenly, as if she'd heard my thoughts, brought a stone in his pocket from the mountains in Spain, it was all he brought. The only thing. His pocket bagging with a stone. It wasn't even precious. It was swirling colours of blue and black, and translucent, and when I breathed on it, all I'd see was my own mist. Numbers were like that for me—there was a bump, she'd put the teapot down on the table—shall I tell you? she asked, almost to herself.

Of course, he said, and I heard the jerkiness again.

I'm so unused to talking about it, she said, her voice warm with hope. And perhaps you don't want to hear.

From you, he said, I want to hear everything.

At the convent I realised there was nothing gorgeous about mathematics, she said. Not like the glowing oils on a painting, that seem like your ardour—not yours, of course—she struggled in a thicket of pronouns—people's ardour.

The silence of years took her voice away, then there was another fling of courage in her breath.

Mathematics seemed like the nuns, stern, clear-faced, austere.

My mother had moved slightly. She was panting under the hanging basket of purple fuchsias which my father watered every day. Even now a glittering bead of water at the end of a leaf threatened to fall into her preoccupation.

More real than objects, she added.

It's an unfashionable thought, but I can see how you'd think that, he said. His voice was warm, rather like a blush rising from the throat to the forehead that can't be slowed. And now they were speaking fast, almost on top of each other.

You can? she asked.

It shows in your work, he said.

It's not finished, she said defensively. There's something I can't find.

But what work could he mean? My mother's work was us.

I felt that you have no interest in anything but the purest relationship between numbers, he said. And sometimes, I'm not sure how you make your deductions.

He touched the back of his neck as he spoke. Perhaps he could feel the prickle of my eyes.

144

So they're not true, she said. My deductions.

She sighed deeply, there was a catch in her breath that was almost a sob.

I'm not saying that, he said.

Often logic seems useless, said my mother, eagerly, the way she would have defended Matti. It gets in the way. There's another logic no one talks about.

Yes, he said as if he knew.

I stopped listening, I was thinking of his hand on his neck, and the longing that moved in me. My sexual longing for my mother's lover, this man as beautiful as the face of God. I recreated his hand in my mind, the exact set of his long fingers. I imagined those fingers smooth on the insides of my thighs.

I've never seen insights like yours, he said.

It's because I worked in such isolation, she said. I've been thinking in isolation for so long.

She laughed, but shyly, to tell him.

It was when Matti was a baby. I haven't had much time since.

I gasped, to think of my mother doing airy mathematics while she held Matti. I clapped my hand over my mouth to contain my gasp.

Why don't you leave? he asked.

Leave! my mother cried. How can I? Though ...

There was a long pause.

My son—I despair of him sometimes and my daughter— how do you deal with a daughter?

Did she say that? Did I really hear her say that?

But, she said, you know I'm the daughter of a refugee.

What's that got to do with it? he asked.

She laughed then, a hurt, sad laugh almost like a wounded bird's cry.

I wanted to reach out and stroke her then. But my mother and her lover scarcely moved, their voices floated in each other's minds, my longing was a long way off.

But there wasn't any point, if the deductions aren't true, my mother said.

Sometimes in your work, you've reinvented the wheel, he was saying. But the wheel you invent, it's always astonishing. What I'm trying to say is that these aren't mere calculations. They're works of the imagination.

I don't know the difference, said my mother.

That's the thing, he said. You cross from one to the other, intuitively.

And that's what's wrong? asked my mother.

Few people can do it, he said. Only a few mathematicians ever.

You've called me a mathematician, breathed my mother.

The air seemed to ease, like water rushing out.

I must show these workings to someone, he said. Someone more senior than me.

No, she said.

It was almost a yelp.

Why not? he said. They should be known.

I gave them to you in secret, she said.

There was panic in her voice.

But I've got to tell, he said. It's my duty. We can't keep this work secret. I would be proud—his voice thickened, so suddenly I knew it was not only my mother's body he wanted—I would be so proud to have discovered you.

He cleared his throat again, it rasped in his urgency, nothing must be in the way of his voice. It was his only ugliness. Did I see his ambition then? I was so young, though I was thirteen. I think I stayed thirteen for years, until—

It'd do a lot for me. My career, he said.

But my mother was leaning over to him, her voice so soft it was just a breeze.

It's our secret, she whispered.

He laughed, a young man's high laugh, almost toppling.

Just for a while, perhaps, he said.

He laughed, greedy, anxious.

A week, he said. And then. Our big moment.

But it's not finished, she said. The conjecture seemed bigger than my examples would show. And—something else, she whispered—I don't want to be known.

There was another silence, another shift in the air.

Perhaps you could try to explain to me how you do your reachings out, he said after a while. The exact processes of your mind.

His voice was as shy, as greedy as if he had never touched her body, so I suddenly knew intimacy comes slowly, wanes and comes again, a stuttering thing.

It'll be like being a girl again, she said warmly.

Some things have changed in mathematics in the last fifteen years, he said. I could show you. But perhaps you don't want—

There are moments—she said.

Would you let us work together? he was asking. Would you teach me to think like you do?

—when you know that God's been listening, after all, she said. Though it's been so long.

There was another silence. They gazed beyond the tea things at my father's lawn, so severely cut in the soft light of afternoon tea, that you could see, as never before, that the grass was clipped to spikes like the hair of my grandmother's armpits, it was not permitted to get long even for a week, after all the work my father had put into it, he wasn't going to let it slip out of his control. A single dandelion gave a yellow, defiant wave.

147

Tell me, he said suddenly, why you won't let your work be known?

My father, she said vaguely. She paused.

The men with knives are all around us, she said.

There was a silence, that was made, as most silences are, of many things. Breathing, twitching, a puff of air across the lake that fluttered silk again. Silence deepened, became whiter than snow.

Frances, said the voice of my mother. She hadn't looked around. It was the knowledge that mothers have of their daughters.

I stood on one leg, blushing, hoping she was talking about me again, not calling me.

Frances, she said again. Stop skulking. Come and be properly introduced.

There was no surprise, no accusation in her voice.

My feet didn't move. But his neck did, with its intricate lacework of curls. He uncrossed his knees. His feet found their balance on the verandah floor. My mother was staring at me through the blue flowers of the hydrangea bush. He pulled himself to stand to stare with her. He stretched to part the branches, and he tipped over the cane table. In one magnificent rushing instant my grandmother's tea-set was a white shouting waterfall. The undrunk tea from the teapot became so many dark patches on worn floorboards. My mother's only heritage, besides her photograph, took a long time to come to rest. Broken white china cartwheeled and seesawed before it was finally still.

No one moved. It was so quiet that as a bird flew above us, we heard the whirr of wings.

My mother turned to her lover, despite the outline of her daughter behind the hydrangeas. Her eyes held him much closer than the mere touch of skin.

And then I realised that with him, she said the sort of things she was made to say.

Did you hear it? she smiled. It echoed. Who'd have thought, that some falling cups can make this verandah echo like a song?

Then she had to acknowledge me. So she spoke without any sense of the future, my mother who had such a passionate sense of her past.

Frances, she said. You haven't met Michael properly. He's a friend of the family. Frances, Malcolm Robertson.

If I'd been Adele and filming this moment, I'd have positioned my mother against the lake, her body carved out by those oily depths. You'd scarcely be aware of her beauty amongst that glittering menace. But in life she was merely standing against a verandah wall that needed a fresh coat of paint. All that seemed to threaten her was a table leg tipped on its side, the raffia unravelling a little.

I've seen your daughter before, her lover said to her, but his arm was stretched out to shake my hand.

You were standing against our kitchen door, I said.

To shake hands, our feet crunched china. The touch of his skin was jagged with sexual shocks.

But you two are so different! he exclaimed. It's hard to believe that you're mother and daughter!

A SHELL CAN SING 2

I was gazing into the blue limitless air of the roof garden when my table was bumped. I didn't look up, I wanted to stay in my silent memories. A chair scraped against the tar of the roof garden floor. Another bump, and there was heat on my arm that wasn't just from the sun. The man in the Hawaiian shirt had sat down at my table, familiarly close amongst the chairs tipped and leaning as if they're telling secrets. He was almost brushing my shoulder, but he wasn't looking at me, he was looking around for a waiter.

They've got to learn to serve, he said. They've turned their country into a holiday camp.

He cupped his hands into a loudspeaker and yelled: Yoo-hoo, waiter. Anyone awake?

I should've objected but I was so glad to meet one of the mathematicians at last.

It's been a bit intimidating, this conference, I said, words rushing out of my mouth because I wasn't a real mathematician and he was, despite his shirt.

My first conference but not my last, I hope, I laughed and blushed in case I sounded presumptuous.

I reminded the back of his head that I was the amateur with my mother's formulae.

I know, he said not quite looking around.

You've read it? I asked.

It was suddenly hard to breathe.

I couldn't make head nor tail of it, he said.

I roared with laughter at such modesty, and all the time I was reproaching myself with my awe of real mathematicians, I'd wanted to be one for so long.

My laughter faded.

Perhaps it's a little out of your area, I said. What is your area?

PR, he said.

It was hard to stop my voice dropping in disappointment after all the laughter.

I'm the person who brought you across the world, he said and there was a note of resentment in his voice, as if he'd carried the burden of me over all those oceans on his sloping shoulders.

He indicated the space of air behind him with his head and said: Great view, isn't it? Isn't it? he repeated, because my thoughts were on the quaking of my stomach.

I moved my gaze to where his face insisted, and there above us the Parthenon hung, pale and smooth as wax, austere, suddenly actual after a lifetime of postcards. But postcards don't show how the air fell away from the sky to pour around the rocks supporting the Parthenon. The rocks were like thrown-down overcoats, crumpled, grey, abandoned.

I turned back, the fat man was waiting for me to praise the Parthenon. His hands were spread on the table. They were pale and unwrinkled, child's hands that needed help.

It's wonderful, I said helpfully.

It isn't, he said.

It isn't? I asked.

No.

He smiled triumphantly.

You only think it's a great view because you've been told it is. But what are you looking at? Some smashed up bits of temple stuck on some rocks. Where would the Parthenon be without PR? he asked. And what are you without PR? Someone with a few squiggles which have no relevance to anyone.

I wiped the fierce sunshine out of my eyes.

The squiggles are relevant to this conference, I said evenly.

But he leaned forward with certainty and he didn't need help, I was angry that I felt sorry for him, his childish hands weren't shy at all.

I'll break it to you gently, my dear, he said. No one at this conference has read your work. I'm the only one here who believes in you.

I struggled amongst the blue tunnels of air. My stomach

yawned, a hole I could've fallen into. I gulped to check the thickness in my voice.

Why have I been brought here, I asked, if my work has no relevance to anyone?

A waiter arrived then, and the conversation had to stop, and I nodded agreement to a drink, and changed my mind because I didn't want to be friendly, and changed it again because I had to be friendly, and I got a handkerchief out of my handbag and blew my nose as if this might've given me strength. I rolled the handkerchief into a ball in my hand, something to clutch. All the time the fat man gazed at the Parthenon that needed PR.

Two drinks, he shouted after the waiter. For good measure he held up two fingers.

I hope he can count, he said to me. You can't be sure here.

We're in the country of the people who discovered proof, I said, my disappointment turning into anger.

I wouldn't know about that, I haven't been keeping up with the news, he said.

It was like a slap.

If it hadn't been for the ancient Greeks, we wouldn't know about proof, we might all be still counting incessantly, millions of examples of the same thing, unable to generalise, I said. Proof makes the world knowable.

I realised my voice was rising, but I didn't care.

Someone else would've been bound to trip over it, he answered. Something as obvious as proof.

Perhaps it needed the Greeks, I shouted. Their particular way of seeing.

Look at it this way, he said. With good PR, your equation will be as familiar—

he turned round to indicate the Parthenon—

as that thing. Schoolkids will know your name.

The well-known equations of mathematics, I said, haven't needed an advertising campaign.

The well-known equations, he said, haven't come from someone like you. Living Insurance just want to say they helped, he added.

I was staring into the limitless blue, not quite listening.

The waiter arrived with the drinks.

To Living Insurance, he said. He ignored the water in the jug and gulped down the ouzo straight, spluttering and coughing and banging the glass down on the table.

The Greeks invented that stuff too, he said.

He threw some coins on the waiter's tray and dismissed him with a wave of his hand.

Who's Living Insurance? I asked after a while.

Exactly. No one knows yet. But they will. Living Insurance funded this conference. Not that they're interested in you. They're crazy about my slogan.

His teeth glared in the sun. He picked up the second glass, he was about to drink it, he remembered it was mine and banged it down on the table. He spread out an imaginary banner against the Parthenon.

Living Insurance is there, he said, at all the important moments. Like it? They did.

He looked back admiringly to the imaginary banner, and bobbed his head as if he was reading along the line of letters following a bouncing ball.

Great, isn't it.

He read it again: Living Insurance is there, at all the important moments.

What moments? I asked.

He remembered me, dragged his eyes off his banner to look back at me.

The moment of your announcement, he said. When you

make it onto the map of mathematics. You'll have to credit them.

He leaned back on his chair.

See, the thing about my slogan is, it has great popular appeal, he said. These academics, no one knows what they're talking about. Who's ever heard of non-whatdoyoucallit hyper squares? None of Living Insurance's accountants even knew how to spell hyper, let alone the other bit.

He grabbed onto the table before his chair toppled.

Six of them in the world! he shouted. Who'd give them funding for a conference? They couldn't get funding for a barbecue! Until I got to hear about their troubles. I said to Living Insurance—he picked up my drink—I said, Look at it this way. All the big conferences have been snapped up. The Greens went to IBM, Coca Cola grabbed the little furry animals, McDonald's gobbled up refugees, Disney landed the hole in the ozone and Colgate nabbed the third world. I told Living Insurance, we can get this little bunch of fools for next to nothing. There's only six of them, plus a few groupies. But we'll tack an international competition onto their conference, we'll scour the world for some undiscovered genius.

His fat lips turned down into a sulk at the word.

Someone who thinks they know something the rest of us don't, he added.

Then he was proud again.

Living Insurance loved it. The academics didn't, but they think they've cornered the market on genius. The six academics said only whackos would apply. But they had to agree, no one else was going to fund them. And look who turned up! You! Plain old Mrs Average Housewife!

He sipped my drink, then dropped his voice to whisper dramatically:

154

Imagine the horror of Living Insurance!

He spread his hands out above the hot table. Behind him, the blue sky danced and fell.

Just between you and me, they even considered sending a starlet here, he said. Someone undiscovered you could coach.

Coach? I echoed. What in?

So she could pretend to be you and expound your theory to the world, he smiled.

But she mightn't know any mathematics, I said.

Any halfwit could memorise a few pages, he said.

He reached over to pat my hand in a fatherly way.

But I said Let's run with this one. The masses will love her. She's such a frump, she's like everyone's mum.

He beamed.

So sit back and enjoy it, my dear. In five days you'll wake up and find yourself famous. Immortality, that's what Living Insurance will give you. Immortality.

I buried my face in my hands, there on the hot table, I hid my face from the ordinary air.

His voice went on, he was saying: There's just one little problem. A university back in Australia contacted me after the *Sunday Times* story. We faxed them your entry. Their mathematics professor got in touch with me. He says your work is not entirely original.

I formulated my mother's conjecture, I said.

He leaned forward, so his tie was flattened against the table's side.

This man says he lectured on something very similar thirty years ago, said Paul.

The air shifted around us then, the past blew into the present, or perhaps it was just a breeze from the Parthenon skittering along the tabletops.

What was his name? I asked.

Malcolm Robertson, he said.

And so the past was blowing through me.

That's when he first leaned on our door way, I said.

Door? Paul asked, just as Grandma Fernandez had asked the nuns all those years ago. What's a door got to do with it?

He probably did take her work and lecture on it, I said. Even though she didn't want that. For him, it would've been a way to keep her as she used to be. Like a fossil in a museum. To keep the tracings of her sumptuous thoughts, her sumptuous body in his heart. But surely he said it was her work.

Hang on, said Paul. Nobody told me anything about a sumptuous body.

I smiled at him then.

It's just an old love story, I said.

There was a pause. I watched the rocks straining to hold up the Parthenon.

He wants a credit, said Paul.

Who wants a credit? I asked.

This Malcolm Robertson of yours, said Paul.

He wants a credit? I roared.

He never published this theory, it was a bit controversial, but he says you got hold of it somehow, said Paul. He said he was a family friend. Maybe you hacked into his computer. Maybe you ransacked his files.

He says it's his theory? I shouted. It's not his. It's my mother's. He got it from my mother, I shouted, I knew I was shouting, I was on my feet holding onto the table, watching the swirling of the years.

If he claims anything else, he's betraying her, I was shouting. Again.

Again? Paul's voice came to me in the blasting light.

Again, I said.

Your mother's a mathematician? She was his student? he asked.

No, I shouted. She was no one's student.

If she's sumptuous, let's get her here—he moved his childish hands—she's bound to be better looking than you. Where's she now?

I sat down on the warm chair.

The Beryl Urskin Home for the Frail Aged, I said.

There was a long pause, I was fighting for breath, it seemed too hot to breathe in the sun.

She'd have written her theory down, Paul said. You'd have worked from something written down.

I didn't need to, I said. It was fossilised in me.

Whether this theory came from your granny or your aunty or your sister, he said, look at it this way. He beamed.

This professor is an eminent man. Apparently he's quite renowned for some part of the theory, though he never published, integrity, something about it was incomplete, he never could quite complete it.

He couldn't complete it, I hissed, because he didn't know how to continue. He didn't know how to move his mind like that. It wasn't his work.

Paul was still smiling fatly.

We can turn this to our advantage, he said. We'll turn a negative into a positive. A collaborative credit with him will do wonders for Living Insurance.

He waved his hand in the sunshine.

It'll do wonders for your credibility. All you have to do is say he helped.

But he didn't help, I shouted. And I won't.

I was hoarse with an old hatred that I can't explain to you, not yet.

157

So you see, there are many moments in a cafe, or in a roof garden of a small hotel when you know that the past will keep unwinding. The way it unwinds for me is something to do with my mother's breasts, the way they were part of my childhood, they were like monarchs pacing in a palace, pent up with power. And it came to me, as I stood on a concrete roof garden far from home, that this is the way of daughters, to struggle against their mothers, to become their mothers, whatever happens. To be like them, be them, be instead of them.

The blue air fell so softly on my unprotected arms and hands that I could say:
   I won't credit him. I'm here to give credit to my mother. To rescue her. To rescue me. To rescue us both.
   Each of my crunching footsteps on the cement roof garden exploded like loss.

It doesn't matter, the past, it was all a long time ago. And nobody cares now, where he stood, what she longed for, what the child that was once me did. These things no longer matter. And yet the past is a passionate, turbulent truth, a truth so dazzling we cannot break free. So it seems.

MY FIFTH LETTER

Grandma Juanita's house

Dear Mum,
In loneliness, I went to the Mother Possum club at the Baby Clinic up near the shops. I should've guessed it'd make things worse.
   The Baby Clinic was bright with talk and yelling babies.

158

Everyone seemed to smile a great deal, as if their lips hadn't been stretched for days. I sat with Zoe on a bench, and too late I realised I'd sat down in the middle of a conversation. On either side, two women talked rapidly, like people trying to say everything before they go home. They jogged fat babies in rhythm. They seemed intent on keeping in time. They'd both rouged their cheeks too bright. They looked as happy as clowns.

You wouldn't believe what they were talking about.

The big problem I face is zips, said one, words jerking out of her in an unfamiliar way so I'm sure she walks round and round deserted rooms too.

Someone tried to sell me a baby suit the other day and I said no, it's got a zip. Have you ever tried to do up a zip with a wriggling baby in the middle?

They don't know what we're up against, she added. She licked her tired lips. Already the lipstick had worn off.

Cappuccino Gold, I remembered from the days when I had time to linger in the cosmetic sections of chemist shops.

Her friend stopped jiggling her baby.

But all I've bought is baby suits with zips on, she said. A whole year's worth. Have I bought the wrong thing?

Zoe murmured and I flattened my back against the wall so I wouldn't intrude, but the movement made the two women look at me. The second woman's lips twitched into a sweet smile.

What do you think about zips? she asked me.

I said I didn't know much about zips.

Aha! said the first woman. Then you're a press-stud person?

But my mind was a black room spidery with emptiness. I knew if I didn't care about press-studs or zips, I was betraying them all.

Then the Clinic Sister came in, large and jolly in a blue tent of a uniform. She was so full of good cheer that she shouted.

She reached out a fat red finger to a cassette player. A nursery rhyme let out a roar.

Let's practise swaying our babies, she shouted, rocking her bulging arms.

Hickory dickory dock, shouted the cassette.

In a circle now, shouted the Sister, you over there, are you going to join us, come on mums, rock away, rock away to the music, rock those little ones, rock away.

Everyone straggled into a circle, swaying babies. I couldn't get out the exit because I'd have had to stalk out past the Sister.

You there.

The red finger pointed to me.

Don't you want to do this for your baby?

So I joined the shuffling circle, lowering my eyes when I passed the door.

Come on, don't be shy, this is just what your baby needs, there's a good mum, you, yes you, look what a good mum she is, look how her baby loves it, he loves it, oh whoa it's a little pink bunny suit so it's a she baby, look how she loves it, rock away, rock away with the music, there's another very good mum over there.

I'm a little teapot, shouted the cassette player.

The women were swaying, the babies were cooing, I was passing the Sister and her big blue jolly tent and her red-faced assurance and I knew that if she walked around empty rooms with her baby, she wouldn't feel any dread.

Move on with the others, watch where you're going, that's it, rock away, rock away, you're new here, aren't you, well, rock away, look how the others do it, just follow the mum in front of you, you'll soon catch on.

We straggled around the circle, straining to do as we were told, swaying and crooning and cooing, stepping sideways and forwards and back while the cassette shouted

Baa baa black sheep

and the Sister shouted: *Beautiful, dear, what a mum you are, what a good little mum, doesn't he love it, good mum, rock away, rock away, that's the way, I'm sure your little one never cries at night and wakes your hubbie, what a mum he's got, rocka rocka rocka rock, look at him laugh, that's the way mum, what a lucky little fellow with a mum like you.*

Little Peter Rabbit had a fly upon his nose

I'd come around the circle with Zoe, I was heading back to the Sister's motherly blueness and in the thumping and shouting and swaying I thought: I must be told I'm a good mum too, I must have this motherly woman tell me I'm doing it right.

That's it, little new mum, here we go, higher, higher with that baby, rocka rock, try to cotton on, dear, just follow the mum in front of you, it's quite simple . . . whoops . . .

Zoe vomited. Vomit fell like a shatter of glass on to the shine of the floor.

The Sister turned off the music.

Stop, everyone, and wipe it up, new mum, before the other mums are forced to tread in it, most of you did that very well and didn't your little ones love it? New mum, don't use your baby's bunny rug for the floor, your baby wouldn't want to be cuddled in that rug afterwards, would she? No.

Then it was show-off time. Each woman round the circle peeled off her baby's clothes, and its muscles and fat were admired. One by one, under the layers of warmth, there was a huge fat baby. Zoe's turn came closer and closer.

Goodness, new mum, she's very small.

The Sister looked me up and down as if she was measuring a horse.

It's true that you're very small, so that might account for it, but I don't know the father, she said.

I yelped that I do.

I felt like I was in school. Do they all think we're stupid because we've had a baby?

Hypatia

THE BODY BEARS NO THREAT

In thirteenth century Italy, Leonardo of Pisa (commonly called Fibonacci), the son (figlio) of wealthy Bonacio saw a numerical *sequence in rabbits reproducing, and wrote in his book* Liber Abaci:

'How many pairs of rabbits can be produced from a single pair in a year if it is supposed that every month each pair begets a new pair which from the second month on becomes productive?'

The number of pairs living at the end of each month are 1 (at the end of the first month), 1 (at the end of the second), 2 (at the end of the third), 3 (at the end of the fourth), and on to 5,8,13,21,34,55,89 etc. (You just add the previous two numbers.) These have become known as the Fibonacci numbers.

My mother, a child of poverty, said that no doubt there were other great mathematicians of the time but Fibonacci could afford not only to write down his ideas on expensive vellum but also distribute the manuscript amongst the influential thinkers. I think she was also a little peeved because she believed in her childhood that she'd been born too late in history, after all the interesting discoveries had been made. Apparently the sequence isn't limited to rabbits reproducing. It occurs constantly in plant growth—the curves of a daisy disc, the florets on a sunflower, in pine cones. My mother used to think that Fibonacci discovered that nature is divine. At least, that nature plans the growth of plants mathematically. But then she realised that all the Fibonacci sequence shows is that in some rare cases, mathematics comes out of nature, not, as she had thought, that nature comes out of mathematics. The real mystery, she told me in her old age, is that most of nature doesn't fit into any patterns that we know. That mathematics and nature have little to do with each other. That the coincidence between them might be just that. A coincidence.
Hypatia

In the moonlight of the stonemason's yard beyond my hotel window, the shapes were stilled as if daylight had them whirling and now they'd come to rest, already part of a death. The rag was still there, I could see the threads of its edges picked out in white light by the searching moon. A breeze stirred an eddy of white dust, and memory surged, almost broke. I shut my eyes against its grit and it was gone. I blew a circle of moisture onto the window glass in a yawn. Then I saw the pram.

During the day someone had thrown an old wicker pram onto a heap of marble dust. It was big and rounded, so the hood almost met the handles. It was on its side, two wheels in the air, but it was built to enclose, so a sleeping baby might think it was still in the circle of its mother's arms, that the circle of her arms will never end.

Against the dark shine of window glass, the fierce moon winkled out thoughts nestled too deep for ordinary daylight.

It wasn't only life I sucked from her breasts.

It hurt every muscle in my body to say it, to say the abyss of it. I knew in that moment that to lose my mother would be to lose my own cells, each one patterned with who she was. I reeled with loss. I backed away from the window and looked around, like a child fearful of the dark, but there was only the neat subdued hotel room around me.

I sucked ice from her as well. That's why I was frozen all those years.

And then I was crawling on the carpet like a mad, wild thing, this woman who wasn't a mathematician after all, just somebody's gimmick.

When is someone going to see me, I shouted into the carpet. When is someone going to see who I am?

My face rubbed salty tears onto the innocent white carpet. There was no answer. The carpet got hot against my cheek, and in the bathroom, the cistern trickled. My watch ticked. A reveller in the street yelled a greeting to a friend. A sudden wind rattled the windowpanes.

I lay on my back on the carpet, exhausted. And then the traffic sang like a lullaby to comfort me, and the moon hid its fierceness behind clouds.

There comes a time when there's no more crying, when there seems nothing more to be lost. I got up slowly from the carpet. My tears hung on its threads like dew on bright morning grass.

You need warm milk, I said to myself, as if I was my own mother.

So I dialled reception, another Fibonacci number, and there was still a spurt of hope as I touched 987. I let myself remember how I first loved big round numbers filling my mouth, as luscious as a summer ice cream. I loved it that there were patterns to the numbers, that I could go away and come back and the pattern waited under everything, patient, rigorous, unflinching, preordained. I remember the love of certain combinations of numbers, long before I knew what made their patterning. I seemed to have known them always.

When I found out about the Fibonacci numbers in a book of my mother's I ran out into the backyard, and ripped at the daisies against the side fence. But I couldn't find the sequence, I was the only person in the world who didn't know which bits of a daisy to count, any real mathematician would see the sequence as if it was printed on the shining petals. I threw the flowers down, their yellow weight bending the long green grass.

But at last I found my mother's conjecture and—the thought came from far away, almost as far as the faintest star—I found the first of a new realm of numbers. So I picked up the phone and it beeped into the night like a helpless child that nobody will come to comfort. When there was an answer I cleared my throat to push away sadness, and asked for warm milk, and gave instructions on how I like it, just a little heat, the milk taken off the fire before it boils, and afterwards, a touch of honey and brandy.

Perimenete, said the voice. Er, you wait.

I waited at the window, and now that the stonemason's yard was shrouded in darkness, I watched the tops of buildings instead, where neon lights smeared the sky with orange and green, and then the night washed its blackness over them, the rhythm would go on until dawn, the neon lights smearing colour and the black night hiding it, and in this continuity there was an odd comfort.

As the minutes crept by, I strained for sounds. At first I expected a footstep outside my door on the carpet, then just a rustle of a step in the corridor, then I strained to hear a clang of the lift doors, or even the sigh of the lift pulleys. There was nothing, only the dim rumble of the street and an ambulance screaming. I became huge with waiting, I filled the room, I was a huge ear. I burrowed under the taut sheets of the white bed, and now I filled the hotel, the hotel was my ear and I was the city waiting, the city was my ear and I was the world.

And suddenly there was a moment when the thought came that overturns everything. That moment, it could've happened anywhere, when I was peeling an orange, getting on a bus, cleaning my teeth. The mind has its own time, its own spaces.

My mind said:

I don't have to save her.

And it came to me that what I know might not be unique after all. Surely someone in the world right then had thought the same way as me, had reached the same theorems, was putting down a pen, completed, satisfied.

It didn't have to be me. I could run away, forget all about the conference, and get on with the second of the new kind of numbers. I didn't need to tell anybody, I didn't need anybody to know. Surely it would be enough for my life to wander in that undiscovered country.

I must've fallen asleep slumped in my chair. I woke with a pen in my hand and dreams of my work drying on my lips. Yellow light was streaming through the curtains and house-maids stood near me, suppressing giggles under stocky hips. I straightened up and they said:

Excuse, and banged the door behind them with fat, derisive hands.

The jokes of a foreign country ring so loudly in a polished hotel corridor.

So I sang under the shower, the way I'd sung when I knew I was going to give birth, inevitability pushing through me like a huge dark rock, now that the labour pains had started. There was nothing else to do but sing.

I don't know what I sang in the shower under those falling points of light. Or what I'd sung in labour. Nothing very meaningful. Probably, in fact, a half-forgotten love song that my father whistled through his teeth when he drove off in his ute to fix someone's gutter and glimpsed over his shoulder, beyond the swirling dust, how frail the house that he'd built to contain his life turned out to be.

In the bathroom mirror, the image of my body floated up after the steam cleared, and I gasped at what I saw. Sadness made me see it more clearly, the way that in a drench of hot sun, you sometimes see the bones of a hilly landscape. My body was made of shadows and hollows, spaces that promised nothing. And there can be such promise in a body, my mother's body always wore a future, as well as a past, you could almost touch it in the skin's sheen. Except for the very old, or the very sad, the body shows no threat of tragedy.

There seemed such boundless knowledge in my mother's breasts.

Until the lake.

As I shut the door behind me, I heard something crackling. Hypatia's letters lay stranded on the expanse of carpet. They were as pale, as stern as her face. It's probably a scam, she'd said. One of the pages was crackling in the draught from the air conditioner. I pulled the door to. I'd read her derision soon, but not yet. I was longing for the rescue that's called love.

TINY SHAPES ON THE FLOOR

The lift was too fast. I dreaded the noise that would come up at me like a slap, the swivel of faces assessing me and turning away, half-smiling, the clambering laughter of young men that claws and topples. The swallowing loneliness of many meals before I fly home. My feet dragged at the stairs. I was back in my childhood, a working-class girl, my parents' daughter, thirteen years old, timid, fierce, old enough to guilt-ily long for my mother's lover, young enough to long for my mother.

Across the dining room, his back to me, C. Denver crouched on the floor. His arms jutted out from his sides like wings, his head was bent. All around him, students milled, unnoticing, tripping into him, but he warded everyone off, he was making a circle with his arms and calling to a tiny shadow on the floor.

Then a bird tripped into the shine of light, a bird flown in through the huge windows. It was slipping on the vinyl tiles in tiny stuttering steps, pecking at the noisy air in jerks, running, pausing, cocking a fierce head. Someone carrying a plate piled with potato chips was arguing

The probability that you just exhaled a molecule of Caesar's dying breath is—

he crashed into C. Denver's arms. A potato chip toppled from the plate to the floor.

The probability, the man continued, is $1-(1-\frac{A}{N})^B$, if N is the number of molecules in the air, A is how many molecules Caesar exhaled and B is how many you inhale. A 99 per cent probability.

He looked down at the floor.

Bugger, he said. One chip less.

The bird was backing, startled.

I'll get you out of here, said C. Denver to it, words smooth as a lullaby. His face was all moist smoothness, without lines. His eyes were hooded like my mother's eyes, as fragile as hers. He picked up the bird. Between his fingers, its chest trembled feathers. He saw me staring. He had the sort of gaze that sees you as if none of you has ever been in shadow, you can be completely discovered and understood, all of you, in a single blazing moment of sunlight. I was standing in the light in front of this man, sure that he saw within a quiver of a moment that I was a real mathematician, as real a mathematician as anyone else in that room. His eyes cut me out from the noise and argument, as if it was just a cardboard background that would soon fall away.

He's only a boy, I argued with myself. He was like the boy my mother's lover was, and look what came of that.

When C. Denver was clambering out of his mother, my face was already lined.

He spoke to me.

I had to do something, he said. The next big boot would've made it just a stain on the floor.

He turned, and I was stranded in the ebbing of his eyes, like a deserted seashore still echoing. All around me was an ordinary dining room.

He took the bird to the windows, old-fashioned, wide-framed windows that towered all the way up the walls, the sort my father would've loved to draw on his plans and afterwards struggled to make. The windows made us all tiny shapes on the floor. He balanced the bird on the window-sill, his hands hovering above its tiny body. Beyond it, the vast sky tumbled blue shouting cascades of air. The bird shuddered on crooked legs, squawked, cocked its head at us all, teetered, and in a sudden flurry it burst into flight, carving with only the tip of a tiny wing great wild soaring circles till our eyes were burnt with haze.

C. Denver turned without noticing me and walked through the crowd back to his dinner and his book.

I couldn't help myself. I found a pen and paper in my handbag. My need to be acknowledged had become desire, wet, panicky, urgent. He must become my lover, the man who'd rescued a bird.

I dithered with my pen. Someone bumped me so the pen zigzagged across the paper. In the end, while my dinner congealed, I wrote:

Could we talk?

I walked through drifts of words that chattered like the titles of my mother's books.

Or is the difficult idea in life, said someone as I pass. *And* is easy. All the argument after Henri's talk was about *or*.

All proofs on that theorem are by Americans, someone else said in an American accent. Me, Goldberg and Phoc Lam.

His friends roared, jiggling half-drunk glasses of wine on their trays.

Well, Phoc Lam is semi-American, one conceded.

Anyone who gets a result in this problem is temporarily American, laughed his friend.

If you let gamma be finite, you can just whisker it up, someone else said.

In that room amongst those conversations, my plaintive note was already gravy-stained.

Could, I said aloud, but no one noticed.

Could. I should have written *must*. *Must* would be the right word for someone of my mature age, self-assured, imperative, confident.

We *must* talk.

If I dropped the note onto his table near his plate, he might well roar with his friends: You know what she wrote? That amateur they let in? *Could* we talk! *Could*? Perhaps she can't. Perhaps she doesn't know how to! What do they think this is, a sheltered workshop?

I walked on through the conversations of people who knew what to say. As I went past C. Denver, I knew that my note could fall onto his plate as tenderly as an autumn leaf that hopes for rescue by the warm rich soil.

But because of *could*, I put it in my pocket. Love was never a rescue for me.

THE CHATTER OF BOOKS

My mother stopped worrying about whether the tea-towels hung straight on the line, and began collecting books with peculiar titles. She'd never known people with books, she told me. Only the nuns. Her own widowed mother acquired magnificent dark oak furniture from Europe, lush red carpets from the mysterious Middle East, Chinese vases wound round with dragons, oil paintings lustrous in gold frames, armchairs with legs as slender as a dancer, statues as high as herself. But no books.

A house with no books, my mother told my bemused father, is a house with no conversation.

Our house had no books.

My mother, suddenly daring, caught trains to the city to buy second-hand books at auctions and fetes. She'd come back with a boxful.

How much? my father would demand.

No one else wanted them, she'd say. I'd pay more for a passionfruit sponge at the CWA than for all these words.

Her eyes were darkly lustrous, no matter how tattered the covers. When we found insects embedded between pages in cocoons, my mother prised them out respectfully.

She asked my father to build some shelves.

I wonder where, my father said. I'll have to give it some thought.

He was buttoning his overalls bib in the rectangle of sunlight.

My mother sighed. So she stored her books in the laundry, in anything that came her way. An old laundry basket, our pram, our baby cot, shelves she erected with bricks and bits of board. She moved the fence palings out (Dad never got around to fixing the fence) and put in more makeshift shelves. After a while there was only a narrow pathway between the books to the copper and the tubs.

Book titles chattered to each other in the laundry. It was a conversation that would have astonished my father, if he'd thought the laundry a place a man should enter. *The Uses of Infinity*, I read. *Medieval Astrologers. Adventures of a Mathematician. The Story of Reckoning in the Middle Ages. Intrinsically Difficult Problems. Human Knowledge, Its Scope and Its Limits. The Exact Sciences in Antiquity. The Number*

Concept. The Golden Bough. The Divine Proportion: A Study in Mathematical Beauty. An Investigation of the Laws of Thought. The Decline of the West. The Present Crisis in Mathematical Knowledge. Patterns of Plausible Inference. Greek Horoscopes. Prime Numbers 1 to 10,006721. The Crisis in Intuition. Euclid's Elements. God and the Universe. Poetry and Mathematics. The Undecidable. Men of Mathematics.

But the chattering said that my mother was planning her future path again, the path she'd lost sixteen years ago when she went to the Town Hall dance. Standing on the chilly laundry floor, I was hot with love and fear for her.

EVEN A TAP

Because I'm always thinking about my mother, I'm always thinking about the lake.

The people in the township called it the Basin.

All my childhood, until the terrible time, the Basin was just a dull brown sheen amongst the wiry branches of the ti-tree. The lake was part of the river but cut off by boulders. The river beyond was a wild force, white with our laughter as we hurtled above it shrieking on the end of a rope swung from a tree and leaping into it so that air was water and water was air and our shouts. The river we respected, it was something to be reckoned with. The lake was not, it was a down-at-heel relation, like us. It was scummed, opaque, too sullen to reflect even the sky. Our front garden meandered into bushland, and the bushland meandered into the lake. In a childhood of strict rules, the sullen lake had no real beginning.

One day men in ties and zippered nylon anoraks pulled up

in a car outside our house, and trekked through the bushland beside our land.

You can't trust government men, whispered Mum and went inside and locked the door.

Stay home from school, she said to me. They might come around pretending they want a drink of water.

I peered through the windows at the men loitering on the shore. I knew the mud of the lake shore, how it would be briefly dry in patches with the imprint of their weight, I knew that their smooth city shoes would be scratched by its ugly hidden shells. The sun streaked jagged from behind a huddle of grey clouds and the men shaded their eyes against a sudden glitter.

It was the lake that was malevolent.

That afternoon one of the girls in my class invited me to milkshakes at the corner store. I knew I should go home because Mum might still be hiding. But the girl's friends were the most popular girls in school, and one even had a boyfriend in the city. I chose a strawberry milkshake like they did. I tried not to notice Dad's old drawing of me as a baby. We sat at Bev Roberts' only table, laminex, chipped, a line of ants marching across its sugar strewn top.

But today Bev Roberts was uncaring about ants. She was red-faced with excitement.

You know what them surveyors found out? she asked. The other girls were gazing down at a photo of the city boyfriend. He was on a stretch of beach, holding a surfboard.

Our lake's five hundred and fifty feet deep, said Bev Roberts.

She rang up her till as an exclamation mark.

What a hunk, said one of the girls about the boyfriend.

It's one of the oldest lakes on earth, Bev Roberts said. If they could get down the bottom, they said goodness knows what they'd find. Bones and things. Of goodness knows what monsters.

Her eyes moved along our faces intent on the boyfriend's thighs. He was in a swimming costume, with a glint of hair frizzing out. One of the girls held the picture up to the light.

It's just leg hair, she argued.

We kept considering the leg hair while we sucked our milkshakes. The corners of Bev Roberts' mouth were insistent, she picked up a wettex, spat on it to make it sag, and wiped around the till drawer as if it was her mouth.

You kids wait and see. That lake's going to put us on the map.

The till drawer jumped open and nudged her bust companionably and encouraged her to lean over the counter to impress us. Despite the grime-rimmed wettex still in her hand, her voice slid into a theatrical whisper as if she was already talking to a group of tourists.

Doesn't it make you think? she asked. What could be down the bottom of five hundred and fifty feet? Eh? You want to know what else those surveyor men said? It's that cold down there in the middle where the five hundred and fifty feet part is, it'd kill a man. Thirty seconds he'd have. If he went in. Thirty seconds. Then his heart would freeze stiff as an iceblock.

I know, said one of the girls. Maybe the hair's growing out the end of his dick.

For a few weeks Bev Roberts was right about fame.

The local paper's headlines were:

OUR MURDEROUS LAKE!

On Sundays, families drove along our dust road in cars that became as powdery as Bev Roberts' nose. Families picnicked where our front fence would be, if Dad had put it up. They

174

forced down picnic blankets on top of the prickly undergrowth. They shaded their eyes with their hands like the surveyors had done while they gazed at the lake's murderous possibilities. I watched the shouts of children floating like bright kites over the lake's brownness. When they'd gone, sandy birds scrabbled for crusts rimmed with Vegemite.

The aldermen were impressed, Bev Roberts told her customers after the monthly meeting of the council.

They say we're becoming a tourist resort, she said.

Her eyes were on her paddock behind the shop.

If it becomes a boom town, she said so flirtatiously to Dad that you could imagine the circle of curlers in her hair were a tiara, perhaps I'll pay you to knock up a restaurant in my paddock. A motel even. I'd have a sign: Rooms so clean you could eat off the floors.

She told Dad that the council was already debating the possibility of garbage bins on the lake's uncertain shores.

They'll be starting to sniff around your place, you being on the waterfront, so to speak, she said. You've got a potentially valuable property. You're right in the hot seat.

Well, I'll be blowed, mumbled Dad.

Your dad's like me, she confided later to me. He's got a nose for progress. We're two of a kind.

After the next council meeting, she hailed me as I went to school.

Tell your father that last night in the debate on the lakeside amenities, one of the aldermen went so far as to suggest a tap.

But the lake glowered on, as it had always done before we knew its murderous possibilities, and the cars and the picnickers eventually found somewhere else to go. The lake held its secrets to itself, as closely as my mother did.

175

Grandma Juanita's house

Dear Mum,
Two visitors today after all the silence and it feels like rush hour.
First there was Jim. He just walked in without knocking into the
bedroom. I'd been considering getting out of my dressing-gown. I'd
been considering that for three days.
  Thought I'd see how you were getting on, he said.
  You've never met him, you haven't got around to that either. His
hair stands up from his scalp, brown but fading into blondness
before it falls on his forehead. His freckles are paler in winter.
He'd ironed his collar, I noticed that immediately, that he'd ironed
wrinkles into the points.
  I actually wanted to see both of you, he said.
  He wasn't sheepish.
  He came over and leaned to look at Zoe big-eyed on my bed.
  Gee willikins, he said, gazing at her.
  I'd forgotten he says gee willikins, it rocketed through me as it
did when I first met him. My jaw clenched. My mind paled. How
could I have had a baby with someone who says gee willikins? I
could kill him.
  He said she had his nose. He got quite teary about it. A nose!
  I said I couldn't see a likeness myself.
  He wanted to play with Zoe but I told him it was time for her
sleep. I was cranky. I don't want to share her. He hasn't been
around so she's mine now. He even said Gee Willikins when she
fell asleep.
  I don't know how I put up with him. Her nose is like mine.
  He left chocolate biscuits as a present.
  His visit made me clean up while she slept, and it was just as
well. Bev came. She shuts her shop up early these days. Too
buggered in the afternoons, she said.
  She's so rude I've always liked her. I never wanted to know

about Grandma Juanita and Bev and grandpa. I didn't want to feel sorry for grandma Juanita.

When Bev arrived, the nappies were blowing on the line in the wind like proud flags, the house gleamed, the carpet was spotless, the baby was still sleeping and I'd got out of my dressing-gown at last.

Bev peered about, even the loose skin on her face darting, ready to judge me. It wouldn't have occurred to her to help.

You're not like your grandma, she said in surprise. You can keep house. That was why your grandpa left her, she said, sitting down confidentially at the kitchen table and waiting for her cup of tea and not bothering to cover her old knobbly knees because we were two girls together.

Your grandma wasn't a good manager. Couldn't manage a house to save her life.

I thought Grandpa left Grandma because she was a bastard, I said.

She liked me saying that.

Too right! she said. A real old bastard.

She ate most of Jim's chocolate biscuits, but she'd bought a present from her shop, six jars of a new line in home-made tomato jam. I piled them on top of the cupboard. Bev Roberts' happy home jam, they shouted.

Hypatia

The parts are as important as the whole 1

After dinner in the dining room I headed for my white room, but on a sudden impulse I got the lift to the ground floor, out of the mathematics conference where I didn't belong.

The ancient ropes cranked the lift so slowly to street level that I was trying to prise open the wheezing lift door before it was ready. The heat and roar of the street rushed up to meet me like a slap. Traffic, crowds, trolley buses, street cafes blurred as I walked, in my sadness nothing was exotic. I watched a group of women exclaiming at a length of material that cascaded on the plaster flanks of a shop mannequin, blazing with sequins. I knew the lonely eyes of women in the houses that I measured for my father's repairs. Women standing in their kitchens, adjusting a teatowel carefully.

It'll make a big difference, that porch cupboard, they'd say, and I heard their voices rise in hope. The family can put their gumboots in there for a start. It'll stop them tramping muck through the house.

And their faces would plead with me, it matters, tell me it matters. And I would stand on one leg slapping flies and looking at the space in their lives where the cupboard was going to be.

Sometimes, if the teatowel she was holding was particularly threadbare, and the woman's eyes were particularly shiny, a phrase of Dad's would pop out of my mouth.

You won't know yourself with a cupboard like that, I'd say.

I knew that when I ran out to the ute, the slam of the wire screen door behind me echoed like a vault.

Oreo, said the women outside the shop, their eyes skimming on the smoothness of the fabric in the window. And though I didn't understand Greek, I understood their voices. It might make life beautiful.

In the haze of white stone around the Parthenon, I watched a workman weave his way amongst broken white columns, hundreds of them, rearing from the ground or collapsed on it. White dust eddied and fell on his shoes, as silent as snow. He stopped, checked a list in his hand, squatted, and while the sun beat on his head like a rhythm, his dark eyes narrowed at a column lopped off at shoulder height. It might once have been grand or humble, it was too worn to tell. He put out his finger and touched the corrugations all along the column's top, as if their rough edges could tell him a secret. He reached for a small fine brush and a tiny bottle of paint beside him in the dust, unscrewed the lid, dipped his brush into the bottle and the bristles came out flaring vermilion amongst all that whiteness. He threw back his head and slowly began painting.

Nothing in him touched the white column now, only the very tip of the sliding vermilion brush. 0030, he painted on the column. He stopped. He studied his handiwork, how perfect it was. In the sudden stillness of his hand, I was remembering my father's hand moving on wood, my father the geometer who could barely count to ten. For the first time it came to me that I learned mathematics not only from my mother but from the spaces that my father's hands moved amongst.

Excuse me, I called out.

The workman looked up into his audience under heavy eyebrows flecked with white dust, he always had an audience, he was as exhausted with questions as the temple behind me. As my mother.

Do you speak English? I asked, despite this.

Some, he said. His eyes didn't bother to find me, in the haze of ancient white heat there was no need.

People looked around at me, the nervous woman whose hair was tumbling out of her hat. I could've asked many questions.

What are you doing? I asked at last. Is there a pattern that's already been worked out?

The workman stayed squatting, he went back to his work, he was about to examine the corrugations he had to paint over.

He ran his finger over them, and I noticed how carefully his finger moved, as if their age could've burnt him.

Or are you trying to find a pattern? I asked.

He looked up at the tired geometry of the Parthenon behind me, at the milling crowd in grubby white sneakers, at the urgent voice that the wind had already whipped away. His mouth moved silently in the heat. He could've given many answers.

My heart beat for his answer, in all that ancient dust, as if it could've been my guide.

I paint the numbers, he said with dignity.

For the first time I saw that I was in a country with a most mocking sun.

I was tempted to go back to my hotel, pack my bag and leave for home. But I walked on. And for the first time in my life, there on a noisy street, just when I wanted to turn back, I discovered that there's something about a road you've never been down before, the way late sunshine slants around the rim of a roof, the sudden intrusion of a lane that leads to anywhere or nowhere, a fence post that's come adrift but leans against the rest of the fence conspiratorially, a muffled conversation that floats up from behind the lace curtains of a basement room, the sudden salty sizzle of meat and onions in a frying pan, the cry of a woman in sex, the cry like a bird's, again, again, again, these tiny things promise to change you, the way time does, in small degrees. I walked on because suddenly a voice in me was urging: go over the brow of that hill, follow that lane, walk down those stairs, go beyond the sunshine, and if you do, you'll be able to start your own life over again, and this time, own it.

Here there was a worn and dimpled staircase between two giant rocks, the concrete poured on like icing on a cake, someone had emptied the concrete over a structure and let it form in its own slow cascades, and then painted it all sea blue so that it lapped up to the shore of a polished passage and a small kitchen brown with the smell of endless coffee making. Here were painted lines on the footpath outside a house, to indicate a porch. Two people had sat there drinking and talking on their porch, and left their chairs still angled for friendship, the rope seats worn stiff by generations of conversations, and the chair legs criss-crossed with wire to last through more. And there, at a deeply-set window, a woman watched me as she peeled potatoes for dinner, her face as wrinkled as a wind-swept sea, as stern. She turned her head, she dismissed me, I floated beyond her thoughts, as I floated beyond my mother's. I'd always been a traveller, never belonging, swept in my mother's sea.

When music whisked out of a lane to my left, a voice and a violin leaping over cobblestones and tumbling across the flat tops of half-finished houses and teasing its way through bougainvilleas dark against the orange night sky of Athens and spreading out amongst the clouds to take the place of stars, I followed where it came from. I seemed to have no choice. I came to a nightclub with a red neon sign in English, Destruction.

I pushed open heavy doors, and blinked into blackness.

At first all I saw was a spotlight on a stage and music that was like a metallic thread whirling out of the dark and unravelling in the sudden glare. There was no frailty in it at all, it was as unflinching as a pattern of numbers. I moved forward straining to distinguish the singer from the spotlight, stumbling into a chair already pulled out from a table. I sat down, bumping into a neighbour, but the music demanded my submission. It wreathed around me, it cartwheeled my heart, I found my hands reaching out to hold on to the edge of the table, as if they could smooth a pathway for me.

I would leave the conference tomorrow, I would leave this country, I would work on the second of my new numbers in silence.

I was with dozens of people, women with long bare arms and smooth shoulders and breasts edging out of their dresses, and men scrubbed and combed. The violinist was trembling on the edge of sad sweet notes that promised if you only listened hard enough, you might remember your dreams. Now the singer glittered into the spotlight, trailing blue sequins in her music, and though she was beautiful, I saw that despite the music she was only the pale plaintive shape of humanity. She sang a phrase over and over, her voice calling out over craggy seashores and carved into the wind, until I took a pen out of my handbag and a paper serviette out of a glass and wrote down the strange sounds, to find out one day what they mean.

sack a po, I wrote.

Then the violin leaped away from her voice and cried a jubilant ending. The woman lifted herself out of her song, shook it out of her long black hair, she was triumphant, released from her music. The audience roared, the spotlight waned, the house lights came on. I was in a dingy room with stains on a white tablecloth and scuffs on a polished floor.

Ti? demanded a waiter to my left. His tie was loose around his neck because the air-conditioning had broken down.

I stood up.

I'm just going, I said.

I hope not, said a voice behind me. It was C. Denver.

He leaned over and picked up the serviette I'd scribbled on. Sack a po? It's s'agapo, he said. He smiled at me, a slow half smile so my heart stretched with it, that same curve.

I love you, he translated. Was this letter meant for anyone?

Hate 1

Hate accumulates slowly, like age, you're looking away, you look back and suddenly it's wrinkling there in coils, irrevocable. While I was looking at my mother and her lover, Dad—who couldn't hate my mother—turned against Matti.

One day my mother called Dad into Matti's room to force a jammed window open that Dad hadn't got around to fixing. His toe tipped over a little box tucked under the bed. Half a dozen pairs of diamante earrings fell on the floorboards, winking. Matti was quite proud that he'd stolen them, even after several beltings.

Now he was trying to squeeze juice out of bits of orange peel, pinching the shining peel in his fingers.

Why did you steal them? I asked.

Don't know, he said. Nicking's just for kids. Easy as pie. I'd rather live a proper life of crime. In fact, to set it off to a real blast, I'm going to kill Dad.

Dad means well, I said.

I watched Matti's slender fingers, how like my mother's they were.

One day I'm going to wag school and I'll get in his ute and I'll drive over him, said Matti. While he's digging someone's drains. Then we'll all live happily ever after. Except him. He'll be buried in shit.

I want to talk to you, said my father.

My father and I were driving back in the ute from measuring up Ed McGraith's new fence. I was wearing last year's jumper, and it was tight across my new breasts. On the warm ute seat

183

I was pretending I was my mother in the arms of her lover, I was lulled in desire to be her with him. All the while we were bumping over dirt roads, my unseeing father and I.

I noticed my father's voice.

He thought I hadn't heard him, he was repeating what he said. And even as his lips closed over his voice, I was thinking of her lover's hand caressing her nipples. His fingers so long and elegant. Perhaps he would use the backs of his fingers, to brush her nipples with the tips of his fingernails. I kept my eyes on the road, to hide the waves of desire that washed over me, so I rocked like a shell in desire in the bush so far from the sea, on the sun-warmed seat of a ute, next to my father.

Have you heard a word I've said? asked my father. I want to talk to you about your mother.

My mother! I shouted.

I peered through the dust-encrusted windscreen.

Watch out! A pothole! I shouted.

Don't shout like that! That pothole's been here longer than you have!

To my alarm, he was pulling over on the side of the road.

Why are you stopping? I asked, struggling with my voice still fuzzed with desire. The engine died into a grey silence. All around us the bush twitched. Tree trunks were hollow blackened lopped off columns, ruined by bushfires. Leaves drooped greyly from spindly saplings. Somewhere a crow moaned.

I want to have a talk, my father said. He turned in his seat so he was leaning against the door, facing me.

The crow cried again.

Sounds like someone mourning, said my father.

It's a place for murder, I said.

But the waves of desire were approaching again as if my body couldn't stop remembering the touch of his hand. I surfed in the waters of desire to be her and her lover. I tried to shake myself free.

I haven't got time for chats, I protested. I should be at school learning things. I'm missing a lot of school, doing all this measuring for you.

My father laughed, a laugh as jagged as the broken tree trunks.

You're a girl, school doesn't matter, said my father.

The blackened trees seemed at that moment stilled, as if they'd been wandering and now, full of knowledge, they'd returned, they were waiting. But every twitch, every shiver of leaf brought desire back, as if it was calling to me from the hills that edge the horizon, and I must answer. So I hotly examined the dashboard, the pattern of whorls on the vinyl under my legs, anything. If I wasn't careful, my eyes would wander to examine my father's crotch. He was after all, I realised with a sickening lurch of the stomach, a man. A man as her lover was a man. I'd seen my father's penis after the weekly bath. In those days, we'd all use the same bathwater, Dad first, then Mum, then Matti. I sat in the swill last. But on bath day, Dad's penis looked intestinally functional, like something he'd tuck away in the corner of his tool box.

Why me? I was saying. Why not Matti?

I have a red face like my father's, his long inquiring nose.

What do you mean? he was saying.

My eyes had fixed themselves in the shadowy folds of his overalls where his legs parted. I was in a delirium of panic. My mind was sliding on the dangling knob that was my father's penis.

My father had been my mother's lover. He must've lain with my mother at least once, to get me. At least twice, to get Matti.

You're not making sense, he said.

Did I say something? I yelp.

I snapped my eyes back to the nearest burnt-out tree trunk, rising no higher than the ute's aerial. I forced my eyes to follow the weary lines of its cracks, and busied myself in the tiny meanderings of ants. My father has lain with my beautiful mother and pushed his purple tool deep into her.

I want to ask you about your mother, he said.

The tree trunk, I saw with a new throb of dismay, was shaped like a penis, burnt out and hollow. I moved my eyes, but every burnt tree trunk was the same, a vista of penises.

Look at me, he said.

I examined long blades of grass instead, the sort that I'd played amongst all my childhood. They thrust from the desultory dirt so knowingly.

There was a noise.

What's that? I shouted.

Only a bird, he said.

Is it mating? I blurted.

My father decided to humour me. He rolled down the window and peered out.

I don't think it's the season, he said. It's just hoping for a worm. Look at me.

He reached over and turned my face to his. But if he saw my eyes, he'd guess. When you long to be your mother and her lover, surely it shows on your face.

Open your eyes, he said.

The sun hurts, I said.

He sighed.

The sun's not out, he said.

He let my face drop.

I'm going for a walk, he said.

He cracked open his door, the way men do, bursting it out to the full length of his arm without moving the rest of his body. I remembered her lover's arm as it stretched out to me to shake my hand, and desire spurted again like warm honey through my body.

I stayed on my vinyl seat listening to the tramping of my father through undergrowth. Twigs exploded under his feet. Ferns broke. I turned and watched the man my father through the back window. I saw how small he was, this man who once towered above me. I saw the concertina of time ugly on his thick red neck. I saw how low he bowed his head.

I folded my arms under my breasts, to touch them, to make my belly cramp again in the ooze of desire. But through the window my father had opened, the bush crept into me. The bird's weight still crunched dry leaves. A spiderweb was hung with dew. The day moved in twitterings and twitchings and whisperings. The bush sighed. My father's movement on dead leaves had faded.

He'd been gone a long time. I didn't want to pretend I was my mother and her lover any more. The crow moaned again. I was jarred out of boredom by silence. It was a day too weary for shadows, but the silence seemed to have fallen around me for minutes or hours, I couldn't tell. I got out of the ute, though the vinyl sucked at my bare legs. I walked in the direction my father walked. Beyond a fallen tree, a deserted sandhill, a stretch of low and desolate scrub, past an outcrop of brooding rock. There was a roaring wind here, a shock after the stillness higher up. I fought against it, scarcely noticing where I put my feet. I kicked a stone. It whirled over a cliff hidden by scrub and soared hundreds of silent feet down to a valley below.

Where was my father?

Dad! I yelled.

The wind pushed my voice back down my throat.

I stumbled along the cliff edge. Bushes whipped in the wind, and stung my face. Stones crumbled under my feet and crashed into dust amongst the trees below.

Wind and bushes whipped me into a frenzy of anger. Why didn't my father think about me? Didn't he realise I should be at school? I was shouting abuse at him with the wind whipping the words away out of my mouth when I almost fell upon him.

There, on a rock edge, my father sat. His legs were pushed up to his chest. Almost at his toes the cliff fell away. If he peered beyond his knees he'd see how tiny the trees of the valley were when they tossed their heads, how from this height they seemed as soft as moss. And that from here the distant mountains pulled at you like longing. But my father had wrapped his head in his hands. He was breathing strangely, his shirt under his overalls stretching and crinkling with his huffing. On the wind I heard noises wrench out of him, bush noises, animal noises, snorting and bellowing and choking. My father was crying.

I backed away. I kept walking backwards long after it was necessary. I opened the ute door softly and crept inside, glad of the warm vinyl.

I had no comfort for him. We were lost, both of us. We were alone, outside my mother, and there was no way to belong.

Matti's jumper, said my mother to my father that last, terrible winter, is worn out. And the cuffs are half-way up his arms.

She pulled it out of the washing basket. The iron sighed on its board.

When I was a kid, said Dad, my jumpers were always like that. My dad said it'd make me tough.

But it has no warmth, said Mum. No goodness in it. See?

She was rubbing it between two fingers, I could almost see her fingers through it.

Even you, she said, should pity a child in a jumper like that. Whatever your dad did to you.

I got nothing, my father said. It did me the world of good.

I stood one-legged at the ironing board as Mum ironed. I put my cold hands on the place where the iron was. Dad had taken Matti outside to teach him how to keep warm without a jumper.

Like my dad taught me, he'd said.

Jump, he shouted at Matti.

Matti jumped like a star into the sky pearly white with snow still withheld. His lanky, fifteen-year-old body tipped slightly at the waist when he jumped.

My mother stared at the ironing board, white-fisted,

Again, Dad was shouting. His voice lashed hate against the windowpane. I shuddered.

Again, Dad shouted.

Dad had taken his belt off to lash the ground with it. At every lash, bits of his lawn struggling against frost flew up but he didn't care.

Again, shouted Dad. The belt lashed at the lawn as well.

And again. And again. And again.

Your father can't give what he wasn't given, said my mother to me.

She didn't realise that she was talking about herself, and me.

As we cut our chops at dinner, I saw for the first time that everyone else's winter cuffs came down to their wrists. And it hurt every muscle in my body that Dad couldn't love his family the way they helplessly were, my brother and his lies, my mother and her lover. Such an enormity, not to love what's there. Unthinkable, till now unsayable.

I suppose that's when I lost pity for my father, the one who recognised the mathematics in me. Because he didn't love my only connection with love.

THE PARTS ARE AS IMPORTANT AS THE WHOLE 2

My mother, being self-taught, may not have known that Clarke thought she was alluding to an old discussion in mathematics. After a childhood with Juanita, my mother felt she knew mathematical objects intimately and understood them better than everyday objects. She was close to being a Platonist, the argument that says that all the objects in what she called the mathematical zoo exist, outside the space and time of physical existence. They weren't created and they won't disappear. The mathematician is like a geologist, discovering, not inventing, the world. In fact, most mathematicians are Platonists when they're doing mathematics though they mightn't admit to it.

But there's another argument which says that there are no mathematical objects out there. Mathematics is just about setting up axioms and definitions and extrapolating from there. Mathematics is a formal game. It has no meaning outside mathematics even if sometimes it happens to co-incide with the physical world.

Both these views are countered by the constructivists, who believe that only when we prove something in mathematics does it become true. We think things into being. So mathematics isn't about ideal forms, it's about what people have in their minds.

At least, that's what Mum told me. She began as a formalist, but Clare influenced her, and after her new numbers she became a Platonist. As for the constructivists, she used to put her hands on her hips and say:

So there's no circles on Mars yet because humans haven't been there to think about circles?
Hypatia

Clarke Denver was the sort of person who gazes so directly that it almost feels rude to blink. I was held in the grip of his gaze as if I was in his arms. I was no longer lonely. We walked back to the hotel together, our feet ringing out in time on the footpaths, and I bought a bottle of Metaxa so I could ask him to my room for a drink.

Where should I sit? he asked. He didn't look towards the white chair austere in a white corner, perhaps he didn't notice. I patted the bed beside me. He sat on the edge.

Make yourself comfortable, I said. Unless you're in a hurry to go.

I laughed to suggest I didn't care. He leaned against the bedhead as I was doing, and my heart lifted as if it was on a child's balloon to see his wavy hair streaming away from his cheekbones so close to me, and the slenderness of his neck where the gold chain slid. He was careful about his shoes on the bed's cover. We hadn't talked mathematics yet. I was waiting for him to bring up the subject so I didn't sound like an overeager amateur. I stared straight ahead to the expanse of orange night melting into yellow neon.

I want to get from love what I get from mathematics, he said suddenly.

Ah, I cried.

Is that what you wanted? he said, and I knew he meant when I was young, as young as him. I thought of my mother then, her young lover sitting on the verandah with her pages of mathematics on his slender thighs.

What do you do at your university? I asked him.

I just lecture about better ways to calculate, he said. It isn't much fun. There was a time—

he remembered his glass and drained it—

when I hoped I might turn into a genius.

He lifted his empty glass into the orange light, like a toast. But his fingerprints smeared the glass.

Like perhaps you are.

I heard the edge in his voice but I took no notice. Not then. I busied myself refilling his glass.

Your work isn't the sort of math that people are doing here, he said. He was the sort of person who changes subjects rapidly.

Is it your sort of mathematics? I asked.

I haven't read it, he said.

I poured myself another Metaxa.

It's hard being an outsider, I said.

The search for an outsider with something to say would've been appealing at first to a lot of mathematicians, he said. Catch a mathematician when we're working, and we don't feel we're using abstractions, some ideas go back three thousands years or more and we work with them every day, they're more real than—

he waved his hands towards the stonemason's yard—

those lumps of stone down there. So when we're at work it's possible to imagine that an outsider could come across a form of reasoning we don't yet have access to. But then we remember that it's a game, not a reality, a game with formal rules that must be learned. So we think that you can't have.

I went to the window and opened it to let in more of the orange night.

What would you say to some geometric devices that helped to find a whole new set of numbers? I asked.

We could all imagine we've invented new numbers, he said absently.

He was more interested in counting famous amateurs on his fingers like a child.

There was Ramanujan, of course, he said. And Fermat was an outsider. And Wronski thought he knew the key to the universe, but at least he had one new sensible mathematical idea. And Grassman—no one took notice of him either at first, because his vector and tensor analysis were ahead of his time. And Kempe with his four-colour theorem—he was a lawyer. So—

he was smoothing the bed cover—

I suppose it's possible that you might have something. But they were earlier on, he added. When mathematics was less sophisticated, when there was a chance that an outsider could come up with a significant idea.

So everyone's sure I haven't? I asked.

Someone must be responsible for making you the winner, but they don't seem to be here, he said. And no one else is going to read it. They'd have to read a lot of background mathematics first. That'd be difficult. Unfamiliar mathematics is difficult. No one likes reading it. You can't skim it. No one has time.

His voice took no account of the bed we were on, our closeness, the light we both gazed at. We could be at opposite ends of the world. I watched the curtains move against the window, so stiff, so formal, so different from the gentle curtains my mother always chose. They moved across my sadness, and I was finding my mother's mind in words for the first time, it was almost as if in the flutter of curtains I was creating her mind in me.

I understand what you meant, I said.

There was a pause.

What do you understand? he asked. He didn't look at me, he scarcely heard my voice, he was deep in his own thoughts, but so was I.

It's as if sometime early in your life you agreed that everything physical was an abstraction, I said. The pen in your hand, the paper, the table, the floor it stood on, the tree shivering with light outside your window, your hand in front of your face, your body. You blurred them the way white light in this country blurs colour, so they did not exist.

He turned to watch me, his face in darkness, reflecting nothing.

So that mathematics could take up space for you, I said. And weight, so you could ride out on mathematics to all the places where the mind can go, mathematics could take you there.

Did my mother say those words? To me? To her lover? I don't remember, but they seem words connected with white curtains that scarcely touch a windowsill. Words that came to me as a voice from my own heart.

Ah, he said.

The neon light outside the window changed to purple.

You're not an outsider at all, he said.

I turned around on the bed, my face towards the pillow. I listened to the slow ticking of my eyelashes hitting the pillow, as I used to as a child awake in the night, wondering if she was out of bed, wondering where she was, what she was dreaming of.

Were you hoping this conference would change your life? asked Clarke.

He was touching my shoulder gently, lifting my hair, as if he'd never seen hair before. I felt the gentle tugging at my scalp, he was examining individual strands of my hair in the purple neon light.

The trouble is, I said, that I've got to do this for my mother, because something happened when I was a child. There was a particular year. A particular summer. A particular day when my mother's lover ... I've never been sure if I called what happened on that day into being, that's the word for it. And now he's claiming ...

I ran out of words.

How old are you? he asked, still lifting my hair.

I turned to look at him. I worried that he could see my neck, that it's no longer like the stem of a flower, like his was.

Thirty-nine and a half, I lied.

A perfect age, he said. You could be my mother.

I put my arms around him and his hair fell softly and covered my neck. He went to sleep like that and even though the neon faded outside the window, through the dark hours he stayed as beautiful as light.

I woke in a room that seemed no longer blank, the walls were softly yellow with sunshine and the white curtains at the open window rippled gold light as they drifted. I couldn't remember why I was happy, I stared with wonder at the glowing walls. I put out my hand to touch the folds of sheet and discovered him, his shirt off now, and his feet bare, and his eyes open and watching me. The bed was warm wherever I turned.

It's like a picnic day, I said. Sleeping alongside you.

Yes, he said.

In childhood, I said. Do you remember them? A sunshiny day, and suddenly it doesn't matter that you've lost your school library books, it doesn't matter that the knots in your hair won't come out, or that you've dripped mulberries on your shirt or that your parents can barely speak for anguish. All that matters on a picnic day is your sunshiny pleasure. All that matters is that there are trees to climb and how your white splashing turns creek water into rainbows.

We nestled into each other then and his warmth shocked me, as if I'd always been cold and not known.

He moved away slightly.

Do you love somebody? he asked.

No, I said. He watched my lips with attention like someone who needs to lip read, then he took the thought into somewhere inside his mind and his face muscles moved while he considered it. He made me think of how voluptuously my mother thought.

He reached out his hand and touched my face with the smooth backs of his fingers, he ran his fingers down my nose and across my cheekbones and the side of my face. He stroked my cheeks again and again until I wanted to close my eyes and take in the gentle sumptuousness of his touching fingers and enjoy it inside my mind, the way he took in thought. I marvelled at his mouth, the little sardonic muscles rippling.

If you were intoxicated early in your life with something, I said, then everything later seems dull.

All the time his hands glided on my face, they were like water, the smooth ebb of his hands. Then he lay on his back and looked up at the ceiling.

Can I show you my work? I said. And try to explain the background you don't know?

He moved his feet against the sheets.

I love someone, he said. It makes me truant.

Who do you love? I asked.

The nightclub singer. I know you hardly saw her, but she's so beautiful.

I turned on my back too and saw how distant the ceiling was, the yawning, dizzying depth of air above me. Under it, I was tiny.

What are you thinking? he asked.

I'm thinking of a room where love might happen, I said. This probably isn't the room.

But I was still held by him, there was something about him I couldn't let go, not yet. There was something about him that brought me closer to my mother.

What should I do about her? he asked.

Have breakfast, it's breakfast time, I said.

In the lift, we stood against opposite walls, watching the floor indicators like the strangers we were.

The lift slid slowly down its ropes. Many things happened in that slow slide. The floor creaked under our feet. The rope sighed on its weight. A corner of carpet ripped away from its moorings. We arrived at the dining room with a jolt you'd usually not notice. I could hear beyond the lift doors the rattle of trays in the kitchen. The doors sprang open with a pant of diesel fumes.

Adele grabbed me.

They've finally worked out a timetable and put you on at the end of the week! On Friday!

I'm glad that's settled, I said.

But everyone else flies out on Thursday, she said.

Paul was at the buffet, having his coffee cup filled.

I want real coffee, he was shouting at the maid about to pour Greek coffee from a tiny saucepan on a small stove. Not that local stuff. It's mud.

She looked up, startled.

I reached over and pointed to the percolated coffee for her.

Let's go, said Clarke.

But Paul was shouting again.

Sugar. I said SUGAR.

He grabbed at me.

Do you know their lingo? This is supposed to be an international hotel! Couldn't one of them learn to say 'sugar'? SUGAR! he bellowed at the maid.

There's sachets of sugar in your saucer, I said. Two.

He looked.

That proves my point! he shouted. One of them should've said 'There's sugar in your saucer'.

Though it was early in the morning, the heat was already betraying him. He found a crumpled handkerchief in his pocket to mop his forehead.

Frances! shouted Paul. Living Insurance must not be compromised by you!

In the heat of coffee and a summer morning, his indignant eyeballs threatened to come loose from their sockets.

I stared from the coffee stains on his shirt to him.

None of us must be compromised, I said.

His eyes bulged.

If you keep up this nonsense about your aunty making up these theories, he said, you'll need some documentation. Where. When. Who. Data, he said. Facts. All this—

he indicated the people in the dining room—

is about mathematics and mathematics is about facts.

It's about ideas, not facts, I said.

Don't be silly, even I know that it's about measuring— what's out there, he said.

He had to mop his forehead again. He wasn't a man to be contradicted. The beads of sweat were already reappearing.

You don't know what you're talking about. How does a plane keep up in the air if mathematics isn't about facts? he was saying.

The connection between most mathematics and the real world may be just a coincidence, I said.

You're a crank, Paul shouted. They're right.

Adele was at my elbow.

Have I told you why I came to this conference? she said to Paul. I saw a map of Greece on my legs. Both legs, she said, smiling at us both and leading him away.

You hear what she said? Paul was hurling over his shoulder so I didn't miss a word,

she's saying that a plane stays up in the air because of coincidence. What if she says that sort of thing to the media? Living Insurance will put me in jail!

Hate 2

In the summer of the year of the lover, people in the town began taking notice of my father's opinions.

Frank Montrose thinks so, Bev Roberts often said over her counter.

Indeed, said her customers, waiting for a chance to ask her if the sugar and the potatoes and the bread could go on the bill again.

It followed that since my father knew about flashings and elevations and key locks, not to mention intimacies like whose bedroom walls in the township were cracked and whose linen cupboards had gone mouldy, that he also knew about the likelihood of funnel web infestations under houses, not to mention bushfires and flooding rains and acts of God.

I've never known Frank Montrose to be wrong, Bev Roberts said.

Indeed, said her customers, some of whom didn't know who Frank Montrose was. But it was comforting to know someone was an expert at everything, and Bev Roberts spoke her opinions with such loud certainty that:

Frank Montrose thinks so
began to be heard on street corners.

Sometimes I meet my own opinion coming down the street,
said Dad, laughing.

It was Saturday and my father worked weekends. He'd
come home for lunch and he was unbuttoning the front bib of
his overalls as he waited for Mum to serve the chops.

Often it's not any opinion I've ever held but I don't correct
it, he said.

He smiled one of his sweet, fluttering smiles so his pride
came to rest on everyone's face.

But my mother huffed, she wouldn't let it rest on her. My
father didn't intend to notice this.

Don't stick your neck out, that's how to get places.

He smiled around at us all.

Give opinions that fit in, he said. Don't get anyone upset.
Go—

he swept his hands towards the floor like water falling, like
our creek falling white onto the rocks below—

go with the flow. It's easy. Everything is, if you want it to
be.

Matti and I were straight backed on our chairs because Mum
was throwing chops from the pan to the plates with her fingers,
her fingers were burning red.

Dad didn't notice this either.

That's not true, Mum said to him.

She was plomping down in her chair, every movement
sharp, she was already cutting her meat, the knife jabbing,
ringing across the plate. Her hair was flossing out of its bobby
pins.

Don't say that in front of the children, she said.

What? he asked, still smiling.

That it's all easy, she said.

His pleasure at explaining life to us was fading so fast from his lips, they were sagging.

Why, is it wrong to say it's easy? he demanded.

He was sitting back, watching her, not touching his food though the lunch had been cooked for him. If he hadn't come home, we'd have eaten bread and butter with my mother.

It's a profanity, she said, to be always reducing things.

She was panting the words over the chops.

A profanity?

My father smiled at Matti and me, inviting us to join in. Profanity? What sort of word is profanity?

His smile was horrible.

It's wrong, shouted my mother. It's wrong the way you make everything so little, when it's not little at all.

You, said my father, leaning on the table and making plates tip,

want everything to be mysterious. So you can be breathless about it.

My mother drew herself back.

Everything is mysterious, she shouted. Nothing may be what we think it is. We may know nothing. Have you ever thought of that? We may be making the entire thing up.

My father's chop slid onto the tablecloth my mother had washed, starched and ironed for this moment. Grease and words spread like brown blood.

My father laughed, trying to gather his children into his mirth, trying to make everything easy.

There's not much left for us to know, this half of the century, said my father to us his children. The scientists have explained it all. We just about know everything there is. We've just about got it all summed up.

You'd be an expert in what's known, said my mother. She couldn't swallow her food too fast.

201

You know it all. You see what lies behind appearances.

She laughed back at him, she lifted her arms to hold back her hair, but she was wrenching it, wrenching her glossy hair almost out of her skull so all we saw was the cruel twist of her face.

You wanted me for my looks and my class. You never thought for a moment who I am.

My father gazed at her a long moment. My mother's hair almost ripped from her scalp. The clock on the mantelpiece ticked. My father stood. He was holding onto the table so tightly he was stretching the cloth.

It's true I was taken in, he said.

So in the silence we knew he must have noticed the hairs on the pillowslips, the teaspoons on the sink, the joy in my mother's face. Silence crackled like a fire between them, and I remember how bushfires devour. We waited for him to say the unsayable. But he turned on his heels.

You were just one of those convent girls taught to pass yourself off as upper class and interesting, he said.

My father left the house too quickly to buckle up his bib front and he had to do it while he backed the ute one-handed down the drive. As the motor droned into the sounds of the bush and became part of it, my mother stared at my father's chops, congealing now in their grey fat on the white tablecloth.

It's a shame they didn't teach you to count, she yelled.

What a family to come from, shouted Matti.

He slammed his way out of the dining room. I was beginning to wonder if my mother had fallen into a trance, she was so still. Then she reached over the table with her handsome amber-skinned fist. She brought it down on my father's teacup, and left it there. She didn't look at her fist.

It was jagged with blood.

And on the tablecloth, her blood was splotched like stars in an unfathomable sky.

It was thirteen days since I'd found any sign of her lover at our house.

When my brother talked about what happened at school, I always edged close to my mother, we couldn't breathe, either of us, we dared not, no sound of his lies should be muted. We'd hear the way they glided, the way they slipped and slithered and frolicked, the way they touched at facts and fell away.

Why are youse holding your breath? he'd ask us.

You, corrected my mother, laughing. He'd laugh too. I'd pick at a bit of dirt on the flyscreen door and puff.

Because we couldn't speak about his lying to each other, it was another of the secrets of my family, that my brother lied. And it was our shame that we were fascinated by his lies, their possibilities. But when I glanced at my mother's face I knew she believed that at the still centre of the lies there was a special place for her where no lies were. Like the centre of the storm, where no movement is. That's the illusion about liars, you cannot imagine they live in an infinity of lies. You believe the liar will not lie to you.

After the lake, I kept expecting my brother to come through the door laughing—that particular high-pitched way he laughed when he'd invented a new story—because you cannot believe in death, let alone the death of a liar.

They always seemed to be laughing together. In the leap of my mother's laughter with my brother, the kitchen was only a tiny room. His open-mouthed laughter went on in my dreams long after it faded from memory, long after the lake. And my mother kept dreaming about it too, I could tell. The way she'd close a cupboard and look over her shoulder at the door when

203

a wind blew it open. Her eyes would be wide with expectation. Till she blinked.

While he was with us, we couldn't stop loving him, my mother and I.

Matti and I were on a bed in a quiet room, maybe it was raining, everything was muffled, birds' songs, coughs, the creaks of floorboards, the branches twanging on the gutter, these things were suspended in a long afternoon. My mother's lover had visited that morning and gone home. I knew by the comb he'd left in the bathroom, his curling hairs still gripped by its teeth, to keep a bit of him in our house till next time. The house was warm with peace again. My feet and my brother's feet were in socks, and there was a balloon in the air, it was drifting, singing, faltering, a foot was remembering to kick, the balloon meandered.

She loves me more than him, said my brother about my mother and her lover. And she's going to give him up because of me.

But she wouldn't, I knew. I already knew too much about passion, how it has its own time, its own end, like any work of the heart, even mathematics.

I gave her a ring, and she said that she'd stop having sex with him, said Matti. Because she loves me, and she knows it hurts my feelings.

I examined his face carefully for its beauty. Liars have beautiful faces, perhaps it's the way their promises ripple out.

She's going to stop him visiting us, he said.

How did you buy a ring? I murmured. This wasn't an important question, but in our family the important questions weren't asked, perhaps not even in mathematics. I wanted the story to go on and on, like the lifting balloon, like our bodies together stretched out on the bed.

I found it in the gutter, he said.

The gutter, I repeated. I laughed in delight, as if I was my mother. I saw that the balloon was yellow light, I watched how yellow light falls and how easily his foot threw it back to the ceiling. My brother was a ribbon of warmth beside me, and his hair was unfolding in blue black shadows on my shoulder.

Did it look like it came from the gutter? I asked.

I washed it, my brother decided.

My brother's lies had no beginning and no end. I laughed under his high-pitched teenage laugh, if only I could be his echo. But I was always stiff with truth, always walking stiffly behind him.

He kicked the balloon, I kicked it back. Between us the yellow balloon sang.

What did she do when you gave her the ring?

She said she loved me. Most of all.

He looked at me.

Mum loves me most of all.

The balloon fell. I almost forgot to move my foot, and the balloon fell as sadly as the moon. But even that my brother might say he could catch and send spinning. Before the lake.

THE PARTS ARE AS IMPORTANT AS THE WHOLE 3

My mother used to say that you don't get around to counting large numbers just because you're human. The Australian Aborigines, for instance, don't have a number bigger than two. Some indigenous groups in Brazil and in southern Africa also live effective lives without many numbers. Francis Galton at the end of the nineteenth century wrote about his travels and observations of the Damaras people in southern Africa.

'When bartering is going on each sheep must be paid for separately. Thus suppose two sticks to be the rate of exchange for one sheep, it would sorely puzzle a Damaras to take two sheep and give him four sticks. I have done so, and seen a man take two of the sticks apart and take a sight over them at one of the sheep he was about to sell. Having satisfied himself that one was honestly paid for, and finding to his surprise that exactly two sticks remained in hand to settle the account for the other sheep, he would be afflicted with doubts; the transaction seemed to him to come too "pat" to be correct, and he would refer back to the first couple of sticks, and then his mind got hazy and confused, and wandered from one sheep to the other, and he broke off the transaction until two sticks were placed in his hand and one sheep driven away, and then the other two sticks given him and the second sheep driven away.'

As my mother used to say, to survive in the world requires noticing the regularities of nature, but it doesn't require mathematising. On the other hand, some people have inexplicable mental abilities so astonishing that Paul Davies has compared it to people being able to jump not just six feet off the ground, but sixty, or six hundred.

About the same time as the conference, late in the twentieth century, there was an Indian woman, Shakuntala Devi, who travelled the world amazing audiences with feats of mental arithmetic. Once in Texas, Devi found the twenty-third root of a two hundred digit number in fifty seconds. Her ability was rare but not unique. There have been other instances, such as two American brothers who could consistently outdo a computer in finding prime numbers, even though they were both mentally handicapped.

My mother found it mysterious why such an ability should have been coded into the human genetic pool—let alone into the genetic pool of her family. It seems, she'd say, as if humans have been prepared for something other than survival.
Hypatia

I couldn't clang my tray down on the hotel dining table too hard. Knives and spoons and coffee cups clattered on the laminex. Clarke was reading the book he kept in his pocket. He looked up.

What's wrong? he asked.

I'm thinking about the precarious nature of things, I said. About the irreversible moment. What we can unleash. Whether it's better to leave things folded up inside each other as they are.

His smile hung on the brambles of her heart, caught forever, and I couldn't untwine it. Because Matti's words unwound unravelled with possibilities, whereas mine were stiff with truth. After the lake, when we said his name even casually, Dad and I—

We had the ute when Matti was—

It must run in the family because Matti was—

all my mother would hear was the sound of his name furrowing into her loss like the skeleton of an autumn leaf.

Pardon? she'd ask. And make her lips follow the shape of our lips, to appear to concentrate. He was to her that blur of evening when the colours can't fight free. He was who she cried for when she cried for other people. He must have seemed like her new beginning when he was born. And when he disappeared, he seemed her ending.

I'm no longer sure why I came to this conference, I said to Clarke who was still reading his book.

I was thinking that what I'd done mightn't be so very important after all. When I finally found it that morning, it wasn't a revelation, it didn't come like God. It slid in, quiet, familiar, insistent, so that later it seemed as if it'd always been there, waiting for me to turn around and look. I felt foolish for not seeing it before. It seemed actual, physical, perfectly formed, from me but not me, ineluctable but warmly intimate, like a child.

Clarke's breath huffed in a sigh. He turned over the corner of a page so he'd know where he was up to.

It's not unknown, a mathematician not wanting to tell, he said.

Being here is getting complicated, I said.

Clarke began to count things off on his fingers again. Gauss didn't reveal things that he knew, essential things, he says. He wanted to leave behind perfect works of art without the scaffolding. And there was Pierce, he knew that the logic of propositions could be done with one constant, it was an amazingly important realisation, and he didn't publish it. There's Fermat's last equation that he didn't tell, of course. You're not the first to want to back out.

They may have wanted to leave things where they were, I said.

He smiled a coolly professional smile as if we hadn't shared anything, even a kiss.

Don't, he said. You might show us some way to reason we don't know.

So we ate our yoghurt together and perhaps it'd be all we'd ever do together, each moment for me twisted at the end with sadness. At the adjoining table, Adele had breakfast next to Paul. I could tell she didn't like him. When a flake of bread crust flew out of her mouth and landed on his collar, she moved even closer and crunched a new crustier bread roll.

A blond student was leaping up on a table and stamping for silence. One of the kitchen maids came forward to remonstrate but he held out his arms mockingly as if he was going to embrace her, and she backed away.

An impromptu entertainment, ladies and gentlemen.

He stamped again. A few groups at nearby tables looked around, settled back into conversation, then they were hushed by their neighbours.

Toshiko, come and help.

A Japanese boy joined the young man. He turned to the room and translated into Japanese. The words moved across the room like an echo I couldn't quite hear. A girl stood up and translated into German. There was a slow clapping to attract everyone's attention, and gradually the room became silent, though now and then a spoken word drifted like a giant shape through the air. At the academics' table an American voice shouted:

Locus is an illiterate word. It's not Greek or Latin . . .

All eyes swivelled towards him. He sputtered to a stop, like a shouting passenger suddenly realising that his train has arrived at a quiet station.

No doubt you know that we have in our midst a world-beating genius . . . said the young blond man. His shirt strained with pride at the attention, and above him the blades of the huge ceiling fans swung. I saw Clarke's face angled like mine, and with a crunch of my heart I remembered the sweet hopeful beginnings of the love affairs of my past, when every movement of my body mirrored my lover's body in desire.

Let this one be for always, I'd think.

I longed to share with him that sweet expectation that we were two halves of a circle that must eventually meet.

Suddenly the speaker's eyes caught mine, held mine. It was a moment like a rock hurled through the air to split my peace in half. But surely he only happened to catch my eye.

. . . in the midst of our mediocrity, I only speak for some, of course—

The blond student was stamping again for attention. The noise of his boots on the table was hammering through my panic. Panic was a crown of heat prickles on my forehead. But in those days, except when I was doing mathematics—that silence—all my thoughts reverted to my mother.

My father shouted at her across the shine of the kitchen floor:
The boy's a liar, just like you.
My eyes jerked up to his, I thought he was glaring at me.
Like you are inside.
The walls of the kitchen heaved in with my mother's indrawn breath.
You're both liars, all the way through, he said to her.
There was no dinner that night except bread and dripping, cut by my father in a kitchen so cold our teeth chattered. It was difficult later to wash the yellow grease off the knife.
He's just like you.
I wished, how I wished he could've said the same of me.
He's just like you.

The blond boy was still shouting ...
She had no need of years of study. It's all obvious to her. She just had to get in touch with the fairies.
And the help of some stolen lecture notes, said a voice from the back of the room.
Some of us know what I'm going to propose isn't real mathematics, some of us know what real mathematics is, the young blond man went on. But we wondered if she could beat the record of Shakuntala Devi, who found the twenty-third root of a two hundred digit number in fifty seconds. However Devi wasn't claiming to be the genius of the world ... So we thought you could manage the twenty-third root of a four hundred digit number in twenty-five seconds, he finished, and

jumped down from his table, startling the echoes of the translators as if they were birds in a valley in the bush.

Even as he brought to our table a piece of paper with a four hundred digit number scribbled on it, I was thinking about my mother's love for my brother.

Hate 3

Amongst the Vegemite sandwiches at school, my brother's lies seemed purple and raw like meat hanging from sharp hooks in the butcher's shop. I squirmed at the names they called him at school, the sounds carried so harshly over the wire netting that divided the boys' playground from the girls'.

But at home amongst the smell of dinners and the endless talk about guttering, my mother and I waited breathless for his face to glow as he told his stories that seemed like endless possibilities.

He was standing on the verandah and I was breaking twigs into the gaps between the floorboards, he stood against the light, my amber brother who had all my mother's love, he was fringed in brightness, and I had to shade my eyes to watch.

I've invented an equation no one's ever thought of before, he said.

My heart squeezed in panic. He already consumed all my mother's love.

I bet it's just something Mum's dictated to you, I said, but I must have been whispering because he didn't stop to hear.

I'll be on the radio, he was saying. They'll write articles in the newspaper about me and I'll have my photo in them.

My twig broke. He looked down at me.

I've signed it, he said. Dated it. They'll say: At his tender age! While he was just a pup!

I don't believe you, I shouted.

His face contracted in pity for my life.

You'll be famous too, he added. Because you knew me once.

I'm ready to tell what happened then. I've never told anyone. Not her, not anyone. But I'm tired of secrets, they've weighed on me all my life. A moment that becomes a lifetime on a verandah already rotting because Dad used soft wood, not hard wood, just the leftover bits he scrounged from other people's lives. My brother glowing with lies and my mother's love. And behind him, the dark lake waiting.

Why don't you get lost, I muttered.

That's what I said the night before he vanished.

Now I've told you, I'm going to lie down. Don't follow me. Thoughts are hammering in my head like the young man's boots at that conference in Athens. Come back later. There's worse to tell you. That terrible thirteenth year. Although, what could be worse?

Go and jump in the lake, I added.

THE PARTS ARE AS IMPORTANT AS THE WHOLE 4

The young blond man dropped the puzzle on my plate. Somewhere in the depths of the room, a coffee cup clinked on a saucer. The paper fluttered. As it landed, a blob of yoghurt claimed it with a hug of grease. In the silence, with all eyes upon me, I was tempted to giggle, the giggle rose in my chest and became a shudder. I found my voice.

All you've given me is arithmetic. It doesn't have any new possibilities, I said into the silence of the room.

Can't you do it? taunted the young blond man amongst his flurry of translators.

My mind caught on details again. It insisted I notice that the drips from the honey had spread across the white laminex table. I took a serviette and wiped the honey up, as if the sheen of the tabletop was all that mattered.

It's not what mathematics is about, I objected. All that's needed is a numerical answer.

I heard the inward breath of Clarke, Adele, Paul. Even the two maids behind the counter had paused. The walls of the dining room seemed to close in, watching.

Well? asked the young man among his translators. I looked back to the puzzle. I saw the way his biro had dropped blue ink in a blot. Perhaps I twitched, scratched, rubbed my nose, one of those gestures you do when you've become your thought, when you do something physical because in fact your body has paled into the dwindling distance.

She's giving up, said the young man's voice.

I looked for his face in the room, but the only image in front of my eyes was my mother. She was a real mathematician. Would she have done a puzzle like this, or refused?

I could've done this when I was a child. If I do it now you'll say I'm not a real mathematician, I said. If I don't do it, you'll say the same.

You had twenty-five seconds and you've used up twelve in argument, said the young man.

I noticed the yoghurt stain spreading like a spurt of laughter across the page. It made me want to laugh again. So I went into the silence of the answer, it came to me and went away. Knowing has always come and gone for me, as quietly as water. Sometimes I'd be flooded by it, then it would recede. So I'd stop, mid-sentence, stranded. I feared these recedings of understanding. On my own, it didn't matter, the way knowing ebbs away. It comes back.

Then the answer was there, as if it always had been, the

way my mother's conjecture had been after all that work. The mind turns, and sees it. If I turned at the right moment, why couldn't I see the answer to anything, to my mother, to my brother. But I didn't ever see those answers. All I can know, all I'll ever know, is mathematics.

Fifteen seconds, said the young blond man.

I'll check the answer, just in case, I thought. I didn't want to make a clerical mistake before these derisive eyes.

Twenty seconds, said the young man.

My voice when I gave the answer quivered like a bird trapped in that fierce room. A bird longing to whisk out the window and be gone.

Frances, called Adele. Frances—

Her voice was lost in cries: She should be in a circus. She could double up as a bearded lady.

Do you feel like truanting now? I asked Clarke.

As I walked out, I saw that crusts of Adele's toast tangled in Paul's sweaty hair.

She only did a sum, he was saying. That's nothing. She said so herself. She may still be an imposter.

Frances, said Adele, ignoring him. I was trying to tell you that my lens cap was stuck on. Could you do another sum now I've got the bloody thing off?

My seventh letter

My house

Dear Mum,
I'll tell you everything, so what, you'll never read it. Jim came here. For once he didn't say I was doing fine, gee willikins.

214

There were three days of dishes in the sink, dirty nappies on the floor, the drains had blocked and gone smelly and the bath was full of washing. It's because I'm so worried about Zoe. She's achingly thin.

She sleeps so much, too much. I can't bear to work when she sleeps now, I can't bear to think of anything but her thinness. I sit and stare at her thinness while she sleeps. I think it's because she knows intuitively about my plans to be a great something and she's trying to starve herself to death so she won't be in my way. She's such a dear little baby, she'd do that for me.

That's impossible, Jim said. He'd been here five minutes and he was an expert.

But babies know what proper mothers are supposed to be like, she knows they do what I can't do, she knows they give themselves utterly.

The way Grandma Juanita gave up her mathematics for Matti.

I came across her diary. Its dust made me sneeze. The edges were crumbling into powder. I don't know what made me open it. I'd never been curious about that horrible old woman. But Zoe made an interested noise in my arms. Was that why? Because of Zoe?

I didn't know you had a brother. My uncle Matt. What was he like? I wish you'd told me about it. About her. About him.

Might he have been my friend?

Though I still think she's a bitch. But maybe she wasn't always. Maybe losing mathematics did it to her. Finish my work, my son, she wrote. Find my conjecture.

It drove me to such crazy sadness, I tell you what I did. I wrapped up Zoe in her warmest clothes and put her in her little sling and walked down our track to the cliff. Everything in the bush caught at my heavy heart, my heart was so swollen with sadness there was scarcely room to breathe.

I got to my favourite clearing. It's near the edge of the cliff and the wind had come up and blown away all the leaves. The ground was grey. Steel grey. I put Zoe down, and found her a fern to play with. And just as I was bending over her, a bird fluttered its wings in a nearby tree or maybe my heart and then it mounted into the

sky and suddenly because of that bird I grabbed my baby. I held
her out. I held her above the miles of silence below.

Get out of my life. You chose to come into it. Now choose to
leave. Go on. Fly.

And you know what she did?

She laughed at me.

My laughing, wonderful baby.

You can have me utterly, my baby. I'm yours. I'll abandon what
I wanted to do. Just like Grandma did. I can't live without my
writing, I can't breathe without my writing, but I'll do it, my love,
my love, my love.

She turned her head, gazed at a row of ants mounting the log,
and yawned. Her carelessness crumbled me. I was on my knees on
the grey ground, I crawled on the grey ground in my pain, I was
moaning like wind rushing through empty spaces, like a wild
animal who's lost her child.

But I had my child, who was yawning.

I rocked myself back and forward on my knees as if someone
else was rocking me, you perhaps, if only it was you, Mum. The
empty sling for the baby was still tied to my chest, and it swept
the grey dirt into little hills.

But when I got back to the house, Jim was there. He said it was
just a matter of managing time better. He's visited us three times
and he said I just needed a few hours with the baby, and then a
few hours with my writing.

I started to scream. I screamed myself hoarse. It was like
childbirth again. I don't know what I said. I think I swore at him a
lot. And then I found myself saying:

How would you know? You're not a mother! It's not just a matter
of allocating time. It may be for a man. But it's not for a woman.
For a woman it's about the allocation of the soul.

I walked back to the cliff alone. I hurled my new manuscript
over it, and my book of sketches. That's finished. So's my life.

Hypatia

THE MICROBE'S DILEMMA

Just before she died, my mother told me about this part of her love affair with Clarke. I suppose she thought I'd reached some age of understanding. She spoke of him with such gentleness in her withered face that she must've always kept him in her heart. While she was telling me, I could suddenly see the beauty she never knew she had.

Clarke didn't seem as fascinated by the way numbers work as my mother was, or as Ramanujan was. As G.H.Hardy (Ramanujan's discoverer) wrote:

'I remember going to see him [Ramanujan] when he was lying ill at Putney. I had ridden in taxi-cab No. 1729, and remarked that the number seemed to me rather a dull one, and that I hoped it was not an unfavourable omen. "No", he replied, "it is a very interesting number: it is the smallest number expressible as a sum of two cubes in two different ways." '

Perhaps you would like me to explain about prime numbers. This is how my mother explained it to me. A prime number is a number which can only be divided by itself and the number one. Two thousand years ago, Euclid proved that there are infinitely many primes, but the problem is that they are, as my mother said, perversely and unpredictably scattered amongst the whole numbers. Many questions about prime numbers are still impossible to answer. No one has found a general formula to generate prime numbers, no one knows how far it is between one prime number and the next. Sometimes tantalising patterns show up. For example, 31, 331, 3331, 33331, 333331, 3333331, 33333331 are primes. But 333333331 isn't! Many mathematicians, amateur and professional, have claimed to find a magic formula for finding patterns and trends in primes but these have always turned out to be false, or, at best, a disguised version of the ancient sieve of Eratosthenes of Cyrene in the third century BC. This is how my mother explained his sieve: to find prime numbers of less than 100, you write down all the numbers from 2 to 100. You circle 2

and eliminate all multiples of 2. Then you circle 3 and eliminate
all multiples of 3. 4 is already eliminated. 5 is the next unmarked
number. Then there's 7, then 11, then 13, 17, 19, 23, 29, 31,
37. I'm getting bored. Apparently the sieve of Eratosthenes
catches 25 numbers, all the primes less than 100.

They're baffling. Computer use has increased specific knowledge
about prime numbers, but after centuries of work, mathematicians
still know very little about them.

No one has counted up to the end of the real numbers yet. Do
we know much about anything?
Hypatia

We ran down the stairs to beat the lift, Clarke and I, laughing
like schoolchildren. With him, I was always light and full of
joy as a child. At least, that's the way it seems now. Until, of
course, I showed him my mathematics. But I'm jumping
ahead.

In the street, tourist buses pumped blue fumes, trucks
ground past so loudly they almost crunched our bones, shop-
pers dodged us impatiently on narrow broken footpaths, a fleet
of motorbikes and an ambulance roared by. But Clarke twirled
on his heels in pleasure.

It's much more peaceful out here, he shouted.

I wanted to twirl with him but he would've heard my
bones creak. Instead, I shaded my eyes against the penetrating
light.

Shall we do some sightseeing? I shouted.

Sightseeing? It was the first time he'd frowned at me. He
began to twirl again.

A set of buildings in one country is only mildly different
from a set of buildings in another, he shouted as he turned.

What about the Parthenon? I shouted.

That's just the geometry of old men, he shouted.

I could've hugged him in the street with the light that bounced off his face and illuminated me so briefly.

Where do you go in the daytime when you truant? I shouted rather breathlessly. At any moment I feared he'd suggest we go past the nightclub in case her smell is there amongst the tawdry daytime dust.

He steadied himself from his last twirl.

On buses, he shouted.

He gazed down the street, shading his eyes from the sun too.

There's one, he shouted, look, down at the intersection. What's its number?

But we don't know where it's going to, I said, not moving.

Going to? he asked. He was turning to run, turning back to me. In his sunglasses I saw I was a woman struggling against her wrinkles. The wrinkles made me pompous.

People usually catch buses to somewhere, I shouted. There's usually the implication of a destination.

You're missing the point, he shouted. When I get a bus, I don't want to make a choice, to intervene.

There was such prodigality in his rosily rounded cheeks. I heard the years yawn between us, an irreducible chasm.

You must be very bored by a world conference on hyper-squares, I said. To spend days riding on any old bus.

I only catch buses with interesting numbers, he explained. Here's a bus, look—

He stared at a bus passing by. 323, he read. That might be a prime number.

It's the sixteenth, seventeenth and eighteenth expansion of pi, I said.

I heard him catch his breath, and my heart filled, to think I impressed him.

Sooner or later there'd be a bus number that was a sequence

in the decimal expansion of some irrational number, I said modestly. It just happened to be me who saw it.

Why have you memorised the decimal places of pi? he asked.

I was about to tell him I learned them to the twentieth place in my childhood but he added: Why would a mathematician bother?

So I blurred my indrawn breath with a cough because probably only amateurs learned pi expansions to the twentieth place in childhood.

Here's another bus, he said. 799. Let me think—that could be a prime number.

No it isn't, I said. But its reverse 997 is and that's the biggest prime number of three digits.

Without you, I must've missed some interesting buses, he said.

I wanted to be fun to be with.

There's a 991, I shouted. That's a prime in both directions, you know, 199, and look, a 389 and that's also a prime both ways. Do you think someone like us has numbered these buses for fun?

He was licking disappointment off his lips. His voice was rather thin when he spoke.

They're right. You could be in a circus, he said.

It doesn't mean that I'm not a real mathematician, I said angrily.

I began walking ahead of him down the street.

If you stick with number games, he called after me,

they won't take you seriously.

He caught up to me, conciliatory.

You're unnerving, he said.

When I breathed out, it was as if I was telling a secret he didn't know.

You're so young you think you'll live for always, I said.

I was hoping he couldn't hear, I was hoping my voice was sliding under the ululating of a police car. Because the first time you admit to anyone how much of life you've lived, you're almost transparent with death.

We could go to a church, he said.

But in the church, he drew away from me again.

You're a believer? I whispered under a ceiling silvered over with stars. He lit candles with such ease.

Three candles? I asked.

My heart sank.

Who's the third candle for?

One for me, one for you and one for your new sort of numbers, he said.

My work's candle slanted towards the other flames and leaped alight. He nuzzled its flare into a tray of sand.

It might all be a simulation, I said.

I gazed into the depth of the church, how silent it was.

This? he asked.

No, I said. Everything. A giant simulation game. If it was, it'd account for the way everything is incomplete.

I turned around. Where before there seemed only shadowy corners, a woman was coming, backing out of the church, heels clipping, skirt swishing, genuflecting. She allowed herself to glance at us as she passed, lips pursed in prayer.

In subatomic physics, I said, sometimes the answer about a particle's position can only be decided when the question's asked.

Do you mean if? Clarke asked.

Maybe, I said, to be agreeable.

Under his long lashed eyelids, I couldn't see his eyes.

I might try to get in contact with the Giant Simulator, he

said. He knelt suddenly on the cold marble expanse. He shut
his eyes, and I knelt to be close to him, to his trembling lips.
I shut my eyes because he did. His eyelashes rested so thickly
on his cheekbones. I waited in the marble stillness with the
wax popping and hissing on the golden candles, and I worried
if arthritis comes on suddenly when the legs get cold.

Clarke opened his eyes as unexpectedly as he closed them.
I traced a streak of blue on the white marble floor, meandering
like one of the veins on the inside of his arm.

We're like microbes, I said, we're in the same dilemma as
microbes might be, trying to wave to the person looking
down the microscope.

He stood up and went out. As he opened the door, the spear
of sudden sunshine struck me. Then I was alone in that dark
vaulted space gaudy with stars. The candles plopped. It was
the candle he lit for my work that had gone out.

So we looked at buildings only mildly different from those in
our own country and we sat in a hot but shady park to watch
a turtle twitch its eyelids, and all the time the moon watched
us from the sky, pale as a hope in a long afternoon that Clarke
would be mine tonight to keep out the despair just for a
moment, because a moment can be held in the hand like a
moth, despite its dusty fluttering. I tried on a fisherman's hat
in a tiny dark shop with white boxes stuccoed with sooty
fingerprints and piled up to the ceiling. Then I put it on his
head for the pleasure of moving my hand inside the lushness
of his hair, and I brushed his face with my fingers, to feel his
smooth unknown boy's skin, I was like a swimmer standing
at the curving edge of an ocean, scarcely able to speak because
of the green moving pleasure of the depths of water around
me. We ate dinner in an open-air cafe and afterwards the
waiter brought three red peaches on a green plate, the water

from a recent washing still streaking their white down, catching in it like tears. The warm air seemed full of conversations I didn't know how to begin, so we went to the nightclub, because that's why he'd been waiting for the day to end.

That night she was dressed in the absurdity of green feathers, shrieking like gaudy birds from her arms, her buttocks, the back of her head.

We blinked in the doorway, blinded by the sudden dark and her feathers. The feathers made Clarke and I conspirators. Clarke made a face at me and I copied it. Our lips turned down in the same derisive line.

But in the darkness, I crashed against chairs. Before we'd reached a table I saw that under the gold spotlight her body had a sheen and sunshine that said what I believed as a child, that nothing else would ever matter but beauty. Not talk, not numbers, not God. I longed for her body, to share it with Clarke. I'd have swooned to watch Clarke hold the amber tumble of her breasts in his hand, his hand stroking again and again to stroke the thrust of her buttocks in wonder that under the pressure of touch, her golden body didn't change, that it was irrefutable. In the dark I was panting to be there when his tongue moved over the indentation in the small of her delicate back, to streak with his saliva the flow of flesh from her knee to the dark secret hair of her thighs. I'd have caressed her thighs as they curved into him, like a curving against the glowing perimeter of the earth. And then I was hot with anger that in the one life I'd been given, I was never beautiful, when I could so easily have been, nose just a millimetre shorter, eyes just two more millimetres apart, my skin coloured by my mother's genes, it was so near, my beauty.

The feathers are absurd, I whispered, my voice a mean thread of spittle on the white tablecloth. But it was the feathers that set her free, she belonged so little to their absurdity, she even danced clumsily, a trembling foot here, a heavy landing there, but it didn't matter, we didn't look at the mere gymnastics of her dance, we looked at the space her body took up. Her body was so intimately bare, she set up a throbbing for possession in us all, I could see it flickering like a dream over every man and woman in the room, the dream that in sexual beauty is all that's marvellous after all, the dream that only in desire can we have anything that's true.

Clarke creaked the spindly chair as he sat down. He had forgotten me. Even as my bones creaked, he did not turn around. I was, after all, a plain-faced middle-aged woman. All I had that was sumptuous were some geometrical devices and the first of a new kind of number.

And so I dreamed another daydream, as I leaned my elbows on the table, taking my space. Clarke and I would be lying in the room where love can happen, with the white-framed windows opening on to blue light. We'd have just made love. We'd be exhausted, and only our feet would move on the sheets, a movement that wasn't even a whisper. We'd be scarcely able to talk but talk would be spilling out of our eyes, like tears. He'd be so close to me, he'd be out of focus, I'd have to move my head away on the pillow to see his face. He'd be smiling, the ends of his lips lifting his cheeks. There'd be a page somewhere, under the bed perhaps, or nearby on a table, these details were on the fading edge of the daydream. The paper would rustle in the breeze from the window, that's why I'd notice it. And there'd be a pencil too, near the paper. I'd roll over, reach down, pick them up, turn on my chest, and write.

He'd say: What are you doing, my love?

I'd say: It's the first of my new numbers. Soon I'll get to the second.

He'd look over my shoulder. There'd be a long moment. He'd throw himself on his back.

He'd say: It's beautiful. Beyond this world.

I'd say: But is it plausible? Is it possible?

He'd say: What's important is that it's paradise, and that I'm in it with you.

Then I'd turn in the bed, and he'd turn, our eyes so close we'd barely be able to see each other, our bodies touching at my breasts, our thighs, our feet. He'd reach down and slide his penis slowly into me, and I'd utterly surround his soft, long, sweet, slow slide, I'd enclose him.

Tell me, he'd whisper, tell me about your three hundred and fifteen pages of work and your mother's conjecture. Tell me. Tell me about your journey from one to the other. So I know who you are.

Perhaps you would like to meet Frieda, Clarke suggested when the house lights came on and we could see the stains on the tablecloth and the scuffs on the floor. We found a waiter whose shirt had circles of damp under his arms and spreading across his chest. Soon they'd intersect. He told us that the live acts had gone home, just now in a taxi, and there would be recorded music for dancing as soon as it could be arranged, for the unexpected departure of the live acts had left the night-club in the lurch.

Gone? Both of them? In the same taxi? Clarke asked, broken.

As we left I saw that the globes in the neon letters of Destruction had all popped, so it was just a grey plastic scribble against a dusty wall. Above my head, a bird in a cage hooked to an open shutter sang out like a warning.

I'm living out my mother's dreams, I said.

225

He didn't ask me what I meant, even though we were standing under a blue streetlight that seemed to take our flesh away so we were only bones.

Funny the things that get said at night, was all he said.

We hurried to catch the traffic lights. We were passing an unfinished house with a second storey that was still only a thought with wires sticking out and already rusting, when he said:

It must be wonderful to be a woman. To have breasts that balloon into a man's hands.

I flickered with hope that he desired me.

Like hers, he said. It's me who should be her lover.

My mouth seemed suddenly loose as it is now that I'm very old. But at that moment, loss made me an ancient crone. I turned my face so he wouldn't notice my lips' looseness. I hid my mouth behind my hand and tried to deflate its swollen sadness. It was one of those preposterous moments when you own love like no one has ever owned it before because you learned it while you watched your mother's breasts. Which once seemed beautiful beyond compare.

He slipped his arm in mine as we walked and I had to content myself with that. When we broke apart to negotiate traffic there was a band of his sweat on my arm. I remember I couldn't bear to wipe it off for days.

At the hotel, he found a bottle of cold wine in his fridge and brought it to my room. We stood at my door while he poured me a glass. I spilled a drop that became a stain on my perfect carpet. We kissed goodnight at the doorway, on the lips, like friends might, except that the texture of dry lips clung, and the kiss deepened.

You won't sleep in the heat, he said. Perhaps I should stay.

No, I sighed.

Perhaps it's a good time to look at your work, he said.

He put the bottle of wine in my fridge. Then he sat on my bed next to me, leafing at last through my pages. The silence deepened, like our kiss. I waited for the pages to curve around his legs, like my mother's work curved around the crossed leg of her lover. The pages stayed stiff.

What do you think? I asked too soon.

He ignored me. I looked out the window as if I'd never seen the view before.

Interesting, he said after a while.

That's the kiss of death, I said. When a reader says interesting.

The traffic waited at the traffic lights.

Very interesting, he said when the lights had turned green, and buses were honking.

At the bottom of a page, he said at last:

The way you use every trick in the book to come up with—

he pointed to the bottom line—

something . . .

His voice trailed off.

What? I asked. Interesting?

. . . no one could've predicted. You're uncanny.

At the end of another page, he said:

You do surprising re-arrangements . . .

Yes? I couldn't stop myself from asking.

And this expansion . . . he said.

Yes?

It's so . . . he said.

Interesting? I asked.

So . . .

He turned a chunk of pages at once, and read again.

Disturbing, he said.

There was a long silence. The traffic lights changed many times. The street cleared of cars. At last Clarke put down my work.

Well? I asked.

I can't keep going, he said.

A new group of cars moved uneasily down the street.

If I kept looking at this, he said, I might get involved. I might never want to go back to my own mathematics. It may seem so dull.

We both wiped sweat from our upper lips.

He closed the folder. He put it on the bed. On the expanse of white sheets, he abandoned it.

I was born at the wrong time, he said.

I laid my hand on his.

Our age difference doesn't matter, I said. At least, not for a few years.

He shook my hand away.

I mean, I was born at the wrong end of the patriarchy, he said. The patriarchy has existed for three thousand years, that's a long time in history, nothing in the history of the world of course, but a long time for humans. It's so long, it could've waited a little longer to end. It could've waited until after my lifetime. It could've waited for me.

He paused.

For us.

For us? I repeated.

Don't you understand? he said. Do I have to spell it out? I can't get involved with someone who's a genius. Where would that leave me?

He went out the door so sadly.

Against my rectangle of window, the hot night slunk like a beaten animal. If I squinted, I could see the shapes of stars the way children draw them, cut out and pasted over the orange sky. I remembered then my daughter's letters, but I was too sad to read them.

Although Frances was an autodidact, I assume that she'd read Roger Penrose, who said that a beautiful idea has a much greater chance of being a correct idea than an ugly one. For example, Dirac, who worked out the equation for the electron, felt that his success was due to his keen sense of beauty. Inspiration seems connected with a sense of beauty. The rigorous arguments come only afterwards.

It was my mother who told me that when Hardy first saw the mathematical discoveries posted to him by the then unknown Ramanujan, he said: 'They must be true because if they were not true, no one would have had the imagination to invent them'.

So my mother must've hoped Clarke would experience a frisson of sensual and intellectual pleasure when he looked at her work. Her problem was getting him to look at it.
Hypatia

FOR THE SAKE OF IMMORTALITY 1

Perhaps minutes later, perhaps hours, I woke to a knock at the door. I switched on my bed light and swung my legs reluctantly out of bed. I moved across the smooth nap of my carpet tentatively. But at the door, I was adamant.

Go away, I said into the keyhole. There's nothing more to be said.

I heard the eyeless corridor behind him, the rows of bedroom doors shut on sleeping people. I held my breath to catch the creak of floorboards as he left.

It's me, said Adele's voice.

So I opened the door.

I'm sorry, she said. I didn't think you'd be sleeping in this heat. She paused. Her cheeks were strained, the muscles in them working.

It's about Paul, she said. And you.

All over her face, shadows played.

Can I come in? she asked.

I stood aside for her, and shut the door.

Would you have something to drink? she asked.

I went to the fridge, and I heard the silence of the street beyond the windows, that short space as one day ends and the next begins, like the stillness in the centre of a dance. I wanted to throw open the window to be part of that fleeting stillness, to be there, not here. In fifteen minutes or so, a drunken tourist would stumble and shout, or a fleet of buses would arrive from the airport, and behind them, tomorrow would roar down the street.

Paul's gone crazy, she said.

I reached for the noises of comfort, the flabby noises like cushions around the head and under the bones of elbows. To fill in the spaces, to ease one moment into the next, to pretend that there are no precipices.

No one's at their best in the heat, I said.

Adele blinked away my comforting.

He's afraid that these people who've funded the conference will sue him, she said.

She didn't take the wine to her mouth. My legs were tired, I wondered if I should sit on the arm of the chair she was in, but that would be presumptuous. I sat on the bed.

Yes, I said.

Because he thinks the media will pay a lot of attention to you, she said.

Yes, I said.

And worse to him than getting sued and losing money is—

she rolled words in her mouth to choose one—he doesn't want to look a fool.

He doesn't want to look a fool, I said.

Women always nod solemnly about the dignity of men.

He's hired an international lawyer, she said. He says the man's a real high-flyer, someone topnotch. To deal with you. The man's due to arrive tomorrow.

I heard the fleet of tourist buses rumble up the road, the squeak of doors opening, the disgorging of passengers. I heard the cacophany of languages float in the warm air.

It's tomorrow already, I said.

Would you mind, I asked, if I get right into bed?

You could just do what he wants, she said. Go along with things.

She passed her hand in thought across her eyelids. Her fingers dragged the flesh.

Many of us do, she added.

I got under the sheet and sat with my back against the bedhead. I slipped down in the bed, beyond politeness.

There's not much to grill me about, I said, the sheet muffling my voice.

She came over, putting her glass down on the way. She stood beside the bed. For a second I thought she was going to tuck me in.

Your mother must think you're a wonderful daughter, she said.

She moved the sheet, touching its fold, perhaps just to hear me more clearly. Her hand collided briefly with my face. My skin reached out to that tiny comfort, my soul perhaps, because the soul is peremptory, grasping, surging always in hope, as foolishly pleased as a child.

To someone else, I said, we could look like figures in a tableau. We could look as if we go back a long way. Our movements, the folds of the sheet, the skin stretched between your fingers, the bedroom drained of colour, all these could seem portentous. It could be a painting called Tryst Between Sisters: A Warning at Midnight.

Her hand still grasped a tiny fold of sheet.

Reality ought to live up to illusions, she said.

She sat on my bed. She patted my legs.

What did you expect? she asked. From all this? Fame?

I propped my head on my arm, so that it was easier to talk with only the night in front of us both. I sighed for all I want, how it lies only under the surface, emerging in flickerings, in the slant of a soothing voice, or after pressure from a hand.

I want to end something, I said. To begin something. The usual things.

There was a puff of cold air that frilled her hair around her face. The air-conditioning came back on. I got out of bed and offered her more wine from my fridge as a celebration. We took turns to sip from the glass, passing it to each other. It was then that she said what she'd really come for.

Have you thought, she said, that you might not be able to begin again? That there in fact might be no beginnings, that the idea of a beginning might be another illusion?

She sighed wistfully.

That all that's possible are tiny shifts?

Halfway down the glass, she said: If mathematics hints at who we are—

She was spreading her arms, slopping wine:

—what's the point? You lot haven't got any idea what it's saying.

When she'd drained the glass, she said:

I read Frege at Lost Property. It had been on the train to Ipswich. Frege says that the straight line connecting two points is there before we draw it, as if we're tracing it. Do you think

I might've got that map on my legs wrong? Mightn't it have been a map at all?

I nudged her gently out my door.

Frege, you remember, is where I began my story all that time ago, and yet here we are, somewhere in the middle. She might've been right, that there are no beginnings possible at all.

Some time later, I woke. The air-conditioning had been working so hard the room was freezing. My body was crusted over with cold. It made me aware that my skin is a shell, only a shell. I found a blanket in the wardrobe and fell asleep again and dreamed that I was only a pale shellfish rocking in a purple sea.

A loud rapping on my door invaded my dreams. It was too heavy for Adele, too certain for Clarke. It had the voluptuousness of indignation. It could've splintered wood. I opened the door mid-knock. Paul was there, a strand of sweaty hair swinging on his forehead.

Take your time, why don't you, he shouted without a greeting.

I was asleep, I said.

A waiter peered down the corridor at us, the woman in a sleep-crumpled nightgown and the roaring man.

I didn't bring you across the world to sleep, he said.

I'm here for my mother's work, I said.

You'll come up for a discussion about your theories in twenty minutes, or you won't be here at all, young lady, he said.

He turned on his heels, hair flying, the corners of his mouth still bubbling with saliva.

Up? I asked. Up where?

The roof garden, he shouted.

I've heard that's your office, I said.

He slammed the door. I sat down on my bed and listened to his heavy plodding down the corridor. I ran through the possibilities of clean clothes in my bag. There weren't any. Unless I wore one of Clare's resplendent dresses. But they'd make me visible, and I didn't want to be visible. I'd been wearing the same cream skirt and shirt since I got here. So I dressed in my crumpled clothes.

But I couldn't deny a spurt of happiness.

He'd called me young lady.

It was exactly twenty minutes since I'd spoken to Paul, but he wasn't there. Though it wasn't yet half past eight, the sun was already hot. The umbrella, sticking up through a hole in the table top, refused to tip over and make a larger circle of shade. After another seven minutes, a man appeared at the doorway, one of the academic mathematicians who sat at the centre table of the dining room at every meal, the neighbour of the man with the bow tie. I remembered my first day, how I expected him to welcome me. He recognised me by a slight tip of his head at my chair. He joined my table, but sat at the far end. He tried to slant the umbrella for more shade.

A basic design fault, he said aloud when it refused him.

We haven't met, I said brightly.

His eyes leaped to some point in the sky.

Hello, he said.

I turned, expecting from the direction of his eyes that Paul had arrived. There was no one there.

I turned back.

I'm Frances Montrose, I said.

He tipped his head again, smiling at a nearby post. Then he folded his hands over his stomach and shut his eyes.

I tried again.

I don't know your name, I said.

He opened his eyes, fished in his shirt pocket, found a business card and tossed it on the table.

Don't call me, I'll call you, he said, it seemed to another chair. He wheezed with laughter and shut his eyes again. I examined the cement mixer on the roof next door, anything rather than look at his card.

And then I looked under the bed

Every day I still searched with stealth through the shadowy house my father built. Two cups washed more recently than the others on the washing up rack. A throbbing set up between my legs. Milk decanted into a jug in the fridge, when we always used milk straight out of the bottle. The remains of jam spooned into a dish, when we always ate jam straight out of the tin. The throbbing between my legs had become a honey-warm twitching deep in my belly. The chairs had been placed more conversationally than they were this morning. The toilet seat had been left up, the way a man leaves it, yet my father and my brother had been out all day. There was the impression of two heads on my father's pillow. Now desire in me was as clear as a shout. Here was a pubic hair like a question mark on the wet surface of the soap.

On days when there were many clues, I lay wetly on my bed groaning to be her with him. If there was a step in the hall, I reached for a book.

I'm working, I'd say to Matti.

Your face is all red. He'd stand smirking before he walked away.

It always is, I'd shout to his back.

I wanted her to tell him everything, tell him all her secrets, all the spidery corners. I wanted him to open all the doors my father hadn't opened. I wanted him to know her utterly, I wanted him to hold her so closely she cried out Daddy.

In my dreams I stumbled through the house examining floorboards, clutching at dust balls, discovering footprints. And every evening at dusk, as my mother watered the flowers in the garden, I searched for an easing in her mouth gentler than the grey light in the sky.

But knowledge shudders, becomes its own question.

My mother was never a good housewife. She couldn't manage a chook shed, I heard Bev Roberts say one day as I ran in for the Arrowroot biscuits Mum had forgotten to buy.

Bev Roberts saw me listening, but that made her louder.

She leaves the washing out at night in the mist, she said. And she never pegs things on the seams, she just stretches them out like billyo. See, she's ruined that jumper you've got on. Where her mind is, I don't know. And I don't know how your sweet father copes, she added.

Dad's not complaining, I said.

The muscles in Bev Roberts' face lumped with greed. I flashed with hate for Bev Roberts' face muscles.

As a matter of fact, he's wildly in love with her, I claimed.

But Bev Roberts was right. My mother had always left tea cups in the sink, pools of water in basins. She always forgot to clean up after she'd peeled potatoes. She wasn't a person to clean her own pubic hairs off the soap, she wouldn't have noticed. She threw blankets over the bed so carelessly when she made it that my father often lost his bedsocks. He searched for them angrily in the rumples she hadn't smoothed out. Her mind, as Bev Roberts said, was somewhere else. A clue, in the end, may mean nothing at all.

And so I came upon the notes.

He'd brought them, the sixteen years of mathematical knowledge that my mother had lost since her marriage to Dad. Under her side of the bed, on the floor, they rose irrefutable, a tower of white paper. PURE MATHS THREE, I read, in the black formal letters of type, notes he would have made for his lectures.

I let the eiderdown fall back into place and got off my knees. Out her window there was a sunset billowing the evening sky with pink. In the harsher light of a kitchen dinner afterwards, my mother wondered why I smiled.

I checked the notes every day, that tower of white. Then knowledge shuddered again, became another question. What if he'd left them there, abandoned, forgotten? What if they weren't reading them at all?

I pulled the pile out and examined them for a clue that they'd recently been touched. A lack of dust, a flake of silky skin. I turned over the page.

Down the margins of many pages, on top and down the bottom and sometimes in flurries between lines was the handwriting of my mother. I knew her handwriting, I'd seen it all my life, the wispy wistful writing of someone blown along in a gale, tendrils attempting to escape but complying. I turned the pages this way and that to read her writing. She'd written theorems, dozens of them, jammed together and whirling into each other, arguing, refuting, sometimes they were piled on top of each other, like someone racing up a mountain. Here with lines so impetuous they streaked across the page and over its edge, she'd crossed out his typed conclusion and written hers instead. And then rethought, or perhaps he'd argued, and she'd seen new possibilities and changed her mind and ticked it. And here, she'd crossed him out again, and underlined her argument. Her scarlet ink played with ideas. He'd become her student.

On the floor beside the notes was her fountain pen. I picked it up, took off its lid and touched its golden nib. A dribble of scarlet stained my finger like blood.

I pushed back the notes, and dropped the eiderdown. It fell around their words like a curtain. I stood at her window to cool my hot face. The scarlet arguments of my mother to her lover were like a gaze of desire that burns the soul of the onlooker.

For a few days I didn't dare lift the eiderdown again. I confined my scrutiny to the placement of chairs, teacups and drips on the sink. The house echoed with my disconsolate footsteps. To be sure he'd visited, there was only one method. I'd have to look under their bed.

He must've visited. The pages of the notes were turned back at the corner to page twenty-three. My mother's scarlet arguments taunted, amended, expanded, refuted, corrected.

My mother's voice rang through the house. I let the eiderdown drop. She was just going down to watch the sun set, did Matti want to come?

There was no answer from his room. She walked often in the evening those days, treading the dust lightly on the road. She was no longer afraid to be seen. The presence of her lover had given her courage. I watched her swaying walk. I lifted the eiderdown again, took out the top notes and sat down on the bed. Most of it was symbols, to me a foreign language. I pretended to be him. I read aloud the parts I could. My voice stumbled. But the house curved around my voice, and the bush curved around the house with bird calls and insects settling for the night. Somewhere there was a roar of music from Matti's radio, somewhere my father swept sawdust, somewhere my mother walked easily along a road. But I was alone with the words of their love-making. The unreadable words of higher mathematics were as intoxicating as kisses on an outstretched throat. I read the way he must've read before he moaned love into her. Mathematics became a chant that dissolved all other sounds. And then I found my silent tongue between my thighs.

FOR THE SAKE OF IMMORTALITY 2

My mother's predicament at the conference made me think a great deal about the survival of ideas. My mother pointed out to me that the author Roger Penrose contested Paul's argument (she wasn't suggesting he was personally acquainted with Paul) that good ideas only survive in a competitive world because they come from the right people, or are aided by market forces. But he also disbelieves that 'superb theories could have arisen merely by some random natural selection of ideas leaving only the good ones as survivors. The good ones are simply much too good to be the survivors of ideas that have arisen in that random way.' He agreed with my mother (they weren't acquainted either) that 'there is still something mysterious about evolution, with its apparent "groping" towards some future purpose. Things at least seem to organise themselves somewhat better than they "ought" to.'
Hypatia

The lawyer leaned companionably across the table. His name was Themis, but he'd said to call him Uncle Tom.

Paul tells me you're from Sydney, he said confidentially. I love Sydney. The little white boats dancing on the harbour. He danced his fingers in the air to show me.

I have many relatives in beautiful Sydney, he added. Three sisters. All with their own businesses.

I'd like it to be clear, said the Professor to the chair, that my seminars call me so I have only thirteen minutes twelve seconds.

239

Everyone turned to look at the chair.

Why's he talking to the chair? demanded Paul.

In the silence he cleared his throat commandingly.

This might be a case of plagiarism, he said to Uncle Tom.

She doesn't look like a plagiariser, said Uncle Tom, looking from me to Paul. Just a nice middle-aged lady.

An eminent mathematician from her home city claims to have had the same idea, said Paul.

Uncle Tom smiled a comfortable smile.

Ideas fall around us like rain, he said. Different eyes may see the same rain.

Paul was blotting sweat from his forehead with a clump of handkerchief.

She claims it's her mother's idea. And she's on in five days, claiming sole credit in front of the world's press.

The Professor had opened his eyes.

The problem isn't just about authorship, he said.

His glance took in the chairs, tables, an empty glass on the railing. He chose to smile at the glass.

The problem is also the theorems. Only an outsider would steal these sorts of theorems.

He smiled at the chairs.

If someone could oblige with a paper and pencil, he told them.

In the business of Uncle Tom opening his briefcase and tearing paper and making pens work, he managed to say to me, One of my sisters is doing very well in Marrickville. Dresses. She'd have something for you—he pointed to my skirt and blouse—better than that.

The Professor was drawing a tree.

Uncle Tom studied Paul carefully.

You might do better, he said to Paul, to use that hanky differently.

This will make it clear, said the Professor, now drawing what seemed to be leaves of various shapes.

Use the hanky as a hat, Uncle Tom was advising Paul. I've read that foreigners with a lack of melanin—

OK, OK, shouted Paul. He straightened it out on the table and laid it across his head.

Not quite right, said Uncle Tom. He removed the handkerchief and folded it in half. The Professor drew leaves while Uncle Tom made Paul a hat.

Every minute, Professor Mitchell, I'm paying a lawyer for this stupidity, shouted Paul.

This will be better for you, Uncle Tom assured Paul. He put the handkerchief with knotted ends on Paul's head, and tipped his own head this way and that to admire the effect.

Mathematics is a tree, the Professor was saying. A mighty tree.

I thought of Clare. They must've read the same book.

The Professor smiled at Paul, then sighed deeply.

With many branches. Space forbade me.

A knotted end of handkerchief dipped in Paul's eye.

This is ridiculous, he shouted, and snatched the handkerchief off.

More and more branches of course as time goes by, the Professor said. He found me to smile at again before he drew wriggly lines radiating from the tree.

Geometry. Algebra. What have you. The tree gets bigger and bigger. Branch upon branch.

Heaven spare us from art, shouted Paul. He leaned over the table. Professor, if minutes matter—

Professor, shouted Paul.

But the Professor was drawing in more twigs. He smiled randomly at the flagpole.

New theories are created, he told it. New objects—of course

I mean mathematical objects—are created. New connections are made. New applications are considered.

This isn't relevant, shouted Paul.

Quite, said the Professor with a quick smile at the chair. Quite relevant.

He closed his eyes to shut out Paul.

Often a twig of mathematics seems to be dying, smiled the Professor at me. Then suddenly somebody discovers something extraordinary and the twig has a new bud. In Non-Reimannian Hypersquares, we are awaiting a new bud.

He shut his eyes. Silence settled on the group. I felt compelled to clarify.

Significant theorems, I said to Uncle Tom and Paul, can't be formulated by a person who isn't in the tree.

The model of a tree is of course imperfect, said the Professor. There are other models.

He began to draw a river. I could tell it was a river by the waves.

Can't you just ask her some questions, said Uncle Tom, to see if she knows her stuff?

They can't, groaned Paul. They say it'd take them months to learn her sort of mathematics. She uses strange backwaters no one's bothered about for sixty years. The hyper what's-it of fifty years ago.

The Professor ignored Paul.

She is capable of leaps, said the Professor.

He showed us what a leap is by drawing two dots on either side of the river, and joining them up.

She leaps to solve hazardous but unimportant numerical puzzles. In her own words, tricks.

My sisters were autodidacts, said Uncle Tom. What training need she have done?

The Professor was joining the river to the tree.

For those theorems, goodness knows, said the Professor. He was colouring in rocks on the side of the river, but he suddenly said: She's got the background of an amateur. In my university, she would've had to read sixty to eighty books for a PhD.

It's not so many, I said. Only about two shelvesful, if you imagine shelves about eight feet long. When I was growing up, I would've read a roomful.

Rooms come in many sizes, sighed Uncle Tom.

Jesus Christ, Paul exploded. Now we're going to talk about the size of rooms.

The room lined with books was five metres by four by four, I said.

Excluding furniture? asked Uncle Tom.

A copper, I said.

Uncle Tom and Paul looked at me. The Professor looked at the post.

And two laundry tubs, I added.

You should be taking notes, Paul said to Uncle Tom.

Uncle Tom nodded at him good-naturedly. We watched him write 'a copper'.

Why wasn't her background established at the start? he asked.

Our university was asked to judge the mathematics, said the Professor. Not her credentials. And I'd like it to be on record that personally I wouldn't like her mathematics, not from what I've heard of it. But I have a faculty to run. Boards to sit on. I couldn't read it. I must say, no one was keen. Even three pages from a crank is tough. Some of them sent in reams! One of them couldn't stop before page three hundred and fifteen!

That was, er, me,

I said but no one noticed.

I left the decision about this ill-advised competition to one of our junior tutors, said the Professor. He got excited about

243

her work I suppose because it was appropriate to the occasion.

He smiled nastily at his pen.

Vulgar.

Can we ask him about it? said Uncle Tom.

We sacked him, said the Professor. I understand he's gone to work in a video parlour.

At last we're getting somewhere, said Paul. You're saying there's something wrong with her work?

Wrong? The Professor smiled at a bird on top of the flagpole. Wrong? We're not discussing right and wrong, like priests.

The Professor picked up his pen again. We all waited for him to draw another part of the landscape, but he seemed to be doodling.

In a long proof like hers, value judgements can enter, he said. The authenticity of a proof isn't absolute, only probabilistic. If it had been known that these theorems came from an established mathematician, my junior wouldn't even have checked them. Symbols and operations don't have a precise meaning in mathematics, only a probabilistic one.

Wait a minute, said Paul. You mean you lot are only probably right. So you could all be up the creek?

A major blunder is made in mathematics every twenty years, the Professor agreed comfortably. He smiled at the Parthenon.

We live intimately with imperfect fidelity. But we are not in chaos. Experiments are repeatable, usage is self-correcting, and the universe is stable.

Paul was beginning to pant.

I think the Professor is saying, I told him and Uncle Tom, that my mother's work has made too large a shift.

The Professor nodded at a bird that had alighted on a chair arm.

New realisations in mathematics usually come in small shifts, he said. That's good, useful mathematics. What amateurs don't realise is that all deep theorems are false, and all true theorems are trivial. I haven't read her work, but given her training, her work will be idiosyncratic. I'm sure I can say that categorically. And therefore—

he smiled at me—

forgettable. So if she did steal it from our eminent friend, you will understand why he never published it. It's a mere doodle. A joke. Like—

he picked up his pen—

drawing a bird dropping under the mighty tree of mathematics.

Another word for vulgar could be spectacular, said Uncle Tom. Another word for idiosyncratic could be daring. Einstein's work was both.

You wouldn't call Einstein's work a bird dropping, said Paul.

Again, a problem of definition, sighed the Professor, looking at me. I don't think Einstein claimed to be a mathematician. He was a physicist maybe—that's not my area—but not a good mathematician.

He looked at my chair, to tell it: He just made connections that were staring other people in the face.

Some people might call that brilliant, said Uncle Tom.

And then he became famous because he happened to coincide with the needs of the publicity machines, said the Professor.

Aha! Just what I've been saying, shouted Paul at me.

Uncle Tom turned to me. Is there a document with this conjecture in your mother's handwriting? he said.

Professor Mitchell put down his pen and stood.

Excuse me, but my twig is calling, he said.

Surely you could find some document your mother wrote

when she was young and in fit mind? Uncle Tom asked me.

The only document is in my mind, I explained.

He patted my arm.

It's a nice story, he said. Almost a Greek legend. Here's the parent. Here's the child. The parent sees behind him, catching up with him, his mortality. He must share his thoughts before it's too late. He chooses the beloved child, who better? So the work is not mortal, but made immortal through the child.

I was aware of a huge heat thumping on my heart, into my blood. The shade of the umbrella had shrunk to a pinpoint. The heat is smothering me, I'm fighting it but I'm gasping. I take a deep breath, to ease my roaring blood.

It wasn't me she dictated it to, I told him, at least I thought I was speaking aloud. She didn't want me to be a mathematician. It was the last thing she wanted. She didn't want me to overtake her, she went to great lengths to stop me overtaking her. I'll withdraw, I added. I'll withdraw her work. So someone else can find her conjecture. The right person. Then they'll have a chance of becoming immortal.

MY EIGHTH LETTER

My house

Dear Mum,
Jim came back this time with a load of nappy pins. He talked on and on about how he chose them until I was getting wild, alright I might be a full-time mother but I think about other things! Having a baby isn't the same as having a lobotomy!

I screamed at him but he just bowed his head. When I was exhausted, he said: There's something out in the boot that you

246

might like. I went out to the boot and you know what? He'd found a track to the bottom of the cliff and he'd rescued my bits of paper and pieced them together and now I've got my manuscript back! My abandoned manuscript! And my sketchbook! He asked could he move in and share the baby with me.

Then he ruined the moment.

We could be a family, he said.

Families! How I hate families! I shouted for so long my hatred of families that the curry for lunch burnt. I had to find something else to eat while he sat with Zoe and watched TV, and then . . .

Her fingers were clamped on her rattle. Then she lifted it. I could see its weight was a surprise. Her wrist drooped a little but she kept on lifting it. Jim reached out for my hand. We didn't dare talk in case she stopped. She shook it. Once. Twice. It was like being in church. Tears began to roll down Jim's face. They rolled down mine too. She put the rattle down. Jim felt for my hand, and held it. His breath huffed. Then she lifted the rattle again and put it to her ear. We didn't dare turn our heads to look at each other, we didn't dare speak. She shook the rattle again, and laughed.

Afterwards I told Jim about it although he'd seen it all, and he told me. We lay on our bed to whisper while she slept.

Gee willikins, he whispered over and over again. The little kid thought.

He cried again, silently so he didn't wake her. I wiped away his tears with the bedcover, and he wiped away mine. In the folds of the velvet-fringed afternoon, we caressed each other in wonder that we've made a baby who picked up a rattle.

I think I'll let him share Grandma Juanita's house and the baby and work time. We might be able to find a new way to be a family. And maybe I'll find something I really want to do. Something I really want to write. Perhaps finding my destiny takes longer than I thought.

Hypatia

247

My suitcase was on the bed with Clare's bright dresses unpacked, flames of scarlet and gold licking the white room and laughing at my despair. There was a footstep outside on the corridor floor. The floorboards creaked badly in that hotel, they didn't properly allow for the expansion of the floorboards, I knew that because I was my father's daughter. My father would've had something to say about the way the door was hung. The other side of the frame would've given the room a sense of greater space. The skirting boards weren't snug against the wall. I tut-tutted over the waste of good wood, my lips making the same sound as his did, years ago. I was not a mathematician, just a handyman's daughter.

Suddenly Clarke poked his head around my door. I hadn't quite shut it, I couldn't quite shut out all my yearning. I quickly stuffed the bright dresses into the suitcase and pushed down the lid. I wouldn't want anyone thinking I'd assumed there'd be a ball.

But Clarke didn't notice my movement.

I thought I had all the time in the world with you, he said, staying at the door.

In the white afternoon light from my room, he seemed younger than before, so smooth his face was a stone. I looked down at my hands, and saw how their skin was crammed full of years.

Getting old probably happens faster than I know, he said as if he was reading my thoughts.

He pushed the door open and came across the room, stepping slowly as if in his head he was measuring time. He saw me watching him and laughed shyly because we were strangers. He reached the bed, its white chenille cover, the rows of upright tufts of cotton, and the roar of bright dresses spilling out of the suitcase. He flicked the tufts of the cover with his fingertips, then put his hands behind his back, a child determined to be honest. Outside the window, shadows of tree boughs swooped and swayed, dancing together and setting themselves free.

There's such hunger in me when we talk, he said.

His eyes were so round and soft.

And there it was again, the errant longing for him like a wildness I couldn't tame, that absurd sense that near him the air had been sharpened, I could feel its points like the tips of leaves. I was poked at and prodded by sexual longing and beyond that, the longing for acknowledgement.

Couldn't you stay? he asked. Stay and read your theorems out. By then things might look different.

You think they might? I whispered, partly for the sad pleasure of whispering to him. We spoke as quietly as if we were back in the candlelit church, talking in spite of the terror that might lurk behind the altar, a column of fire that could consume us or make us gods.

But you won't be here, I said. No one will.

I might truant, he whispered as softly as the air.

There was a pause. He was so close to me, his lips moving as if they're kissing. His leg touched mine, now his elbow, now his hand. It was almost as if his blood was flowing into me, knowing me, every nook and cranny of me, understanding me as no one ever had.

The air-conditioning surged suddenly through the ceiling vents. We both turned our faces to the ceiling. Adele's slip of paper near the window fluttered. We both put out our hands to it, to hold it down, the same action, mirroring each other. He saw its urgent writing and read it aloud.

The desire on one hand to go on and on, to lean towards infinity

On the other hand, to be caught, completed, with no more yearning.

What's this? he asked.

It's Adele's. I should've given it back to her, I said.

He read slowly, his mouth moving over the words, he took the thought into himself like my mother always did. Or at least, that's what I imagined. And in that moment my mind flowed over a thought, ebbed, flowed over it again, because of him or despite him, sometimes these distinctions are so difficult they don't matter.

Don't know what that's about, he said.

The thought came back, I held onto it before it receded.

It's about mathematics trying to trap infinity, I said.

His breath huffed. His breath was sweet, jaded, impatient. I floundered against the wall of his breath.

No one cares any more what mathematics is about, he said.

His eyes were flat. Were they flat before? I couldn't remember.

He sat on the bed.

It's an out-of-date question, he said. Anyway, it's irrelevant to a real mathematician. Mathematicians do math. The others talk about it.

He reached out, he dragged at me to sit with him on the bed, silently.

I resisted.

We try to trap infinity because we can't bear what's incomplete, I said slowly. We. I. I can't.

I stood staring down at him.

You'll never fit in if you don't stop talking like this, he said.

He was still patting the white bed beside him.

And it's about my mother. And me. She's always been mathematics to me, beautiful beyond compare, unbearably elusive, unbearably unknowable, I said, then petered out.

We fell into a silence while the shadows on the wall waved in great wild arcs.

Whose are these? he asked.

It took me a while to focus on his hands. He was caressing Clare's brilliant dresses with his child's hands. It took me a while to focus on his question.

A friend's, I said.

He was fingering the brocades, silks, taffetas.

Why haven't you worn them? he asked.

Why's that important? I asked.

He lifted up pink silk, and rubbed his smooth cheek against it. He was lost in the dream of the dress. It was no surprise when he said: I'd have fallen in love with you if you'd worn things like this. They make such promises.

I looked at his bent, smooth neck. For a moment, I was dizzy with memory. It was my mother's neck I was looking at. His hair grew out in whorls, like hers did. His hair was the texture of her hair, the colour of her hair.

In the lobby I turned a corner and ran into Jan Symonds, ringed by the sunlight outside, carrying a take-away coffee. Some of it spilled on her spotted green dress.

I'm so sorry—I began.

She said the words that were always told in the newspaper articles about me.

Frances Montrose! I've been sitting up there in my room reading frantically—

I wasn't watching where I was going, I interrupted. Forgive me.

But her voice went on.

I'm going back to that old math every one else ignored, she said. The math that was your starting point.

Coffee was trickling down her skirt onto the floor.

Would you like me to find a damp cloth? I asked.

It was brilliant, she said. The way you knew to start there. The way you followed that instinct. I'm poring over your work, I want to know every shift of your mind. I'm skipping everyone else's lectures. I'm going flat out, reading that old math so I can understand your paper. I've only got four days till you're on. It's a race against time, I'm reading till dawn every night. I can't talk to you now, I don't know enough, but I'll want to talk to you then.

Ah, I said, my suitcase heavy in my hand.

My voice was a rush of desperation.

Would you—I asked.

Her mouth was bright, lipsticked, admiring.

Would you like me to buy you another coffee? I asked.

A coffee? she asked. I've already got one. Oh, look at that, I must've drunk it.

She tossed the empty cup away into a nearby bin.

I'll run up now, back to work, she said. It's hard to just call you Frances, isn't that funny, I want to call you Montrose, the way you'll be known in all the books—

I put down my suitcase. She smiled dazzlingly and disappeared. The coffee on the floor puddled. I vacillated, because there are choices, after all. I moved towards the door, and back to the steps, I moved between shadows and sunlight. My wavering feet smeared her coffee puddle. I went to the door and thought: I've run away all my life. I went to the steps and thought: My daughter would say Jan Symonds and I are both losers. It takes one to know one, she'd say.

What hasn't been told is that just then, the lift opened and Professor Mitchell strode out. His colleague faltered behind, tightening his belt to hitch up his trousers. I held my breath, waiting for a nod or a word. The colleague saw me and looked away, stretching his hands by his sides in embarrassment and hurrying to catch up with Mitchell. I wasn't sure that Mitchell saw me in the small lobby, because of the odd movement of his eyes. But as they swung out the door, he said loudly to his friend:

The way things are going, next year we'll probably be funded by a circus of juggling cockroaches! Look at that view of the Parthenon! Its grandeur knocks me out every time!

He stumbled over my suitcase.

My feet moved so slowly, my life was implicated in each step. I stopped by a roadside kiosk, and lingered, uncertain. Outside the kiosk, a woman talked into a phone. I had no one to telephone, but I waited. Lingering was an old habit. The waking up, waiting, watching the drift of a long white morning, slowly talking yourself into the self-important sunshine. The lingering at night, waiting, the mattress that cushions against the next long white drift of morning.

The kiosk owner poked his head out of his tiny window and gathered his English in his head. Above his head, cigarette lighters on strings jiggled, all decorated with naked blonde women with buttocks like ripe yellow pears.

You want? asked the kiosk man.

Newspapers pegged like washing on another string shouted volcanoes in Asia, massacres in Europe, the death of an actress.

I pointed to a carton of juice, so I could lean against the kiosk. My head hit the rows of pear buttocks into a frenzy. I moved and examined the faces coming towards me in the street. Here was the face of an old man, his eyes as hidden as caves. Here was a woman with long tendrils of hair falling and bouncing on her red coat. Here was a group of young men laughing, striding in ironed jeans towards my sucking, middle-aged face against the yellow buttocks. In the end, you don't stand against a kiosk wall for long. Your handbag nudges you. You remember who you are. You pay the kiosk owner, slapping coins on the scratched plastic saucer as if you're in a hurry, as if there's somewhere you must go. As if you have somewhere to go. You pick up your suitcase with lolly papers blown against it. Where it's been, there's an island of bared footpath until the next gust of wind. You walk counting the stones in the road. The traffic shouts, you do not shout to it. You allow its din to push into your layers of silence, layer beyond layer, you give yourself to it. The meeting and parting of the screaming traffic, the pattern or chaos that is now inside you, that is your only lover.

But taxis purr promises at street kerbs. A promise that you can fall asleep and dream again and this time the dream will be different. There'll be no more frenzy. No more spiralling down. Taxis don't spiral, they unwind the hubbub of streets. They follow the clear intentions of the streets laid down by sensible city fathers. Swaying on the back seat of a taxi, you could wake up and find there's one clear pathway taking you out into a sky so bright you're riding along the shining perimeter of the world, at last.

There was a taxi outside the airline office. A woman inside had lips so glossy they almost reflected me clutching my suitcase amongst the travel posters of yellow beaches shaped like smiles. Near the counter, a cardboard cut-out girl in a bikini was careless of how precariously it clung. The lips of the woman behind the counter fought against a weight of gloss. Or perhaps it was that I was shipwrecked on an island of carpet, my face marooned. She touched her own smooth skin with her rounded fingernails.

You can't fly home yet. You can't change your ticket at

this stage, she said. It's a package booking. Anyway, there aren't spare seats for weeks. Have you got accommodation? Just go back and wait it out. You should've known not to bring your suitcase along. You can't board an international flight in high season at the onset of a whim.

So I walked away and lingered again, this time outside the airline office. A wiry mat prickled my soles. I gazed at the perplexities of the street until the shop windows and doorways and street railings and bus stop signs and traffic lights and meter boxes weren't shop windows and doorways and street railings and bus stop signs and traffic lights and meter boxes at all, but just the light and shadow of the mind's drifting. Behind me the automatic doors of the airline office whooshed open and shut as if they were heralding birth and death, birth and death, birth and death. Until the lipsticked woman came out from behind her counter and strode down to the straggling queue of customers to yell: Would you please use your sense and get off our mat!

So I looked inside the taxi and there was a back seat that was almost a mattress, and dusty windows that would frame and filter the light outside into the distant dots of a TV screen. But still I hesitated.

You can't leave—you're needed.

Adele was in front of me, standing between me and the taxi. Her irises gripped mine. I knew that grip, that clench of the heart. I'd gripped like that, holding on to people who might give me meaning. Clarke. Harry. My mother.

Needed for what? I said.

In the roar of the traffic we were in a cave of silence together. Every pulse of the body sounded like a shout. I even heard the brush of her eyelashes against her cheeks.

I'm sorry about your film, I said.

That's when at the mouth of our cave, the taxi honked.

I was racing across the squares of the footpath, my hair, my suitcase banging against me. She was wheeling on her heels as I clambered in. She still hadn't moved from where she stood.

Greek money crinkled in my pocket. I peeled off the largest note, peeled off ten more, surely enough to get to the other side of the country and bring the taxi driver back alone. I dropped them on the front seat beside the driver. He found an English word: Where? I didn't know the Greek words for anywhere but here. My mind was blank of the name of any Greek town.

I shrugged and pointed straight ahead. He shrugged. He released the handbrake, still turning to search my face for meaning. Then his saints jangled orange beads looped from the windscreen mirror. He'd been a boy in church, he understood. He drove into the sky, that merciless blue.

Once a woman lovelier than light bathed in an old-fashioned white porcelain tub while her lover, handsome and younger than her, sat on the edge of the tub reading the words of Georg Cantor to her, and her children watched through a crack in the door. The mother's breasts and the man's words billowed and rose more astonishingly than steam. After steam has cleared, you might think they would all see more clearly, but the spell still held the girl, those breasts, those words.

The girl watching didn't look at her brother watching, because she thought there was no need. Later she was to wonder about the exact angle of his face as he looked at the man who came from beyond the tiny township, from cities and bustle and noise. But she was memorising her mother, to learn how to become her, and possess the lover.

And the boy, jangling with lies, stories, hopes, boasts,

schemes, terrors, his history and his parents' history—what did he long for?

Talk to me, my mother was saying, but not to me. To Matti, who was listening to the Goon Show and laughing his high-pitched teenage laugh. He didn't look at her. He turned instead to the brown silk-covered speaker to hear the next joke.

Turn it off, she was saying. I want to talk.

Did you hear that one, he screeched to no one in particular. He saw me watching. Did you hear that one?

I need someone to talk to, my mother said. Her voice was thin and firm. It slid under his laughter, toppling it.

I need someone else's mind, she added. To blot out mine.

She reached over and turned the radio off. His eyes were flames of light.

You've got a husband, he said.

He turned the radio back on.

She went to the stove. She banged a saucepan on the hotplate. From the radio, jokes darted, cutting each other to pieces in their haste. My mother's face shone with tears. My brother drummed his fingers on the table.

Then something happened, I don't know what. The planet spun outside the window. The afternoon light faded. A bough twitched against the guttering outside. It was a tiny shift they heard when I heard nothing.

My brother turned the radio off.

He moved behind my mother at the stove. His arms circled her. She turned slowly in his arms. They clung to each other then so sadly, wiping tears with a limp tea-towel. The saucepan crackled with heat. I didn't dare move from my seat. The handle fell off the saucepan with a bang.

My mother turned round to me.

Why didn't you tell me the dinner was burning? she said.

At dinner they sat close together, and passed the salt so gently.

Out the grimy back window of the taxi, I saw that Adele was wading in the traffic like an old woman who couldn't swim on her own. Her arms, frantic to make a taxi stop, could've pulled the sky down. But everything roared past her, and jammed to a stop while a lorry reversed. As we eventually bumped into motion again I looked back and she was a tiny figure heading in the direction of the hotel. I'm the mirror she needed to look into.

We are mirrors for each other.

AND THEN, THE MIRRORS

My father saw the shape of many things. He saw the shape of a wall cupboard that would suit the unusable place between the fireplace and the wall in the MacDonalds' front parlour. He saw that if the Johnson's roof was lifted there'd be space for an upstairs bedroom for the twins. He saw that the Greys' foundations had to be reinforced or the house would subside.

He had, they said, a good eye.

But his good eye was for other people's lives, not his. He lived somewhere beyond his life in the house he built to realise it.

All that calamitous year, what my father talked about most was the old tap in the front yard. Every Sunday when he mowed the lawn, he talked about finding a washer for the front yard tap.

I'll have to get them to check, down at the hardware shop, he said.

But he didn't. He was a shy man. He just kept talking about

it to us over Sunday lunch. Next time I went with him to the hardware shop, I reminded him. Dad blushed a little.

Not now, he said.

Another problem? said the shop assistant.

My tap, said my father reluctantly.

Then because the shop assistant didn't move, I asked him to check through boxes and to take apart the second-hand taps lying in a pile in the back room. I knew the shop as well as he did.

Sounds like you ought to give this tap the shove, said the shop assistant to my father.

He was an old man with a fat backside as he bent over boxes.

That bloke just didn't have his heart in it, said Dad afterwards. I knew they wouldn't.

You're their biggest customer. Complain to Mr Carter, I said. Mr Carter was the owner, and too bored by hardware to be in the shop in the yabbie season. But we both knew my father wouldn't complain.

The tap became a cause for my father. Whenever we went out on a job together, we had to drive back through the town slowly. It was my job in the passenger's seat to peer through the dusty hardware shop windows. If the rude shop assistant was behind the counter, we'd keep driving.

There's someone else behind the counter, I was able to shout one day.

Dad screeched to a stop and left the ute in the middle of the road. He confided his problem tap to the new shop assistant, who was not much older than me. I stealthily examined his buttocks as he bent over boxes. Their curvature was rounder than a girl's. Perhaps they were pulled by strong muscles. Something deep in my belly spurted with desire, there amongst the grimy boxes of the hardware shop. I was wondering about the buttocks of my mother's lover.

But the new shop assistant was yawning.

This tap business sounds like a storm in a teacup, he said.

My father flinched. I blushed for my father.

But Mr Carter was there, now that he'd caught all the yabbies for miles around. He stopped yawning over the new saws he was unwrapping and came over.

Sounds like you've got a bit of living history in your yard, said Mr Carter. He scurried the young man back to the saws.

You think so? said my father.

Might be worth looking into, a tap like that, said Mr Carter.

He was a man who delighted in a search. Within seconds he was examining catalogues and phoning city firms. His lips tipped down to show the importance of the tap. My father's lips tipped up into one of his sweet smiles. His chest puffed with pride. He stuck his hands in his front pockets.

This tap of yours might have been there before the whole place got subdivided, said Mr Carter.

He stuck his hands in his front pockets too.

If taps could talk, said Mr Carter. He laughed.

Heh-heh.

My father laughed too. Heh-heh.

See, he values a professional like me, said Dad later.

But Mr Carter's interest couldn't solve the mystery of the tap. Frowning over my mother's pen at home and dropping blots, my father wrote to the Water Board, calling out for the spelling of certain words.

Does concern have an s in the middle? he asked.

Water Bored looks funny when you write it out, he said.

I'll post it, said my mother, pulling on a cardigan. I'll pop down to the post office right now.

The question of the tap continued to give suspense to his mornings as he buttoned the bib of his overalls in the small rectangle of sunshine through the window he'd built.

It's unique, that tap, he'd say.

The question is, whether it's better to get a new tap or preserve a bit of living history, he'd say.

It's becoming an odyssey, my mother murmured to no one in particular.

My father fluttered one of his halting smiles at her. He had suspected her scorn.

That's just the word for it, he agreed.

From then on, my father quoted my mother.

My wife calls this tap an oddity, he'd tell people.

Whenever he'd have to go to another township, he'd pop into the hardware there to root around in their oldest boxes, just in case. He waited for the Water Board's reply. Has it come, Mum? he'd ask as soon as he got home.

The year of the dripping tap might've become two years, or even a decade, but one night, coming home in the dark, he backed the ute into it.

Years later, I found the letter he'd written to the Water Board folded neatly into a tea-towel at the back of the kitchen drawer. My mother hadn't posted it. If government men nosed around our tap, they might notice her.

THERE WERE ALWAYS MANY MIRRORS

My father refused to buy pictures for the house he'd built for my mother.

I've got a picture in you, he said when they were getting on well. And why pay for a dog when you can do your own barking?

The walls are blank, she said. Like silences.

But my mother and father were still chatting amiably at

mealtimes, so as a compromise he collected mirrors. There were often old mirrors left behind in houses that people had left, or at the tip.

They save them for me, he said as he dragged another from the back of the ute.

He enjoyed being somebody people saved old junk for.

I'm carving out a place in this district, he said to me as we stood looking at the latest spotty mirror on our lawn.

He was always given mirrors grown imperfect with age, so that when you gazed at them you could think you were looking into rain spots or a toss of gravel or a drizzle of water or the murky depths of a lake. But he didn't hang them, not for months. He leaned them back-to-front one on top of another against the walls in the loungeroom and dining room. He was not a man to care for the house he'd made.

It stinks, he'd complain as he put a new one amongst the old. There was an accusation in his voice against my mother. So she would quickly dust, and bathe the mould in bleach, and over time the new mirror would settle in with the old ones and they'd all become invisible, another obstacle to skirt around in the rooms of our lives. They might have stayed there ringed around the walls until the house fell down but one day when my father banged the door, a mirror shattered on the floor.

Bad luck for seven years, my father yelped and crossed his fingers.

You must've propped it in a wonky way, he shouted at my mother.

He spent the rest of the day hanging mirrors. There were so many he hung several in every room. When my mother protested, he drove the nails in harder.

Wouldn't want it leaping off the wall when you were checking the bags under your eyes, he joked.

You were never quite sure of distances in my father's house. The watery, ancient images swam out to meet you, part of you collided with another part, your underarm with your neck, your smile with your eye. My father hung distorted mirrors to reflect the beauty of my mother.

Then one day, it was after Matti, it was a Sunday, that weekend disappointment of an uneventful Sunday afternoon, there was an absence in our house that was something other than Matti. Something essential seemed forgotten but I wasn't sure what. I wandered around the house dragging my hands on surfaces, like a blind woman checking her possessions with her hands. My hands trailed on the dust of tops of tables, dressing-tables, desks, the doors of cupboards, wardrobes. All the usual surfaces were there. It was only when orange clouds were thrown across the evening sky like curtains that I turned my eyes to the walls. They'd become blank spaces again, reflecting nothing. My mother had taken down the mirrors.

Because mirrors are like lakes, like that lake.

THE FOUR
MISSING DAYS

As I travelled in my taxi across the mainland of Greece, I saw nothing for myself, if I ever had. I saw it for my mother. She would've poked her head out of the taxi window to comment to Matti on this village, houses suddenly in a cluster after the stretches of slopes so gentle in the morning light and shadow they could be clouds. On this roadside cafe with old men sitting in sunshine, their stick hands clicking on worry beads. They were probably children here together once believing as they slid off old men's knees that they would never grow old my mother would've said. And here was a group of old fishermen leaning on the side of the travelling fishmonger's truck. They were bent legged, their trousers the colour of the Aegean when storms sting it into sailor blue wrinkles. As they touched the fish for sale they fingered their life stories, because there's never a catch silver or slippery enough to match an old fisherman's memories. My mother would laugh at the shepherd sneaking his goats like hungry children into the gardens of Nick's Fish Taverna while Nick visited a relative in a distant village. Her eyes would see the shepherd's crook whittled in the shape of a winsome snake; all day his fingers slid around its smooth and curving neck, she'd say. She would see the toddler pudgy as a cherub of the paintings in European galleries as, thumb in mouth, he gripped his mother's doorway and gazed at the lane endless with secrets. And the knot of older children chanting a game: Anglia, Gallia, Deutschland, until the rough stone walls echoed like the shining depths of a marble church. This village, she'd remember, was mentioned by foreign travellers in their journals when Fibonacci was discovering his number sequence.

The old men on their wooden chairs in the sunshine pushed caps out of their eyes to watch my taxi from Athens all the

way down the road. Afterwards it would rumble back again
as they shouted in argument: Of course it's the same taxi as
the one that came through before with the foreign woman in
the back. The same back bumper bar, held on with the same
bit of fencing wire.

Sometimes you're sure you know someone as if they
shared your heart. This knowledge has nothing to do with
words. It's given in the curve of their body, the clutch of muscles that guard their mouth, the eyes as collapsed with memories as your own. You feel you are like old lovers with this
person, when one quiet nod says more than a week of young
passionate embraces.

But you look at many things and boast knowledge. Even
a line of washing seen out of a taxi window tells about lives.
Those wet pyjamas, cuffs worn, seams unthreading, that
nightdress edged with a bit of torn lace, those underpants
with slackened elastic. Those flowered sheets, drooping with
damp stains, that line of misshapen nappies. You look at a
line of washing and you guess a family's secrets, you guess
what's hoped for, what's hidden.

You know nothing at all.

ONLY A TINY MISUNDERSTANDING

The taxi was in a country of stiff black grass. The road was
a blank between dark hills, like something left out of a story
like an unsolved mathematical problem that the edifice of
thought ignores. This was not the shining perimeter I wanted.

What's the black grass? I asked the driver. My voice was
thick with disuse, after a silence of hours.

He looked around at the woman on the back seat who
didn't know where she wanted to go.

I tried again, hoping that somewhere words in **Greek and English** collide.

What, grass, why, black, I gabbled.

This time his glance only went as far as his shoulder. He flicked off a speck of fluff.

Fire? I tried. Sun?

It was hardly worth shrugging his shoulders for the woman in the back.

We passed a plateau with rows of empty chairs and tables around a small building that must be a cafe. The sun was so fierce, the cafe seemed a mirage on a silver sheen.

Stop. Drink, I croaked from the back.

This time the driver didn't bother to shrug. He pushed the accelerator down, and shrouded a man lounging at the cafe door in a whirl of dust.

An earthquake? I asked the driver. We were passing a huddle of houses, low, so close together there was no light between them, made of stone the colour of dust. But they'd been split open like nuts at a Christmas feast. Here was a chimney towering alone. Here was the sun and shadow of a staircase with the house gone. Here were walls, zigzagged with cracks like slowed-down lightning, waiting to tumble to the earth. There were no belongings, no chairs, beds, tables. The houses gazed sightlessly at the dusty blank of the road that they'd one day become. But at night they must've dreamed in the silver drift of stars.

Boom? I tried again to the driver. Boom! Boom!

He didn't even look in his mirror to see the woman in the back exploding lava into his car.

Suddenly a hen flapped over a lower wall, garbling surprise at its own flight. Its wings shook out a brilliance that was shocking in this dark landscape like something that should not be seen. It skidded to its feet in front of the taxi. The driver stopped. The madwoman at the back was chattering more sounds.

You probably have children, I was saying. To be so careful of a hen.

I wondered if I should reach over and shake his hand. But he was swinging his face around to me, and speaking.

I searched his face for meaning, the high cheekbones holding out the skin the colour of earth, the lined forehead, the black and hooded eyes. Three of his front teeth were edged with gold. He uttered another sound and tipped his head skywards.

Yes, I agreed eagerly. I was so eager, I clucked like the hen. Chook-chook-chook.

I flapped.

That's just how it flew, I agreed.

He stared at me in disbelief that I didn't understand him. I wanted him to think I did, I wanted to be in accord with him. I clucked again. Then I tipped my head like he did. I hoped I was imitating flight.

Behind his lids, his pupils twitched. Something ticked in his dashboard. Perhaps the heat was drying up the car. We both waited for meaning. After a while he turned to reach beyond me. His hand pushed past my breast to open my door from the inside. Then the taxi was like an insect in this scorched landscape, one wing flapping, the other shut close to its body.

We waited without words.

Perhaps he wanted me to see the deserted village. I looked helpfully towards it. I wondered if, now that I had his attention, I should try to sound like lava again.

Boom, I shouted, giving the sound great import. Boom boom.

He turned in his seat. Perhaps he'd resume driving. I was about to swing the door shut but he was banging on the dashboard, his fist clenched. Knuckles whitened his skin, his

orange beads bounced, his metallic saints lurched. He shouted
again. His fist dented the roof.

Touristes, he shouted.

He pushed against his door so it flew open. Then his car
still like an insect had one wing at the back and one wing at
the front flapping. He was still shouting. Dust clouded in and
claimed the inside lining of his door with silent urgency, and
the vinyl pockets on the door, and a map and a bottle of ouzo.
He was out on the road and crossing around in front of his
taxi, pivoting his body by a hand on the bonnet. Dust billowed
at his feet. His body jerked to walk. Behind each jerk I saw
that the grass wasn't black, wasn't grass but mound after
mound of tiny fans a lady might flutter at a ball, purple,
orange, grey, brown but spiked with thorns.

Wild thyme? I asked like an eager horticulturist as the driver's face filled my open door. His spit cooled on my cheeks.
He obviously didn't want to discuss horticulture. I wondered
if I should've been afraid. His hand was reaching in, he was
pushing past my knees to my suitcase. It grazed my knee and
he'd pulled it out onto the road. He was pulling at me and I
couldn't resist, his body was tight muscled and wiry and I
have the loose soft body of a woman whose days have been
cushioned by chairs. He let me go and I tottered in the dust
like the hen. He walked back around the taxi and climbed into
his driver's seat. He rolled up the windows.

I wiped a circle in the brown coating on the passenger
window. He was doing something at his dashboard. He didn't
look up. Dust rimmed his eyebrows. Already it was slinking
towards his eyelashes.

He started the engine and did a U turn. He wound down his
window and the sound of a soccer crowd cheering in triumph
unfurled all the way down the road. I stood there till the dust
settled. It even settled on my hands.

Too late, I wondered if all he wanted was more money. Eventually everything peters out.

When a liar tells a story you listen to the story and you listen for the lie. It's another kind of waiting. You clamber through words as slippery as seaweed drifting. You'd depended so much on words. You want and you don't want to find the lie. At the same time you watch the storytelling face, the eyes, the lips, the pull of storytelling muscles. The storyteller knows how to make you long for the story not to finish and at the same time for the story to finish. Most of all the storyteller knows how to make you long for the story to be true, that completeness. This longing is ancient, as you strain you know the longing of tens of thousands of years of humans in your body. That longing's even in the stones of the earth, in its dust.

A large bird swooped over my head. It was so low to the road that I should've heard the thump of its massive wings. But there was no sound. Perhaps that was because of the dust, sticking to everything, muffling sounds like snow does, a restless, drifting brownness.

Or perhaps the soundlessness was because of what I already knew. That I could keep walking down this road. On and on, free, uncontained, unknowable.

There was a laugh. A woman stood at the doorway of a house intact amongst the rubble of other houses. She twitched a duster, she'd come to shake it and to see who got out of the taxi. The hen with its shocking emerald green feathers scuttled at her feet.

Where am I? I shouted. You speak English?

She raised her hands from her sides like birds' wings. They

dropped. We stared. Her clothes were brown like the dust. She was part of the earth already.

Help me, I shouted.

She scooped up her hen. Her face was stilled angles of dust. Her body blocked light. But when I moved my head slightly, there was a passageway behind her with a cone of yellow light from a high staircase window. Dust in that cone was a golden dance.

I leaned my suitcase against my legs in the middle of the lonely road. I needed friendship, coffee, food. Perhaps she'd understand pi. It was her ancient ancestors, tormented by the way some lengths wouldn't fit into ordinary arithmetic, who thought up pi. I looked around for a stick.

Perimeno, I said brightly, as Adele would've.

I scraped a circle in the dust, prodded the circumference and the diameter, drew an arrow to outside the circle and wrote the Greek letter for pi.

She clicked her tongue.

I threw down the stick in triumph and stretched out my hands and smiled like a lost relative come home. But she was cocking her head on one side. So was her hen.

Thoughts tugged each other across her face. She made up her mind. I was a foreign woman dressed for a city, shattering her privacy as if it was glass. She turned with her hen into the dance of gold, gold that danced every day the sun shines, and shut her door behind her.

Perhaps all I did was poke in the dust like a child.

So there was nothing to do but pick up my suitcase and walk down the road. The dust had already drifted in to cover the tyre tracks.

Only when I'd walked into the hills did I remember my mother saying that the ancient Greeks hated the idea of infinity, and that's why they'd invented pi. Apeiron, they called infinity. Something despised.

WHAT A CIRCLE IS

The winter Matti disappeared was the worst in living memory, people said. There'd never been such endless mist, such constant frost, so many days of snow. Mists swirled like a wraith outside the windows, rolling away so you thought it had gone, then rolling back mockingly. When Matti and I were younger, we'd pretend that the mists had cut us off from the township.

We'll starve to death, we'd shout and shriek with laughter. Death seemed an improbable adventure and afterwards you had a hot dinner.

They dragged the lake for Matti for three days, the lake of five hundred and fifty feet. Three days of hope and anger and the nights grey with mist, starless, moonless, sleepless. Three days and three nights and my mother stumbling through them, sure she knew the outcome. It was plain in the way she bent over the oven, plain in the desultory way she slopped water into the kettle.

Matti's body wasn't found.

Men came from other townships to help, men my father didn't know and men he'd grown up with. They stood heavily on our verandah at the end of the three days, their black rubber boots shiny with the lake water still trickling off. Two of them swayed with drunkenness. They'd had to swallow gin to keep out the cold as they dived. My father handed round cocoa because my mother's hands were shaking too much. The men didn't look at her. They looked at my father. He was known to be someone with a bit of vision. A respectable man, carving out his place. He was more respectable now death had touched him. He wasn't a man to have a son who'd merely run away.

Five hundred and fifty feet is bloody deep, they said.

You could make a horror film down there, one of the drunk ones said. All sorts of things are oozing through the slime.

He hit his forehead with his open hand in memory.

I found something interesting, he said.

My mother moved.

Something of Matti's?

Her voice was disturbingly high. I moved to put my arm around her, but she eased herself away.

Who's to know? Kids, these days, the man said.

He put his cocoa down and fumbled in his pocket. His pocket lining hung whitely.

This was stuck in the mud not far from the shore, he slurred.

It was a bangle, silver, a perfect silver circle.

Interesting, isn't it? he said.

That wouldn't be Matti's, my mother said. Her voice was cracking.

Just thought it might be of interest, the man said.

In his drunkenness, he sounded peeved.

My father spoke to placate him.

It is of interest, said my father. Nice bit of soldering on the join.

That's all you found? said my mother.

You could hear the gaps in her voice, gaps where Matti was supposed to fit.

I'm afraid so, said the sober man.

But you can't give up, cried my mother. Unless you haven't been searching.

Hang on, said one of the men. It's been a bloody freezing three days.

He'd finished his cocoa and was standing, nodding to the others to hurry them through their cocoa.

If we could barely survive it in our wet suits, how could he—

I don't believe, shouted my mother, that you've looked for him!

My father grabbed her, held her, he was saying into her face, but twisting his head to the men:

It is an interesting bangle, see they don't do that sort of hammer work any more, there'd be a bit of history in that, nice bit of work, I'm a bit interested in history myself.

But he couldn't cover the pain in the screams of my mother.

You've killed him, screamed my mother.

I'm afraid we'll have to go.

The sober man was shepherding the other men down our path and speaking to my father.

The police will be along soon, he said.

His voice just came in tendrils through my mother's scream: You've been waiting for this chance! Haven't you? Biding your time! It's taken years but hate lasts forever.

The men all stopped on our path and shuffled.

I'm sorry, one of them said.

Why didn't you take me? my mother was shouting from my father's arms.

Why couldn't you have left him his young life and taken me?

One of the drunken men, the one with the bangle, suddenly moved, he came stumbling back down the path to the verandah where we stood, and held the bangle out to me.

You might as well have it, lassie, he said.

I took its hard, sad weight.

Dad and I knew the search was over by the clang of the gate behind them, and the slams of doors of vans and trucks and utes and cars. It was too misty to see.

My mother's voice still hung in the mist.

Did you see their knives? They must've had knives! I always knew they'd come back.

I often thought later that if Dad hadn't been so respected, maybe Matti wouldn't have been presumed drowned.

Throughout that terrible winter, PURE MATHS 3 was covered in dust which rotated in balls when I lifted the eiderdown. The top page was folded down on The Infinitesimal Calculus. There was no scarlet argument on it from my mother.

I put the bangle that maybe was Matti's and maybe wasn't Matti's on his dressing-table, now that the drawers were oddly quiet and his bed stripped to its black and white mattress. All the noise and amber light that was him had gone. He would've liked the silver circle of the bangle, its clear simple geometry more visible than him, if he'd been tossing in the Basin's depths. I left it there, just in case. Only the dust noticed it.

Then one day, a year later, maybe two, I moved it. It was still heavy in my hand but its weight wasn't sad any longer. I polished it with the cuff of my sleeve and put it in my blazer pocket and it stayed there, bumping and shining through what was left of my childhood. It was there when I found out that kisses are sweet and that pi has an infinite number of terms because a circle is a regular polygon with an infinite number of sides. That discovery was sweeter than kisses. My body rippled silver in the old excitement. I felt in my pocket for that shining circumference of countless arches, and wondered if there'd ever be an arch that I could slip through.

But for my mother, it was the end of mathematics. The end of her meetings with her lover. The end of her life, though she kept on living, for life can be tauntingly long.

WALLPAPERING

There was a great mathematician Sofia Kovalevskaya, who had lived as a child with her parents and many servants in a grand but decrepit house in the countryside in Russia last century. When money was short and the walls of the house were damp, anything that came to hand was used to re-paper them. It so happened that Sofia's bedroom was papered with old lecture notes on calculus left in the house by her uncle Peter (a gentleman mathematician) on one of his occasional visits there. The servants had no interest in or understanding of calculus and pasted the pages up in random order. Sofia was a rebellious, lonely child and it became the amusement of her life to stand at her wall trying to work out how the pages should've been placed. She'd only received the non-mathematical education normally offered to girls at the time, but when her father saw her eventual understanding of calculus, he provided tutors. Sofia Kovalesvskaya later became recognised for her brilliance in mathematics. She was professor of mathematics at Stockholm University, she was awarded the coveted Prix Bordin of the Paris Academy of Sciences, and she was the first woman to be elected to membership of the Russian Academy of Sciences. For all the honours heaped on her however and the resources which she was able to command, she struggled through her short life with the constant problem of how best to love her daughter, and how to share her time with her, a struggle not unlike my mother's struggle with me. Sofia Kovalesvskaya died at forty-one, at the height of her fame.

My mother knew about Sofia Kovalesvskaya, and used to say that Kovalesvskaya's work on series showed who she really was. I don't think that's possible, but who am I?
Hypatia

The disappearance of my mother's lover after the lake was another secret. He'd come in secret. He disappeared in secret. But one night, at midnight, the light in my brother's room was on. I heard the slop of her slippers, the clank of a bucket, the thud of something dense. I went to the edge of light under the door, and pushed it open.

What are you doing? I asked her.

Fixing up your brother's bedroom, she said. Your father's not likely to. Now they've both gone.

I should've shouted Both? Who's both? But I stood marooned in years of secrets.

She didn't say it again, didn't turn her face to me. Night and day stretched on without explanation.

The next night at midnight my father stood at the door. His feet were anxiously pigeon-toed as he watched my mother. It was easier, after all the things that had never been said, to be anxious for his house rather than his wife.

You could've said, he complained. I would've got you some proper paper, you just had to say the word. Some Sandersons in a floral maybe, or a stripe, with a nice frieze at the top. Something to catch the eye. Something other women would choose.

He peered.

It's just a lot of scribble. Why would anyone paste up scribble?

She'd taken all the furniture out of the room. His voice came back to him, like an answer.

She didn't turn around to look. She was too busy slapping on glue. And her eyes were yellow, glazed, and the cobwebs behind them were glittering. Sometimes she took my breath away, she was so much like my brother. She worked feverishly, in a wild anger, while I followed her, handing her the next sheet of paper and cleaning gobs of glue off the floor.

You're leaving a lot of gaps, my father said next time he visited us as we worked at night. People are not supposed to be able to see bits of wall underneath. You'll have to do something about the gaps.

His feet were uneasy on the floorboards, like a man who wasn't in the house he'd built.

I'm a professional tradesman with a reputation to keep, said my father. What if someone sees this mess?

My mother worked on, deaf, glazed-eyed, almost sleepwalking.

One night, my mother took the kitchen stool into the room, the stool we used to sit on while she cut our hair. My mother's sagging body on the stool was precarious. But she filled in the gaps with any pages that came to hand. She got impatient with me if I dithered. Now their order didn't matter, now it was almost over.

Afterwards, she stayed in bed for three weeks.

She's been overtaken by the fumes, my father explained to me.

And the whole thing will have to be done again. It looks like a dog's breakfast.

But he didn't touch it for years. His household was sliding away from under his control, and now he couldn't deny it.

She'd wallpapered the room with her lover's lecture notes, and with her refutations.

The next winter, with more mists and damp, the ceiling in my room began to crumble. I waited for my father to come home so I could show it to him. He came home very late these days because he'd been elected Mayor of the district.

We stood under the swinging light shade and looked at the ceiling. A lump of plaster had fallen onto my bed while I was at school. It had survived intact amongst the soft bedclothes. It looked like a country fallen off a flattened map of the world.

Another job to do, my father sighed. I'll have to get to it soon.

He was putting on his robes, off to an Extraordinary Meeting, he said, of the Council. That's why it was held so late, he said. He had a very helpful assistant mayor, Bev Roberts. An invaluable ally at all times, my father said.

I asked my mother if I could move into Matti's room, since it was spare. She was sitting by the window, waiting for the post, though it was long past dinnertime and the postman had been hours before.

You can sleep there for the time being, she agreed. But don't get too comfortable. You might have to move out, anytime.

My years of watching my mother at night had made me sleepless. She was sleeping again, but now I stayed up to number the pages on the wall she'd pasted up out of order. I felt, in her disordered world, I owed her order. Many corners of pages were lifting off the wall, but I didn't pull them off and reposition them.

Beside the window, my mother had pasted Maths 3: Bernoulli Numbers. Her lover had typed at the top of a sheet and the black print lectured down the page.

Then my mother had begun her scarlet arguments:

More interesting is the fact (underlined) that Bernoulli denominators are always divisible by 6. You haven't said there are other ways of calculating Bn. If n is even ...

Then the writing with its tendrils wandered onto another page that I couldn't find anywhere near the window. Nights later I found the argument down behind the door just above the skirting board:

... but not equal to zero, Bn is a fraction and the numerator of Bn/n in its lowest terms is a prime number—do they know that? What's more, the denominator of Bn contains each of the factors 2 and 3 once and only once.

He'd written back: B20/ 20 is 174611. Not a prime number AT ALL.

She'd circled his argument with red again and again while she'd considered her response. Just above the light switch some weeks later I found a note she'd written to herself. She was still thinking about Bernoulli numbers:

Tell him $2n(2n-1)Bn/n$ is an integer and so $2(2n-1)Bn$ is an odd integer.

In a margin, she'd written: Frege said that the straight line between any two points is there before we draw it.

Her lover hadn't argued with that.

I drew arrows in different colours to follow the path of her lover's mathematics, and hers. I used single lines for her, and double lines for his. I used all the colours of the spectrum. Slowly the sad empty room became as bright as a rainbow. It was like drawing two different journeys across a map, her journey and his. It took the rest of my adolescence. And though I joined up many arguments, by the time I'd left school, I could see how different two journeys could be.

Where memories go 1

I came at last to the plateau I saw from the taxi. It was bordered by two houses and a cafe. There were rows of weathered chairs expectant in the sun, and only a man and a priest under a circle of shade from a plane tree. I sank into a chair in the shade. I eased my hot stockinged feet out of my shoes. The cafe owner came out. He flicked a tired tea-towel across the grit on the tabletop. He watched me struggle with a mime of drinking.

Nero, he said.

He waited for me to repeat it after him, and corrected it.

Nero means water, he said in perfect English. And afterwards, do you want coffee?

Yes, I gasped.

Metria? he asked.

I remembered the word. Metria means sweet. Yes, I said, But I hadn't answered it right.

Neh, he taught me. Neh means yes.

Sweat was pouring down my face despite the shade.

Neh, I repeated, dry throated. Neh means yes.

No is ohi, he said. He tossed his head as he said it.

Ohi equals no, I repeated. He corrected the toss of my head.

Soon, you'll learn.

He shook his tea-towel as he went. It flapped against a brilliant sky.

Against the wall of the cafe on a table were piles of plates, forks, glasses and paper serviettes. The paper serviettes were weighed down by a stone. I was too tired to put my shoes back on so I walked across the plateau in my stockings. I lifted the stone and took a few serviettes back to my table to blot up the sweat that trickled down my face, down between my breasts. The top serviette was stained with lipstick in the shape of a kiss.

I sat staring at the kiss, how intense it once was, how it had faded.

I'd thought I would be able to put these images behind me.

The waiter returned with water and coffee. The coffee slopped into the saucer but he refused to notice this. He wasn't my servant, his people were not servants, he wanted me to know. He'd turned his back to my table before he'd put the cup down. He walked into the cafe with long strides, someone who makes sense of things. I wasted one of the serviettes blotting up slops. And on the outside of the cup there was a looping of coffee grounds like a veil.

Two tourists had arrived, a boy and a girl, blond, pale, young. They arched their thin backs to let their knapsacks fall to the ground. They wore thick shirts unbuttoned in the heat, and their paleness had the fragility of lace. They seemed part of the light on the road they'd come from. In this gnarled landscape their faces were transparent with youth.

The girl raised her arms to free her hair from her hot neck. Her arms were rimmed with blonde hairs. A silver bangle slipped from elbow to wrist.

The waiter was walking back against the sky towards me. I had to squint to look up at him. He held another cup of coffee and a piece of baclava on a battered silver plate.

He put the cake and coffee down. This time he lifted the cup and wiped the slops from the saucer.

No money, no money, he said.

Ah, I said, waiting.

He didn't go, he bent over a chair so he leaned his weight on its back. That way, his shoulders were broader. His hands were furred with black hairs.

This is my cafe, he said out of his brown felt face.

I followed his gaze and took in the concrete buildings festooned with crimson bougainvillea, the man and priest still talking, the tourists easing themselves out of the weight of their knapsacks, a white goat tethered to a stick, two hens scrabbling on the path. The cafe owner's stomach above the back of the chair moved of its own accord against the sky.

My brother has a good hotel, he said. Very clean, very quiet.

He nodded towards one of the houses as if it was a friend. A man lounged by the door of the cafe, one foot on the ground, toeing the dust, watching its eddies, the way they subsided.

No thank you, I said. I want to walk down that road.

I smiled because the road's blankness was suddenly as sweet to me as life. Something inside my chest was dancing as lightly as dust in sunshine.

But your suitcase, argued the cafe owner. He reached down for the handles, to test its weight. It was heavy with bright dresses I'd never worn. And my work. And my daughter's letters I hadn't read.

Ohi, I said.

The cafe owner shrugged, lifting his hands away from his sides like the old woman. He remembered his tea-towel, flicked more dirt off the table and walked away. The serviette with the kiss floated after him.

The cafe owner's brother stayed by the door looking at the hens. He didn't look up. They stretched out long necks of turquoise towards his hand, in hope.

A rope dripping spangles

After Matti and the lake, there were terrible summers. The whole neighbourhood was gripped by a fierce brown hand of heat. It seemed to grip us forever, helpless, motionless. The air was dull. Only tough boys went barefoot in the dry prickling grass, their soles as grey as the desultory soil. I let whole sentences drift by before I wiped the sweat and flies off my face.

Yeah, I'd say, whenever a comment was expected of me.

In that endless brown summer, no one was burgled, no door catches broke, no kitchen shelves collapsed, no one needed new bedrooms or porches or sheds, the entire fabrication of the town lay still, stunned, waiting for the sky to relent. Even the front lawns didn't grow. Rosebuds weren't watered, even by jugs or kettles. No one dared waste a drop, and the roses were thorny sticks of memory under a sky so defiantly blue it reflected my squint. Dad, without work, sat in darkened rooms behind curtains closed to the heat, and whittled.

After Matti, I was always jostling to stand near my mother, sit near her, to be the one to pass her a cup of tea. Secretly I'd warm the place where she'd been sitting, cradle the bowl she'd eaten from, use her hairbrush, touch her clothes hanging in the wardrobe. I waited for the moment when she'd put her arm around me, then I'd at last be contained, contained at last in her. So I didn't notice when she went mad. There must've been a moment.

My father bought my mother a vacuum cleaner, to cheer her up. It had a snivelling whine that echoed in the head like a roomful of mosquitoes. One day I watched my mother vacuuming. Sweat was splotching my mother's blouse under the arms and between her breasts which seemed after Matti and the lake to always point in sad triangles towards the floor. I'd already dusted, and now I watched her hips swivelling with the demands of the vaccuum cleaner, this way and that across carpet. Not all her hips would turn at once, now that my mother had loose hips. Her upper buttocks were resistant, reluctant, they took their time to be acquiescent. Sometimes she'd tuck her skirt up into her pants like a woman laughing in a frolicking sea, but her legs were now goosepimpled and veined as if love and hope and thought for Matti had kept time away, but now it was rushing over her, pulling at her skin, her blood, drowning her in sadness, like my brother. When she wiped the mirrors with turps and newspaper, she met my eyes and smiled. In the sudden reflection, her smile floated. She moved the mirror back and forwards as she wiped and the smile lay on it like water, not belonging to her. The heat and the sky had faded everything out of me, even loyalty. I went out into the backyard and I shouted amongst the screaming of the cicadas and the endless drone of blowflies:

I can't stand it.

I went back into the house weakened by my own fury. My mother was putting the vacuum cleaner away, winding the cord around her arms, those round strong arms she often held behind her hair. I suddenly wondered how long I'd been outside. She didn't turn as I came in. There was a quiet, intent set to her lips. Then she said:

Your life hasn't started yet.

How long is it, she asked my father one day, since Matti? How many months?

Her tea was going cold in the white cup in her lap.

He was whittling. He'd taken to whittling model cars. They were lined up on the mantelpiece now, a Customline, a Simca, a Humber, a Vanguard, a Holden, and an Armstrong Siddeley.

How long? she repeated.

My father shook his head.

A while, he said.

Can't you fix something? she cried. Instead of making those silly cars?

She stood. Her cup slid to the floor.

Watch it! he shouted.

It bounced. She came over to his chair. She was shaking the chair's arm.

Is there one of those cars for each time you remember? Or don't you remember anything?

When my father didn't answer, she wrenched his whittling out of his hands. It fell on the floor too.

Watch it! he shouted.

It had broken.

She snatched at his knife. She held it trembling towards him. He pulled her arms down to her sides and pinned them there. She was screaming now:

How long, how long, how long?

Her mouth was big, and full of bubbles.

When there was no more crying, he carried her to her bed.

He told me this story afterwards, his voice breaking.

It's her nerves gone, he said. She's forgotten who I am. She must've thought I was one of the men with knives. And she expected me to count.

It was thirteen months since Matti.

From the roof of our house you could see the river winding to the ocean. The ocean was eighty miles away, so most of the river's journey was invisible, something you had to believe in. It would have been easier to believe that it wandered into the grey and waiting sky. Between our house and the river were reeds so brown and dense that you had to push them to walk through. That's all changed now, of course.

There was no smell of dinner when I came home from school. That's how I sensed her absence, because that's where home started for me, the smell of potatoes she'd cut up and boiled in the saucepan, the smell of things nurtured in secret. So panic started.

Mum, I called, and my voice was already high, but surely it would be alright. The lounge cushions were still rumpled from where Dad sat to put on his shoes, and she'd left the milk bottle on the kitchen table after her last cup of tea. A full milk bottle, untouched, the cream thick and congested yellow at the top. The teapot was cold and when I lifted the lid, I saw the pot had been washed out and a handful of tea leaves thrown in. But no water. And the kettle had boiled dry on the stove and was starting to blacken. I pulled it off and the pain from the heat was a scream, my scream for my mother. I was running now from room to room. I didn't look just at beds and chairs. I checked walls, ceilings. Only the terrified look at ceilings. I ran outside to the garden. On the path the raffia washing basket was piled with clothes she'd wrung but not pegged out.

My heart was an abyss for my mother, I was fighting for my life, for my mother's life. I rushed down to the garden shed. The door was stuck, another of the things my father never mended. I ripped at the door, again, again, and the hinges gave way. The door flopped onto the ground. I found the spare extension ladder. I rushed with it to the house. I propped it against the house. From the roof I could see everything, the river winding into the sky, the township struggling into the bushland, the church steeple, the school, my schoolmates laughing in the street, Bev Roberts' corner shop. The line of pines around the cemetery spiking the sky like arrows. The lake. The brown reeds by the river. And a figure in brown by the river. In a sudden gust of wind, the brown flapped. An angular brown bird beside the river. It was the brown of my mother's winter coat.

I'd been up a ladder a thousand times in my life and yet time slowed as I climbed down and on the last few steps the ladder fell away from the house, pivoting on my weight.

I picked myself up, I was hurling myself through the reeds, screaming, tearing them out by the roots, losing my way and finding it and losing it and finding it. At last the glittering river and I was stumbling over mounds and rocks and there was my mother on the bank. Looking startled at me, remembering who I am.

I found her there in the grime of the river bank, my mother, my child. When I stroked her, that soft part of the arm between wrist and elbow, so smooth it could be newly born, at that moment I could no longer remember if I came out of her or she came out of me. In our touch, differences merged.

All I could do was hold her. Her head lolled against my shoulder while she followed with her eyes the reeling world, the trees tipping on their sides, the rocks sliding, the river standing on its banks. I watched it all with her, the way she did.

Then her head slipped onto my lap, where I've always wanted it to be. My mother was giving her weight to me, at last. Her trust.

I had so much hope when I was young, she said. Despite the ... knives.

Yes, I said. Oh, yes.

Her head moved amongst the shine of her hair. She found comfort against me. I stroked her face and she allowed me to. She was even letting my fingers brush her lips.

At the convent, they thought I had a future, she said. They thought I was a genius.

I wanted to concentrate and remember everything about this moment. The exact weight of her glossy head, the amber glow of her skin lit up from inside like cellophane, the sweet curve of her lips. When I was old it would make me young, when I was sick it would make me well, when I was lonely I would hold it close, this repairing moment. I didn't dare look away from her eyes but I took in every detail to know it all, the grey of the clouds and how they fitted together in the sky. I memorised a post leaning in the water making a v with its own quiet reflection. I memorised the loops of a mooring rope dripping spangles. I memorised a bird sitting in the centre of its own ripples. I memorised the exact texture of grime.

There was one nun, she said. There was something odd about her voice, something choked, in a flash of heat I wondered if she'd swallowed something, if there was an obstruction, if my mother would be taken from me now that her warmth was in mine as we crouched beside a river.

I was the nun's favourite, she said. For a while.

Her voice was thickening more. I fought panic. It was only the cold evening air in her voice, only the grey air, and her exhaustion.

She was my nun, she said. For a while.

Her eyes were glossed with tears, her lips crinkled in memory.

But one day my nun took me by the hand, she said. She led me into a garden I'd never been in before. I hadn't even known it existed. And I said that, I said: I didn't know this was here. It seems like something that happens in stories. That there's a secret passage in a wall, and you go in and come out into the sunlight and there's a special garden.

My nun smiled at me and said:

This is my special garden. It's only for my dears.

I told her I hadn't been in a garden, not a real one, since my father.

My mother's eyes turned to me.

Did you know my father died? she asked.

Yes, I whispered.

My mother never took me home, my mother explained as if I was a stranger.

She left me at the convent for ten years. She never visited me. She said my home was the convent now. But suddenly it was going to be all right, because in this special garden, the air was pink with the smell of roses, like the garden at home was. Roses smell like sunshine in some gardens, did you know that?

My mother's eyes were not on mine, they looked up at the sky so urgently that I twisted my head to see if there was someone else there. There was only me.

Every evening my father walked in the garden with me, she said. In the last of the light. He broke pink rose petals to show me their lushness. He showed me how to look for insects. He showed me where bees suck. And in my nun's garden, it was as if I was back with my father. And I told my nun, I said:

The smell's so wonderful it makes me think that I'm in the smell of my father's pink roses.

And she said: You are my perfect little rose. She was kneeling, touching my face, see, like this.

My mother touched my face.

See how my fingers almost don't come away from your skin? That's how she touched me. As if we were stuck together. My nun said: But your father's not here. I'm here, and I love you, and you're my rose now.

My mother's head lolled. Her voice lisped.

The nun was breathing on me. She was holding me so tight I couldn't breathe and she was asking me if I loved her. There wasn't room to breathe with her so close, so I wrenched and hit and ran out of the garden. I hid in my cell. She never spoke to me again but I didn't mind. I didn't want to be anyone's rose but my father's. I didn't want anyone to touch me but my father.

My mother in my arms was seven years old, a little girl lying on a narrow bed in a strange room that's not her home, her father dead, her mother gone. She leaned on me more heavily, she was an unbearable weight, like a lopped branch.

That's when I found numbers, she said. I could bear their touch.

Her eyes slid onto mine unexpectedly.

How much of a genius do I have to be? she screamed.

Around us, cockatoos screeched. They cut up the air, like scissors do. And crows moaned in the trees.

Her face drooped, her energy was spent. Saliva dribbled from her lips.

I could have said a thousand things to my mother but we'd been strangers all our lives. I fought for words but they slipped out of my grasp like river eels you try to hold in your bare hands. I was gasping with the weight of her as we crouched in the grime. The grey river ruffled over a sandbar. I should have found her then in words at last, but for me it was only mathematics that came whirling out of the dark and made sense. I suppose that was because I am my mother's daughter.

We can't believe that the story will only be partly told. Maybe to others, but not to us, we don't deserve incompleteness.

We yearn so much.

WHERE MEMORIES GO 2

At the cafe on the plateau, the priest and the man under the circle of trees stood up from their coffees. They walked towards me. I expected them to veer around my table, but they stopped. I squinted up at them. They didn't look at me. They spoke to each other in Greek.

After a while the priest turned to me. He was dark against the sun, everything, his eyebrows, hat, the pouches under his eyes, his cloak, it all hung ponderously, he gathered everything to himself.

My friend, he said to me slowly, so each English word was like a medal he flashed in the sun,

my friend thinks you are Maria. Are you?

I shaded my eyes.

No, I said.

Maria from America? asked the priest.

No, I said.

You are sure? asked the priest.

I don't understand, I said.

My friend, he is very sad, his mind—the priest's hands smashed together in the air—my friend loved a woman called Maria. It was a long time ago. You will excuse us.

The priest's dark lips almost smiled. His eyeballs had the fierce sunbleached whiteness of the cafe walls. The man his friend was small, in a suit too short in the arms. He looked at the ground, not at me. He rubbed his nose with his hand. His cuffs were worn and disappointed. He lifted his head to look only at the priest.

My friend, the priest said to me, is a simple man, but good.

I saw that they were attached to each other by more than the priest's hand on the man's shoulder.

I will convince him you are not Maria, if you're sure, said the priest to me.

A hen clucked near the cafe walls. I stared at its brilliant feathers. A mad possibility of shouting

Yes! I'm Maria!

and following the priest and the sad man into another life eddied like the dust under the hen's claws. The dust settled again.

I am not Maria, I said.

The priest gently steered the man away. I could make out some words. Ohi Maria. Ohi Maria.

Behind him, his cloak spread like the leaves of the plane

tree, it swayed against the man's legs, his heels, his sad, loose trousers, it dragged at them like a net, like time, and for a second moment I wondered if I should've allowed it to drag at me.

Dead. It was such a hard word to say, I was sure that was why she didn't say it. A simple monosyllable but it rises so high in the mouth it blocks thought. I go over the moment again and again. My mother sagging on the kitchen lino.

No one said dead till much later, not for years. Nor did we talk about it in the long time after. Even Dad stood fiddling with the paintwork in doorways, forgetting what it was he'd come to say.

We lived in a quietness that was not silence. My brother's disappearance became another secret.

My suitcase leaned against my legs. My handbag was strung on the back of the chair. And the road unravelled in front of me, a blank space I could fill in.

I had been walking for minutes or hours, I couldn't tell, and still there were no houses, only hillsides slipping away and caught by ancient terraces, like the pleating of a fall of material. The way my mother might've pleated her skirt when I told her I was going to marry Harry.

She'd been sane for months, we thought she was no longer mad.

Can you reason with him? she'd asked. Do you fight?

I'm surprised when we argue, I said. I don't see the arguments coming. But afterwards, I can see how we got there.

And she'd gazed at the lake and said:

But we never see anything till afterwards.

Here the earth was the colour of rust, but it smelled of heat and flowers and goat dung. The noise of bells came on a gust of wind, each bell a different note, like a thought. The hills were like monsters hurled down and now elbowing their way back up to the sky. Behind the hills there was probably a field, olive trees shining silver in the light, a shepherd, a house.

Now as I walk on through the dust, I don't want to be a mathematician. All I want to do is watch eddies of memories tumble.

There was a noise, a shout. I wheeled. It was only an old man against a tree. The tree was too ancient and withered for shade. The man had resigned his legs to the sun and stretched them out. His thighs gripped an open, half-drunk bottle. He opened his mouth again in a laugh, and grabbed the bottle and waved it in the direction I was heading. Liquid in the bottle slopped, yellow as the sun. He shouted more words.

Thalassa, I heard. Kita ti orea thalassa.

I shrugged and turned to go on walking. And then I saw what must have been in front of me for a while. A swoop of sea, a sheen of slowly rolling silver. I couldn't move for the incomparable rolling silver of the sea.

The old man shouted again and thumped the ground beside him so that dust spiralled. He was indicating that I should sit and toast with him the incomparable sea. But I was a woman with memories tumbling out of me like light out of the sky. I laughed back, to think that I could sit under a tree to watch the sea.

I'm a bit busy, I said.

Though it demanded an audience, this sea, moving in silent grandeur into the sky and onto a beach. There was a huddle of shacks and a long fishing net stretched out on rocks to dry. And a truck, white and battered, starting up. The motor resisted, and its resistance floated into the air, and the silent sea dissolved it. The truck lurched forward and now it was noisy as it began its journey up the hill. I waited for it to go past, to dwindle so I could begin my silent journey again.

The truck drew level with me and braked. The driver looked down from his high seat at the old man under the tree and the foreign woman dressed for a city and carrying a suitcase.

Ti kanes, he shouted to the old man.

At home, amongst an interchange between two strangers, I'd go on walking, I knew how to be polite. In this new country I stood on tiptoe snatching at words, to at least hold their shape in my hand, to try to still them for a moment. But they whipped away as if nothing was said.

Ohi, I heard. Neh. No. Yes.

I began walking.

The driver pushed open the passenger's door and suddenly spoke English.

You understand him? he asked of the old man.

No, I said, startled.

Where are you going? he asked.

I have something urgent to do, I said.

He looked up and down the road empty of houses, traffic, offices, shops, telephone boxes, electricity wires.

Urgent, eh?

He pursed his lips and nodded as if he understood. He leaned black hairy elbows out his window.

Have you found somewhere to sleep? Or are you going to sleep on the beach, like a mermaid?

I smiled, and turned to go on walking.

You must be careful in this place, he called to me.

What of? I asked, unwillingly turning.

In this place, he said, the day fades so slowly, you do not realise, you stand on the beach watching the beautiful sea, you think the day will last for always, then suddenly—

297

he exploded his hand out like a star—
suddenly there is no light—poof!
His hand exploded again into a star—
light goes the way love goes.

I was turning to walk on, but the old man was shouting at
the truck driver, words rushing out of his mouth like spit. He
ran in front of me to block my way. I heard . . .

dipla sti thalassa.

He wants to offer you something, the truck driver called.

I saw how the loose skin on the old man's chest trembled
as he skipped.

I don't need anything, I called back. I was still walking,
and the old man was running backwards in front of me, his
bare feet on the road as light as a child's.

This man is not a good man, the truck driver called after
me.

Most of us aren't, I said.

The old man stopped so I had to walk around him.

He betrayed, called the truck driver.

Most of us do, I said.

He sold his first child to buy goats, the truck driver called.

I stopped in the sun at the insistence of the truck driver's
story. He'd got out of his truck to tell it. I turned around, took
a few steps back. The old man was squinting or smiling, I
couldn't tell which.

Then his wife had another child, said the truck driver, but
he sold that one too. And another and another and another,
says the truck driver. She had fourteen children but he sold
thirteen of them for goats.

The old man smiled in the sun and nodded.

I examined the dust at my feet so I couldn't see the old
man's trust in the truck driver, so I couldn't see his wife, her
swollen stomach, the plump arms of babies, how they twined.

So I couldn't see her sadness as her body split with the children she'd lose. After a while I found something to say.

He must be very rich.

The old man still smiled, scratching his underarm.

The goats died, said the truck driver.

In the pause we all watched the sea, its slow rolling.

This isn't what he wanted you to tell me, I said to the truck driver.

No, agreed the truck driver.

Well? I said.

He has a house on the beach. You can stay in the house. You give him money and you can sleep there, the truck driver said. What's the urgent thing you have to do?

Think, I said.

There's an old woman living by herself nearby, said the truck driver. She can arrange food, water, everything. She won't be any trouble to you. She doesn't speak. She hasn't for years.

I swallowed.

The men were shouting, bargaining, arranging a deal. I watched the sea.

Everything, said the truck driver to me. You have everything.

The truck driver was sitting back in his seat, turning on his ignition. The old man had gone, walking down the hill towards the sea.

You didn't tell me the end of the story, I was shouting to the truck driver.

He leaned out his window.

What happened to the fourteenth child? I asked.

That's me, said the truck driver.

I followed the old man towards the sea.

THE WOMAN WHO LOST THIRTEEN
CHILDREN 1

My house was a boatshed, the concrete on its floor so roughly laid its corrugations were like the seabed. The walls were rocks balanced on rocks, wooden beams and chunks of wood. The roof was olive tins, hammered flat, red with rust, but they made an assertion like a distant shouting: ELLAZ. Ellaz, I knew, means Greek. There was a canvas camp bed dipping in the middle and lopsided with a broken leg and piled with thin grey blankets and coarse sheets and a dented pillow. The door had been wrongly hung and opened inwards so that to shut it I had to step backwards or flatten myself against the opposite wall. Damp cobwebs hung from the rocks, grit crunched under my feet. The only light was from the doorway and the gaps between stones. It was the least polite room I'd ever been in.

Perfect, I said to no one. I brought my suitcase in from the pebble beach outside and flung the door shut and flattened myself against the wall just in time. I lay down on the bed to think, to decide, as if there was still a decision to make.

But there wasn't. I'd run away from the conference, and that was that.

There was a noise at the door, a jangle, a thump, and I was struggling off the bed, my legs waving in the air like a cockroach. The door burst open. It was an old woman with a back so bent her face almost reached the apron tied around what was once her waistline. Her eyes scarcely met mine. She looked at the floor and the walls and then she turned and dragged through the doorway a mop and a broom and a bucket brimming with water. Though I could only see round mounds of pebbles behind her, I heard the ocean sigh.

I moved forward to help but she waved me fiercely away. She went out again, and came back holding another bucket with a wringer attached. She picked up my suitcase and handbag and handed them to me, but all the time she didn't look me in the face. She gestured towards the back wall that faced the ocean.

But I shook my head at this broken woman. I took the mop. She grabbed it, she struggled for possession of it, and as the mop twisted she looked me at last in the eyes. The sea had no glitter compared to the pain in her eyes, and no strength like the strength of her hands. So I deferred against the wall while she wielded the wet mop, because I knew who she was. I was the woman who had chosen to keep secret my mother's theorems that lead to numbers no one has ever thought of before, and she was the woman who had lost thirteen children. I was the one who crouched.

She scuttled spiders and dirt and in a moment we were both coughing. She came over and pushed me away from the wall. I jumped at her touch, as guilty as if it was something I'd longed for. She prised me away from the wall. She struggled with a latch. Suddenly the back wall shifted. There was the turquoise sea, standing upright and roaring towards us, and she was nodding to it as if it was her friend.

She didn't speak to me but she pushed me towards a chair on a tiny porch the size of a doormat. As I sat, the sea was frenzied with light and the wind whipped the surface into angry currents. Waves scurried head downwards like crowds in a subway, not daring to stop and look around. I sat facing the endlessly sighing sea.

My boatshed was a place of dreams. Sometime in the middle of the first night, I woke to air pouring so coldly between the gaps in the stones, it felt like the ancient silver of moonlight. I sat up amongst my grey blankets and checked my body, expecting to find I'd become a silver ghost. And at dawn I woke to see on my grey blankets a broken bird clawing the sweet earth one last time before it closed its eyes forever. I reached out and touched the bird. The bird was my other hand. I traced my hand to my arm, my shoulder, my face, my mind.

When the spell of a dream's gone, there's only sleep.

Now there was a knock on the door, the door of my father's house with a customer waiting, the door of my hotel and Adele waiting, the door of my boatshed. I heard it above the rise and fall of the waves, the whirring and rattling of the beach of stones, the suck of water.

I opened the door, backing with it and side-stepping the bed.

Just a minute, just a minute, I was shouting.

I put my head around the door. On the step there was a cup of coffee and a glass of water and a bread roll on a metal tray. The tray was dented so it flared in the morning. No one was in sight on the beach or on the winding road. The only sound was the beach stones and from somewhere behind the hill, the clank of goat bells.

I walked out on the beach. There were three houses off the road to one side. Two looked uncared for. Perhaps someone lived in them, it was hard to tell. There was the blackened exhaust pipe of a tractor sticking up behind an ancient stone wall, and beyond that, a field of furrowed grey dirt where perhaps potatoes grew. The third house had a line of washing pegged meticulously between olive trees. Olive tins brimmed with pink and red geraniums and a bougainvillea vine was so thick and ancient it was like a pillar on which the whole house leaned. With the sun behind, it was festooned with flowers the colour of my mother's skin.

A figure appeared at a window. I raised my hand to greet her. She went away without waving. In a second she was back, shaking a rug, making it whip the air.

That day

*My mother told me this story when she was dying, in a voice so
faint, I had to put my ear against her ancient lips.*
Hypatia

There's another day. I'll say it, and let it go. It all happened
a long time ago, and time buries everything in the earth.
Another day, another afternoon. Matti was still with us. It was
a time of sudden heat, just when we were preparing for that
last terrible winter.

There had been, on the top of the notes under the bed, a
picture, blurred from a gestetner machine. It was called Even
A Slave Boy. An ancient Greek man stood with folded arms,
his followers behind him, looking like him. Perhaps it was
Socrates. On the ground, he'd drawn a diagram, a square on
the diagonal inside a large square. Socrates and his followers
were patient, knowledgeable, righteous. The ground was dust-
less. A boy, far below their towering figures, was half-naked,
on his knees, considering. You could see that till this moment,
the world had been for him a teeming chaos. But Socrates
waited. He knew, you could see from the picture that even the
folds of his garments were convinced, that with thought and
care even a slave boy could trace the mind of God.

It was amongst her lover's notes, a picture of the belief that
mathematics is outside of us, waiting to be discovered.

It was on this picture that my mother's scarlet pen had
laughed about apeiron, the ancient Greek word:

Apeiron, the word for infinity, meant something as dull, as
grubby as a dirty handkerchief. (As my apron???) They
didn't want anything so incomplete as apeiron. They wanted

a simple, underlying pattern. So spell-binding, it stopped thought.

But the day I have to talk about, Matti was still with us. I was early home from school again. Her lover had let himself in the house. I don't know how often he'd done that before. I'd crept up the front steps to see them again, my mother and her lover. They weren't on the verandah, or in the garden. But the spare key was in the door, its metal ball chain dangling.

I was hot with shock at that careless key, the chain swinging at my touch. She'd been calmer lately, no more nightmares, no waking in the night, she answered the door to Dad's customers. But she still locked everything behind her. She wouldn't have left a key in the lock.

I heard, from inside the house, a noise. A throat clearing, his throat clearing, that anxious noise as if all obstruction must go, not any bubble of saliva or clutch of phlegm must impede him. It was him. He was inside. He must've unlocked the door with the key and left it there.

Did the throat clearing come from my parents' bedroom? Was he in my mother's bed with my mother?

The cough again, more imperative.

It was from the kitchen, he was in the kitchen.

A sudden breeze fluttered a note sticky-taped to the wall. I hadn't noticed it before.

Can't quite remember our arrangement. Tomorrow, I hope. Dashed off to a deceased estate's library sale. They're just giving the books away.

It was written in my mother's ink.

Her lover was in our house, alone.

I prised off the note, folded it into my pocket. I was suddenly full of rage against him, that he'd broken the rules. He should've taken the note down, she would've meant him to. He'd left the note there careless of my sudden return. Careless of my brother. Careless of my father. Careless of her, whom he loved. The thought whirled like a tornado into my dark spaces.

Didn't he know her? Didn't he love her? Loving her meant loving her secrets, making them his secrets.

Suddenly that dark wind had blown me out beyond the road, beyond the steps, the path, the gate. I was crouched between the ancient roots of a giant angophora. I rested my cheek against its calm strength, it was silent, close, indifferent.

But in the kitchen of my home fifteen metres away was the warm, moist precision of the man who was my mother's lover. His shirt gaped to make my breath huff in wonder at his smoothness, his slenderness. Even his fine hands moved like songs I'd remember if I thought hard enough. His muscles knotted in his arms as he held my beautiful mother.

I decided to go inside the house. He'd imagine, at the creak of the hall floorboards, that I'm my mother back early. He'd turn, those handsome arms stretched to enfold her. His eyes would be points of light before he realised it was me.

I'll put on a cuppa, I'd say, my schoolbag clattering on the lino.

Mum shouldn't be long.

He'd have been reading lecture notes, the ones my mother had written on. He'd have been sitting—did I decide he'd be sitting or standing?—he'd be sitting legs crossed, shirt unbuttoned to show his skin stretched so winsomely across his bones, the tremors in his chest, his eyes tipped up and set like a cat's in his face, those eyes that seek you out in the room, to separate you even from the air around you.

He'd speak then. What would he say?

I thought I'd wait here for a bit because it's a while before the next train, he'd say.

He'd smile slowly, uncertainly, this thirteen-year-old girl whose name he didn't remember. There's such warm suspense in a slow smile.

His hands would be fiddling with the pages of his notes, unsure in the presence of a thirteen year old whether he should keep reading or put his lecture notes away. He'd decide to be polite because it's important to show the young how to behave. He'd put his lecture notes away. He'd turn his gaze to me.

I'd fill the kettle, glance out the window while the water boiled to check the roses, how many petals the frost had browned, just like my mother always did. He'd notice that. I'd empty the teapot. His eyes would be prickling my back.

I know you take milk, I'd say proudly.

And then, in our ordinary kitchen, when I was standing at the sink, he'd say:

I'm astounded.

That I remembered you take milk? I'd say.

The fine lines under his eyes would be twitching with recognition. He'd have pushed his notes aside to be sociable, no, I forgot, they're already in his bag.

I'm astounded at how wrong I was. You're so like your mother, he'd say.

Out the window, the ordinary day would pulse. Somewhere far off, a dog would bark. Leaves would twitch on the ground. It would all be as it always was. But my head would be ringing with joy. That the words had been spoken at last, that someone at last had thrown a gauzy cape around my misshapen red face, my bony legs, my purple elbows, the blue veins that already crossed my hands, my bleached lips, my long and earnest nose. Someone had looked deeply into me, at last, and seen that I shared my mother's beauty.

You're almost her, he'd say.

As we filled in the silence by sipping tea till my mother arrived I'd lift my arms behind my head like she did. My body, like hers, would measure thought.

For a moment in time, I'd be her, with him.

So I walked into my father's house whistling as if I had no knowledge of his presence, I turned into the kitchen, I skidded my bag against the wall.

My mother's lover was at first only a shadow leaning, arms crossed, against the kitchen table. I was suddenly aware of how the fatty flesh on his arms bulged. I hadn't noticed fat before.

I saw you crouched in the bushes, he was saying. What were you doing, weeing?

It was one of those moments again.

What did you say? I asked.

You heard me. Weeing.

Something inside me was crumpling.

He's so bad mannered, my head was shouting. No one in my life had admitted to nakedness, and he was using a word hot and stinking with nakedness. Oh, he'd been naked with my mother, and my mother had been naked with him, but it was not admitted, not a fit subject for talk. And no one, no one in my world would wee in front of another person. Did my mother know he thought like this? I reached out for the working board, my mother's working board, the scratches of our family, our comings and goings, our history that suddenly seemed so gentle.

You knew I was watching you out the window, didn't you? he was saying. You were enjoying being watched, weren't you? As you weeed?

I was struggling to hide my burning face in my arms, I was so embarrassed at his bad manners, that's all I could think, that suddenly he'd lost his manners.

Little animal, he said.

My mother wouldn't like to hear you say that, I said, I wasn't shouting yet.

I've had my eye on you, he said.

I'd reached the rough edge of the working board but it wasn't the working board at all, I was holding onto the rough edges of his hands that had seemed so smooth. But now he was grabbing, yanking. I was screaming, stumbling to the knife drawer, which was toppling, falling against my shins. And still he was yanking at my clothes, laughing, saying more words like wee and animal and little, I bent for a knife but he pushed me and hurled the knife out of my hands, it arched over the kitchen like my voice, my voice was spiralling over his laughter, my voice was screaming for my mother. Then he seemed to be using the knife inside me. It was his penis.

My mother when she came back wondered why the kitchen table had been pushed out of its usual position, why the chairs were toppled, why the drawers were upended, why there were knives all over the floor. Why I crouched in my bed, like a wild animal after all. Why I stayed there for a week with my head turned to the wall, unable to speak.

There's blood, she said when she washed my sheets eventually.

But there were no answers to her questions, there could be none, when in all our conversation it was as if her lover had never existed, never existed at all.

And there were no answers to my questions: with all my daydreams, did I call that terrible moment into being? That moment when everything turned?

When I left my bed, it was the start of that terrible winter.
So I've told it at last and it can be buried.

My house

Dear Mum,
Mum, we're not hollow. Last night, I came across an old book
about women's bodies. It must've been Grandma's. It was
published before your birth. Maybe she was trying to find out how
her babies would be born. How you'd be born. It opened at a
picture of a closed brown fist crisscrossed with strength as if it
wanted me to know. Cross-section of a womb, the caption said.
There was not even room for a baby. A baby would have to fight
back those towering walls. I'd thought we were empty bags,
gaping, flaccid, waiting. I thought that's why we lived such waiting
lives. Why you did. Have you ever seen this book?
I cried over that picture, I rippled its smoothness with my wet
tears, I cried for me, I cried for you. When I reached up to put the
book back, my fierce womb roared.
Today my story allowed me back inside its cushioned softness,
my story, I'm inside it and it's inside me. My heroine no longer
dies. I think I'd succumbed to unnecessary sadness. I've rewritten
the ending, astonishingly fast after months of anguish. Now I'm
rewriting, and suddenly it's easy. I float above the type-written
pages like a bird, inspecting where to land.

Love from Hypatia

The day deepened. The sea glinted turquoise in the gaps between the stones of my boatshed, then emerald, grey, silver, gold. The glints became changing patterns on my bed, on me, on the walls, on the other patterns. We moved, my boatshed and me, inside the patterns of the ocean, my boatshed a transparent shell moving inside the sea. I drifted into sleep and woke and moved again into the patterns of the sea's light. And I eased into the sea's sighs and it heaved itself up to my shed and rolled away. I drowsed in the turquoise sighs of the sea.

Sometime on that first long morning, I walked on the stone beach. I bent to finger sea shells coated with a pearly sheen, I touched their spiraling history coiled up, the present nestled against the past. A man strode up the beach when the sun was so bright I had to squint, to mend his nets drying on the rocks. The nets were threads of yellow, orange, brown, now knotted, now loose, now knotted, now loose. He sat with his back to the ocean, cutting, knotting, he dragged more net towards his lap, his lap swallowing folds of net as he worked. He looked up from heavy grey eyebrows as he knotted, he checked my gaze, he barely nodded his head. He had work, and I was a woman with nothing to do but urgently finger the coils of her life.

I went back to my shed. In the turning, turning light of the sea, I wanted to think about it endlessly, that mother, that childhood. I knew that the movement of all that sea outside my window could be charted by the same simple differential equation, yet every breaking of a wave was different. It seemed very important to me then that from simple equations, complicated things happen. I wanted to hold each memory up to the turning light of the turquoise sea. And as I tossed on my canvas bed, drifting between patterns, I thought of how events seemed to take a particular shape, but how they could just as easily have taken another. Where the line is drawn is arbitrary, no matter how inevitable it seems. How much it seems like truth.

Another knock on my door. A meal on a metal tray again, the same dent flaring like meaning. A bowl of aubergines and tomatoes, bread still in its loaf, yoghurt, water, a cloudy red wine that was surely homemade. I opened the door and looked out. The old woman toiled up the hill. Beyond her, the waves paused between certainties, then plunged, like the mind does. The old woman had dwindled now to her hair, tousled in a sudden wind. Her hair was a blaze of white light.

So I sat eating my breakfast and watching the sea. I'd said I had to think. That was what I'd come here for. That was what the journey was about. With each bite, maybe at this moment I'd work out how to live, what to do about my mother. I'd weigh the big issues: love, betrayal, ageing, failure, death. That'd do for a start.

But the mind is always errant. Only one question moved in me. It wasn't the big question I expected to have to answer. It wasn't, after all, about life. Or maybe it was, because the divine and the trivial often slide into each other, as if they're part of each other. My question was: how did she cook the aubergines?

Certain things come in a blaze of white light, that perfect coalescence of colour. A certain movement of the mind, the realisation that we are different from what we thought. Even as her door slammed behind her, I knew I must sit in her kitchen.

As I stood at her front door, her ancient face clotted like the sea's furrowing. She took the empty tray with the merest nod of her head. She was wiping her hands on a white cloth, one of those people who clean everything, even the air around her seemed more shining than it seems for me. I kept standing on her doorstep smiling. I smiled for so long that at last she tipped her head behind her, to her dark and gleaming corridor.

The other day

Dad divorced Mum and married Bev Roberts. Mum kept living in the house he'd built to house the dreams he'd had when he was young. I moved out when I married Harry, to begin my freedom, but I'd driven up the mountains three times a week to visit her ever since.

This is freedom? You would laugh.

I've been missing the convent, my mother said to me one day. Holidays at home are nice but this one's been too long.

Behind your grandmother's back, you made your usual screw-loose circles with your finger.

Besides, my mother said, it'd be safer there. They don't let men with knives in.

Grandma's really crazy, talking about her father's enemies, she laughed in the car on the way down the mountains. What enemies would a dull family like ours have had?

I should've realised how little I'd talked to you. But I still didn't talk. Not then. I just gripped the steering wheel and kept in my lane.

I put my mother in the Beryl Urskin Home for the Frail Aged in the city. She didn't seem to notice that there were no nuns, only nurses. She called the nurses Sister, and the matron Mother. No one argued with her.

If that's the way she wants it, that's OK, said the matron.

When asked, my mother nodded yes, she liked it here.

There's too much freedom out there, my mother said. Here, you know where you are.

For outings she went down to the ditch when it rained.

I took you away from school for a week, and remember, we sat together on a lonely beach up the coast and watched the sea take the sand away in its rolling, and bring it rolling back.

What are you going to do now, Mum? You asked behind your knowing eyes.

Now grandma's defunct, you added.

You were thirteen at the time, the age I'd been when everything happened.

I went back to teaching, and waiting.

And then a small thing happened, a tiny thing that didn't seem at the time like a beginning. I'd often been exasperated by my students and literature. One day I ordered a girl to come to my office after school for detention. When she knocked at my door, I'd forgotten her misdemeanour, but I was in the habit of giving one hundred lines.

What do I have to write? she asked. Her hair, I remember, was frizzing out of a bobbypin, the sort of hair that's grey and wiry right from the start. There was a mole on her cheek which stretched when she gaped. She was sullen and heavy and her chins tucked into each other in mute resentment. She wasn't going to grow into a pretty woman, nor a clever one. I was almost going to tell her to go home, but it was a school that demanded strictness, so I led her into an empty classroom.

Irony is the mocking distance between what is, and what could be, I dictated.

She yawned. I didn't blame her, it was a hot, sleepy afternoon. Every twitch of the roof in the afternoon heat startled me. There was no sound but the clicking of her biro and her laboured breath. There was nothing to do but watch her, nothing to think. From whimsy or a dull hope that it might lessen the work, she didn't write the dictated line straight across the page, as I'd expected. She wrote irony in a column all the way down the page, then a column of is, then a column of the, then a column of mocking. By the time she'd handed me four pages of my sentence deconstructed and arranged in mocking columns, I'd decided to end the irony of my life.

I skipped out of the school as if I'd been a child waiting out a detention. Which in a way, I was.

You were still thirteen, and I'd like to know, I'd like to understand who a daughter is.

There's some old books I have to read, I said. Stacked away in Grandma Juanita's laundry.

THE WOMAN WHO LOST THIRTEEN CHILDREN 3

The old woman led me into a kitchen full of potatoes. On a table that took up most of the floor space, a tumble of potatoes trembled at our footsteps, nudging and wriggling, nudging and rolling and lying still, relinquishing clumps of brown dirt as they rolled and pressing them into the table, rolling and threatening to topple over the table's edge, stopping because of a metal strip around the table's edge, rolling and rumbling back to the centre. Against the walls, sacks of potatoes were humped. Around the table were two large bins of potato peelings, three bins of potatoes soaking in grimy water, and three empty bins. High above the potatoes, a shrine ticked on the wall, battery operated, with a red glow and a pale young Christ. And then there was the sea, shocking in its sudden wildness, contained within a window frame but leaping in blue silence through her kitchen, a torrent of blue brilliance on her walls, her shrine, her face, her potatoes. I had forgotten the sea.

The old woman beside me pointed to the clock and picked up a knife. Potato juice ran along its blade. Perhaps I was meant to understand that she was busy and I must go, but I didn't want to. I wanted to stand in this blue light near her amongst the smell of potatoes. She picked up the next potato and began to peel it.

I told you a long time ago that I never peeled potatoes with my mother. And yet the most important moments of my life happened in kitchens. I learned to count with the daily collection of eggs from our hens, brown eggs nestling on an old green plate and spinning at my touch, breathing dirt and bran and grass. I watched the big brown clock on the kitchen mantelpiece measuring time so I thought time had a kindly face. The first words I read were labels on my mother's cannisters, flour, sugar, tea, and when I was tall enough to look inside them and find coffee, salt and rice instead, I learned that words are as slippery as love. I fell in love in my mother's kitchen, with my mother and mathematics. I learned about my brother's disappearance when my mother sagged on the kitchen lino. And when her lover grabbed me on the kitchen floor and forced me down, I learned we all have such appalling power, such appalling frailty.

So that as I looked around the old woman's kitchen lit blue by the sea, the walls stained with steam but hung with photographs of her lost children, the kitchen chairs worn down by conversations and arguments, its familiarity didn't surprise me at all. A kitchen, in its own way, is as much a place of the spirit as a cathedral.

So I pulled my chair up to the table of jiggling potatoes and sat down. The old woman looked up angrily at me, her knife

raised and flashing above the floury whiteness in her hand, as
roundly smooth as a breast. I'd always fitted in with what
other people wanted. But this time, I didn't. I jumped up, went
to a drawer and there was a knife, just where I knew it would
be. I sat down again, side by side with her, I was her mirror,
except that I was clumsy and her hands moved like a sculptor,
baring the potato of its skin and shaping it into its new life.
She watched my clumsiness, sniffed, worked on. I watched
her jab out an eye with the point of her knife. I did the same.
She almost smiled. We went on peeling potatoes. We threw
the naked potatoes into the bin of water. There was no sound,
just the crunch and chopping of our knives and the plop of
water, and the potatoes rolling on the table to take up space.
The shrine ticked. Somewhere, goat bells rang. The sea shed
its silent light.

When the sea light began to make rainbows on the walls,
the old woman stopped peeling and rolled up her sleeves. She
took a soaked potato out of the bin, chopped it into chips, and
threw the pieces into one of the empty bins. It gleamed whitely
on the bin bottom, at peace at last. I put down my knife,
wondering if I should help with the chopping. She looked
questioningly at me, and her lips twisted into a rare smile. She
picked up my knife, patted my hand, and put the knife back
into it. I peeled, she chopped. A rainbow from the sea glanced
on her knife's edge as she worked. I peeled so clumsily that
she had finished chopping all the potatoes into chips when I
was peeling the last one. She came over to me, took my knife
away, laid my hands flat on the table, took my potato, finished
peeling it with one deft twirl of her knife, washed the potato,
chopped it and threw the pieces on top of the third bin.
Together we dragged the bins of chips out the door into the
corridor. She covered each with a damp tea-towel.

We came back into her kitchen. She smiled at me and there

was a rainbow in her face. She plucked at my sleeve and pulled me to a tap. After my clumsiness with potatoes she despaired of me, she took my hands and washed them like a child's, soaping them until I wore bubbling gloves of soap, lifting with her own fingernail the potato dirt from under mine, rinsing the soap off under a clear fall of water, drying my hands gently on a soft towel. A wind moved across the ocean and the rainbows in her kitchen leapt and ricocheted and collided in her face.

I would've liked to reach and touch them, but I didn't. My hands reached out so clumsily to my mother.

She wiped down the kitchen table, now the work was done, and nudged me into a chair. Suddenly she was girlish, all flurrying swinging skirts despite her bent back, her slippers worn at the sides of her feet. She went to a shelf and brought back a box. She put it on the table. On its lid someone had stuck a painting of a blonde pale woman with white shoulders and a fan. The woman was being kissed by a handsome man in a velvet blue frockcoat. The picture was lifting at the corners. She saw me smiling at the picture. We caught each other's glances, and laughed. I was still laughing as I opened the lid. Inside, there was an eyeball.

The woman shuffled to the shrine. She crossed herself and kissed the face of Christ. Her lips lingered on his. I saw with a jolt how untried his young face was. She pulled a tumbler from a high shelf with difficulty, filled it at the tap, put it down, poured olive oil into a teaspoon, poured the teaspoon of oil into the tumbler. When she put the glass onto the table, the water with its green sheen of oil leaped and swooned.

Some oil spilled on the shining surface of the table, but she didn't notice. She sat with her back to the red glow of the shrine.

She reached into the box and dropped the eyeball into the

tumbler. Her face was cocked above the glass. Her lips moved, she might've been mouthing a spell or a prayer or just grunting, I couldn't tell. She stirred the water with a teaspoon, the ordinary movements of someone in a kitchen. The green oil scattered in shining beads. At the bottom of the glass the eye was huge, glaring, monstrous. She lifted the teaspoon out. The water stilled. The only sound was the ticking of the shrine. She scrambled to her feet, she was smiling, satisfied, whatever the eyeball had told was sufficient to please her. She touched my hair and my face so gently.

When her son in his grinding white truck arrived to pick up the bins of chipped potatoes, we were sitting, the old woman and I, on chairs side by side in the sunlight to watch the sea. Around our white coffee cups, the coffee grounds were looped like arms. His shadow fell over us. His mother jumped up to greet him. She cupped his face so gently in her hands, as my mother never cupped mine. I was unwilling to smile, childishly staring at the sharp line of the horizon, waiting for him to go. I was bursting with words, but not for him. For his mother.

He dragged a bin of chipped potatoes to his truck. I knew I should offer to help, but I stayed in my chair. He saw my hunched shoulders.

How long have you been helping her? he asked convivially.

I pretended not to hear. Surely he could work it out himself.

He grunted, and pulled the bin up on the truck.

I told you, he said as he returned for another bin, to be careful of the light here.

He went inside the house.

The sea is oreo today, he said when he came out. Oreo. It means beautiful. As beautiful as anything you can dream of.

I've worked that out, I said.

He lashed the bins together, and latched up the back flap of his truck. But he didn't go. He leaned against his truck and dug his hands in his pockets, determined to have a conversation. I was determined not to. We both stared at the sea.

After a while, he brushed his hands together and pushed his body forward away from his truck as if he was about to walk around to his cabin and drive off. His mother plumped back down in her chair, looking from her son to me, wondering.

Sometimes, he said, the seas are very heavy going.

I found something to say.

In heavy seas, every tenth wave is bigger than normal, I blurted.

He stopped. He leaned back against the truck and began to smile.

Every tenth one, eh? he smiled. For a second I thought he was going to count waves as they rolled in.

On average, I corrected myself, anxious to speak now and a little embarrassed because whenever I thought of something to say, there was only mathematics.

On average. Even though it just looks like waves heaving and collapsing, I added.

His mother reached over and took my hand. Her son didn't seem to mind. He was still smiling, the smile moving up his face.

I'll watch out my window tonight and keep a tally, he smiled.

You'd think the size of waves are unpredictable, I said, floundering in his smile and her ancient hands with skin as wrinkled with life as a lizard's.

But in unpredictability there's often a pattern, I added.

Because we look for it? he asked. Or is it there?

You're asking that? I murmured.

I've had a lot of time, he said, to ask things. A lot of silence.

Yes, I said.

Then, because suddenly his smile was like the curve of a wave we were both riding on, I was toppling like a wave into saying:

If we make it all up—

He was still smiling.

—how can we choose what to make up? So we can bear it? My voice was puny against the crashing sea.

He waited until the breaker swirled almost to the road's edge before he said:

Whatever we choose, the waves keep rolling in.

Suddenly we were both laughing like conspirators who'd shared a secret. His mother creaked in her chair, her hand jerking in mine, her mute mouth open with laughter too. Then he sighed and turned back to check the latches on his truck.

It's hard to talk, he said, so close to his truck that his breath puffed the dust that coated the white duco. So many memories get in the way.

Here? I asked. You mean, Greece?

His eyes rested uneasily on the glinting ocean.

It was hard to be the chosen one, he said.

You were the chosen one? I asked.

Of course, he said. All the others were sold. I was the one who was kept.

It's painful to be chosen? I asked.

Everything depended on me, he said. I wanted to run away.

It's another moment, the sort my mother denied.

You wanted to run away, I repeated.

The past was too big. It takes a lot of getting over, he was saying. But it can be got over. Bit by bit.

It can be got over, I repeated.

He got in his white truck and slammed the door. But he wound down his window to say:

Thanks. That was a great talk.

He didn't wave as he drove away. We were left, his mother and I, on the white silent blank of the road.

Happiness was suddenly an expanse as wide and full of light as the ocean in me. I put my arm around the old woman, and found a stick in the road. I was pulling her with me, I was finding a spot where the dust was deepest. She came so readily. There, in the heat of the sun, I drew the first of my new sort of number.

I'd like to say that it reached her, that the ancient Greeks were right, that mathematics is a language which everyone understands. That it's for all of us. She hobbled around the symbols, herself a bent stick, glancing, gazing, shuffling, exclaiming.

What do you think? I asked her. Can you see that if I change this function—

I showed her

—that I'm in a new land of numbers?

I had no idea what she made of it. But when she came to grip my hands, her face was drowned in light.

Orea, a trembling voice said.

I was staring at my symbols in the dust. I turned slowly, to see who'd spoken. From the blue horizon of sea to the white horizon of earth, there was only me and an old woman, bent and mute.

Oreo, she repeated, stronger now.

At that moment, I didn't mind if she was the only person in the world to know about my new sort of numbers.

I peeled potatoes with her another two days of rainbows. Afterwards, we sat in our chairs side by side to watch the sea.

The surf's up, I said into her eyes that were now so merry

I couldn't remember her earlier sadness. All around the bay, rocks clanked as the waves pulled back out to sea.

She laughed at me, her face on one side, quizzical.

There's nothing at home for me, I said. The trouble with overtaking your mother is that you're on your own. Unsheltered under a violent sky.

I had forgotten my daughter.

The old woman stood up to make me another coffee. She wouldn't let me make it, she was sure I couldn't learn the deft movements of her hand as she moved the tiny pan of coffee grounds and sugar over the heat.

At night I sat alone with my metal tray on my lap and a candle beside me dancing in the wind and almost blowing out and recovering to dance again. I worked on the second new number, searching for a path into a bewildering country. The sea was so black I couldn't tell where it became the sky. It was so starless that if you wandered in it, you'd be lost.

Sometimes I put down my pen to look at it.

You've had your turn, I whispered into that starlessness. You've had it twice. In your own life, and in mine, even though you didn't want that.

Sometime on the third night, when I'd finally put away my work and gone to bed, there was such a moaning at my door that I imagined a wild wind was tossing the ocean. I pulled at the door. It flew open too fast, I had to jump out of the way. Something had been leaning against it, a deeper darkness.

Who? I whispered.

There was no sound, only the moaning. I searched for a cat, or a child who'd lost its mother. I had to stand on the step to see an outline. It was the air that spoke to me, so clenched I knew it was her. Then it loosened and I knew she'd stepped over the threshold and come inside. There was a rustle of sheets. She was in my bed.

So we lay for the night in each other's warmth, the woman who never reached her mother, and the woman who had lost all her children but one, and sometimes we rocked each other, and sometimes we moaned, and sometimes we laughed.

SOME PEOPLE WOULD'VE CALLED HER BRAZEN 2

When my mother went into the Home, I didn't take down her wallpaper in Matti's room just in case one day she came back. It was tattered and peeling. Strips of it lay on the floor.

Then, after the house had been boarded up for a few months, I drove there from the city one day. Dad's new ute was in the drive, and there was a dribble of white powdered plaster down the path to the door. Dad had just replastered the walls of his house. In Matti's room, the pages of mathematics were gone. Bev Roberts was by his side with the thermos.

Can you manage without me, love? A bit of girl talk,

she said to him flirtatiously as if we were going to compare lipsticks.

She took me out to my mother's kitchen. She shut the door.

I'm sorry to say it about your mother, but if I hadn't seen it with my two eyes, I wouldn't have credited a woman could be that brazen, she whispered.

Love letters. Among sums!

Ah, I said. I couldn't think of anything else to say.

She drank most of the thermos herself in the horror of my mother, the tea steaming down her gnarled throat.

Your father and I, she said, tossing her head towards Matti's old room,

are laying ghosts to rest.

Her face was dusted with white plaster. She could've been a ghost herself.

Not that you'd have known what they were up to, you being so young at the time, she said.

I didn't stay long. But as I was leaving, she said suddenly, an afterthought:

You ought to lay some ghosts to rest, too.

When I was backing down the drive, my father came out of the house. I stopped and wound down the window.

I want you to know, he said, leaning in, sweaty, warm, wrinkled,

that my wedding day to your mother was the happiest day in my life.

It was such a good marriage? I asked, touched.

No, he said.

He had a smear of white on his forehead.

But I thought I held heaven in my hands, he said. For a while.

His blunt hands in the air were estimating the length and depth and breadth of heaven, as he'd always estimated the length and depth and breadth of rooms and land and wood and pipes and glass, calculating by some sense I'd never considered, the exact distances between the span of his fingers, between the tip of his longest finger and some point on his wrist, elbow, shoulder or neck. It was the first time I'd ever looked at him in awe. He was a geometer.

There are many ways, I saw, to be a mathematician. I owed my geometric devices to him.

A WINDOW CAN'T CONTAIN THE SEA

I'd like someone to discover another picture in a pile of notes. I'd like that someone to be a teenage girl longing for splendour. I'd like her to come upon it unexpectedly, say under a bed where lovers lie, or at the back of a wardrobe where diaphanous clothes hang. I'd like to think that she'd pore over the picture, that she'd put it away and take it out so many times it wore out along its creases.

There'd be an ancient woman lying on a bed in a room made of wedges of moving light. The woman's life has bent her body, but not quite broken it. Her worn dress sags to show breasts exhausted by the tuggings of many children, but her cheekbones hold out her face in a way that's almost triumphant. Inside the bend of her body is another woman, perhaps her daughter, just waking, her hair still tangled with sleep, her face still moving into its morning shape. But she's gazing out of the picture with eyes that have the glitter of an animal suddenly freed, such fine glittering points that you know the picture cannot contain her, as a window gazing out to sea cannot contain the sea.

There's a moment you know when you are not your mother, after all. You're like a black stone on a beach in a black night. The stone is almost the night. Almost. It's the almost that rescues you. Long before dawn there's an edge of light against a deeper darkness, and at that edge, you know that the stone is not the night. So your mother falls away from you.

And then there's a long white dawn, so long it's like those days in childhood when you couldn't remember the beginning. Was there a beginning? But then, who's ever to know when a beginning happens?

At some time in that long white beginning, I put down my

pen and took out my daughter's bundle of letters, and broke
the string she bound them with. I sighed at their endlessness,
and began to read them in the blue light from the sea.

MY TENTH LETTER

Our house

Dear Mum,
I've had a shock. I read Grandma Juanita's diary again. I had a
look at the sum at the back, that goes on for pages. Most of the
sum—I suppose I should call it a conjecture, you would—most of
it's in blue ink, blots dropped, the symbols drawn with such
difficulty. Sometimes she's crossed them out in her scarlet ink and
redrawn them. At first I thought you and she must've sat together
at this kitchen table, perhaps exactly where I sit now. When I look
up, white curtains gauze against trees. I was trying to imagine you
in this house as a child writing this down, your feet not quite
touching the floor, your hand slipping on the wooden pen handle,
your tongue sticking out in concentration as you rounded the
numbers and letters. You wanted so much to please her.
   But here, and here, and here there's almost a reluctance, the
pen seems to loll, splattering blue to hide the line before, and here
Grandma has crossed out your work so angrily, her scarlet nib has
pierced the page. Have I misunderstood, I wonder. Were you all
along a rebellious scribe? Have I misunderstood? It is yours, isn't
it, the writing of these stumbling, fading sums?
   Or—the thought breaks, wavers, chills—as I touch the faltering
letters with my blunt fingertips—am I touching at last the silent
secret of your life? Was it Matti my uncle, not you, she meant to
make a mathematician?
   Now I examine his schoolbooks, I could persuade myself the
handwriting's his, there's his v and his a, and there's how he does

326

t. All his proud flourishes. He must have been vain, preposterous, extravagant. How could a brother and sister be so different?

So perhaps there's another story I've never heard. You weren't her scribe. You weren't at the table. You were somewhere else, perhaps at the doorway over there, picking at bits of paint, your mind moving with hers, your mouth moving with her conjecture, your eyes reaching out like arms to touch her glossy face, to say:

I'm the child who will remember your soul.

But she turned her back to you. You saw by the determined slump of her heels in her shoes that she would never turn around. It must've been such a sad paradox to her, that you didn't look at all like her but you were just like she'd been as a child, such a painful reflection. Matti was the chosen one. And here's the proof of how reluctantly he dragged his pen against her fierce will while she dictated her life work.

All my life I've never known that you were waiting for your life to begin.

The baby has taught me so much. My own childhood.

Your daughter, Hypatia

The Remainder of
a Lifetime

Joanna's door sprang open at my touch. She came into the passage, a potato in her hand, its peel spiralling onto the shine of the floor. She put the potato and the knife in one hand and led me through the house to her stove. In a deep wide pot, lunch was simmering, eggplant and tomatoes and meat. She put down the potato. Her breath was coming in little puffs, her old withered cheeks were plump.

Daughter, she said. The word was almost unsayable in her mouth. She pronounced it with such difficulty, the way I've always done. She went to the sink, washing her hands in the silver run of water. She dried them, and came towards me. She pointed her finger to her chest.

Joanna, she said. Daughter.

Joanna! I shouted.

I told her my name. In all our time together, we hadn't needed names.

Daughter, she said again.

I sighed.

Are you telling me you're someone's daughter?

Daughter, she said again.

She was moving to an old wooden box underneath the window that held the sea.

Daughter, she said.

I'll have to teach you another word, I said laughing.

She opened the box and took out a fold of tissue paper. Inside was a tiny dress of finely wrought, exquisite lace.

Daughter, she said.

She moved her hand as if she was still making the lace, as if she'd never stopped. Then she laid it on the open box lid and took out another fold of tissue paper, another dress, this one white and bright with embroidered yellow flowers.

Daughter, she said.

She moved her hand, she was embroidering it, her face soft with a faraway look. She took out another fold of tissue paper, another dress embroidered with a geometric design in blue and gold, another, another, each one painstakingly beautiful, each one a sad pool of colour in the room.

She had laid out the twelfth dress and was unfolding the thirteenth when I said:

You made thirteen different dresses.

The most painful things come slowly.

For thirteen daughters, I said.

You lost thirteen daughters, I said.

We held each other so closely.

When Joanna came with coffee and biscuits to my room, the sun was high, the floor was scattered with unfolding pages of Hypatia's letters and I was still reading.

She touched my cheek, and gazed at the letters.

Till that moment I hadn't noticed I was crying.

I pointed to my breasts, and showed a smaller stature than mine.

My daughter, I said.

She wiped away another tear that had settled in the lines around my mouth. Her eyebrows were raised.

I spoke again.

I have, I said, a daughter.

It was an announcement that startled us both.

Hours later, I came into her kitchen. She was at her stove. She pointed her finger at me, and indicated the table where we could eat and watch the sea.

No, I said.

Athens. I realised I was shouting, and touched her clock on

the old mantelpiece, its hands rolling around until nine o'clock in the morning.

Athens, I repeated. Athina. How can I get there? Nicholas ... drive ... Athina?

I wasn't sure if she understood. I pulled out of my pocket my daughter's letters.

Her smile dropped. Her mouth struggled. A sound rumbled behind her lips.

Athina? Daughter?

Suddenly I was holding onto her and laughing and crying and shouting:

Yes! Daughter! Athina! I've got to read my mother's work out, and then go home to my daughter.

Tears streamed down my face, while Joanna wiped them with her apron.

My daughter, I repeated.

The words seemed big, almost unsayable.

I've never known her, there's never been any space for her, I said. And all the time, she's been wanting a mother. It's me she wants. Can you believe that?

Joanna led me to a chair. I sat down, laughing, crying.

It's as if my daughter's just been born.

Joanna, uncomprehending, sat beside me and held my hands.

As if a nurse in the hospital has just come in, and said ...

Joanna smiled.

Ti? she asked.

As if the nurse said ... This is the real beginning, after all.

In the warmth of Joanna's smile, I was blurting:

In those letters, she hasn't realised it, but she's saved me and my mother, she found my mother's work written in

Matti's handwriting, my mother forced him to write down her work, and that can be dated, because he drowned—maybe—or maybe he just ran away—

Joanna nodded as if she understood everything.

All those times when it was Matti she dictated her soul to, not me. Because he was to be the mathematician, and I was to be nothing at all.

After a while, Joanna laid a cloth, plates, cutlery, a basket of bread. She led me to the table. She poured two glasses of her home-made wine, it leaped red and winking from her old stone jar. She spooned out lunch, and it spilled on the blue-checked cloth in its richness. Then she sat next to me, pursing her lips.

R-r-r-r-r-r, she said.

Pardon? I asked.

R-r-r-, she said.

Surely this wasn't a Greek word.

R-r-r-r, she repeated.

Perhaps I shouldn't notice. I gazed out the window at the sea's slow movements and pretended nothing unusual had happened. But she was doing it again, so insistently I had to look around at her.

R-r-r-. She was like a child imitating a noisy engine.

Embarrassment made me shout.

Nicholas! You're being Nicholas!

She must've been miming Nicholas in a battered white truck bent over the steering wheel, rounding a corner, scattering chickens in a village, dodging a herd of goats, racing past wide-eyed children and sleepy old fishermen, shattering the peace of crowded village houses with orange pumpkins on their roofs as he headed towards Athens. Then I saw that her hands on the steering wheel carved such an effortless path across the sea, it strained to follow her.

334

It was difficult to fold Hypatia's letters into my suitcase, they were crammed with such joy for me. Sobs still broke the flow of my breath. I lingered in the shed to pull sheets and blankets off the narrow bed and fold them, thinking of them swirling in tub water with Joanna's hands as she washed them. I held up my sensible cream clothes, brown with dust and bedraggled, and on an impulse I put on one of Clare's dresses instead. I considered scarlet brocade, but I didn't want to look like a streak of my mother's ink. I chose purple crepe instead, with an elegant tight skirt. There was no mirror in the shed to mock me.

In my tight purple lace, I watched a wave heave. It required all its effort, like something that must, must go on. Now the water was a wall so clear, light twinkled in it, then blurred on the clanking rocks. And I laughed aloud in my purple lace at the boast that I've done anything at all. I'd merely gone on a journey to a particular destination. All I had was a pile of theorems and in the history of mathematics, there have been so many. But I had a daughter, and a granddaughter, and soon I was going home.

There was a roar and a grinding so loud I leaped from my chair and grabbed my bag. But still the khaki road stretched emptily up the hill, where blue smoke drifted. Someone had started the tractor, that was all, now I saw its chimney belching smoke behind the brown stone wall.

I turned back to my chair, amongst the grinding noise of the tractor that had even silenced the sea. That's when I caught sight of Joanna's metal tray, propped against the wall. I caught sight of the reflection of my face.

It was someone else's face, that was what I thought at first. A determined nose, intent intelligent eyes, a patient, friendly mouth. I looked behind me to see who'd stepped silently into the room. There was no one, only me. It was my face. It wasn't my mother's face, it wasn't my mother's beauty. It was plain, a little red, but it was part of my history. I had the right face, the right face for my life.

Frances. Frances, I heard Joanna call.

I looked out again, but there was still no truck. Only the tractor edging towards the road, roaring and belching and bumping and turning now into the road up the hill.

Frances.

High on the driver's seat of the red tractor was a small dark figure, a woman, Joanna. She peered down the hill, saw me and whisked one hand momentarily away from the steering wheel to wave to me.

Get down, I shouted. You'll kill yourself.

She threw back her head and cackled with laughter as I ran behind her.

Stop it, I shouted. What on earth are you doing?

Everything about her shuddered with the tractor's roar, her ancient breasts, her chin, her skirt pulled up to her thighs to make way for the gear lever between her knees.

Get down, I shouted again. I was particularly scandalised by her legs. Her face had been crushed by time, her laugh fragmented it into a hundred lines. Her body had been bowed by fourteen children. But her eyes danced and her scandalous bared legs, they were the pale slender limbs of a girl.

She was patting the seat beside her. She wanted me to joy-ride with her. I baulked. The steps up to the seat were so far apart, that in Clare's dress I'd have to hurl myself at them like a high-jumper.

Athina, she was shouting, her voice soaring out from her broken teeth, her jiggling wiry hair. She ground into a gear

336

change and heaved the steering wheel with as much strength as the ocean. Athina, she shouted again.

Above the din of the tractor, her laughter swooped like the blue sea behind her. It was my confusion she was laughing at, and her reckless plan. She knocked her girl's white knees together in merriment. But still I stood on the road until she shouted:

Joanna—Frances—Athina!

There was nothing to do but hitch my purple skirt up around my waist, and climb up beside her.

We ground and roared through tiny streets of starlit villages, and waved to the long ribbons of people who leaned in doorways. Joanna still hooted with laughter when she caught my eye, and now that I'd abandoned sense, I laughed back. There was nothing else to do in the shuddering jumble of noise.

Oreo, she shouted as we roared through a quiet valley.

My answer slipped out of me before I had time to consider. Oreo, oreo, oreo.

Suddenly she was talking fast amongst the dance of noise, words spilling out of somewhere they'd been stored, waiting for this moment. I think she was telling me the story of her life, she was elated, as if she'd lived it for the telling. One hand moved over her mouth sometimes, as if she shouldn't have allowed these words to tumble out, but all the time her other hand glided on my arm as she steered, like knowing feet over a rocky path, the feet of a young girl foolishly impatient for love and stealing out of her mother's house. I nodded to please her. In the roar of wind, she had to shout to confide in me. She was telling me of her beauty, her hands left the steering wheel to move in the shape of a winsome body. She was telling me of her first kiss. She was telling me about a young shepherd she couldn't stop kissing. He minded sheep for a rich man. But her parents wouldn't allow her to marry the shepherd. She had to marry the rich man instead.

That's what she seemed to be saying, though I wasn't sure, you know how few Greek words I spoke then. But later, when Nicholas talked to me, he told me the same story.

To ride through the darkness with Joanna and her story, to read my mother's work at last and then to go home to my daughter, this seemed at last my life's beginning.

Sometime deep in the dark night, when we were roaring into another village lit only by the moon's reflection on white-washed walls, a truck honked behind us.

Nicholas! his mother shouted. She ducked her head and pushed down the accelerator. It took the entire length of the village, a terrible bend in the road and a big hill to climb before she found the brakes. In the sudden silence, we were as hoarse as if we'd been shouting in triumph all our lives long.

Nicholas carried his mother off the tractor. She was so stiff, it took her a while to unbend.

Your turn, he said, holding his arms up for me.

I'm fine, I said.

But I couldn't unbend either, I'd been so cramped in the seat and confined in the purple dress, and I was glad of his strength. We collapsed onto the large front seat of Nicholas' truck, giggling in our exhaustion like schoolgirls, and after the shuddering tractor it was like sitting in the pink sky amongst billowing clouds.

Nicholas left Joanna at the house of a relative, startled and crumpled in a nightshirt, on the outskirts of Athens.

I'm glad you told me about wave sizes, he said as he steered his truck on to the Athens–Patras freeway. Beyond his face, I glimpsed the sea, still rolling in, whatever I made of it. Some-times it seems that it's only the sea that's not preposterous.

Does your mother know what I'm about to do? I asked.

What are you about to do? he asked.

I'm deciding that, I said.

I slept then, my head against the back of his seat, and I dreamed that I was resting on the warmth of his arm. But I woke to find him bent over his steering wheel. Out the window the buildings of the grimy grey city were slipping by.

Which hotel? he asked, smiling to see I was awake.

I told him its name, and explained it was near the Parthenon.

Of course, he said. Hotels are always near the Parthenon. No one is allowed to forget who we once were.

From behind his seat, he pulled out a thermos of coffee, and fresh bread wrapped in a tea-towel.

I drank and ate, and then held the spare coffee cup for him and broke off hunks of bread for him to chew.

He parked in the parking yard of my Athens hotel.

You've got half an hour before you're on. You want me to come in with you? he asked.

As he tugged on his handbrake, his hands were grimy with hairs. They weren't like my mother's hands at all.

I'm not a city person, but for your big moment, I won't mind staying, he was saying.

You might be the only member of my audience, I said.

He flung open his door while buses screeched behind him, and came round to open mine. I didn't move.

Shouldn't you hurry in? he asked.

I've got a few minutes, I said, and took his grimy hands, and his fingers arched like rainbows on my breasts.

In this truck, if you tip your head upwards there's not a landscape outside, I told him. Just blue light streaming. And the windows of your truck are white-framed, I added. And open out from a space that's honey warm.

He kissed my open mouth, his lips moving right around its circle. Afterwards he said:

I'd like to talk to you for hours.

You want to find out about mathematics? I asked.

About you, he said. I want to find out who you are.

In the lobby, we found the hotel manager.

All gone, he said. Gone, gone. The mathematicians. You're too late, too late.

But I came to explain my work, I said.

Everyone gone, he repeated. And no rooms for your talk. All gone.

Nicholas took the manager by the shoulder. They talked together, Nicholas' voice flowing like his hands, rippling colour, that rainbow foreign languages make in the air when you don't understand.

The hotel manager grunted, and hurried off.

He'll let you lecture in the car park, said Nicholas. It's his own space, but his car's at the wreckers'. It's the space next to a stonemason's yard. Will that do?

It's how mathematics was done in the beginning, I said. Just scratchings in white dust. All I'll need is a stick.

Just in case, I put up signs in the lobby
9.00 am. F. Montrose. Car park.

There might be someone still here, I said.

At nine o'clock, I stood against the stonemason's fence.

Adele would've liked to film this, I said.

Nicholas found dust on my purple skirt to brush off, and combed my hair with his fingers.

Do you know exactly what you're going to say?

No, I answered. I'm not going to say what I planned to say.

I gave my talk to Nicholas, Adele who turned up as if she'd heard me mention her name, and Jan Symonds who arrived a minute late, breathless.

Did you know I'd stay? she asked.

Yes, I said.

I took a chance you'd come back, she said in her lilting accent. I have to hear your mother's theorems.

You can read about them, I said.

She looked startled. I suppose she'd been reading so much, anticipating that I'd reiterate the mathematics that won the competition.

There's something else, I said. I invented these geometrical devices, and they gave me this idea. They allowed me to keep track of a change that could happen here

I drew in the dust—

and a change that could happen there—

I drew in the dust again—

I've been trying to break into a new country of numbers that could explain so much of what we don't know. And I've failed. I found what I thought was the first new number, and I've been looking for a second, but maybe it's just a mirage. I seem to see it in flashes, I'm almost there. Then it disappears.

Jan's face was intent, frowning. Then something happened. Two things, really. There was a shout. The hotel manager was looking out the window. He saw Jan Symonds' tissue pink dress, and my bedraggled purple one, and assumed we were both ladies in the audience needing chairs. He brought them out. Jan Symonds didn't notice hers at first, he had to tap her on the arm and point. Her dress rustled against my

341

thoughts, as my mother's dresses used to do. That's the other thing that happened. It was that rustling that moved my mind.

Then it disappears, I repeated because I knew they were expecting me to speak and I had to find some words, any words.

But I could barely speak for the white knowledge that blinded me. I was drawing in the white dust, with Jan Symonds kneeling beside me and shouting, I'm not sure what she shouted, but it didn't matter, because at that moment, I'd linked a theorem over here with a theorem over there and I'd found the second number. Like the first number, it slid into my mind in silence as if it had always been there, as warmly actual as a child.

I heard Adele say: This isn't what it's supposed to look like, is it?

And Jan said: It's amazing.

As the dust settled, Adele asked her: She really has found a new sort of number?

She makes everything we took for real look like mere imaginings, said Jan. I don't know what's real, and what's been made up. There just aren't distinctions like that any more. She's found a new way to think.

So she'll be famous? Adele asked.

I will be too, said Jan. For discovering her.

Even in that moment, she glared at Adele with her camera and said:

I discovered her mathematically speaking, and that's the only way that matters.

But Adele said proudly: I got it all. At least up to when she started scribbling so fast. After that, the tape went funny.

I flew home to you, my daughter. And to my mother's diary, in case she'd written something that was, after all, permission.

342

Ten years later, after many letters between us, Jan sent me an article published in America: 'A quiet revolution—the first fifty Montrose Numbers'.

It caused a storm amongst mathematicians that took these last thirty years to calm. By that time, if you saw mathematics as a tree, you might make out a new twig against the sky. If you saw mathematics as a river, it tumbled over a new sandbar on its way to the sea.

And that's why, Hypatia, Great Men and Women of Mathematics has an old fashioned shaky video still of Jan Symonds and your mother about to place their bottoms on chairs in a car park.[1] If you look closely at the photo, you'll see your mother is scruffier and dustier than usual. Younger too, though I thought then I was so old. Those shapes behind us, they're plaster statues of angels. Beyond the fence, but perhaps it's just my memory filling in the shadows, I can make out Nicholas' white truck where we fell in love. Some people said that I loved him because of his mother. I loved him because he knew how to love, though in all our time together we never talked mathematics, he knew nothing of that. It didn't seem to matter.

There's a photograph of Juanita, the one who began it all, but the publishers didn't want to use it because she'd turned her face away from the camera when she was a daughter of a widow with a fortune, and waiting for her happiness.

But she was so beautiful, I said.

They peered closely.

Was she? they asked doubtfully. And then I doubted, too.

You must include her, I insisted. It all began with the shape of her breasts.

So they did.

---

[1] Living Insurance is there, in all the important moments.

These details seem important to tell you. Because inside every person and every object, even a mathematical object, is enfolded the incomplete story of many lives, leaning towards infinity.

But I was foolish, I see that now, to try to find my story's beginning. Because we only come in part-way through our stories, and we die before their ending.

Glossary: what Frances didn't explain

It's probable that Frances had drawn inspiration from Kate Llewellyn's poem, Breasts, reprinted in The Penguin Book of Australian Women Poets *(ed.) Susan Hampton and Kate Llewellyn, 1986, Australia.*

Opening the invitation

Page 7: 'Observing her as she returned home in her carriage, they dragged her from it and carried her to the church called Caesareum, where they completely stripped her, and then murdered her with shells. After tearing her body to pieces, they took her mangled limbs to a place called Canaron, and there burnt them.'

(*Socrates Scholasticus*, Ecclesiastical History) quoted in Women Sum It Up *by Diane Farquhar and Lynn Mary-Rose, Hazard press, New Zealand, 1989, p. 12.*

Seances and Mathematics

Page 12: My mother, despairing that I would never understand Zeno's paradoxes, borrowed this explanation from The Main Stream of Mathematics *by Edna M. Kramer; Fawcett Premier, 1951, pages 318–320. I still don't understand, I'm afraid.*

Page 22: I suspect Grandma Juanita didn't talk about tree roots at all. My mother was probably conflating something Grandma Juanita said with the work of Cheryl Praeger, an Australian mathematician, who in the late twentieth century worked extensively in algebraic graph theory, geometry and computational group theory, and also carried out work on the relationship between the root system of trees and their height distribution. See Women Sum It Up *by*

Diane Farquhar and Lynn Mary-Rose, Hazard Press, New Zealand, 1989, p. 79.

My mother's armpits

Page 30: The subtitle of this biography was taken from the painting by A. Gorky called: 'How my mother's embroidered apron unfolds into my life'.
   Although my mother was a great mathematician, she was in some ways charmingly naive. She assumed that because Juanita never finished the quilting on her apron, Gorky's mother didn't either. I've seen the painting and I don't think that it's about an apron at all.

Undressing and the soul

Page 37: Cantor's words are quoted in Pi in the Sky: Counting, Thinking and Being by John D. Barrow, Oxford University Press, New York 1992, page 198.

Dressing and the soul 2

Page 43: People who haven't had a mother who's a mathematician mightn't know that Omar Khayyam, author of the Rubāiyát, was the greatest mathematician we know about between the fifth and the fourteenth centuries. He classified thirteen different types of cubics for which he'd found solutions. He used the early clumsy techniques of the Greek geometers. My mother said she was like him, an algebraist in choice of material, but a geometer in method.

Triumph

Page 64: To kindly protect the anonymity of the boors who attended this conference, Frances has borrowed a make-believe mathematical term from The Mathematical Experience by Philip J. Davis and Reuben Hersh; Penguin, Boston 1981.

The quotation from Bernard Riemann, the nineteenth century German mathematician of extraordinary intuitive power, was from Jacques Hadamard: The Psychology of Invention in the Mathematical Field; Princeton University Press 1945.

Fame

Page 99: My mother had no memory for places. I think she scarcely noticed Athens. So Adele's Winged Victory statue probably wasn't in Argos as she said. On the other hand, maybe my mother didn't say Argos. Frances didn't really say this interpretation of Archimedes' famous moment—or if she did, she borrowed the thought from Mathematics: The Loss of Certainty by Morris Kline; Oxford University Press, U.S.A. 1980, page 29.

Page 102: Frances never did give back the slip of paper with the sentence about infinity on it. In fact, she passed it on to me. However, I have traced the origin of the words, and know that the owner of the pigskin handbag copied it out of The Mathematical Experience (quoted above).

Time rushing over her

Page 108: The Venerable Bede's finger counting scheme, drawn a
thousand years after Bede by Jacob Leupold in 1727, reproduced
from Pi in the Sky p. 50 (quoted above).

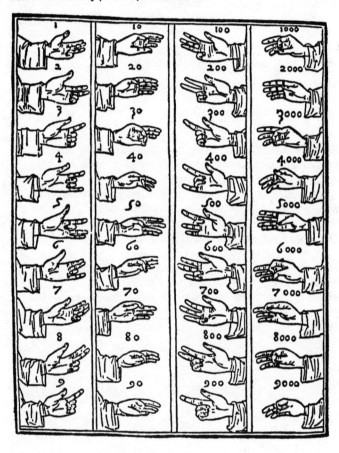

The body bears no threat

Page 162: Frances has borrowed this line from the essay by Luce Iragaray: 'And the One Doesn't Stir without the Other'.

The parts are as important as the whole 2

Page 188: Sources for the discussion on Platonism, constructivism and formalism: The Mathematical Experience (quoted above), pages 318–320, 370, Pi in the Sky (quoted above), page 222, and Peter Boyle.

Page 191: Frances would've shuddered at the first comparison, the one with Wronski. Wronski wrote a four-volumed Oeuvres Mathematiques, as well as five books on cultural messianism, not to mention his systems of history (which were to do with the negation of inertia).

But as Davis and Hersh wrote: 'It would take a profound student of eighteenth-century mathematics to tell what, if anything, is new or useful in the four volumes. I am only too willing to accept the judgement of history that Wronski deserves to be remembered only for the Wronskian. The doors of the mathematical past are often rusted. If an inner chamber is difficult of access, it does not necessarily mean that treasure is to be found therein.' (Quoted in The Mathematical Experience, page 59.)

The second mathematician, Hermann Grassman, who lived from 1809 to 1877, published a book called Die Lineale Ausdehnungslehre. Because his work was somewhat mystical and obscure, he was ignored for many years. He is now regarded as a genius. (He also was a Sanskrit scholar and translated the Rig Veda into German.)

Arthur Bray Kempe published an epoch-making and novel proof on the four-colour conjecture in 1879, but Frances couldn't really take comfort from the mention of his name. He was a barrister, *but when he published he was already a member of the London Mathematical Society.*

The parts are as important as the whole 3

Page 204: Galton's quotation has been taken from Pi in the Sky *(quoted above), page 36.*

Page 206: C. S. Pierce shared Zeno of Elea's view of space as an undivided whole that cannot really be broken down into parts. We can find scattered locations in space, but space is always more than the sum of these isolated points. As Rudy Rucker says, we can pick out higher and higher infinities of points from an absolutely continuous tract of space, but there will always be a residue of leftover space, of continuous little pieces, infinitesimal intervals over which the actual motion takes place. He quotes Godel who said 'Summing up all the points, we still do not get the line, rather the points form some kind of scaffold on the line.' According to C. S. Pierce, a truly continuous line is so richly packed with points that no conceivable set, no matter how large, can exhaust the line. 'There should not be just one point between all of 1 and 2, 2 and 3, 3 and 4, 4 and 5, 5 and 6. There should be absolutely infinitely many.'

Rudy Rucker: Infinity and the Mind: The Science and Philosophy of the Infinite, *Bantam, New York 1981, page 88.*

The Microbe's Dilemma

Page 215: The discussion on prime numbers was greatly assisted by The Mathematical Tourist: Snapshots of Modern Mathematics *by Ivars Peterson; Freeman, New York 1988, pages 20–28.*

Page 220: Frances is again confused, this time conflating a remembered conversation with Clarke with a recent conversation with Mike Woolfe, who suggested that we share with microbes the dilemma of making contact with whatever lies outside the test tube of our known world.

However, I must tell you that despite such confusions, she was a sprightly old lady and partial to a flutter on the dogs herself, for which she evolved a system so excellent, her own betting grandmother must've turned in her grave. (Not many historians acknowledge this betting system, despite the grandeur of her eventual estate.)

Page 223: The discussion about the survival of ideas was taken from The Emperor's New Mind: Concerning Computers, Minds and the Laws of Physics *by Roger Penrose, Vintage US., 1989.*

For the discussion of beauty and mathematics, see The Emperor's New Mind *(quoted above) page 545.*

For the Sake of Immortality 2

Page 243: Behind the Professor's statement that Einstein drew connections that were 'staring other people in the face' was the knowledge that the physicists of the time understood Lorenz's transformations better than the mathematicians. In fact, Lorenz's transformations weren't accepted by mathematicians until Einstein accepted them.

Wallpapering

There have been mutterings from some quarters that the notes pasted by Juanita on the wall are a mere fiction, not part of Frances' history at all: worse, these mutterers quote a recent Australian work of fiction (Painted Woman) *in which the heroine (coincidentally also named Frances Montrose) painted the story of her life on the walls of her house.*

Frances was acquainted with Sofia Kovalevskaya's autobiography, A Russian Childhood, *and in her old age, she may have reinvented her adolescence in keeping with Kovalevskaya's story.*

Page 279: I'm afraid this isn't Juanita's mathematics at all. She was quite a borrower, I can see that now. She stole it unreservedly and unrepentantly from the mathematics of Ramanujan, as documented in The Man Who Knew Infinity *by Robert Kangel; Scribners, US, 1991.*

I can only say in my mother's defence: who better to steal it from?
Hypatia

JUANITA'S DIARY

20TH FEBRUARY 1947

So pretentious to write the year, as if I or anyone else will read this.

I write this instead of mathematics. I'm a mother now, not a mathematician.

First night back here out of hospital, kept waking up to check Matti hadn't frozen. So tiny. And that he wasn't feverish. Asked Frank to ask his customers the Bradbridges how many blankets they were putting on their baby.

How many? Frank worried. How many blankets, he repeated. How many blankets.

As if there was going to be some incalculable number!

But he's been in awe of me since the birth, so at lunchtime he was able to report that last night the Bradbridge baby had only a nappy and a singlet on.

And they'd left the doors and windows open. It was, he reported, a very hot night. A no blanket night.

20TH MARCH 1947

Matti's asleep and I should pick up my notebook. Had a deep suspicion that underneath everything I've worked out, there's a big conjecture, a pattern. Felt I almost knew it and the feeling of almost knowing gave me such elation, it soared me through the first of the labour pains.

But perhaps finding the big pattern isn't for me. My professor at the convent said that there are some people who just specialise in finding nice examples, that's all they can do.

I don't think he was talking about me.

What if he was???

There'll be time while Matti sleeps. He'll sleep quietly in the background while I work. Now all I want to do is write about the mist. It's all around the house so I can barely see the bush, the bush is white, there is no sky. Against the windows the mist trails up, sometimes thinning to show the grey of scrub, then closing into itself and its white silence. It's too cold and damp to walk with a new baby in my arms. And where would I walk to? The houses along the road a mile away are weekenders, doors shut, gates that rust on their locks. The shops two miles away just sell bread and potatoes and meat, there's nowhere to pause and finger and pretend to consider, just to keep the silence outside.

13TH APRIL 1947

A bell clanged through the house when the baby was dozing off. Ran to the doorbell. Just a slippery doorstep. Then remembered the telephone. It hadn't rung for weeks. At first with a spurt of fear I thought it was my mother. Only her old friend from cards. A brown sherry voice because she'd been drinking all day. As always! A wall-to-wall chatterer. Today she kept saying You're alone out there? I was frightened. Is she going to tell my mother I'm not coping? I was squatting on the floor. Frank still hasn't made much furniture. A shell of a house.

No neighbours I suppose, she said. So I said lots, the next gully is crowded with new houses.

Her name. Starts with K. Katherine? Kate?

A backyard on your own's the loneliest place on earth, that's what she said next.

My heart lurched. I looked out the window. My backyard is hundreds of miles of bushland.

You were always so strong, she said, and it sounded like an accusation.

A pause windy with sighs. Then: Your mother been in touch? she asked.

First inkling I had that this phone call was about more than it seemed.

My abandoning mother: the endless silence of the convent with the other children gone home for holidays. When she finally took me away it was ten years too late. We sat in her pink parlour watching the days. Sometimes we touched each other's arms as we'd seen friends do.

Mum's busy, I said.

Your mum's always busy, she said.

For a moment her voice on the black telephone cord stretched between us like a giant hand, caressing us both. Then her voice lurched.

It's the great love affair, she said. That no one talks about.

I thought she meant herself and my mother. The rhythm of a drip from the gutter was drumming in my head. Love—how oddly that word falls onto the floor of this house. I remembered their arms looped around each other like vines.

A mother and a child, the greatest love affair, the drama of that bond, and no one talks about it, she repeated.

She wasn't coughing, she was crying. She rang off.

Sat under the telephone in case she rang back. Would have liked it. She didn't. It kept coming to me through the day that my mother's old friend sounded like my mother. Perhaps over the years, they'd taken on each other's mannerisms, the way some old dogs do with their mistresses. So finally they seem to have begun together.

Didn't do my mathematics, didn't think any. Nothing, only this.

Had to go down to S. on the train for more nappies. Why does a tiny baby need so many clothes? Raining. Frank couldn't do Mrs Mac's fence because of the mud so he stayed home. He wouldn't shop for nappies for his own son. Suppose I could've waited for a sunny day but when? Suddenly going to the shops was like going to a party. I put on my green taffeta dress with its swirling flared skirt. He wouldn't even drive us to the station, he wants to save the ute for work. So angry, I screwed up my return ticket and had to find instead a smile for the ticket collector.

On the train, a woman sat next to me. Another non-stop talker, save me from them. Her father had left her mother for someone her own age, a girl. She wasn't a girl! Then she told me her name! Twinkle! She was allergic to all vegetables, she told me, and then she unwrapped the greaseproof paper off a tomato sandwich to have a quick bite before she got out at the next stop! But a tomato is a vegetable, I told her. She argued.

A tomato is a fruit, she said!

I shut my mouth. Without my mathematics, I'm becoming a cranky person. I thought that I shouldn't get angry over a tomato sandwich eaten by a stranger called Twinkle.

Then on the way home, something unexpected. I fell in love. No one in our carriage, just Matti and me. He was asleep so sweetly. Suddenly my mouth was a glowing secret, my lips were locked on it, my thoughts glowed like particles in a suspension, waiting. The faces on the platform, I didn't search them as I used to, they rushed by, other people have nothing to do with my happiness. My baby made me feel that everything, after all, might have meaning, and I might be there to discover it with him.

He's mine, I kept thinking. For always. Mine for always.

He's instead of my father.

6TH MAY 1947

Rain stopped.
The conjecture will unwind in me.
But all I write are these notes.

7TH MAY 1947

This morning I called to him above his cries. He stopped crying.
He turned his head and looked at me. I swear the look he gave
was trust. We held a gaze. We shared it. I almost forgot to
breathe.
He saw me.

9TH MAY 1947

3 am. Breasts

10TH MAY 1947

Where are all the people in the world? Doesn't anybody ever
walk down this track?

11TH MAY 1947

My mother's friend again. No one's rung since her last call.
Could hardly speak, haven't talked to a soul for days except
Frank and is that talk?

Sometimes loneliness is better than company.

She went on and on about how hard I must be working, all those nappies. I couldn't bear it any longer. I said that a baby isn't about nappies. She totally missed the point.

See? That's what I mean, she said. You're cranky. Worn out. It's all those nappies.

She'd decided she was going to call me once a month.

To stand in for your mother.

I've never needed my mother, I said.

She crashed the telephone in my ear. I suppose it stopped the argument. Listened to the swirling noise a hung-up telephone makes. Hadn't heard that noise before. It's quite companionable. Then the switchgirl asked me what I was up to. Watchar up to larve?

Haven't got back to my conjecture for days. Not even to its possibility.

Rain again.

To be alone with a new baby in a kitchen takes all the bravery there is. More bravery even than mathematics.

ABOUT 20TH MAY 1947

Frank woke up late today. Please leave quietly and don't wake the baby, I said. Again. He slammed the door. He never times it well, in summer there are always blowflies in the house when he's gone out the door. My Matti woke, of course. Sat him on my lap, we watched the fire together. His eyelids closed. And then, in the warmth, drifts of the conjecture came into my head, nothing to do with the rain, the baby, Frank's anger, my loneliness. Or perhaps everything to do with it. This drifting possibility, it felt

360

like it's always been there. Wanted a pencil, but didn't want to disturb him.

Stuck my foot out, pushed a log deeper into the fire. The equation was like a voice, insistent as a voice. My skin was prickling in the shower of gold heat from the fire. For a second I thought: It's the baby talking inside my head.

Put the baby on the sofa. Stood, wanted to brush the equation away. Matti woke and cried, I had to feed him, he was overdue. But the voice ignored me, ignored him, it went on talking.

I was running around the house looking for a pencil, no pencil anywhere and the baby by this stage screaming. But I had to record the voice. Went back to the loungeroom, saw the newspaper screwed up to go in the next fire, smoothed it out. Wrote in margins. All the time the equation talked in my head and the baby screamed on the sofa. The voice stopped. Sat down beside Matti and cradled him.

The voice started again, dictating. It made my original idea look quite dull, and I'd been so proud of it. Put Matti down again and wrote. And only when the voice stopped, did I feed my baby.

With my baby on my lap, sometimes I feel I am my father. Don't remember much about him, just a smile, a warmth so even the air knew when he'd come into a room. On Friday nights he always sang something that sounded like wind moving through pine trees. One day I sat on his lap and told him I wanted a dog and he gave me a white goat instead that leapt and skipped. My mother screeched about its droppings on the floors. Father said they didn't matter. He cleaned them up himself. Sometimes the green hills rose around us like questions and my father was an enigmatic stranger in a muddy paddock. Once he ran upstairs clumping mud and hid in the attic amongst the spiders while our house was suddenly full of strangers. Our spare paddock filled

*with dung from their horses. Go away, he mouthed at me when I
crept up to the attic. Are they chasing you? I whispered. He drew
me onto his lap and I stayed with him, trying not to look at his
eye socket, the gap where his eye should have been, the flaps of
skin that always seemed sad. We trembled together. Panic has a
smell. A long time before the strangers went away. He died when
I was, I don't remember when he died. Or what town he was born
in, or why he came to this country. Or why he hid, and why the
strangers came. Why they killed him.*

*Sometimes I talk to him in dreams, I'm shouting in my dreams,
and waking with words drying on my mouth.*

The baby, my future, is taking me into my past.

22ND MAY 1947

*Threw the newspaper with the scribble on the margins into the
fire. The scribble looked so urgent. But it isn't. That part of my
life is ended.*

*Later: It doesn't matter. Something much more subtle has come
to me. And yet, when I got that first two line idea, I'd thought,
what had I thought? I felt like God.*

*Is this how God felt, a few days on from his original creation?
That he could've done it better?*

WINTER 1947

*One of those bush days when everything is rock still, no wind,
not the flutter of a leaf. Ran out to the washing line to get Matti's
singlets and in all the stillness my movements seemed extravagant.
Muddied the hem of my new dressing gown. (Frank had complained that I'd been in my old dressing gown most of the day as*

I went between stove and copper, and a couple of minutes of mathematics while I waited for the potatoes to boil. He said since I was his wife, I ought to make an effort. So I went to the shops and bought this new dressing gown.)

I came inside, careful with the door, Matti was asleep and I didn't have the easiness to cuddle him, not yet, I'd been alone without an adult conversation for three days, I was rock-stiff.

Frank home late and gone just after dawn, it was too cold to take Matti to the shops, the delivery boy just left the groceries on the step and didn't call, I was looking forward to saying hello not that he'd talk to me, I'm just an old woman to him. The postman hadn't blown his whistle, even the birds were silent. I'm ashamed to be so needy. Three days of solitude and I was lifting the black telephone receiver to see if the switch operator could hear me, and when she said You again? I shouted Sorry. I was twisting my head this way and that to peer through the scrub to the letterbox, gazing up the road to find an eddy of dust from a car.

He heard me, he cried himself awake, I let him cry a while, reluctant to begin again with him, like an insomniac slow to admit that the night is over when morning comes. Carried him to my bed for a feed. We had a long slow feed, for my sake as well as his. Twenty minutes on each breast, and he sighed happily and eased into sleep. Dozens of dull chores to do and I was imprisoned with a sleeping baby across my chest.

And then I heard it. A slither of utter gentleness across the roof, and near the gutter, leaves drooped under a new weight, a sound so soft it could be under my skin, my skin strained to hear. A pat on the windowpane beyond my head. A wrinkle along the walls. Blades of grass twitched. A drizzle of moisture down the drainpipe. Between Matti's sighs I worked it out, my astonishment was a laugh, I had to clap the laugh back into my mouth, Matti stirred, but slept on. I mightn't be able to get back to my mathematics today. But now I know that mist has a sound. It's the sound of the earth thinking.

4TH JUNE 1947

Frank has put his back out and he'll be two weeks on the sofa because it's too lonely in the bedroom. His chatter is like a mosquito in my head. So I had company after all, and he held the baby while I put out the washing, cut wood, made dinner. Not so much washing and ironing with him wearing only pyjamas. He's very particular about having clean and ironed overalls. Sometimes he changes twice a day. We only talk about our childhoods. It seems to be all we have in common, that we were children once.

The doctor comes in regularly on his rounds. I kept the washing out of the lounge room. I give him little bits of paper with IOU Five Pounds because I can't walk carrying Matti to the bank. Asked him for a lift into town and we sat rattling on his back seat, Matti and I, all the way to the shops. It was two days before the delivery boy was due and we were running out of food.

What were you doing when it happened? the doctor asked Frank when he first visited. He knows Frank well, Frank put in his new floorboards. Frank has a big boyish wide-mouthed laugh and a smile so sweet you realise he's still only a child.

I was picking up a feather. Frank's one of those people who repeat jokes, so he said it again, jerking with laughter and pain.

Even on his back, he showed off a way he's invented to hold the baby, his arm extended, Matti stomach-down lying on his forearm like a tiny plane. He said that it's easy looking after a baby. Nothing to it. I said: Don't do your back in.

I went into the kitchen and leaned against the stove. What a nuisance he is, what a nuisance.

In the pale blue afternoon light from the mountains I saw that my Matti's upper eyelids have begun to look like my father's hooded eyes. I was panting with happiness. It's better for him if he looks like his father, a proper Australian, but I kissed his upper eyelids, that are Daddy's.

6TH JUNE 1947

Carried my Matti through the morning, a morning as grey and damp as me. When he laughed up at me, my face was as stiff, as ancient with dread as a Sphinx.

And then he slept after his feed, and I sat with this notebook. There are only words in this notebook. My mathematics is abandoning me again, like a mother who won't come back no matter how loudly you cry.

7TH JUNE 1947

There should be a sister, an aunt with a jolly lipsticked smile, many cups of tea, chats over the clank of the washing up while the baby laughs on a blanket on the floor. That short sentenced, gasping talk of mothers.

8TH JUNE 1947

Perhaps motherhood is like old age, when you lose your passion. Perhaps by Spring I won't want to be a mathematician any more. Is old age really like that? Does this wild errant need fade, like the colour of eyes do?

10TH JUNE 1947

Frank's back is better but now no one's asking him to repair anything. He offered to mind the baby while I got my work done because no one is visiting so they won't find out! I pretended I wanted to sit in the garden to mend socks but my notebook was on my lap. Except that no mathematics would come.

Getting more examples that ought to be true but how to prove them?

I wrote this instead.

12TH JUNE 1947

Left Matti crying in his cot for ten minutes, blocking my ears, hunched over this notebook. Not my mathematics. Writing words has become my lonely addiction, but not my love. Matti is, of course, my love.

18 JUNE 1947

Sometimes now he turns towards sounds. During the early morning feed, Frank, lying beside me, woke up and blew his nose. Matti stopped sucking and turned to see. His beauty spins my heart, that slow turn of a tiny head.

1ST JULY 1947

I'm doing mathematics again. Blank pages look like hope. I'm hacking my way through such untidy thoughts. How do I know if this is a successful way to think? My professor at the convent said that the untidiness is part of the process.

Some people specialise in just finding nice examples. Collecting them, like a botanist. But the real mathematician finds the meaning of it all.

That's me. That's me. That's me.

3RD JULY

Tried to work on mathematics today with Matti on my lap looking around the edges of pages. Saw him smiling his joyful, toothless grin. I turned to see at what. A blank white wall.

What's wrong with me, that I want mathematical excitement when I have a beautiful child? It's as if I keep forgetting who I am.

4TH JULY

4 am I woke from a dream that Matti had written a letter to me. Frank woke up. Told him about the dream. That in it Matti had said he wants to spend his childhood in the orchard with the white goat. We haven't got an orchard or a white goat, Frank said.

6TH JULY 1947

Yesterday I was in terror that Matti had grown out of his daytime sleeps and I'd never be able to get near this conjecture again. But today he slept long sound sleeps and I scribbled. I'm nowhere, nowhere near. It glimmers sometimes. Only sometimes. As I look, it fades. Did it really glimmer just before I went into labour? Why can't I recall it? Or even the moment of elation when it seemed to thrust itself suddenly into my conscious mind and everything eased. Is this all I'm ever to have, the memory of ALMOST discovering?

Hunched over my notebook writing in pencil, I seem drawn into some deep well in my mind. Morning seems stuck onto evening with a short bend in the middle. I heard a familiar sound nearby. It must've been connected to an object in the room. It was connected to moments in the past. Nothing was moving. My eyes ranged the shapes in the room. I found the telephone. It was ringing. The voice on the other end said: Mrs Montrose? I paused, fighting my way out of the mental jigsaw. The line clicked in impatience. I tried to remember my life. This house. My father. Frank. My child. The jigsaw came together. So I'm Mrs Montrose, after all. The call was about broken bathroom tiles.

When I'm in my mathematics, do I hear when Matti calls? Do I remember who he is?

I must get to this conjecture before he's much older. I'll give myself till Spring. By mid-Spring he'll be awake and I promise I won't keep trying to be a mathematician.

7TH JULY

Today as I hung out sheets and they wrapped around me wetly, I laughed aloud at my promise of yesterday, that I'd find this conjecture by Spring. Why, September is Spring—that leaves me July, August and September. Look how little I've done since April. How can I consider myself a mathematician? My notebook is full of endless examples that many would argue weren't even connected. How can I dare to weigh the importance of that against my baby? How dare I say: Please child, don't grow up, don't wake—so your mother can finish her work.

10TH JULY 1947

I'm scribbling again, a new equation today. I let Matti cry when he woke. I didn't check the clock to time his cries. I worked till the equation resolved itself.

I told him this as I picked him up, It may prove quite trivial in the end, but I had to get it down. You knew I was coming. You've got to understand. Spring's not far off.

16TH JULY

It's left me. My mathematics has left me. I tore up strips of paper. I put my head down on my notebook. I half-dozed, half-dreamed. I let my Matti cry for fifteen minutes before I picked him up. As I fed him, my tears dropped on his downy head. They glittered like panic. He looked up, startled. He saw my tears. He cried all afternoon.

20TH JULY 1947

Last night a new equation, connected to the last one, started scribbling in my head as I pushed the pram round the house. Matti and I were alone. I'd turned the lights off, and the rooms were dappled with silver moonlight. Then, in the quiet rhythm of the pram wheels and the baby's head lolling at last as heavy as a flower, while my mind was with my baby, the equation began, no feeling of effort, more the elation of remembering. Symbols were arranging themselves like the dappled moonlight on the walls, a repetition there, not there, there, not there. As we passed the dressing table I slid open my drawer so quietly. The next round, I took out my notebook. The next round, I wrote the first symbol, I must've paused, and Matti jolted awake. So I walked a few more rounds of my silver house again. Then I found the rest of the equation.

This morning, I got out the notebook and read. I stood with the notebook in my hand, and cried with love for it.

It's not the original conjecture. Maybe it's better.

This morning the postman's whistle and a letter from Frank's younger brother and his wife in the city. They're planning to drive up here one day. Would that be alright?

Frank asked me to write back to say yes, any time.

But you'll have to do something to the house.

I asked what he meant.

Make it look like we live here. Not pigs.

I have a baby, so even if I have no mathematics, I'm not alone. I must learn how to be alone with my baby.

21 JULY 1947

Matti needed carrying for nine hours, and then, just as the moon edged around the gum trees and made the dining table gleam like dark water, just then a pattern came for many of my equations. All? I hadn't been thinking about mathematics, I'd only thought about my baby. And now. Is this the idea everything will lead up to, and fall away from? Might I be like Euler, doing mathematics while he tossed his children on his knee?

It's far better than the conjecture I got to before Matti came along. And now I know that mathematics is a map of something I don't know but most deeply believe, in this bewildering landscape.

How can I have felt like God, when now I really do?

23 JULY 1947

It's not the big conjecture, after all.

24 JULY

It's a pattern. Of something else, if only I can work out what it is.

25TH JULY 1947

Put Matti in the pram in the afternoon to walk through the chilly winds. My mind's so muddled, I needed the wind to blow through it. The more I work at my conjecture, the more I don't know. I can't keep track of changes. So many loose ends, that flap in the gales of my uncertainty.

·26 JULY 1947

He coughed through the night, but there was no fever. I'm shrivelled in guilt that I walked him so far in the pram yesterday. I caused his cough.

27 JULY 1947

Yesterday Matti slept uneasily through the day. I got out my notebook but I did no mathematics. No longer seemed marvellous. Not now, I thought.
*   All I wanted to do was worry about him.*

*Saturday morning, Matti peacefully asleep, Frank laying foun-
dations down Valley Road, and I was in my silent house, in the
silence of my mathematics. Outside, the bush twitching in
sunshine.*

*A car on the road. I postponed the realisation of the sound, I
don't know how much time passed, it might have been five
minutes, five hours. A knock at the door. Another, so I got up on
my chair and looked through the top of the window. I wouldn't
have opened it to Frank's customers so I could keep working, but
it was his brother, his sister-in-law, their two children. What were
their names? Then I realised it didn't matter, they knew each
other, I wouldn't have to introduce them.*

I put the chair in its proper place and let them in.

*The children, two boys, drew in breath and asked what all the
balls of paper on the floor were.*

*I was blushing in front of mere children, I didn't know how to
explain. They picked up a ball of paper, smoothed it out and read.*

*What, you just throw sums up into the air if you can't do them?
they asked.*

*I saw with surprise how much paper there was on the floor,
and several old cups of tea on the table, and peelings of a
mandarine.*

*George told them I must be figuring out some household
problem. George, of course, and Mary.*

He said I must be such a help to Frank.

Had to clear the sink to make them a pot of tea.

*Matti woke, so I got him up and it was a relief to take them
for a walk down a bush track to see hundreds of miles of green
trees, it seems like a view of forever, except for an eruption of a
mountain on the horizon that rears like a body wanting to be*

touched, it pulls at my mind even when I'm in the kitchen washing dishes and I glance up at it. I'd like Matti to love it. A landscape like this becomes in time the mind's landscape. I'd like to tell that to Matti, but today the bush was stiff and scrawny, and the creeks were too deep in shadows to see.

Matti's mouth lifted when he watched a sudden flight of birds. His smile like the curve of a wing.

Mary held a wildflower on its stem. She said it was just perfect. Like life, sometimes.

We never quite meet eyes. She's older than me, and when I first met her, I asked her what giving birth was like. I wanted so much to know. She said it was 'wonderful of course'. She has thin ungenerous lips with lines at their ends, like thorns. She didn't meet my eyes then.

I showed her children how ants scurry.

As a parent, I would make a good father.

But mathematics is more enfolding than any mother.

Afterwards, when Frank heard they'd been, he fretted that they'd had to look out at his view through dirty windows. As if he'd made the view! And they hadn't admired him because of my faulty housekeeping!

6TH AUGUST 1947

No mathematics, only window cleaning.

11TH AUGUST 1947

A good day yesterday. Squeezed in two hours of mathematics by getting up three hours earlier.

Sometimes ideas catapult in, splintering everything. I fear and

*love them. Sometimes I think that the pattern of the conjecture is
already worked out in me, and all I must do is learn to wait for
it.*

*My mother's friend telephoned again. Was I busy? Was I man-
aging? She'd won again at cards or bingo, I couldn't tell, Matti
was screaming too loudly to hear.*

*I hope you're getting enough sleep, I heard through the tangle
of Matti's screams.*

*Women age terribly when they don't get enough sleep for a
year or so, she said. Their faces never recover.*

AUGUST 12, 1947

*The strange rasping again in Matti's breath. Tonight when he
was in his cradle I could hear it across the house. Stuck my finger
down his throat in case he'd swallowed one of his beads. Peered
down. Just darkness.*

AUGUST 13, 1947

*There's not much to tell. Frank went late to work to drive Matti
and me to the doctor.*

*What's wrong, girlie? he said in greeting. Did he call me girlie
when he visited us to look at Frank's back?*

*I stripped Matti's clothes off, his chest is so thin, has this hap-
pened suddenly while I've been immersed in searching for my
conjecture? It crunched my heart, that thinness.*

*He listened to Matti's thin chest. He said he couldn't hear
anything.*

It might be nothing. Or it might be asthma, it comes at night like a bad dream. Asthma might be why he's so thin. It strips the flesh off their bones.

I asked if there was a cure.

It may ease with time—if there's enough time, he said.

He said that of course I was keeping the house completely clear of dust, cleaning every day.

My dust balls chase each other under the sideboard while I think. Not that I told him.

Dust would be bringing the asthma on, he said. You must dust every day, he repeated.

When am I going to have time for mathematics? My appalling heart was still objecting.

I must wipe every object in the house twice a day, everything, with a damp cloth. Wet mop twice a day, as well.

It may save his life.

His life.

My father's life.

Go to the Baby Health Clinic every week, are you doing that already? No? What are you doing with your time?

Did he say that? Or was it my guilty heart?

They'll keep an eye on this mother, on me.

Get pregnant again, girlie, he said. You mightn't rear this one.

A young woman walked up the steps into his rooms. Was she a girlie? I don't remember her.

13 AUGUST 1947

If I can't do mathematics, my mind feels silenced. I cannot live in a silenced mind.

15 August 1947

Mrs Bradbridge gave Frank The Women's Weekly for me.

It'll come in handy, she said.

Full of recipes and stories about happy mothers who aren't sneaking off to do mathematics.

It came in handy to tell me I'm not a woman. There's only one place where I'm not a woman, but unfortunately it's the only place. I am not a woman in my head.

And the head, sadly, sadly, the head is everywhere.

August 17, 1947

I'd thought when you held your baby, you held the future, but when I hold Matti, I hold my past.

Matti's skin is my father's amber skin, his brown and hooded eye, his eyelashes so glossy that in their curl they catch light, his proud and regal nose.

I hold my father's past. I am the keeper of my father's past.

August 20, 1947

My mother's friend on the phone again, what's her name?

I asked the question on my mind, I said: Did you know my father? Why did he leave Spain?

She sighed, this isn't why she rang. He was before my time, she sighed.

She said she thinks of me as my mother's daughter.

But surely she knows why my father was in hiding, what he was hiding from, who knifed him, why no one was ever caught.

The thought popped into my mind that my mother killed him. But no, that's impossible. She loved him. She was good with a rifle, but he was knifed. It's just that I never trusted her. I never had a woman friend. I've never had a friend. Only Daddy.

Into the silence she said that my father was from one of those hot-blooded countries where they're always arguing politics.

She said I was lucky I lived here.

I told her how Mum said I was always in danger.

She agreed that I look like him. She was getting impatient. It was all a long time ago. Anyway, she met Violet after it was all over. So I had to ask who Violet is.

What? she asked. So I had to ask it again, had to ask who Violet is.

Violet is your mother.

Sometimes worlds fall away like flesh off bones, just with words.

All night, Matti coughed. He cried all day, exhausted. Will he ever know me?

SEPTEMBER 2, 1947

A letter from the Baby Health Clinic. Was I feeding Matti two meals a day as well as his milk?

My heart widened to a chasm big enough for me to fall into. I only feed him one meal! I hadn't thought of two!

What have I been thinking of?

Moonlight was glossing a dining room table in my childhood. There was a baby who'd died, could it have been my sister? Did I have a sister? I wade through memory that drifts like mist. An old woman near the glossy kitchen table, but in my childhood all adults looked old. Her old fingers were pressing into the table top for support. One of her fingers was missing, there was just a stump, and I was trying not to stare. When she took her fingers away, I wanted to examine the tabletop, to see if the stump left a fingerprint. I knew that she had lost a finger because of a rose thorn. Why did I know this? Perhaps she was my wet-nurse grandmother, Grandma Johnson. Is that true? I didn't know her first name either.

Your baby died, the old woman in my memory said, of malnutrition!

Around the gloss of the table, everyone was quiet, their breath withheld.

Malnutrition! Her voice thin with accusation. In a family as wealthy as this!

For years after, I heard her question, it rang in my head amongst the chanting of nuns: How did it happen? Wasn't the mother watching?

When did my mother stop watching, and let my baby sister die? Did she send me to the convent to protect me from the men with knives? Or to protect me from her? Or was it so she could follow her first love, gambling? Or did she gamble because of what life had done to her?

SEPTEMBER 5, 1947

So 'his' house is a pigsty.

When Matti slept, I turned out drawers and cupboards. But I haven't this womanly knowledge. There's no mother to ask. There never was.

Got huge accumulation of washing under way. I expected praise, but Frank says proper people wash on Mondays. Another row. But this is what I must learn. The most grievous lesson, to subdue the equations that come leaping out of my head.

True Australian Sponge Cake (from Mrs Mac)
(SHE said true)
1 cup sifted self-raising flour
¼ teaspoon salt
grated rind ½ lemon
1 ½ tablespoons lemon juice
5 egg yolks beaten till thick
5 egg whites
1 cup sugar
Sift flour and salt together x four. Add lemon rind and juice to beaten yolks, beat till thick. Beat egg whites till thick. Fold in sugar   (FOLD?)

Add egg yolks. Fold in flour ¼ cup at a time. Bake in ungreased pan in moderate oven. Remove from oven. Invert pan 1 hour before removing cake.

SEPTEMBER 15, 1947

Mrs Bradbridge sent a knitting pattern for a jumper for Matti through Frank. Shop bought things won't keep him properly warm.

Everyone's lending a hand, Frank said. It makes him important, having a sick child.

Be good, sweet maid.

Getting quite adept at purl following plain, as if one day it will save my life.

No mathematics for five long long weeks.

SEPTEMBER 25, 1947

Lust, I read today in the newspaper. It seems a word like rake, belonging to men. But does anyone know lust till they're a parent? The lust for a single life. An early night alone to forget a bad day. A soft fold of sheet to burrow into. And the mind's silence.

After long days, the return of a husband, though he'll be wet, exhausted, hungry and silent, can seem like the second coming of Christ. Poured myself some of his sherry, not enough to hurt the breast milk. Made it last a long time. Time paused, waited for my sip, raced while I sipped, paused when I put the glass down. Women with babies have to have a lot going on in their heads. A lot to think about. A lot to say for themselves. If someone asked.

I'm not a natural woman, I want my mathematics so much.

SEPTEMBER 26TH 1947

Tried Mrs Williams' asthma cure (Mothballs in a jar of warm water: hold the baby over the steam)
 Stupid old busybody.
 It made him worse.

SEPTEMBER 28TH 1947

Turned out spare room, wet mopped.
 Cleaned out rubbish near incinerator because Frank thinks fumes are upsetting Matti's breathing.
 Such guilty housework.

SEPTEMBER 29TH 1947

Breathing eased 5 am.

October 1st, 1947

I wonder if Frank has been frightened of Matti, like I have. But last night Matti laughed when Frank came home and Frank, flattered, held him and bounced him. I didn't like the way he held him, it was on the edge of my tongue to say: Don't do it like that! You'll break his arms!

But I didn't.

So I went out into the garden, into that dark sticky perfume that floats up from the bush. I looked at the window and Frank was holding Matti up in his long white nightgown that I've sewn into a bag. An angel in a bag against a lit up sky.

Panic is turning us both into parents.

I stayed out in the garden, and on a sudden breeze it came to me that motherhood and mathematics are both a grand and absurd creation.

October 3rd, 1947

Today I found him bent forward in his pram, his face close to his toy bear. I settled him back again, my mind on when he'd fall asleep.

Have you noticed what he's doing? asked Frank, panicking again.

The kid keeps falling forward.

I went and looked. He was bent forward again, it was true, his face was near the bear again.

Something's wrong, he can't lie back any more. Put your ear near his mouth, he probably can't breathe.

Wrong? I said. Our son has learned to sit up.

Shopping yesterday, I bought stockings and new socks. At home, Matti held the socks and crumpled the crinkly paper they'd been wrapped in. He brought his tiny hands together around the ball.

He's put it into his mouth, said Frank. He's trying to eat it. That's how hungry he is. You're not feeding him enough.

So I explained that babies use their mouths to test things. The Baby Clinic Sister told me this only yesterday, but I didn't tell Frank that.

He's testing things? Frank asked, suddenly making the baby sound like a scientist.

I said yes, and that of course I've been watching and waiting for this, because ever since he was born, my mind has been on my baby.

OCTOBER 4TH, 1947

Matti well all week.

Working in my mathematics notebook.

There's a voice that argues in my head: You said you'd be a full-time mother by Spring, the voice argues.

I argue back: It's early Spring. I've got a week left. Maybe two.

OCTOBER 5TH, 1947

Each morning I mop and wet dust and if he's still asleep, there's time for mathematics.

He's sleeping well today and the mathematics is inside me, and I'm inside the mathematics.

OCTOBER 6TH, 1947

Argument with Frank—he's blaming me for the milk Mr Graham brings. It might be watery but I can hardly be blamed for what goes on in the udders of cows.

Matti's sleeping but the white paper of my notebook glares at me like teeth. It seems that if I stop doing the mathematics, it recedes, I can't call it back, like I can't recall time. Pulled a page out of the notebook and crunched it into a hot angry ball. He wasn't asleep after all, just lying quietly in his cradle. He roared with laughter.

My baby and my mathematics, they both show me why I'm alive. Perhaps Mr Graham is watering the milk.

OCTOBER 8TH, 1947

A new command from Frank. Washing to be done only on Mondays because then we know where we are with the week's water. Not sure of this logic. Why can't we know where we are on Tuesdays? Or Wednesdays? Ah well.

Very dry winter. But last night, v. heavy rains. When I tapped the tanks this morning, maybe ten more gallons.

From now on, I'll bring water from the lake for washing and the garden.

OCTOBER 9TH, 1947

Sketched a rather good pulley system to bring up lake water, v. simple, v. good. Frank vetoed it. I am to carry it up by the bucketful

like other women do, or otherwise we act as if we own the lake.
Act like a real wife, he said.
Act???

Yellow jonquils poked through a white picket fence like children
sticking out their mocking tongues.
Spring, I yelped.
Matti howled.
They're late winter blooms. Spring's a few days off, I said into
Matti's puckered face.
In the soft morning light, a theorem came, two, three. But
they're not related to the conjecture. Or are they? I can't take
them any further. I keep losing track of the changes one alteration
brings. There must be some way to keep . . .
My mathematics seems alien to me now, moving beside my
mind but not in it, like a creek beside a bush track.
Maybe Matti will find this work I'm about to give up. He will
read my examples and work out why they're true. He'll have been
wondering who his mother used to be, this body of water I once
was. When he reads my work, he'll understand.
I'm so sad, it's a relief when he cries for me.

OCTOBER 12TH , 1947

Matti tried to prop himself up on his elbows on the table. He
seemed to be waving at me. Is this possible?

October 13th 1947

My mother's friend rang. I held Matti on my hip, no afternoon sleep now for him. My time is almost over and I'm not any closer to my conjecture. Unless all the examples I've found are only a tiny part of a pattern.

You don't want to talk, you resent me, said Dora. That was her name! Not Kate! Not Katherine! It doesn't even begin with K. It's Dora!

She said I was angry because I think Violet's failed me. There was a clink of glass on a table.

She said that my mother was the only girl, and one girl was too many in her family. She was farmed out, kept in a barn with the dogs for warmth, made to work as a maid from the age of six. She couldn't give you what she wasn't given.

Matti squirmed on my hip. I turned to him, I wanted to gaze at him, at the hope of his tiny face.

Much later, I put Matti in his pram and rocked it while I looked for my mother's telephone number amongst papers so untouched, grit scraped like a warning. I don't know my mother's telephone number. Nor her history. Nor what to say to her. The switch operator let the telephone ring for a long time. I rocked Matti. A voice answered, my mother's housekeeper. My mother was out playing cards. She might be out all night. She might gamble the night away.

October 15th 1947

Still clear of asthma. I've become such a good housewife, though some would dispute, like Mrs damn Bradbridge.

Your roses aren't doing too good, she said, sticking her long nose through the fence.

I hope one day it gets stuck!
Must wean.

*Mixed up cereal with a bit of banana and a drop of honey. I
didn't want to wean. My sadness slowed even the hands. Matti
gurgled with the fun of having his bib on. Food for him is my full
breasts. All he did was to play good-naturedly with the spoon. His
tiny tongue was always in the way. Feeding him banana was like
plastering a wall. Soon I was flicking bits of honeyed banana off
the furniture. Then we had a long slow feed from my breasts, the
sort he loves and believes most deeply in. I watched the evening
streak the sky. After a while, I turned off the modern dance music
from the radio. It was him and me together in the darkening
house, we filled the house and ballooned in our peace. Only the
sound of his sucking interrupted the silence. He stopped sucking,
began again, stopped, began again. Afterwards . . .*

OCTOBER 20TH 1947

*Made a compost heap according to Frank's instructions. It's so
easy to please him, so hard to please myself.*

*Chip heater. Chips too large to get a fire going. I had to take
them out and cut them up again, with Matti on the lounge room
floor and my heart thumping that there might be a sudden break
in his breathing while I was out in the yard.*

OCTOBER 25TH 1947

*My baby has learned my breasts like a song, he folds himself in
this flow between us and sucks himself to sleep while his toes
twitch in bliss.*

Wean him!

Or Mrs Bradbridge's nose will sniff that out too!

With weaning, this flow between us will falter. I jostle with regrets, that I never caught the moment, I never said I will live in this moment with my baby, this time with him will never come again. No, I was always impatient, always longing to get back to my mathematics. I wanted to live and mathematics was life. And so time has taken his bliss from me and all I have left is paltry scribblings in a notebook that amount to nothing.

OCTOBER 27TH 1947

Planted lettuce seed while Matti slept. Found black snake, worried all day that it might follow me into the house and strike Matti.

He coughed ten times through the night. Asthma is always worst between three and five in the morning. I stood by his cot listening, willing the dawn.

OCTOBER 28TH 1947

Dusted orange and lemon tree with DDT while Matti slept.
Pests fell onto ground.
Cleaned pine needles from gutters.
That'll please the gossips.

NOVEMBER 1ST 1947

Bushfire smoke everywhere. Tanks v. low.
Haven't dared to leave Matti in the garden for his sunbake since the snake. Their venom most powerful, the Bradbridges told

Frank to tell me, in early Spring, and much weaker at the end of Summer. If the baby's going to get bitten, Mrs Bradbridge said, make sure he gets bitten in late Summer!

NOVEMBER 2ND 1947

Bushfire on ridge, but wind changed direction.
 Every night Frank taps the water tanks accusingly. How do you wash 10 nappies clean in the puddle of water you can carry from the lake?

NOVEMBER 10TH 1947

It's a long, slow relinquishing. I washed the windows inside until they gleamed. What sad anger is it that I would stand with my hands in the grey swill of washing water rather than hold my miracle child?
 What do you do with a child who's fed, bathed, dressed and wide-awake? Those huge waiting eyes? His face went red with sobbing. Blotched with it. I scooped him up and then the phone rang. As I went to it, I banged his head against the door. Though he roared, I sat him against the wall and clamped my hand over my free ear. It was a wrong number but at least it's a conversation with the switch girl.
 Excuse me, she said, clearing her throat. But it's my goiter mucking up.
 I took the baby back to the sofa, I was softer now, because of a conversation about a goiter. I propped him up and held him close. Even his scalp was rage red. When he'd calmed, I settled back on my heels and explained.
 Without the mathematics, I'm hollow

As if my insides won't stay up

When he's a grown man I'll wish he was a baby again with my arms around him. Now he's a baby I wish he was a man so he would talk mathematics to me.

While I was explaining my mathematics to him, his hand lifted out of the circle of my arms. It rose uncertainly, I watched in wonder, it was level with his shoulder, level with his ear, it hovered, it undulated. He was waving, he was really waving at me. I ran behind the chair and waved back, he waved again. I ducked behind the door, waved, he waved back. I waved from behind the cushion, from under the table, from behind the radio. I got the bath mat and held it high and waved from behind it and he waved back. We didn't smile, we panted, he was panting with knowledge and I was panting with awe, the awesome moment in the white blankness when my baby reminded me who he is.

Now I know how to solve it all. He'll be a mathematician, in my place.

DECEMBER 1 1947

Tomorrow morning at dawn I will tackle Mr Graham about the milk.

DECEMBER 2ND 1947

Mr Graham's horse so quiet on the dirt road, he was collecting my jugs before I noticed. I heard him running the tap! Our precious tank water tap! Then the chink of pots against cement. He'd taken them with him to the tank. It came slowly to me. He's been watering down our milk with our precious tank water! Not even with his water!

I heard him plonking the jugs down on our footpath just as usual. It was Matti's cries which made me stamp down off the verandah.

Turning the water into milk, Mr Graham? I roared.

I had to sit down on the steps with him and wipe his face with the handkerchief I found in my dressing gown pocket. So I didn't tell Frank. Secrets are safe with me.

DECEMBER 10TH 1947

Three days of rain, and the tanks singing.

DECEMBER 11TH 1947

Tanks overflowing, and the backyard flooding from the water spout, and the lake rising. Waded out in it to rescue spade and rake and wheelbarrow and some of the woodpile, before the rush of water swept them off.

Frank said how wonderful for the apple growers on the slopes and the little farmers.

How wonderful for me, not having to carry water from the lake for a while. That's half an hour a day saved, but not for mathematics.

A fight with Frank. He's had afternoon tea with Mrs Bradbridge in her back parlour. She'd just baked a cake and it smelled like home, he said.

As if there isn't a home here.

Later, he said he'd like to have a wife that embroidered in the evenings. What about an apron? That'd be womanly. Mrs Bradbridge has been doing her chairs and curtains and she has some stuff you can have. Lots of different colours, some of it really flowery.

I'd prefer to do some equations, but I can't say that.

DECEMBER 16TH 1947

Made scones following instructions in Commonsense Cookery Book. Made two lots, hid first lot in compost they were so burnt!

Greeted Frank at lunchtime with flour from forehead to ankles, and Matti like a little snow man.

Good little woman, Frank said.

He'd brought tiny bits of Mrs Bradbridge's leftover materials. What a muddle of colour her house must look!

DECEMBER 18TH 1947

Matti full of beans. The Doctor said he can't hear asthma in his chest, it's the weather, he said, the change in the weather has cleared his asthma.

But what about the change in the mother?

What about the mathematics of the world, that won't change because of this woman's life!

JANUARY 16 1948

This is how it happened.

I lay Matti on our bed while I cleaned out my dressing table drawers. Face powder, dust, bobbypins. Suddenly in the dust of powder I saw a new way in to my conjecture. After all these months! I glanced round at Matti, he was watching gum trees toss out the window, I ran for my notebook, and behind me there was a thump. A scream. I ran back into the bedroom. The bed was bare, just a long white stretch of guilt. It was only then I heard my baby screaming. I thought so ponderously, I had to work it out: That thump was my baby falling. I rushed around to the far side of the bed, there on the floor, his eyes so black and full of terror or tears, I can't say which. But he's alive, he's crying, or is it me who's crying? It was my tears splashing him, and suddenly he was kicking his legs together in applause, he was laughing.

At night, I tried to confess it, I had to confess to someone.

The baby fell today.

We were eating dinner. There was a crumb on Frank's mouth. He fell, I said.

What were you doing to let the baby fall? That's your job, to mind our baby. You haven't got anything else to do, he said.

Babies are always falling, I said. It happens with babies. That's how you know they're growing up. Trust me, I know, I'm a woman.

He paused then and licked the crumb off his lips.

Babies often fall?

Always, I said. They're always falling.

JANUARY 30TH 1948

Tonight, Frank tumbled Matti, getting him wild. It was time Matti went down, so I stopped the game.

Frank said later, over his whittling That kid's a chip off the old block.

He'd let the fire go out. I could've hit him.

Which old block???

FEBRUARY 10TH 1948

He crawled. Chuckling at every step, tottering, slapping his hands on the floorboards, he crawled like a worm in pyjamas. When I took them off, I kissed their dirty knees.

Only tonight I realised that he crawled not towards, but away from me.

FEBRUARY 15TH , 1948

After the last feed tonight, I'll pack my notebooks, including this diary, into a cardboard box and staple down the lid. One day Matti will find it in the attic, the pencil almost too soft to read, the paper crumbling to powder. I'll be dead then but he'll be a mathematician, he'll read my words, my work, he'll find out who he came from.

Please understand, my love.

Finish my work, my son.

Find my conjecture.